I0748959

ARMAGEDDON'S PRINCESS

ANTHONY PACHECO

Published by Deep Mountain Studios
Hardback Edition printed and distributed by Lightning Source

Edited by Salvatore Biancardi
Cover Art by Eve Venture
Cover Design and Layout by Kate Strawbridge, Dwell Design & Press
Interior Design by Anthony Pacheco

Library of Congress Control Number: 2013932355

http://anthony-pacheco.com

ISBN-13: 978-0-9883652-4-7

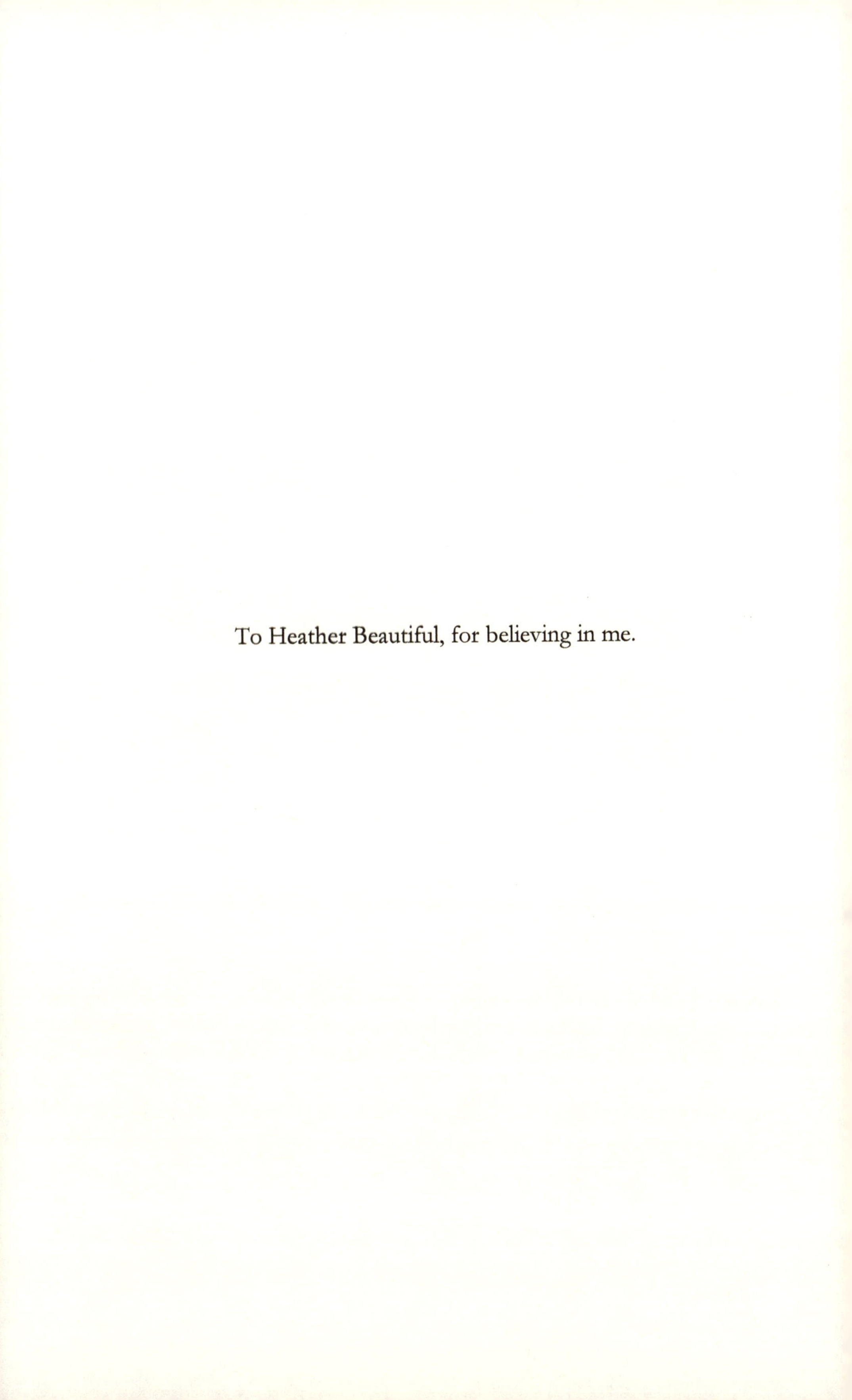

To Heather Beautiful, for believing in me.

"LEXUS, YOUR HUSBAND IS an unmitigated pain in the ass," says Mitchel, the other Husband, as soon as I take his call.

I would sigh and bang my head on my workbench, repeatedly, except this is full video and I'm working on disassembled explosives. Separated, the stuff that explodes is inert, but either way, banging your head on over-two-decade-old chemicals is a bad idea.

I wave my hands and the holographic interface around me disappears. Mitchel is one of those men with a long fuse to a big bang, both in and out of bed, so I give him the once over after turning down the magnification on my work glasses.

Hunched shoulders. Frown. One hand tapping with a stylus. Eyes that simultaneously say "kiss me now" and "you're pissing me off."

Oh yeah, he is about to burst, and that's partly—okay mostly—my fault. The last time we were in bed together, I was so exhausted from fieldwork I nodded off while he was, uh, bleh.

"Sweetheart, which Husband is that?"

As if I didn't know.

"Bill. Can we divorce him, please? Bring out the nurturing woman I know is somewhere in there, and break the news to him tenderly."

I laugh, and Mitch gives me a smile. Divorcing Bill is a long running joke in the family—even Bill uses it.

Bill is the junior Husband, and very assertive. Which is why we all married him, but still, periodically, he gets on the other three's nerves and I, as the only woman in the marriage, am the 'neutral' party usually assigned to broker a deal—or prevent bloodshed.

"I'm sorry, Husband One, but I'm very fond of Husband Four. He's rich, and he has this girth thing going for him."

"You're so predictable. Why is it you always bring that up when we talk about him, anyway? Trying to make me jealous?"

Okay, this conversation is finally going somewhere. I have Mitch pegged. He's lonely, which is my fault. And the fault of Husband Two and Three. They took the two dogs and went fishing. I should have seen it coming but I've been busy with this stupid bomb.

Thinking about the bomb, something clicks in my brain. The assembly and the economy of parts lend itself to a line-run manufacturing process. This bomb could be Chinese made. The Mad Bomber, my internal label for the bad guy, probably didn't make the bomb himself.

At first, I thought the bomber used war-era parts. Now I see that's not the case; it's an actual war-era bomb.

Now I'm really pissed.

This one didn't go off because at some point it suffered EMP—a directional electromagnetic pulse—but someone used its un-sabotaged twin for a bit of industrial vandalism. Nobody died but the material damage was annoying. The client is paying me many credits to nail who did it, so I'm burning the midnight oil to deliver. Plus, someone using war shit for his or her own gain just pisses me off. I get all stabby-stabby, shootie-shootie.

Back to Mitchel, I realize his complaint about Bill is just a symptom.

"I always use intimate little details when talking about other Husbands to put you all in your place."

"Oh? What do you say about me?"

"I refer to you as 'he who stole my girly virginity at a tender age,' which is very distracting to the others. They wonder how young I actually was."

"Hey! That implies that I took advantage of you when you practically ripped my clothes off."

I smirk. That's exactly what my other Husbands think.

Mitch is fighting another smile but it finally comes out. Then he chuckles.

"Ha. Anyway, Bill wants my next day on the calendar."

"Well you told him *no*, didn't you?" Bill should know better. I let them broker calendar dates amongst themselves, but everyone knows I botched my last day with Mitch.

"No, I am calling to tell you that I said yes."

"What? But I miss you. I wanted to be with you!"

"Sorry. He had a convincing argument."

Oh no! Bad male! Bad!

"This wasn't a trade, was it? Please tell me he didn't bribe you with credits."

Now Mitchel is grinning ear-to-ear. "Yes, he did."

"Mitchel Jameson Toulouse! And how much am I worth?"

"Five-hundred."

"Mitchel!"

Mitchel laughs. "Sorry, Honey, but it's your own fault. There is only so much Lexus Pie to go around. I don't like mine falling asleep while I'm worshiping her breasts. This is a fitting punishment."

I sigh. "Fine."

"Oh it's the 'fine', is it now?" He crosses his arms.

"You're mean. You know this case is important. You know how much war shit bugs me. And here I was going to offer to meet you in my office!"

His eyes go wide. "Really?"

"Well, forget it."

"No way. I'll be there in ten minutes."

"Forget it."

"I'll give you the five-hundred cred."

"*Mitchel!* I'm not the family whore! We have a sex-bot for those games!"

"I'm coming over there. You will be naked by the time I get through the door. You will take the credits. Are we clear on this, Lieutenant?"

I scrunch my face at him. Mitchel was never in the Military. *Lieutenant* my athletic butt. "Or what?"

"Or I will call Bill and tell him he can have the second day too." Mitchel is grinning again, and it's all predatory.

"What!? Is he planning something?" This doesn't sound good, not good at all.

"Leaving now." He stabs a button and the video turns off.

"Ahhhhhhhhh!" Screaming doesn't make me feel better. Why, why,

why, why did I get married at all, much less four times? I have no one to blame but myself.

Well, this bomb isn't going anywhere. I carefully lock away all the parts, and quickly compose some mail to Chen, a Chinese Investigator I frequently work with. I send him all my data and a hundred credits. If he needs more, he will tell me.

I sigh, snap my sidearm to the side of my desk, take off my clothes, and lie on top of the workbench, staring at the ceiling. The mirrored ceiling over the workbench lets me practice posing my tall, curvy figure. I shamelessly pose this way and that, feeling silly yet very much alive. I practice making bedroom eyes at myself.

In actuality, I can't wait for Husband One to arrive, and I've already forgiven him for calling me Lieutenant. It's not that I feel bad because I nodded off on him—I was serious when I said I missed him. Mitch is my first love, and being apart from him hurts.

It takes him ten minutes to get to my office, which is impressive. The climb is 4,167 feet from the base of the mountain, a four-mile drive. He must have had his car on auto at maximum speed.

"You're pretty damn sexy laying there for a fifty-three year-old lady," he says, peeling out of his clothes.

I stick my tongue out at him. I'm in damn good shape for a fifty-three year old. It's the "blessing" of multiple regen series during the war. Sure, I stay very fit, but it's easier to take care of a forty-five year-old body. Nobody outside the family knows my secret. I let people assume that I just look that good for my age.

I start to giggle because he's not wearing undies and then he jumps on me, kisses me, putting his hands all over me. He paws and sucks on my breasts, then presses fingers inside me and swallows the sound I make. I gasp and squirm and soon we're having naughty intercourse right on my workbench. Oh, I need him. I need him not because I feel bad for falling asleep, but because I love him.

If Mitch is annoyed with me, he sure doesn't show it. His passion consumes me and soon I'm mindless.

I take the credits when he points out, in a rare moment where his lips are free, I can use them to buy Bill something nice, which he pointedly reminds me I have not done in a while. Husband One isn't the smartest guy, but he understands people. He and the maid/sex-bot Cazandra keep the family tranquil.

* * *

"Priority call on line three," Bob, my office computer, tells me sweetly. It wakes me up instantly, but Mitch just grunts and snuggles closer. I grab him so he doesn't roll over and fall off the workbench. "A Mr. Scott, CEO."

Scott. Scott is a Constitutional Enforcement Officer. I've never dealt with him professionally, but our respective territories overlap, so we keep each other appraised. I also run into him on occasion at Government seminars.

This call will not end well.

"Privacy audio only, connect." Mitch doesn't need to know work details. Line three is official Investigation business. As if Scott would be making a social call. I think he just hangs upside down in dark caves when the sun comes up.

"LT, this is Scott."

"What up, Scott?"

"Bacon, Washington." Bob is listening, of course, and instantly brings up a map of Washington, projected on the ceiling. Bacon is in central Washington, in the middle of nowhere, somewhat close to the Grand Coulee Dam. Nothing but desert and wheat fields, as I recall. Or maybe apples. Oh yeah: wine. Big business, wine is, out there.

"Double homicide," Scott adds. "A mother and her daughter."

I grunt. Ick. "Why me?" Anyone who knows anything about Investigators knows I don't advertise for homicide. I saw enough dead bodies in the war, and the purge. And Scott knows everything. Maybe literally.

"My field comp got a red flag from your agency on this one."

I feel the blood draining from my face and the room grows cold.

"Were they found tied together, facing each other?"

There is a long pause as the silence gives me my answer. Scott may encounter or force the occasional death, but he doesn't normally deal in murder.

"Yes," he says, as if he's having trouble speaking.

"I'm taking a hopper. I'll be there soon."

"Got it." Scott disconnects. Only a CEO would be un-frazzled by Investigator use of an orbital hopper. Actually, I used to think nothing bothered Scott; he has the emotions of a work bot. His sudden anxiety disturbs me almost as much as the fact that I've seen this crime before.

I get up, pushing Mitch off. I feel dizzy. Mitch says "Hey!" and stands up, grumpy I interrupted his post-euphoric nap.

"Mitch, can you hand me that wastebasket?"

Mitch nods and hands it to me. He really is a sweet man, really he is.

I promptly lose my breakfast.

CHAPTER 2

IN THE HEAD, AND of all the things I should think about, I'm really thinking how I should remodel the Military-sparse look and turn it into a real girl's bathroom.

I'm also cleaning myself up from Mitch's joyful incursions and brushing my teeth. He's a funny man, Husband One. At home, he's tender and sweet (unlike my other three naughty males), but if I get him somewhere outside of home, all of a sudden ravaging my body is the name of the game.

I enjoy it, and he knows that. But does the man have to paint me with his stuff, as if marking his territory?

Actually, considering I have three other Husbands, maybe that's exactly what he's doing.

"We have a problem," Bob says in my ear. "The nearest hopper is in Portland. Even the private ones are rented out."

"Portland! What the hell?"

"Volcano erupted in China. Rescue crews, the entire Pacific Region Volcano Research team, along with all of their equipment, etcetera."

Ugh. Ever since Glacier Peak went active, every volcano researcher, which admittedly is not a big number, moved to the Seattle area.

What is left of Seattle, anyway.

Coupled with the active Mt. St. Helens to the south, these scientists have a lifetime of active study right here. Volcanoes that go boom are natural disasters outlined in the Constitution for resource priority. I cannot remember my priority, but I'm sure local Investigator hopper use ranks way down there.

"It's not a long drive to Bacon, a couple of hours. I suggest—one moment. Incoming Military Call, Line Zero. MOF/B-12, AI."

Manned Orbital Fighter/Bomber, number twelve. Artificial Intelligence calling.

You know, if I didn't just have hot wild monkey sex with Husband One, this day would go down in the category of 'The Big Suck.'

"Connect." I consider having a sub-vocal conversation, which Bob could pick up, but decide Mitchel would think that is rude, even though I'm in the head. He respects my privacy greatly, no need to rub my sub-vocal ability in his face.

"Lexi."

"Arune."

Because of their speed, Military and commercial flights are exclusively drone equipment, with one significant departure: NI Pilots. Me.

Maximum combat efficiency is a result of Uplinking a human and an AI. The war powers that be made the MOF/B; the most badass flying machine ever built. Indeed, we ended the war with them, and Arune was 'my' MOF/B just as I was 'his' human Pilot.

Arune and I have a history. A real history. Towards the end of the war, we both went a little crazy.

Okay, maybe a lot of crazy. One time, on the way to the moon to help build the launcher, we had sex. Not Uplink sex, either. Physical sex.

Today, such stuff is normal. Back then, Arune and I, we were *pioneers*.

"I saw your hopper request and looked at the hopper queue. I'll be on your pad in about ten minutes." His masculine voice is assertive, smooth, with that little accent of his.

I open my mouth to argue, and then shut it.

"Okay."

What could I do? Say, "Sorry Arune, I lied to you and the therapist when I said I could climb back into the cockpit?" Or how about, "Sorry old friend, you were nothing but a vibrator to me that blew stuff up while playing taxi?"

Fuck. War shit.

* * *

When I come out of the head, Mitch gives me a juice drink. The wastebasket is nowhere in sight. It's the little gestures like this that really touch me, and I actually feel a little emotional, especially now that I have to kick him out while he's obviously worried. To my Husbands, I'm their rock. She who is never fazed. The war hero. The Investigator.

Before all of that, I was a girl. Sometimes I wonder if I should give it all up and just go back to the person I used to be, yank my implants and cyber gear, and deal with life on its own terms.

Then I wonder if that's feeling sorry for myself. Then I start wondering if I'm losing it. Then I usually take some snorf and don't think for a couple of days while my Husbands look on and frown.

Back to Mitchel.

"Sweetheart, I'm going to get dressed now, so I want you to leave."

Mitch gives me that look. He doesn't like to see me upset, because it happens so rarely. His inclination, as always, is to support me. To be there for me to lean on, to be the man that he always has been, all these years.

Oh, I love him!

"I can help you get into your field suit."

I shake my head. "I'm not wearing a field suit."

You can't 'fly' a MOF/B in civilian getup.

"What then? Was that a social call? Did someone die? Who…"

He looks at me, finally parsing my comment. "Oh."

He gets dressed, and I just watch. I try to burn his image into my mind, something normal. Something real. Something good.

Someone to come back to.

Plus, he has a nice ass.

He kisses me and is almost out the door, when he turns to me.

"You know, I just figured out that I'm the only one you call *sweetheart*."

I smile.

"I love you, Lexus Nancy Toulouse. You come back to me. Or I shall be angry." He gives me a wink.

Then he's gone.

* * *

My complex on the top of Mt. Si is rather large for a one-person operation, but going solo does have its advantages. I often walk around naked, but walking nude through a high-tech armory built for a fully equipped squad (why did I do that?) makes me feel silly.

I stand in front of the security locker. There are several different ways to open it. I pick the one that matches my mood.

I give it the finger.

The big locker opens with a *hiss-thunk*, and I survey the contents.

War shit. I hate it. The war was so bad the survivors destroyed most of the leftover advanced war tech. We burned the automated factories down, pushed the orbitals into the sun. We erased the tech knowledge from the books and the nets. The book/net part would not matter too much, but it sure made us feel better.

No chance of the enemy coming back, they were all dead: the people, their livestock, their pets, anything bigger than a hamster.

Total War. Genocide Plus Plus.

The locker beckons me, and for that, I'm fearful.

Many strange things happened during the war, so we decided a certain percentage of gear be kept in reserve, in case some of the bad things reared their ugly heads again. Leftover kill bots. Genetic mutations. Nano. Stuff flung out into space on a long return orbit. Some bad guy in stasis, hidden underground.

I take out an aerosol applicator and spray myself. Soon I'm hairless, hair turned into a fine mist with a funny smell. When the can is gone, I will have to use one that causes hair to fall out, making a mess. The can, being a Military design, even interfaces with my mil-grade internal nano regulator. No one makes the good nano stuff anymore, just as no one makes the good neural linkage equipment.

The Military kept most of their neural interfaced stuff for a rainy day, but supposedly stopped giving soldiers neural implants, rendering the equipment useless. The other branches of government, the Investigators and Constitutional Enforcement Officers, could keep their personal crap if they wanted. Not many did. I tried to get rid of mine, really, I did, but since I had no support for that effort, I failed.

"Bob, run a diagnostic on Suit Z12." Suit Z12 is exactly what I loathe: neural interface equipment, built during the technological height of the war.

"Fully operational, power at one hundred percent. Shall I extend the rack for suiting up?"

No.

"Yes, Bob, thank you."

The armor rack slides out and lowers. The armor is ready to go—all I need to do is back into it.

No time like the present.

At my wrists, the bottoms of my calves, and at the back of my neck are interface receptors, the entry point into my neural overlay, a lattice of bio and cyber on top of my nervous system. As soon as I'm in the suit, the male ends caress these NI points, almost like a lover.

Then like that lover, they penetrate me, snapping into place with a little *click-click-click-click-click.* Then the waste tubes are next, and I shudder, their insertion designed to feel good.

I hate it.

I want it.

The suit closes around me. It really is a second skin, technically three skins; a thin inner bio-layer, a memory gel above that and a harder, but flexible, outer layer. Air, water, waste processing and the scrubber ads bulk, but it's all micro small and powered by solar with a collector lattice, the power stored in BerTech accumulators.

The helmet automatically forms around my skull and the faceplate unfolds, locks into place and the soft hiss of the pressurization test fills my ears. When the check goes green, the faceplate neatly folds back but the helmet stays over my hairless head like a hat.

People who do not know what Z armor is think that because the material is thin and can fold back unobtrusively, it's "light armor" and therefore not as effective as a large armored shell.

Those people would be wrong.

"Interface complete," a woman's sexy voice sounds in my ear. I snarl, and turn off the audio interface. Using Active Thought is faster. Without neural receptors, the best one can do is sub-vocalize. Real war armor simply reads thoughts used for sub-vocalization.

The enemy went beyond that with their Net, and in reply, we went one more step with Uplink. Thankfully, the war ended before someone invented anything freakier, because beyond Uplink must be the old Christian God.

I look in the mirror. There I am. And I hate it. I don't hate it because the urinary extension went in and felt good. I don't hate it because it put a hose that feels like a penis in my anus and felt good. No, I hate it because now I just feel like *me*. There is no special feeling. The cyber interface is unobtrusive, I feel utterly normal.

Except I'm not normal. I'm a killer masquerading as an Investigator and Wife.

Suit Z12 doesn't make me a killer. It just reminds me that I am one.

It's an enabler, my combat suit.

I got the suit, might as well finish playing dress up.

—Bob, open the NI weapon locker.—

—Aye, aye, ma'am.—

The locker opposite me *hiss-thunk* opens.

"Hello, pretties. Did you miss Momma?"

Yeah, war vets. Over the years, a fifth of us killed ourselves, literally a twenty percent suicide rate. And there was a reason for that.

But they say the Military is just a more violent reflection of society. Things weren't much better at home. In some ways, they were worse.

The ground trembles as Arune lands. I'm sure if I had neighbors, they would be outside watching the spectacle, but after the war was over I claimed Mt. Si as repurposed Government land now attributed to my Investigator agency. Nobody saw fit to argue.

Too bad—it's not often a self-aware, anti-gravity orbiter lands in your backyard. Visually, it's amazing to watch, the technology used no longer acceptable to society, and thus rare.

* * *

A MOF/B is beautiful. It looks like a futuristic spaceship designed for atmospheric flight, and that's exactly what it is—flat-black composite deadly sleekness that sometimes haunts my dreams. There isn't anything stealthy about a MOF/B. Its main function is descent from orbit, blowing the crap out of anything it wants to—a tad hard to be stealthy as the very air around you ignites from the compression of your atmospheric entry.

The MOF/B uses a push-pull gravity accelerator, either attracting to a larger gravity field or pushing away from it. It's the smallest orbiter housing the device. The inventor types have been trying for years to cost/shrink the grav bubble ever since. They say, in my lifetime, I will be able to buy a bubble car.

There he sits on my landing pad, connected to my compound with a cute, redbrick path lined with flowers. The juxtaposition makes me want to laugh, the sound pressing up against the back of my throat, raw and joyous. He's big, sleek, menacing—so beautiful it hurts.

His cockpit access pad lowers and my suit's audio channel automatically clicks active. The suit is still attuned to Arune's command tree even after all these years.

"Lexi. Good to see you and I'm not saying that to squirt nano up your ass. I've missed you," Arune says in my ear.

In answer, I burst into tears.

I can't breathe. I can't think. Fear of Arune, love of him and desperate longing; self-loathing, grief, fear of what I will find in Buttfuck, Washington washes over me in a wave of throat-tightening, stinging tears.

"Oh my God, you're actually crying! Shit. Stop that. Shit. Get in the fucking cockpit before you embarrass yourself!"

"Only my office comp is watching," I manage to sputter.

—Ocular irritation. Clear visual inputs.—

Ack! Now my suit is telling me to get a grip. I quickly slap my two field cases into the lowered cargo loader and hop on the pad.

The orbiter has a living area/cargo bay about the size of a large Gulfstream cabin. The cockpit, however, is quite small, designed with several interesting features negating a large size. As the pad nears the top of its run, the cockpit chair descends from the inner-bubble, and I throw myself into it.

"Lexi..."

"Arune. Please. Lock me in and Uplink."

"Your heart rate..."

"For the love of everything, Arune. Uplink!" I beg. I'm on the verge of hyperventilating. If I don't calm down soon, my suit will tranq me with mood-altering drugs, which would suck for Investigative work. I need to be analyzing, not high.

I can always get high later.

"I've been ground-side for over twenty years. I need it, I need it and I need you. Please. Please…"

Arune is a mass of Think Goo, but he has emotions. To see me in such a state is probably stressful.

The chair raises and snaps into place. *Hisssssss.* The small cockpit comes alive with readouts befitting the high-tech marvel that he is, but most of them are covered in dust, and I feel guilty for abandoning him.

Probably right when he needed me the most.

My helmet reforms and seals around my head. *Snap.*

Tendrils move from the chair, and my suit opens at the base of my neck. They enter, and I feel one of their little touches, sliding across my skin, caressing me, connecting along the channel provided by my neck receptor.

"Yes!" The start of the connection is euphoric, mental foreplay.

"Ah!" says Arune.

My mind expands. We expand.

—Uplink!—

RAPTURE!

CHAPTER 3

LIKE MANY OTHER DESPERATE war-era innovations, Uplink to a self-aware quantum computer is a direct rip-off from several science fiction stories. The tech heads, desperate to overcome the neural social linking giving the Union such a speedy decision-making advantage, could not—of course—copy the technology they hated, the technology that destroyed every last iota of the individual. Instead, the neural scientists figured out a way to take neural linking to the next level.

Instead of destroying my free will like Unionization, they gave me the capability to interface with someone else yet keep my identity. Unlike the enemy, I could only do it in cyber-time. All the other links are just reflex links. No Uplinkage with my armor, for example. Just pure, lightning reflexes.

I was one of the first to get the neural interfaces. Generic Military Neural/Uplink Receptors, they called it back then. Only they never used the word "generic" around the first to get the implants. I just assumed it would be for armor. If I'd known an implant would make me a Pilot, and what that really meant, I would have said *no fucking way*. And it wasn't just a receptor—it was a neural overlay, the cyber that interfaces with the nerves and the receptor.

I wanted armor and faster reflexes, not bombs. But after the body count went up, who was I kidding? Bombs just let me do it without seeing faces.

That's water under the bridge, as they say. Now here I am, in Uplink, with a war machine I previously went on a murderous rampage with, and then had sex. My eyes are the ship. I look around my landing pad for the first time using enhanced optics. Beautiful view, from the top of Mt. Si.

—We need to talk.—

Arune likes to chat but I want to float.

—Let's lift. I need to see stars.—

With a MOF/B we can get to Bacon just by flying, and quickly, but I don't care. I want in space. Now.

—Lifting.—

—I'll call PS Traffic Control.—

I suspect Arune has never even talked to them. Everyone else simply gets out of his way, and that includes anyone contracting with PSTC.

—You always were one for politeness.—

"Puget Sound Traffic Control, this is Zebra-Zero-Zero-One-Two. Requesting priority flight path for the following coordinates via orbital descent." I send them a squirt of our destination and my Investigator cert.

I'll give them this, PSTC is nothing if not professional. They reply immediately, a young man's voice full of confidence. "Zebra-Zero-Zero-One-Two, here is your ascent and descent path. We really appreciate you contacting us. If there is anything we can do for you, ah, Investigator, please let us know. PSTC out."

"Path acknowledged. Thank you PSTC."

PSTC is a privately owned system covering the Pacific Northwest, and you can either pay-as-you go or contract with them. As an Investigator, I pay them a small yearly retainer because they offer me a significant Government discount. I don't use orbital vehicles or aerial equipment much, but when I do, I don't want to haggle over making sure something doesn't run into them while I should be thinking about a case.

Then again, I'm not thinking about the case right now, and that irks me.

Arune interrupts me feeling sorry for myself.

—Sliding into their ascent path. Oh, and we need to talk.—

Oh, Uplink partner communication, I love it. It's faster than anything imaginable. Faster than Active Thought. Faster than Union speech. It's a harmony of our souls.

The holographic path appears before us. Arune moves into it smoothly, accelerating.

—We will. Checklists first.—

I send mental commands to one of his subroutines and a readout starts scrolling in my eye. The interface sends the data right to my eyeballs via my nervous system.

Wow! He's loaded with everything, and "everything" on Arune is some major weaponry able to deal out destruction both pinpoint and overt. It's as if the war never ended.

Arune, they let you lift with that?—

—Heh. I break their decisions into thirds.—

—Eh?—

—I believe that one-third of 'them' feel I should be segmented out for spare parts, one-third feels we might need it, one-third feels like they are just humoring me. Forget about that, we need to…—

—Okay, I buy that. Yes, yes, talk. I'm sorry I lost it on the pad. I'm just human, you know.—

—What? Not that. What, was I your last Uplink? A normal relational reaction within parameters on the response matrices.—

I mentally roll my eyes at the machine talk Arune slips into when he is nervous or stressed.

—Yes, so what…—

—The medical diagnostic I ran on you has a yellow flag.—

Oh, great. Wonderful. I'm sick. Fuck. Could this day get any worse?

—What?—

—Your Lib-Gee has reset itself.—

—What? How? What does that even mean?—

—Don't know. I do know it's not supposed to be at the default, which is what, fifty/fifty? Do you know what it's supposed to be set at?—

—Ninety/ten!—

In the war, I took radioactive bullets to my internal woman parts. The wonder surgeons brought me back, but my ovaries were toasted and my uterus damaged, and they had to remove it all. Regeneration doesn't work on the human reproductive system—instant menopause at thirty.

Except, soon afterwards, some genius med-head finally figured out women sex hormone levels and the related neurological inputs. So they planted med-tech in me to give me a sex drive. On the hetero/homo scale, they set it at what I tested out as before accepting my commission—ninety percent/ten percent.

Like all the other crap they crammed into my poor body, it is a prototype, given to me by a society feeling guilty for abusing me to save their asses. It works, but it is not perfect by any stretch. It gives me a ferocious craving for sex instead of augmenting my romantic feelings. It drives me, rather than me driving it, but as the years slipped by, it stopped mattering if it was the tech or me. I stopped caring.

Replacing it now cost upwards of *five-hundred thousand* credits because of its molecular construction and the way it interfaces with my other cybertech, like my artificial thyroid.

When I found out about the cost all those years ago, I decided an 'almost' working Libido Generator was good enough.

There are worse things than craving sex every day. Sometimes twice a day.

Okay, once, I had sex ten times in a single day. Four Husbands can have its advantages.

Now, apparently I am fifty percent gay. Well, dip me in shit. I don't *feel* gay. If I am gay, I should be humping the maid-cum-sex-bot Cazandra that Bill brought home as a wedding present to the other Husbands—like a rabid weasel, because she's one of the hottest bots ever to walk the Earth.

Yah, Bill was popular for a long time with that one. Husband One thought it was great, and Husband Two and Three loved someone doing household chores, giving them more time to slack off fishing and hunting. I was somewhat jealous, but I got over it. Mitchel and Bill were happier for it, and in all honesty, after she arrived, my girly parts got the occasional much-needed break.

I like sex as much as any other woman with an 'enthusiastic' Libido Generator, but still: four Husbands.

—Wow. Is there any indication for how long it has been at default?—

If anybody could tell, besides my gynecologist, it would be Arune.

He literally knows my body better than I do. He can read and parse the data from my neural overlay, and it touches every part of me.

—With the available data, I can extrapolate to almost a year.—

—Ah, hell. About a year ago one of my perps decided to get even. He zapped my hotel room good with an EMP gun before trying to gut me with a knife.—

—Oh, that had to suck.—

—It did, I was wearing a silk slip, not battle armor.—

—What happened?—

—My contacts HUD went offline and I fell over, I was so dizzy. Vash, Husband Two, shot him repeatedly with my needler.—

I was more pissed off that someone interrupted my spectacular man-fuck more than anything else. Vash is gay, but he married me for a reason, and every so often that takes precedence over his sexual preference.

Stupid perp. Everyone likes to assume I'm the famous family muscle. Compared to Husband Two and Three, I'm dog chow. They are like me, except thirty-five percent meaner. And that's not a figure I pull out of my butt but from the old-school combat scale.

—Didn't someone do a full diagnostic?—

—Yes, but no one asked what the Lib-Gee should be set at. All the ones after mine are post-operative adjusting. And I'm overdue for my girly exam. Shit.—

—Oh well. Maybe you should get a new one.—

—I guess.—

Maybe menopause would be preferable to whatever I am.

—We're at the apex of our hop. Here are your stars, my Love.—

I look at the stars, so many stars, unfiltered by the atmosphere, bright and lovely. The sight tugs at me, and all the worries of the day slide away, lost in the pinpoints of light.

And the planet below is beautiful, so very beautiful.

—Ohhhh…—

—You're an incurable romantic.—

I can exchange thoughts, even sub-conscious ones, with Arune, but he can't 'read' my mind. It's similar to 'talking' in my armor, except, faster and 'broader.' He does know what I'm looking at, of course, since

I'm using his sensors to do so.

—That's why you love me.—

—No, I love you for your body. Your breasts, specifically. *Boobs.*—

I mentally laugh as we head down the descent path. That's a terribly bad joke for Arune, considering our history. I chuckle all the way down to the landing pad.

I also review all available info on Bacon, Washington. Since I am thinking in Arune time and not Lexus time, the amount of data I absorb before we touch down on the dusty pad is very efficient. Arune makes Bob look like a solid-state calculator.

—Bacon? Am I missing some pre-war social context? Did they raise pigs?—

Arune sounds curious, mainly because he didn't exist pre-war. The time-period fascinates him mightily. When he found out I had a Masters certification in pre-war history, he would Uplink with me every chance he could get so he could spend the virtual hours asking me questions.

—Don't ask me, it's better than Mossyrock. Probably named after some dude named Bacon.—

—Mossyrock? There is no town called Mossyrock.—

—Is to! Somewhere near Mt. St. Helens. I've been there.—

In fact, I think that's where I gave Mitchel a blowjob for the first time. The area has some pre-Collapse ruins (which, of course, drew me in) and we saw the ancient road sign and stopped. We trounced around in the woods looking for mossy rocks for tourist pictures.

—It's not on a map.—

—Would you put some ruin called Mossyrock on a map?—

—Got me there. Anyway, there was a welcoming committee at the pad, but all of them except the CEO (tag: Scott) just now ran off. You're not Investigating a CEO are you?—

Investigators are the only people with jurisdiction over CEOs (other than CEOs themselves). CEOs have jurisdiction over the Military, and the Military has jurisdiction over the Investigators. It's a three way dance I initially thought was stupid, but wonders of wonders, it works. So far.

—No, but something is off. Homicide, referred to me by Scott over there.—

—Not unheard of.—

—The homicides share characteristics of an earlier case.—

—How early?—

—I…—

Ah hell, I can't finish the thought. My brain doesn't want to go there. I'm feeling like I'm tainting Arune by talking about it, which is stupid, because he's smart enough to…

—War shit.—

Arune finishes it for me. He uses the same phrase copiously. Indeed, I may have gotten it from him.

—Yes. Sorry, Arune. Before we met.—

—Okay. Landing cycle complete. Lexi?—

—Yes?—

—Be careful. I know you desperately needed to Uplink, but I'm glad it was me. I missed you. And I'm very fond of you. If something in this stupidly named town happens to you, I will be angry.—

I'm simultaneously amused that he sounds so much like Mitch but also worried, because I know the combat load he has. Then again, he has other ways to make his displeasure known.

—Okay. I will. I promise.—

—Disengaging.—

And just like that, he's gone.

I have to be honest with myself; I have no idea how that makes me feel. People are under the impression it's as if part of you is missing, but that isn't true. The best I can describe, it's being high on outstandingly good drugs, and then cold stone sober in an instant. Which is the normal state? I could not answer. I don't know.

The tendrils slide back, my helmet half deforms, but before the chair lowers to the pad, an access panel pops open.

I snicker. The top is a lighted mirror, and inside the box, my old makeup compact. I ignore the compact and take out a cleaning cloth, wiping my tear-streaked face.

The chair lowers and I slide onto the pad, standing, and my helmet created eyewear tints in the glaring sunlight. Scott has kept his distance, so I stride over to him.

We shake hands, always a dance in armor.

I look into his eyes.

There I see something I have never seen from Scott. Fear. He's trying to hide it, but you can't hide a fear response from an Investigator in war armor.

Scott is not afraid of telling me something. The MOF/B is freaking him out. My combat suit is freaking him out.

Scott is afraid of *me*.

* * *

The landing pad Bacon has set aside for official Government use is in the middle of nowhere, set on a hill several miles away from town. I look around. I'm in a desert, this portion of the landscape set aside for fallowing, it seems. Or perhaps nobody wants to irrigate it. It's lonely, and starkly beautiful in that unique Eastern Washington way.

Tumbleweed blows by in the distance. I expect to hear someone playing the harmonica any moment. I turn my attention back to Scott.

"Scott."

"LT."

Scott isn't a good-looking man. He looks like a cross between a tech nerd and a weather-beaten forest ranger. To his credit, he has an athletic look, which I find somewhat attractive. His CEO uniform, armored and distinctive in its black and dark green motif, makes him look official, and must be intimidating to lesser mortals. He's a man of few words, and a master at economy of action. He's a very good Constitutional Enforcement Officer. Some say the best.

I used to think of him as an unemotional *asshole* that still needs to get over not being breast-fed. Now, I'm starting to suspect he's just like me and carrying baggage around from the stupid war.

I can sympathize with that greatly, but now Scott is just pissing me off.

"Start at the very beginning. Leave nothing out. Start with how the Office of Constitution Enforcement is involved with a serial killer."

The words 'serial killer' seems to rock his world. For a closely guarded man, I must be Daughter of the Old Devil.

His eyes flash and he recovers in record time. "What, right here?" He looks pointedly at the MOF/B behind me.

"Here and now."

"Look…"

"Are we arguing? Are you actually going to argue with me in front of Arune? On a *murder* case?"

It is then Arune releases a steam cloud from the back, his timing impeccable. Scott almost jumps and it's all I can do to keep from laughing.

I just look at him, and he blanches. He knows my combat record, and to see me with the MOF/B in question has him completely unnerved.

"Lieutenant…"

The rank card. "Major, the war is over, but I'm not over. I was never 'over.' My title is Investigator."

I take a step closer to him. He actually steps back.

I don't relent. "Since the first two homicides occurred before OCE was even founded, I didn't think this was even remotely OCE related. Do I need to turn this into an Official Investigation, not just an Investigation for Hire? Tell me, did the little red flag cause you problems? I'm the last person you wanted on this case, correct?"

Scott looks at me and deflates. He hunches his shoulders, slouches. He can't look me in the eye.

My look doesn't soften but my heart goes out to him. Whatever Scott is, whatever is going on, he isn't an evil man. Scott is a good man, I remind myself. One of the good guys.

I also remind myself even the good guys screw up.

"You're right. All of it," he says.

I just look at him, my emotionless expression a void. One quarry once described it as 'the light-absorbing nothing look from Hell.'

"There is a psi-operative involved," he finally says. The admission sounds like he had to rip his own heart out to tell me. "That's how County Safety found out about the murders before they were reported."

"A cyber operative?" This doesn't make sense. Cybercrime is a dime a dozen. County Safety usually deals with it, and if it is especially bad, they hire an Investigator, sure. But still…

"No, psi, not cy." He takes a deep breath. "Psi as in psionics."

"Psionics? Like the Humanoids in those ancient Jack Williamson books? Mind over matter shit?"

Juan, Husband Number Three, makes me read his old sci-fi books because that's what he likes to talk about when we are alone and chatting. They're fun, but sometimes the Military parts give me the willies. I like his fantasy books much better. I can read those forever. In fact, last month I found a few really good ones he hadn't read yet and I pranced around in my panties making fun of his lack of geekiness.

Then he threw me on my bed and fucked my ass until I thought it was going to fall off.

Heh. I bite my lip to tell my stupid Lib-Gee to shut the fuck up.

"Exactly like that," Scott says. "Except not through, ah, rhodomagnetics. Through dark energy manipulation."

I suppress a shudder. That sounds suspiciously like Unionization, but my brain kicks in and I know it can't be. I have a sudden appreciation on why I haven't heard of this before.

Everyone hated Unionists and their use of dark matter and energy to rip out a person's soul.

I look at his face, willing it to display a lie. Scott betrays nothing, back in his CEO zone.

It's official. This is the strangest day of my life. At no point during my infamous existence has a day gone so weird, so quickly. Only Mitchel has grounded me in reality. Now I'm waiting for a call, something like 'This is Bill, Mitch ran off with Cazandra; he's pimping her out in Vegas while they live in a trailer with their Persian cat named Jet.'

I consciously remove the scowl from my face. "I take it back. Don't tell me everything yet. I don't want to know right now."

He visibly relaxes.

"You can help me with my gear," I say, heading to Arune's cargo hold. "The lockers have wheels."

Scott doesn't even frown that I have reduced him to a porter.

As we're trucking my gear to his waiting SUV, I finally get a clue.

"Are you psionic?" I ask him.

"Yes, of course."

Well dip me in shit.

CHAPTER 4

SCOTT'S SUV IS FANCY, expensive and powerful. I can feel the torque kept at bay. I deduce there is a mil-grade accumulator housed in the engine block.

"Look, I'm sorry," I tell him as we enter wine country. Grape vines stretch on forever on either side of the dusty road as we head north.

"No, don't apologize. Geeze, one moment you're psycho-killer bitch about to drill me right on the pad with your needler, and the next like my mousy secretary, apologizing for no reason."

Ah, Scott is back to being Scott. Good.

"Well I'm sorry, you big dork. War shit just sets me off, that's all."

He grins and then actually laughs. "You should have seen us all as your MOF/B descended. It was like the Finger of God dropping from orbit. The locals literally ran off, and since I was wearing armor, I decided to piss myself. Holy crap that was the most awesome-scary thing I've seen in a long time."

I laugh. Arune and I didn't even consider our method of arrival, a battlefield insertion drop. Let Scott keep his illusions.

"Just tell me, do you know anything about the prior murders?"

"Jesus, you're so intense. *No.* I shit a brick when I saw that red flag. No."

"We'll get to your story later, but I need to warn you. This is bad stuff, Mr. Scott. Psycho killer rapist stuff. The details will be ugly."

"R-rape?" Scott almost drives off the road.

"Yes. Both of them, if it's the same guy. Or even if it's a copycat."

He's quiet, and I glance over at him. He looks as if his world is coming apart, so I look out the window at Bacon instead. The town is not so much on a hill as built into it. Terraced streets go back and forth, east to west, most of the buildings and houses facing south.

From the data I reviewed in Arune time, after the war, Bacon eventually turned into vineyards, acres of grape vines genetically engineered not to hork in the frozen winter. Today, beyond the grapes are apples and beyond that wheat. Bacon is a diverse farming community, untouched by the ravages of time, good middle-class folk making a decent living. The wineries pull in quite a bit of credit.

Considering no one is making French and Italian wine anymore, that's not surprising.

We drive through town, which is in the hills. Folk are peeking out at the SUV. Scott continues to drive northwest.

"Who found the bodies?"

"It's in the file."

"Who found the bodies?" I have no desire to explain to a CEO my Investigative methods.

"The Husband-father."

"Where is he now?"

"With his parents. He looks like the walking dead."

"Any other children?"

"No."

"Vet?"

"No."

"How about the parents?"

"No."

Hmmm. Getting a list of vets in the area isn't going to be easy. There are no official records for that, and many vets don't exactly like to advertise.

I see many interviews in my future.

—Bob, queue up the County Coroner. Tell her I will be ready in about three hours.—

—Aye, aye, ma'am. I have messages from all four of your Husbands. They heard about the MOF/B and are worried.—

—Tell them I will speak to them later. SOP on this one, Bob, by the numbers.—

—Aye.—

After passing a County Safety SUV guarding the winery and thus the crime scene, we pull up to a farmhouse, which I deduce is seasonal living quarters for grape pickers. Harvest should be in about three weeks. The farmhouse is offset from a winery (the sign said *Riversage Winery*) by about 200 yards, and off in the distance I spy the main house, where the family lives. Used to live.

Scott puts the SUV in park.

"Let me see the search waivers."

If he's surprised that I just assumed he would collect them for me, he doesn't show it. He flips the driver side visor down and grabs a stack of papers. In most cases, I would be verifying these myself. With a CEO at my elbow, I don't need to do that. If something were not legit, he would be the first to know. Unless he wanted to hang me out to dry, that is.

I think showing up in a MOF/B took care of that angle.

Searching beyond the crime scene without permission is a bad thing. I could lose my license. Be sued. Have the Military Police arrest me. Be shot at by the owners or stakeholders with no recourse.

I commit the names and signatures to memory. I have signatures for everything that constitutes the winery. With one exception, I also have the neighbors' surrounding property that borders the fences, not including any structures or vehicles. Standard stuff, good deal. I appreciate that he understood to use real paper, an archaic Government custom in use by Investigators more so than the other two branches.

Nothing says 'pay attention this is official' like a real piece of paper.

One tear stained neighbor release had all the boxes violently checked—full permission. That sometimes happens too. A distraught friend, crying his or hers eyes out while trying to make a decision about consent.

And I thought my day was shitty. I vow right there to stop being a little girl and do my job.

I drag out the first locker that contains my Crime Scene Investigation bots. I activate them before opening the locker. When I do, they spring out and start walking around, delicately. They will record everything in 360 hi-res and look for small clues better than any human could. One bot looks for footprints or outside clues, and it skitters here and there. The rest, after looking around, line up at the door, waiting for someone to open it.

Scott looks vaguely uneasy. I surmise he probably has never been this close to an Investigator working in the field before. The bots don't exactly move like bugs (their multiple articulated legs are designed for maximum stability so they almost seem like they are gliding), but they *look* like big bugs. I think they are somewhat cute, scurrying here and there.

Then again, I had sex with my MOF/B, so my definition of cute probably sits outside the middle of a bell curve.

"Did you do any field prep?"

"I gave the house comp orders right out of my field manual. I confirmed it killed the circulation, sealed the house, all of those things," he answers.

"How long are we going on?"

"From County Safety's crime comp, the TOD estimate is four hours, sixteen minutes."

Oh. The bodies are still fresh. How did Scott get here so fast?

Ah, I get it.

—Arune, is there a sat floating up there, one of the older lookieloos that went on standby after V-Day?—

—Yup. Two, actually.—

—Send them activation codes and start IDing anything that moves in or out of Bacon for a hundred kilometers. And don't tell anybody. Ever. Make sure they're not transmitting any telemetry, that they're storing everything local.—

—Ooooo. Done. What up? —

What I'm doing is a total invasion of privacy to anyone not on a common road. It's naughty.

—The bodies are still warm. The killer could still be in town.—

—How did OCE get there so fast? And why?—

Arune says aloud what I am thinking.

—I have a theory. I'll give you a full brief onboard.—

—You will?—

—I would never keep anything from you, Arune. You're like Husband Number Zero to me.—

—You're just saying that to get in my pants!—

—Ha. Lexi, out.—

I open a channel to 911 and bypass the operator, going straight for the County Safety dispatch channel.

"County Safety, this is Investigator Toulouse. Do you have any potential suspects in the Gifford murders?"

"Safety Officer Sam here. Negative, ma'am, the crime comp has a very high percentage on the stranger factor, so I have the entire County monitoring just about everything there is to monitor. If a mouse farts in the field 4.5 yards southwest from your position, we're probably going to pick it up."

"Good deal, Sam, good deal. Any strangers in town?"

"An entire tour bus of bicyclists and winery hoppers."

Score.

"How long has the bus been in town?"

"Since two hours before the murder estimate. They plan to leave after a catered dinner."

"How old are they?"

"Ma'am?"

"How old are they?" Damn, I hate repeating myself to people that know better.

"Sorry, Investigator. Young folks without kids, except an older gentleman, a photographer."

"Sam, is the photographer on common property?"

"Yes ma'am, he's on vid right now."

"Send me his picture and anything you got on my piggy-back channel."

"You got it. But Investigator, he has a rock-solid alibi. I haven't interrogated him, but we can vouch for all of their movements since they got here. Standard safety waivers for using the bus."

I sigh. People can be sheep sometimes. I would never sign a monitoring waiver.

"Okay. If he starts acting strange or bolts from town, let me know. How about the bus driver? How old is the driver?"

"She looks like around fifty, ma'am."

I frown. "Okay, watch her too, Sam."

"Okaaaay. You going to fill us local yokels in, Investigator?"

"It's murder Sam. Murder most foul. You might want to consider who you want me to scar mentally for life with a debrief."

"Ah, okay." He sounds depressed.

"Sam, how old are you?"

"Excuse me? What..."

"Just yanking your dork, Sam. Bad Investigator humor. Jay-Kay."

"Okay you got me there. If you're asking if I was an Adult during the war, yeah. I was."

"Thanks for all your help. Toulouse, out."

Only, I'm not kidding.

Not kidding at all. There is a reason the first thing I do is find all people old enough to be vets. It's a terrible cliché, but I know far too well the horrors of war don't end simply because the fighting stopped.

I look at the picture of the photographer. He has a good Nikon. He looks like just a guy. The still turns into a video, and I watch him reading a book and sipping coffee. Something strikes me as off, though. I watch the video again but can't put my finger on it.

Crap. I can't figure it out.

—Bob, I want to know everything about this person. Run him Pri One through MatchUp, have them put a real person on it. Tag that expense as 'Bacon 01'.—

—Acknowledged. Running now.—

—Thanks Bob. Any other messages?—

—Chen called. He might have a lead on your bomb.—

—Yeah! Go Chen!—

Chen is a good Investigator. I wonder if the volcano has given him grief.

—Also, Mr. Gifford has paid for part one of this Investigation in full, with the standard retainer. He signed an Alpha contract.—

—Okay, thanks Bob. Toulouse, Out.—

An Alpha contract is my carte blanche to Investigate this murder all the way to a Judgment for a fee of up to one million credits, all expenses paid, monitored by a standard forensics account auditor.

Mr. Gifford is pissed. Pissed and *rich*. It's a reason why homicides avoid rich people. Their family hires agencies like mine.

He could have hired another agency, perhaps a team based one, and they simply would take over. The red flag on the case would let me hover over their shoulder, but I'd be out my fee. The best I could hope for is a subcontract.

That he went straight for me shows he's angry.

This is good. Angry is good for him right now. It will keep him from the abyss. It will keep him from destruction when I tell him what happened to his Wife and daughter.

Speaking of destruction, I put my hand on Scott's arm. He startles, but looks at me, eyes sad.

"I should leave you outside, but I'm not going to. I'm not even going to ask, but I have to warn you. You can go in, but what you will experience will be bad. You may never be the same."

"I..." he looks at me. "I have to see—with, with my own eyes."

I grab his hand with my other gloved hand, cursing that I can't just touch him with real skin. "No! It's more than see. It's smell. It goes everywhere. You will taste death, actually *taste* it because it's so thick on the air. And that won't even be the worst. My equipment has the potential of revealing the entire murder. This will be just like the war. In this case, it might be worse. No matter what you did to get your CEO slot right from the get-go, this could be worse."

Please Scott, please. Just stay in your car. I'm mentally begging him, but I know what he's going to say, I know it.

"I have to, LT, I have to."

Sometimes I hate men.

I get out my second locker and position it by the door. My CSI bot army, still lined up, waits patiently. I put my hand on the doorknob, and I can hear an old-style electronic lock disengage, pegging the house's age as pre-war. It has prints on it, all filed away by the print bot.

I turn to Scott once more.

He steels himself.

"How long have you been a precog?"

He isn't even bothered by the question. "All my life. Over the years, I've gotten better. I've been augmented, but we can talk about that later."

I nod. "You saw the murder, but you didn't see the rapes, did you?"

"No, I didn't," he whispers. Silent tears are now running down his face. I'm destroying this man, and I can't stop. I would sacrifice him to solve this case, and he knows it.

"You lied by omission to me, didn't you? You said there is psionics involved, not that the killer is a psion. Psionist. Whatever you call it. You were sleeping in Coulee City for that hydropower business I heard on the net, and the murder invaded your mind. You're the rogue psi op, aren't you?"

"Please, LT, I'm sorry. I'm not supposed to get involved like this, but you don't know what it was like. It was bad, really bad."

I gently pat his face. "No worries. I'm the one that's sorry."

Scott is a good man. He doesn't deserve murder in his life.

Scott grins weakly, wiping his eyes delicately with a gloved hand. There is a reason you're not supposed to cry in armor. "There you go again, apologizing for nothing you did."

But he knows why I said it. He knows. His eyes thank me.

"I'm going to be actively recording," I say, partly because he's a CEO, partly as a warning. I turn on my active link to Bob. I take a deep breath and open the door. My CSI bots go forth, and I smell death.

* * *

I am a righteous woman. I don't like Investigating homicides, but that's because of one body too many in my life, not because the details of the crime affect my mental health in real-time.

When I see a dead body, I see a puzzle. I know I should feel something for the victim's state, but I don't. It bothers me that someone killed someone else. It doesn't bother me that the victim is dead.

For that reason, I mostly quit taking homicides. They constantly reminded me I'm not a normal person.

I will take on a homicide Investigation with some reluctance, because sometimes the details of the crime piss me off. Like if the murderer used war shit.

And that's why I love being an Investigator. I can do something about the crime. That little detail is everything. I'm not a powerless observer. I can avenge the wronged. The society we built from ashes takes a very dim view of crime, especially murder.

My righteous fury doesn't splash harmlessly against a wall—I become the tip of the spear.

The house smells as it should—as if the air scrubbers are off while two bodies inside and the summer heat flowing around it. The house is in shade, but it's still hot.

A path appears before me on my HUD, and I remember to send the telemetry to Scott. My floor CSI bot has made sure there isn't anything I'm going to tread on and screw up. I'm sure if it had advance thoughts, it would want me to float, somehow, around the room. One time I actually walked off the trail it blazed and it came zooming back, beeping and waving its little antenna in some type of electronic angst because its initial sweep was still in progress.

Like I said, cute.

Cute like the farmhouse. The walls have art of grapes, wine, people drinking wine, and beautiful, naked women. The floors are hardwood and clean, the furniture old but of the sort that's stain proof. My little trail is taking me to a media room.

That's not exactly unique. Media rooms are usually sound shielded so as not to disturb sleeping people.

I walk slowly and do a thermal scan, looking for bad guys.

Pausing, I get out a little half-mound device and place it on a tabletop. Immediately it activates, and starts pinging. It's a motion detector, and in my HUD, I now have wire-forms for the bots, Scott and myself. I could use my suit detector, but old habits die hard. It is better to receive broadcasted data than it is to send it. I don't care if someone shoots the detector, but I do care if they shoot at me.

Scott has been quiet so far, carefully observing. The use of the detector, however, crosses some tactical line with him, and he speaks up in a flat, neutral voice.

"You don't think someone is here, do you?"

I turn to him. It's a good question.

"No, but people sometimes commit murder to get at an Investigator. It happens, so it's a good procedure."

"That's sick!" I can almost hear him thinking. "What about a bomb?" he asks. "That would be easier."

"Yes, but some are looking for the personal touch. Nevertheless, CSI bot #2 is a bomb sniffer. It's x-raying everything and anything, and has a chemical sniffer that's okay. He's linked right to Bob, and Bob is programmed to make sure I don't do something stupid and blow myself up."

"Did you have anybody try to kill you like that?"

"Yes." A good follow-up question, one that brings up bad memories.

"A vet. Pissed off you ordered him to do something which he never forgave himself," he says with confidence.

"Yes." Damn, he's good.

On the other hand, seeing as how he outranked me during the war, he may have encountered that exact scenario himself. Maybe, I'm thinking, there is a reason Scott is always in his armor.

A few more steps and we're at the media room—and the crime scene.

I frown. Not because there are two dead bodies, but because it's immediately different from the first time I encountered something similar.

A mother (tag: Jennifer Elizabeth Gifford), her hands tied to her daughter's, which in turn are bound with a connecting cord to a ring screwed into the floor. She's on her side.

A daughter (tag: Layla Elizabeth Gifford), facing her mother, hands bound to hers. Their wrists, interlocked with their hands, bound in duct tape, make for a nightmarish scenario.

Around each neck is a pink silk scarf, tightly wound.

Just like the prior murders. Here, the scene departs from the other. Each is wearing lingerie—the mother, a black silk slip and the daughter, a young pubescent girl, obscenely wearing stockings and a garter belt. The victims of the first murder were naked.

"Is this the same as the other murders?" Scott sounds like he is working on being dispassionate.

"Mostly—the victims of the prior murders were nude. Other than that, this looks all too familiar."

Scott frowns. I decided to fall into teacher mode to keep his immediate mind off the implications of the scene before him.

He can fall apart later.

"What do you think the cause of death is?" I ask him.

He looks puzzled and wrinkles his nose. "The cause of death *appears* to be strangulation with the scarves. That's what I saw in my dream. I'm not too sure though, I have not seen a strangled person before. I think their eyes would be bulgy, or something. What I felt in my dream was different. I think."

I walk around the bodies. "Somewhat. There are burst blood vessels and discoloration beyond decomposition you can look for before removing the scarf and looking at the neck. The lungs tell the rest of the tale during the autopsy."

That's not how they died, though. In a few moments, I should have…

—Warning: Unauthorized nano intrusion detected, Level 3. Internal regulator short-term insufficient. Suit neutralize?—

Bingo.

—Report nano composition.—

—Pheromonic enhancers with endorphic riders.—

Sex enhancers. Nanos that dose you with pheromones, activate the pleasure center in your brain and increase the blood flow to your genitals.

—Do not neutralize.—

—Recommendation: neutralize. Override required.—

—Acknowledged. Override: Don't neutralize.—

—Recommendation: Seal suit.—

—Acknowledged. Override: Do not seal.—

Gosh darn I love Active Thought arguing with the overpriced war armor that makes me feel like I'm twenty-five years younger and about to go to battle. This is fun.

Actually, it's pretty fucking distracting.

I turn to Scott.

"They ODed. On nano. The bad guy injected them with a nullifier, and then about five minutes later, sprayed them with sex enhancers, enough to kill them. If this is like the other murder, then before they died of toxicity and neural overload he raped them and their bodies responded as if it was the best sex in their lives. Only, mentally, it was not. They were mentally aware of their unnatural state, but the artificial sex-response, even if they didn't die from toxicity levels, would've driven them mad."

"That's fucked up!"

"It's evil. Pure evil," I admit.

"Nobody makes injectable nullifiers that can work that fast, and you can't OD on sex enhancers," Scott says, stating the obvious.

I give him an even look. "Nobody—nobody *today* makes that stuff." Scott was Home Guard. There was a lot he didn't see, so it's forgivable he didn't clue in at first.

"Oh Sweet Jesus. Are you telling me this is zombie tech?"

I purse my lips at the use of an ancient religious expression with the word "zombie." I understand why soldiers like Scott, back home trying to keep our borders intact, would use it. On the front lines, however, we never used 'zombie.' It's hard to think of someone with such a beatific, angelic face as a zombie. We just called them the enemy and left it at that.

No, it was fucking scary enough without thinking of them as zombies.

I nod.

"How come my armor isn't screaming bloody murder?"

"The nano is for girls only. When the newly converted plugged themselves into the Happy Network, their females lost a lot of drive, not just sex drive, until they were acclimated. To keep them happy, they doused them all regularly with the stuff. Then they made it for Collaborators. So they could, you know, get used to it."

Indeed, I owe some of my libido to conceptual reverse engineering. My internal regulator eventually killed the stuff when I ran into it last time, but the data made it back to several scientists who took the information and ran with it.

Yay. Lucky me.

Also, Scott's post-war armor kind of sucks. I'm not sure how it would respond to war-level nanos. I feel no need to go into that here.

"Is there enough still here that it will be affecting you?" Now he's concerned.

"It will, and soon."

He opens his mouth to say something, but shuts it as the CSI bots give me the go ahead to examine the bodies, and I approach closer.

I unseal my gloves, and receive more protests from my armor, requiring more overrides. I put on normal latex, very tight fitting gloves.

I approach the girl. I'm eager to examine her first, because there is one thing I left off my prior report, left it off on purpose. A detail I left off because I knew, even back then, that the murder was so sensational that if the details came to light, some sick fuck might want to recreate it.

That was before everything went to Hell, of course.

I get on all fours and switch on my helmet light. One thing about the armor, the light is many times more powerful than my field light.

Rigor mortis has set in, but it's far from a full rigor. I gently pick up her rear and look at her from the back, and proceed with an examination. Even that quick look tells the tale: just like the first murders, he sprayed her with a first aid spray so she would not bleed.

I have to get up close for the exam, and the proximity has the nanites in me good and proper and I feel euphoric. Instantly I regret not letting my armor take care of it, but the information is very valuable. It's the exact same response, the same nanos, the same *modus operandi.*

I ignore it, but I'm sure my flushed cheeks and dilated eyes make me look terrible.

I turn to Scott, and he looks like he swallowed a worm.

"I know what you're thinking. That I'm violating her." I stand up and go to him. "Trust me with this. You, me and the Coroner, we're the only ones who are going to give these two victims a voice. The dead need us, Scott, they so very need us."

I'm high and my thinking has a certain euphoric clarity to it.

"What happened here was monstrous. A physical examination is what she would want. She wants us to get the bad guy. Wherever she is now, she's relying on us to find him and get him."

He nods.

I keep his attention. "I want you to finish examining the bodies. Your dream is the only reason we're here. If there is any justice in the world, there has to be a reason for that dream. I don't know how your precog works, but don't you think there is a reason? If so, you need to go all the way with this one. You need to set aside your guilt and help these two in death."

Scott abruptly sits on the sofa.

"I tried, LT, I really did. I just didn't know where to look. When I figured it out it was too late."

"You calling as soon as you did may be what catches the killer. The first rule of crime scene investigation is getting to the scene as soon as possible. The clock is ticking. Time is our enemy. For Investigators it always has been. You could not help them then, but you can now."

Scott nods again, but he's frowning. "I'm not an Investigator."

I place my hands on my hips. "Fuck OCE. Even without your psionics shit, you're an Investigator, Scott. The moment you walked through the front door, you sold me your soul."

He pauses for a long time, face blank. Then his expression crumples; he looks troubled.

"I only get snippets from the future in dreams, not in the waking world. Precog is really just a side-effect of true psionics."

Well dip me in shit. What else can he do?

"Better than a poke in the eye with a sharp stick." I counter.

Finally, I come clean. "Scott, I can't do this. The nano response has me tripping. I'm too high. You have to help me. Please."

Scott examines the bodies. He does everything I ask. He looks for semen, and we don't find anything. Looks in their mouths. Sniffs. Examines for bites, looks under the fingernails. The bots will get all this, of course, but they can't do any abstract thinking, so it's important to look at the bodies as soon as possible to spot anything wrong.

It takes us an hour.

"Did you see what he looked like?" I finally ask.

He doesn't hesitate. I guess he feels the cat is out of the bag or that confidentiality will prevent problems or maybe he even has authorization to scrub my data. With a CEO, it's possible.

"No. I saw through her eyes," he says, looking at the girl. "She was just looking at her mother, feeling high, feeling turned-on, feeling horrified, feeling, feeling like her body was on fire and her mind was trapped in a different body, not hers. Feeling as if she died and went to Hell. He was standing behind her. Then she started begging him as the scarf went around her neck. Begging him to kill her. Begging him to fuck her even though he was choking her with the scarf. Pleading. Her heart felt like it was going to burst. Then she felt like she was floating, and finally she felt pain, pain in her chest, and her vision went red and she—felt nothing more."

I am speechless; what could I say? Fuck. Now I feel like a total bitch.

"I didn't understand why she kept asking him to fuck her, but now it makes sense."

I take a deep breath. The nano is finally dead, the response gone. All I smell now is corpse.

Good, because at one point while Scott was examining Jennifer, I almost felt turned on enough to draw my needler and shoot myself in the head.

Fuck. This is going to be a one-way trip to a therapist for both of us.

Scott takes a deep breath, and then looks like he regrets doing that. "LT, where were the first murders?"

Why do people ask questions they don't want the answers to?

"Alsace."

"Where is that?"

"Was. France. Near the German border."

"Mother fuck!"

Yeah, it pretty much sucks.

CHAPTER 5

ON COMMAND, THE CSI bots begin their inspection of the bodies. Scott and I search the house while they do their job. We don't find anything interesting at all. We take the trash, the garbage disposal contents, the air filters. I change out the filters for the replacements right by the HVAC, and turn the house system back on.

This takes another hour. With two of us, it's taking a shorter amount of time to look for evidence and run the checklists, even while Scott is an amateur. It's a sobering wake up call to my solitary existence.

Then Bob drops a bomb.

—ICDA has a scene reconstruction. Program available on request.—

Whoa boy.

I give the house commands, and the windows go opaque, the doors lock, and the lights dim.

"What's up?" Scott looks curious. At least his color is back. Watching the bots swarm over the bodies is sure to remind him of some war shit he wants to forget. I know it does with me.

"Investigators use ICDA—Investigation Crime Database and Analysis. It's a big honking supercomputer. We're talking war shit—the computer used to design the AIs, so when paired with all the crime data known to man, it knows all about human behavior in a disgusting amount of detail. As the bots and I collect data, it goes to Bob, my work comp, and Bob sends it to ICDA. It's an expensive system to maintain, but worth it."

"ICDA—as in, Cheyenne Mountain ICDA? I thought that was

some old Defense Agency thing."

"Cheyenne Mountain, yes. And no, that's also where the ICDA hardware is."

Scott's expression darkens again. Or still. I can tell he's been to Cheyenne Mountain because what little happiness he was holding onto for dear life after seeing the murder scene has dripped from him as if I squeezed it out of his body with my armored fists. I can almost see it pooling at his feet, turning black.

"Between the details of the prior murders, your dream description, and the data from the CSI bots, ICDA thinks it can display a reasonable facsimile of the crime as it occurred."

"Whoa," says Scott. I give him a stiff smile. "How is that possible?"

"The CSI bots are finding forensic evidence, and ICDA matches that with M.O.s and details from prior crimes going all the way back to the beginning of recorded history. Even the lack of evidence has meaning, a profile. Data analysis doesn't get any better."

"Kick ass. Let's watch it."

"No," I say and give him a look. "It's too intense for someone untrained."

"Damn it, I'm a vet. I can handle it."

"This is completely different. This recreation is post-war tech. Not war tech. It's going to push…"

"Fuck that. You've no idea what it's like being a psion. I can parse it."

"It's gonna be bad."

"Damn it! You special ops freaks think you had it bad behind the lines. Well fuck, LT, what happened at home was sometimes worse. You thought Edinburgh was bad, you should have seen Honolulu. Yes, I'm righteously pissed some evil sexual deviant serial killer obliterated the Gifford family. Well, at the end of the day, I can go to bed and say, 'at least that wasn't fucking Honolulu'."

Scott is shaking.

I put a hand on his arm and rather than flinch away, he visibly relaxes.

"I'm sorry. I didn't know."

He frowns but then gives me a small smile. "Yeah, I'll let you apologize for that one."

I smack his ass. The armor causes my hand to sting; I'm still wearing latex gloves.

"Hey! Investigator abuse!"

I grin. "Call a MP and report me."

He chuckles.

* * *

The County Coroner team comes and collects the bodies, both collection techs wearing perpetual frowns. I express my desire to be there at the autopsy.

I look over at Scott. I still think this is a bad idea, but he's right. I have a bit of arrogance, but I don't think trying to ease him into the underworld of sex crimes and murder is a bad thing.

From the second locker, I get out four projectors and arrange them around the media room. I bolt them to the floor, the reenactment can confuse the senses, and tripping on one isn't pleasant.

"This is going to feel real," I warn. "It will use all of your senses, and if you get close to the actual reenactment, ICDA will take that as a signal that you want to be plugged into the scene as the person you touched. It will give you a full sensory dump and give you touch, too. For you, it will use your armor's sensory feedback system. For me, it will give me a narrowband wireless Uplink. So don't touch any of the images. You need training for that because you will feel everything ICDA thinks the victim felt. I'm serious. No touchie."

"Wireless Uplink?" His eyes are almost bulging out of his head.

"Z model armor functions."

"I had no idea Investigator tech is so advanced."

"Nobody does. And we keep it that way," I warn.

I give him an even look, but think better of asking him to leave again. "You need to put your holster on Level 4 retention."

"My holster? Why—oh." Finally, it's sinking how serious I was when I said it's going to be intense. He doesn't back out, however.

Macho men, indeed. I actually sigh, and he actually slouches. I guess that makes us even.

"Sometimes it helps to move around the scene," I say unceremoniously, and then I start the simulation.

* * *

The man is menacing and shadowy. No face is visible because the software doesn't want to make a mistake in identification, and that makes the reenactment more horrific. Jennifer and her daughter Layla, however, look all too real. They are lying on the floor, feet and hands bound with restraints you can buy at any sex shop, mouths gagged with pink scarves. The software doesn't know how they got there—otherwise, we would watch that.

They are already wearing lingerie. Interesting. I will need to review the tags associated with that to see how ICDA came to that conclusion. It has not been running thirty seconds and already I have valuable information. Where did he make them put it on? Or, more disturbingly, did they put it on willingly because they were *seduced?*

The thought of it makes me shudder, and I refocus my attention on the scene before me. The man reaches into a duffel bag and pulls out a self-setting eyebolt. He puts it on the floor and presses a button, and the ring sets itself in the floor with a muted pop.

Both victims' eyes go wide. It's now, I think, that they suspect what is going to happen.

The man grabs Jennifer's wrists and drags her over to the eyebolt. He connects a cord to the bolt and then to the restraints on her wrists. He unties the pink scarf and tosses it away. He undoes the ankle restraints and places them back in his duffel.

"This doesn't feel right," Scott says. I look at him and his face is a strange blankness. He actually looks like he's glowing, a wispy, violet aura surrounding his body. Abruptly he grabs the butt of his auto pistol, he yanks on it but it doesn't come free from the holster.

"You leave my mother alone!" he screams as his helmet forms around his head.

I'm a solo Investigator; it has been years since I worked with a partner. Years and years, in fact, so my next stupid action is somewhat understandable. What I should say is "End Program!" What I actually say is "Scott! It's not real, take..." and grab his arm, meaning to finish my sentence while yanking him away from the reenactment.

Stupid, stupid, stupid! I may have made fun of Scott's armor, but it is real armor nevertheless. It is also active—the helmet reforming should have been my ultimate clue—and I touch it with my hands, my unarmored hands, wearing only the latex examination gloves.

His armor performs exactly to spec, and shocks the Hell out of me.

Zap! Living fire goes through my hands and into my body. I crash backwards onto the floor, banging my head hard enough to see spots. I'm disoriented. I have crashed into the holographic Jennifer. Wait, that means...

—**Uplink request acknowledged.**—

No!

Scott stumbles and seems to snap out of it. "LT, what happened?" He reaches out to help me up.

My armor replies in kind, but that happens like something at the end of a tunnel filled with water. Dimly, I see Scott take a jolt through *his* unarmored hands from *my* armor. He falls back, and slumps to the floor on the holographic Layla, his eyes going wide with terror.

"Mommy! Help!" he screeches, sounding like a girl.

I can't think straight. I try to form words, and can't. I try to subvocalize, and I seem frozen in place. My head is swimming from the shock and the nasty bump, I don't know if I can open a channel. My ears are ringing and I try to reach out to Scott.

—**Uplink established, simulation engaged.**—

end program end program end program

My vision is going dark.

end endendend

My vision clears and I'm on the floor, bound by my wrists, wearing nothing but a black silk slip.

No!

I scream in pure terror.

"Scream all you want, Jennifer. No one can hear you," says the killer, as he moves towards Layla.

"Please, please, don't hurt my daughter," I plead.

He laughs.

* * *

No nononono stop please no nonono it's supposed to hurt it's supposed to hurt it's supposed to hurt no nono oh my god no oh god oh god help me please no nono Layla no don't touch her no no oh god no

no

Layla

I love you too baby hold on

oh no oh no

Layla come back

come back

please come back

nononono

why can't I cry

end

i'm dying

end program

i can't breathe end program

fade

i'm dying

scott help

dim

help me

scott!

blackness

* * *

"YOU LEAVE MY MOTHER ALONE!"

The room explodes.

I'm no longer at the ring but flying through the air. I smack against the blank projection wall and crash to the cabinets below it. My vision returns and I see the room is in shambles, the shutters on the windows exploded outwards, the door blown down the hall, furniture broken and askew. Holographic projectors busted in half, everything broken. Dust is actually falling *from* the ceiling.

Scott is in the middle of the room, standing there looking puzzled and dark.

—IF YOU DON'T ANSWER ME RIGHT FUCKING NOW I'M

GOING TO FLY OVER THERE AND RIP THE GODDAMN ROOF OFF THAT MOTHER FUCKING HOUSE!—

—Arune?—

—Finally! What the fuck? I get this weird-ass medical telemetry from your suit and when I finally ignore your privacy setting and broadcast, you ignore me?—

—Equipment malfunctions.—

—Are you alright?—

—Still have some issues, will get back to you.—

Boy do I ever have issues.

—Don't fucking forget it.—

No sooner than Arune leaves the channel, then Bob's PDA puts through a call from 911 from a young sounding woman. "Investigator Toulouse, this is County Safety! There seems to have been some type of kinetic shockwave at the farmhouse. Are you okay?"

"Sorry about that. A minor equipment malfunction. No problems to report."

There is a pause on the other end as if she doesn't believe me.

"Acknowledged. 911, out," she says instead.

I turn my armor to passive. Scott's helmet deforms and he walks towards me with hesitant steps.

I sit up, leaning against the broken cabinets. He comes up next to me and slumps down, and we're both sitting next to each other, looking at the broken room, sunlight streaming in from the shattered windows.

"LT."

"Scott. How's your day so far?"

"Not so good. Been raped once and murdered twice today. You?"

"I've had better days."

We sit there and look at the wreckage.

"Scott?"

"Yes?"

"I've never been…"

I can't say it. I can't. I feel so dirty, so ashamed, which is stupid because it was an accident, it was not even real and even if it was, it was not my fault!

But it sure was real at the time.

He turns to me, fearful, and sorry. "I'm sorry, LT, I had no idea looking at something so real would drop me into that state."

"It was ultimately my responsibility. It's my equipment; this is my crime scene to control."

My voice is hoarse and shaky.

He looks at my face.

"Go ahead, LT."

Oh no, no. Not again, "I don't want to!"

"Go ahead."

"No!"

I can hear her voice in my head, *Mommy I love you… Mommy I…*

"Cry. Cry for Jennifer, for Layla," Scott says.

I do. He holds me, and I do. Then I realize I'm crying for the both of us.

Stupid man. He will pay for that, oh yes he will.

My job, I conclude, sucks.

CHAPTER 6

I LOOK AROUND THE room after I get a hold of myself. It's an impressive display of instant destruction. Shockwave indeed. Only the sofa somehow remains unscathed, but the cushions are all over the room.

"Psionics?"

"Ayup."

"How come I have never heard of this before?"

"You spec-op types went Investigator, with a few exceptions. We from the Home Guard went CEO. The psion unit was part of Home Guard during its development, with the intention that we'd branch out later. So, follow me here. The war ended, and we all split in three."

"Yeah? So?"

"So follow the trail. CEOs don't socialize with the only other people who can arrest them when they make mistakes. And, you know, it's classified."

I contemplate that.

"That's an exaggeration. The arrest rate for CEOs is virtually nil. Still, I can understand. Why did you slip into that, um, whatever it was?"

Scott turns to me. "Look LT, it's not true precognition. When a psion is in a certain state, they are just seeing. It could be the future—although for me that comes in dreams. It could be the past. It could be the present. We don't know how it works. But once you start dealing in the fundamental stuff that makes up the universe, strange things can happen. Forget about time, the progression of it. The capability isn't linear."

I stare at the place where the women…

I interrupt my own thoughts. "That's the second time I've cried today. I think I'm losing it." I hate saying it but Scott needs to know what he's dealing with.

Scott thinks for a while. He shudders.

"What?"

"I just realized we're going to have to watch that again."

I nod and look at my hands. Scott looks at his. Second degree burns for both of us, mine are worse than his. Fuck.

"There is a first aid kit in the car," he says.

"I just need to put my gloves on. You're going to need to help."

I spray his hands with a kit from the locker we dragged in.

I almost pass out, but we get both of my gloves on.

—Skin trauma Level 2 on the hands, administering first aid. Watch heat levels.—

Bah, not as if I'm going to go stealth.

But then again, considering how this day has gone, maybe I shouldn't tempt fate.

"What's next? Clean up?"

"Hell no, like I said, the clock is ticking. This was an equipment malfunction. Understand?"

He nods. I'm already following through, as I interface with my PDA though my armor and get busy nuking the recordings. No one is going to find out our dirty little secret. *No one.*

I finish the deletion. "I need to get out of this forsaken place and just think. Then we need to eat something, we need to speak to Mr. Gifford and finally we need to formulate a plan for the tourists in town. Then either today or tomorrow, we need to interview the neighbors."

It's two in the afternoon, the previous hour spent trapped in Hell.

I spend ten minutes walking aimlessly around the grounds, followed by my CSI army (battery level: 80%). I spy a ladder to the roof of the winery, the building where they actually make the wine. I climb up and Scott follows me, and we peer out over the landscape.

It's pretty, here, flatlands to the south and east, the Cascades to the west and north. Fields of grapes surround us, neat rows of green in the sandy soil. Scott doesn't say anything. His look is blank.

I get out a flask from a utility pocket. I drink and the whiskey burns. I hand it to Scott.

"What is it?"

"Scotch."

"Canadian?"

"No, scotch, from Scotland."

"Holy crap." He takes a swig, then another, and hands it back to me. "How much do you have left?"

"Not nearly enough."

"Can I be Husband Number Five? You know, to guarantee my share of the Scotch?"

I chuckle and lay down on the roof, hands behind my head. Scott does the same. A white, lazy cloud goes by, heading east.

After about five minutes, "That was a terrible joke," I say.

He grunts. "At least I actually joke. You're as infamous for your lack of humor as for your exploits."

What? I turn to him. "I joke!"

"When? And sarcasm doesn't count."

"Uh, well, um, fuck. Wait! Today I opened my armor locker by flipping it off."

He actually snorts. "Whatever."

"Are you saying that I'm an unemotional, humorless bitch?"

"Yeah, pretty much."

"But that's what I used to think about you!"

"What the hell? How do you expect me to act around an Investigator? Or did you forget about the Ring of Checks and Balances?"

"Ah hell, I would never arrest you, Scott."

"It's not being arrested that had me worried. It's not living up to your standards, and in the end, looking down the wrong side of your needler."

Okay, I can parse that. Still, I harrumph.

We watch another cloud float by us. Up here, it's not so bad. I almost feel normal.

But I'm not.

I don't know if I will ever be normal.

I scrunch my eyes, fighting tears again because I know I'm losing it.

"After Gifford, I get the second whack at him," Scott says.

"Yes."

I try to pretend he isn't fondling the hilt of his combat knife.

Before we leave, we hose ourselves off. I put the water on hot, wishing I could feel it through my armor.

* * *

While Scott is driving, I check in with Arune, and send a personal note to each Husband. This town called Bacon has an old-money charm to it, with an abundance of shade trees and landscaping to break up the ever-present wind. It's a sleepy neighborhood, and although the affluence of the place is downplayed, the houses are multilevel and must be expensive. There are even yards with white-picket fences.

"Did you meet with Gifford personally?"

"No, I was dealing with County Safety," says Scott. "They seemed only slightly annoyed that I showed up in town. Sheriff Sam might be out of his league."

"Don't be so sure. Sam is salty."

"Okay."

"With Gifford, let me do the talking. Don't be surprised if he seems more bitter and less grief. He's going to blame his Wife. At this stage, that's natural. He'll have a lot of self-loathing, too."

"It bothers me we didn't find her sidearm," Scott remarks.

"Yes, that makes me feel there is another shoe going to drop somewhere."

It's a big house, built, I think, when they incorporated Bacon after the war. From the outside, the house smells like money more so than the others do.

There is a County Safety SUV parked on the street. A man gets out, an older man with a folksy gait to his walk. He's wearing two pistols, one on each thigh, and a combat knife that almost could be a short sword. His handlebar mustache curls up and despite the grey hair, he looks like he could bench press me all day.

He is indeed one salty dude.

"Investigator, Officer. Name's Sam. I'm the Sheriff."

We all shake hands.

"What did you find?"

I look at Sam wearily.

"Evil, Sam. Pure, unadulterated evil. There isn't a name for the vileness we encountered. It was like the war, except worse because now it stands alone—rape and murder in one of the most heinous forms imaginable."

Sam deflates, much as Scott did earlier in the day at the landing pad.

"Ah, Hell. The Giffords are good people. They don't deserve anything like this."

"Anybody have any beef with them, Sam?"

"No. We were all happy as a clam. Now…" he trails off.

Murder is rare and rape is even rarer. Stranger rape is the rarest of them all mostly because of a lack of unarmed victims. Spousal rape and date rape are more common, but still, even those have been trending downwards since the end of the Cyber War so long ago.

Child rape is all but unheard of. The last time it happened in my neck of the woods, it was someone going crazy. He had the idea that if he didn't get his daughter pregnant, the war would start all over again.

Indeed, that's the most common scenario: a person touched by the ravages of war finally snaps. Either they kill themselves or they do something Really Bad.

Fuck. I'm not sure I'm the best person for this. I briefly consider calling Chen, the first non-vet Investigator. He's a big city man; he's seen plenty of modern crimes.

I decide I like Chen too much to bring him here.

"That photographer guy acts normal, but ever since you had us watching him, something about him bugs me," Sam adds.

That's interesting. "I'm doing a look up on him."

"Okay. Like I said, he has a rock-solid alibi. The bus has been tracking him since he got to town, and he hasn't gone anywhere except to take tourist pictures."

Sam shrugs, and then he peers from me to Scott, scrutinizing.

"Are you two okay?" he asks me. "You've a bump on your head, Investigator. You look a little pale."

I favor him with a weak smile. "We had an equipment malfunction, and I didn't have my helmet fully active."

"Ouch. Well, The Missus told me to remind you to eat food. I tried to explain to her about how eating doing a murder investigation is somewhat difficult, but, well, you know."

"Thank you Sam."

"There's going to be a Safety Officer here for at least a day. I'll be in the SUV if you need me."

Sam 'moseys' back to his vehicle.

We walk up from the street to the front door of the house, and Scott sub-vocalizes through our impromptu channel.

—Sam doesn't believe a word you're saying about the 'malfunction.'—

—I know. Still think he's out of his league?—

—No. His folksy shtick is just an act, too.—

I say what we're both thinking.

—Vet.—

—Yup.—

—I hate to say it, but I think Sam is probably better adjusted than both of us put together.—

Scott smiles weakly as I touch the announcement pad by the door. Then he grimaces.

—The thought of food might make me barf, by the way.—

My stomach rolls at the image and I give him a glare.

A distraught woman in her thirties opens the door, looking weathered and burdened.

"Investigators, come in."

On the porch, I make introductions. "I'm Investigator Lexus Toulouse, and this is Officer Scott from OCE. Officer Scott is assisting me in this investigation."

"I'm Paul's sister, Jaycee—Jaycee Gifford." She frowns at Scott but doesn't say anything.

"I'm very sorry for your loss, Ms. Gifford." She nods, looking like she's choking back tears. She shuffles us to a den.

Mr. Gifford is there, staring at a media wall of smart glass. The video isn't home movies, rather some mindless show about fly-fishing. He turns it off when we come in. Paul Gifford is a middle-aged man, looking ten years older than he should. His brown hair has grey flecks, and he's well-muscled.

His eyes are dead. I've seen dead eyes like that before.

It hurts to see him this way. It hurts to see anybody this way.

An older couple joins us, the parents and owners of this lovely home, who introduce themselves and sit on a love seat.

Gifford looks at us, pain flickering briefly in his poufy, dead red eyes. He doesn't get up. I think he wants to, but doesn't have the energy.

"I will need to talk to Mr. Gifford alone for now, please," I tell everyone.

Jaycee shakes her head. "What you can say to Paul you can say to us, we make decisions as a family."

"No ma'am. I'm not going to have a conversation about the Investigation contract. I need to eliminate, formally, Mr. Gifford as a suspect because the peculiars of this crime link it to the War Authorization Clause. Even if you were not paying me, I would be here interviewing."

Every one of them, including Paul, looks like I put a puppy on the floor and stomped on it with my armored boot. Arf! Squish! Blood-splatter.

Jaycee looks like she's going to hyperventilate. "W-WAC? Are you saying that what happened to Jennifer and Layla might have something to do with the war?" she asks. The parents look as if they are going to keel over.

Unfortunately, I'm tiring of dragging this out, so I drop my bomb. "Not might—is. This crime relates directly to the war. There is no doubt about that, it's an inescapable conclusion supported by evidence and personal account. The Military will soon become involved. We need to have Mr. Gifford cleared as a suspect before the MPs arrive or I could lose control of this Investigation."

The mother bursts into tears, and the other two lead her out. They leave Paul, who seems strangely relieved. Grief, anger and relief fill his face, as obvious as if someone painted those emotions there.

The door closes. "We're very sorry for your loss, Mr. Gifford," I say.

"Call me Paul," he says, tersely, speaking for the first time. His voice is hoarse, as if he had been shouting.

He probably has.

He turns to me. "They were raped. Both of them."

"Yes."

"He did it like that so each could watch what was happening to the other."

"Yes."

I can feel my heart pounding in my chest.

He rubs his face. "I want to laugh, about the war. Isn't that strange? Partly because I was convinced someone I knew did it, partly because my whole family avoided war casualties, yet here it is anyway."

I need to grab control of this interview, so I go off my script. I wing it. I sit down in a chair next to him, and it creaks under the added weight of my armor. "Paul, I know you didn't do this, but I have to ask my questions anyway. Why did you feel someone you knew murdered them?"

"It was planned so perfectly, you see. I was in Portland, meeting with distributors, going over our predictions for the harvest next month. Everyone was on vacation, getting ready for the long harvest hours. Jennifer and Layla were out there all alone. The grapes we have are only one portion of what we make wine with—we buy the rest. They were taking care of the vines, it wasn't a hard job."

"How did you find the bodies?"

"When I got home, the house was empty and I didn't see them in the fields, yet the car was in the carport and so was the truck. I rang their phones and they didn't answer, their phones were in their rooms. That's when I started to worry, and searched processing first, then I—I—went to the farmhouse. And found them there. Oh God, the lingerie, the moment I saw it, I knew they were dead. That's not anything either of one of them would've worn."

He shudders, and tears fall down his face. I put my hand on his arm.

"I know this is hard for you, but time is of the essence. We got on this case early, and we must use that advantage."

"I—I know. That's what Officer Scott and Sam said when we talked." He takes a deep breath, calming himself—or about as calm as he could get.

"What time did you discover them?"

"It was 9:40 AM."

"Does your car keep a driving log?"

"Yes."

"Okay, that's good, I'll download it. Is there anyone that would want to harm you, or wanted to harm your Wife or daughter?"

"No. We're not the most prosperous winery, but everyone local is our friend, we're a part of the community. No feuds, good neighbors, respected, happy employees. The wine business is very good."

It would be, Washington being one of the biggest wine producing regions in the world.

"How about money? Did anyone stand to gain financially from their deaths, or from your grief?"

"No, the business has been in the family ever since Bacon became a winery town."

"Did your daughter have a boyfriend?"

"She did, but they broke up when he moved to Ottawa."

"Did she ever complain about boys wanting to sleep with her?"

He shakes his head, and actually gives a weak smile. "No. She was the reigning school lead in Three Gun. Nobody messed with her, ever. Most boys were afraid of her. She used to complain about it."

He leans back on the couch. The dead eyes go deader.

"Until today."

"What was the name of her best friend?"

"Rachel. Rachel Barrett."

"And your Wife's best friend?"

"Neighbor. Anna Wilcole."

"Thank you, Paul."

"How—how did they die?"

He deserves to know. My voice stays perfectly steady and I don't hesitate.

"They were injected with a nullifier, and then given a powerful nano drug. They overdosed on a synthetic sex enhancer."

"Oh fuck, oh no." He takes a ragged breath. "Wait, nano? How? How can an injected nullifier get rid of their nano regulators without surgery? They had the best!"

"That's part of where the war comes in. Both the nullifier and the drug are relics from the war. Military grade."

"From the Union?"

"Yes."

"No. No." His face, already ashen, takes on a new pallor.

Our techs have yet to recreate the Union nullifiers. They were that powerful and advanced. One dose will destroy any internal regulator, rendering the body defenseless against nano attacks—which is why my Z armor specifically has an *external* regulator. It's cyber system, using no organic tech. Nano against my armor is useless.

Not many people know, but the nullifier was everything to the Union. It purged the body of any defenses, and that paved the way for the linkage hardware via a massive nano series we called "The Cocktail." It was as insidiously effective as it was evil.

"Paul, this is going to be hard, but I have to tell you more."

He nods, looking very fearful.

Out of the corner of my eye, I see Scott grab a wastebasket.

"I have encountered this crime before. I have positive indications your Wife and daughter were victims of a serial killer."

"Oh no. Why? Why them? What did we do? We just make wine! We never bothered anybody!"

"I don't know the answers to those questions, but I'm going to find out."

"Did you find their pistols?"

"No, but we have not searched your house yet."

"Why? If this was a stranger, why didn't they just shoot the fucker? My Wife and daughter never went anywhere without their auto pistols. Why! Why didn't Jennifer kill him? Why, why, why, why!"

He breaks out into a sweat. Scott hands him the wastebasket, and he throws up water, and then dry heaves.

I'm burning with anger and the look on Scott's face actually is frightening in its quiet intensity.

What happened to Jennifer and Layla was monstrous. What Mr. Gifford is going through is, unto itself, a terrible ordeal.

I give him a 50/50 chance of making it to next summer. Only the thought of vengeance may keep him alive. And once I catch this bastard, and I will, what will he do when all this is over?

Worse, what will I do?

What will happen to me when the anger is gone and all that is left are perverse memories?

Mommy I love you… Mommy…

* * *

We're driving back to the winery to search the main residence. Before we left, I asked Sam to have Safety search bottling and processing. I don't think anything is there but it's best to be sure. Sam takes it as an insult when I offer to pay for the expense, so I don't push it.

Both our stomachs are sour, but Scott and I sip on a protein drink anyway.

Ick. I fight nausea, a side effect of any intense simulation. And of the fact that this case just absolutely blows. And that I'm a wreck.

And that I've been raped.

—Dr. Mary Wheaton, Coroner, on Line Three.—

—Thank you Bob, connect.—

"Hello Doctor. I'm putting you on speaker. I have a CEO helping me."

Modern Coroners are Investigators with a forensic pathology background, always carrying some type of medical certification. Once I send her the body, she is my subcontractor. Not only do I pay her an initial fee (which I then bill the Gifford family), but she also gets a percentage of the total payout for the case. If she provides evidence that helps catch the bad guy, she gets a bonus. If the bad guy meets Justice, she gets an even bigger bonus.

Coroners sometimes even go at it in the field, indeed many families or corporate interests just hire a Coroner to make a death investigation end-to-end. The primary difference besides the medical knowledge is that I can, and will, travel.

If I ran into trouble with an Investigation, the Coroner would be the first person I turn to for help. It's not just the credits. More so than other Investigators, Coroners hate homicides. They take it personally. Well, I take that back. They hate murderers.

"Investigator. I called about two things, well three. One, I'm not going to delay the autopsy. I got nano probes going bat-shit over here. I need to go now; I'm worried about toxicity breakdown."

"Roger that."

"Second, I'm sorry I didn't talk to you first, but I have strict protocols when encountering WAC flags. I entered the required info into Zero Net and now MPs from Fort Lewis are on the way."

I groan aloud and glare at Scott when he grins. "Best to play it by the numbers here, Doc."

"Thanks for being a good sport. The third thing is I read both your old report and the notes you've sent me thus far. This is bad juju, Investigator. Let's just ignore the fact you're dealing with the crime of the decade. I'm not a particularly post-war religious woman, but the way these two died was about as evil as anything ever was. It was like being Unionized. We're talking the depths of Hell. He violated them in every sense of the word."

"Yes," I manage to get out. Oh, I know Doctor. I know all about this murder. Oh how I know.

"Anything. Anything you need from me, you got it. I need to get started, but please, Lexus. Be careful. I know your reputation both as a war hero and as an Investigator, but I have to say it. Be careful. Your Justice needs to be swift and complete, but this zombie tech is bad juju. Nullifiers and sex enhancers were not the only bad things to come from that Hell Hole, not even close. Mary, out."

Oh don't I know that too, Dr. Mary, don't I know that too.

Scott isn't smiling anymore.

I get out the flask and belt one down. I hand it to Scott and he does the same.

"I should warn you, I have an addiction-prone personality," I tell him, leaning back, watching the road.

Scott glances away from the road for just a second, giving me a curious look. "Alcohol?"

"Mostly sex, but yeah, alcohol, drugs, whatever."

"I see. And I understand. I won't feel sorry for you though, but that's mostly so you don't kick my ass."

"Ha. Also, my Lib-Gee is malfunctioning. Apparently, I'm now fifty percent gay."

"They call that 'bisexual'."

"Whatever."

"I guess being addicted to sex and having four Husbands works."

"It sure does make things easier."

"What happens if you're in the field too long?"

"I try to avoid that. But I'll turn to other things. Alcohol, pot, snorf, what have you. Mostly snorf. Snorf is good."

"I got some good B.C. weed in my hotel room in Coulee City."

"Ooooo."

More silence.

"You know," I say casually, "if I wasn't raped this afternoon I would probably call one of my Husbands and have him stay with me tonight. Now, meh, I think I'll just get drunk. Or Uplink. Maybe both."

He nods. "Are you going to tell them?"

"Someday. I don't know. I think they will figure it out when I swear off sex, forever, and go on a snorf binge. How about you? Are you going to tell anybody?"

"I'm hoping I can just channel my rage into killing that fucking bastard. Then I will spend a pile of credits on an overpriced Bellevue companion, perhaps a set of twins, and go back to brooding unnecessarily twice a month."

I chuckle. "Unless you are related to the victim, you have to be an Investigator to go on a homicidal rage on the perp."

"As your *de facto* assistant, that's implied. Article 42 from Section 15."

Huh, I didn't think that clause meant that, but he's a CEO. He would know. "Ah, well, dip me in shit. I better not cut you loose then."

More road.

"Scott?"

"Yes?"

"If I go crazy, and I mean war frenzy, make it a head shot. Okay? Please."

He doesn't hesitate. "Yes, if you do the same for me, yes. Of course."

I hold out my pinkie. "Pinkie swear."

He holds out his, and now our armored pinkies are clutching each other. He holds my hand like that all the way back to the winery, and somehow we both control our emotions all the way there.

* * *

I was doing okay until I walked into Layla's room, and now I'm not.

It was once a happy room, for a thirteen-year-old. Now the happy things in the room tug at my heart viciously.

Please, please, don't hurt my daughter.

I push that false memory aside and look at others.

I remember how I was back then. I was outgoing and self-confident, in outwards appearance. Inwardly, I was a normal teenage girl. I was looking at boys, they were looking at me, and I had just started exploring giving myself pleasure, which I felt vaguely uncomfortable with—not because I thought the pleasure was bad, but because I knew my mother would want to talk about it and that was just something I didn't want to talk to her about.

A bad man murdered Layla Gifford at thirteen, in one of the worst ways a thirteen-year-old girl can die.

I looked around at the pictures of the boy bands, the targets she had hung up on the wall with small groupings circled, pictures of friends, normal stuff.

Please, please, don't hurt my daughter.

Mommy I love you… Mommy…

I'm breathing too fast and it's making me feel sick. It's not supposed to be like this. I'm the Investigator. If anybody on the planet could deliver vengeance for Layla, it's me. It had to be me. It's what I do. It's who I am.

Or, is it who I pretend to be? I start to shake. *Oh my baby, I am so sorry.*

—High levels of anxiety detected. Normalization required.—

That's my suit geek-speak for 'calm the fuck down or I will tranq you.'

I practice breathing techniques. It's impressive armor. I can scream, shout, throw up, get shot, get pissed, just about anything—but if it thinks I'm going to lose control, *pisst,* there goes the happy drugs.

So I calm down. If I'm going to get high today, I'm going to do it for real. I think about Layla. If Layla is to receive justice, I need to get it together. She needs me. She needs me. I wasn't there for her earlier, but she needs me now.

"Are you okay, LT?"

I'm a closed woman. Nobody except my Husbands go in, and even then I open the door just a little way and they have to work at it to get to the rest of me.

I look at Scott, all pensive yet tall with that man-in-charge look. Just what is my relationship with him?

He's more than just an ad-hoc assistant, more than just sharing a traumatic event. I believe Scott, the man, is simply one of those rare people who don't judge others without knowing who they are. I have only worked with him for a few hours. I wonder, where do the psionics end, and the man begins?

I decide on brutal honesty.

"No, not really. I'm—broken." The last comes out a whisper. Admitting it drains me.

"Oh, LT, I'm so, so sorry." He sounds crushed and guilty.

I frown. "Hey, I told you that because I like you and trust you, not that I blame you."

"I know, it's, okay. Okay. I asked if you were okay, and you gave me an honest answer. Still, I'm not blameless, and for that I'm sorry."

I suppress a sigh. "I accept your apology if you will accept mine."

"Yes, I do."

"Now that we're done playing touchy-feely, can you please call me Nancy?"

He cocks his head at me. "Oh? Who calls you Nancy?"

"Nobody. Only you. It's your private Secret Squirrel pet name for Investigator Lexus Nancy Toulouse. Maybe it will make me smile. Maybe it will make me not so humorless. Maybe it doesn't remind me of my platoon."

"Okay. Nancy it is. Nancy is a good name. You look like a Nancy."

I give him a little smile. My newfound awkwardness, at least, is stalling the freak-out.

We find Layla's rifle and carbine. We don't find her pistol, and a holster is missing.

This detail is starting to bug me. Killers will take trophies, but when they take guns, they usually have a plan to use them on someone.

Something else is starting to nag at me. It's not just the fact that the killer struck in a war zone and then all the way out here. Some detail is trying to come to the front of my brain, but I'm so out of it I can't think straight.

I mentally shrug, and grab her laptop and comm pod.

True to Paul Gifford's word, we don't find any lingerie beyond long, warm tees with funny sayings that are now sad. Some pictures in the house feature them all in the nude, which isn't out of the ordinary.

We don't find Jennifer's pistol either. I take her laptop and pod.

Sam's boys and girls find nothing in the big warehouse-like building. I find one crying in a dark corner. I give her a hug. She simultaneously looks grateful, embarrassed and like she wants to kiss me.

I curse my malfunctioning hardware and wonder if I'm putting out the girly pheromonic red light.

CHAPTER 7

WE'RE DRIVING TOWARDS THE Coroner. The slicing and dicing most likely is over, but she also has a forensic cyber tech that can snarf the data from the laptops and comm pods. I can do it but it's a pain in the ass, and my client is rich. I can afford to take the fastest route to any relevant data.

Arune buzzes me on my sub-vocal channel.

—I spy me a hopper that just dropped an armored carrier.—

"Bah."

"What?" asks Scott.

"MPs, incoming. They didn't drive over, either."

"You don't sound too happy."

"I'm busy."

"Well, now you know how us lowly CEOs feel."

"Can it. The investigation rate for MPs over Investigators is almost five times that of Investigators over CEOs."

"Heh. Busted."

We pull up to a pleasant building in Ephrata, the seat of Grant County. The main door unlocks and slides open for us. I notice the nearly invisible, but quite heavy, security. It's not that the doctor has enemies. Her equipment is very expensive.

An attractive young girl with big, curious eyes walks into reception, barely five feet tall. She is wearing a stylish red synth-silk blouse that shows off her boobs—impressive boobs, actually, for such a small woman. She has on a miniskirt and black stockings. "Investigators. I'm the tech head of Wheaton & Associates. My name is Bambi. Do you have any cyber gear for me to play with?"

Bambi? Parents today and their naming conventions for their kids. She looks so eager I almost burst out laughing. I smile instead.

"I have two. And their communication pods."

"Yum! Actual hardware. Associated with a crime. I know it sounds bad that I'm happy, but I can't help it. I spent all my savings on the training and I've been waiting tables to pay off my hardware."

"You subcontract?"

"Yes. I want to be my own Investigator, specializing in cyber. I've started working here because I get exclusives on any tech business."

"Growth industry," says Scott, which is true. The advent of civilian quantum computing makes cybercrime very complicated.

She puts on gloves and takes the laptops. She actually rubs one over the front of her blouse. "Oh yes, Baby-Cakes, let's go into the backroom and you can show me what you got."

Ha, kids these days.

"Oh, sorry. Follow the blue triangular trail to the theater. Dr. Wheaton has buttoned up the lab tight. You won't be able to talk to her face-to-face. Now if you will excuse me, I need some alone time with my dates." She leaves, humming happily.

Then I notice that Scott is looking at her tiny butt. It is a shapely butt in a black mini-skirt, but still. It's tiny.

"Scott!"

"What?"

"She's like, twenty. Maybe twenty-one. She could be your daughter, you perv!"

How can he even think about anything remotely connected to sex, anyway?

"Sorry, I like my women young, smart and sassy."

"As opposed to?"

"Surly and sarcastic," he says pointedly, leaving off the word 'old.'

I smack him, which makes a 'boink' sound and accomplishes nothing.

A blue triangular trail appears in the air before us, and we follow it.

* * *

It's a small observation room, but having one is a nice touch that I appreciate. Video only goes so far. We peer down to the scene below.

Fully buttoned up in hazmat suits, Dr. Wheaton and her stocky assistant are working on Jennifer. Autopsies never bother me and I can even do one under direction (having seen much worse in the war, of course), but one look down at the lab nearly causes me to faint. For a brief moment, I get a sense of vertigo, as if it's me down there peeled open.

—High levels of anxiety detected. Normalization required.—

Oh Hell. My stupid armor has given me nothing but grief all day. You could even say that it was really the *armor* that raped me, through my Uplink receptors. I vow to take it off once outside.

I practice breathing again while the duo finish a little bit of something. Finally, Dr. Wheaton pauses.

"Mrs. Toulouse, Mr. Scott. This is my assistant, Dr. Ivan."

"Please, call me Lexus."

"You bet. Before you ask," she waves around the lab, "this is all a formality. I have a bunch of nothing. Cause of death: heart failure due to nano overdose. Homicide."

She wrinkles her nose. "There were three nano packages the perp delivered, and one first-aid spray application. The nullifier, the sex enhancer and the most disturbing, an evidence DNA Eater that he, and I'm just going to assume this was a 'he,' sprayed in all of their cavities and injected into their stomach with a needle applicator. The only difference in the bodies was he sprayed Layla Gifford's genitalia with a first-aid spray at the start of the assault."

She crosses her arms.

"All of those things were zombie tech. I can't tell you where in the Union they came from, nor when manufactured. I want to assure you I have modern equipment, and serve on a Level One certification board for forensic pathology. We actually service all of Central Washington, not just Grant County. Even a Coroner who served in the war would not be able to pull out anything more."

She sounded very confident. I nod. "Why were you worried about toxicity?"

"Because we had it. The programming of the DNA Eater told it to eat any biological material foreign to the victim, but it also caused a runaway cancer like effect on their body to produce more of it. In other words, it was feeding off their bodies to create more of the evidence eraser. The tissue conversion started about five minutes after the bodies got here."

Ick, ick, ick. I've seen or heard it all, but *ewww*.

"Would the biological evidence I gathered at the scene be of any use?"

"Only for non-biological compounds, and that will take time to parse. He sprayed a huge amount of the evidence eater on both women. We're talking half a *liter* of nano solution *each*. And this was zombie solution, the stuff was better, hell, *is* better, than what someone can manufacture today."

Interesting. I'm even starting to flinch less at the word 'zombie.' Only a bit, though.

"Sorry I can't give you more. I hope your other CSI bots collected useful clues beyond the bodies. I will certainly waive my percentage retainer."

I shake my head. "No, Doctor. You actually were a big help."

She tilts her head. "I guess. Still, normally I provide much…"

"Doctor. I know you're going to watch the ICDA recreation. It will be bad—so fundamentally nasty that it will chill your very soul and you may never be the same. And don't under any circumstances plug yourself into the recreation. Believe me when I tell you, emphatically, your fee and cut are well earned."

"I, well, thank you, Lexus for your confidence in me, the business, and the warning."

I have never worked with Mary before now, but I like her. She's nice and seems smart.

Mary gives me a serious mommy-like look. "Need any muscle? I'm not great in a fight, but Ivan here was actually the lead doctor on the Trans-Siberian Sniper Team for years."

I whistle. "Not right now, but if do, I'll beep you."

"Yes," says Ivan, voice gruff and wintery with a heavy accent. "Is good if you call. Much pleasure in capturing this bad man. Yes, I would enjoy that very much."

I nod and he nods back.

Wouldn't we all Ivan, wouldn't we all.

Mary waves over the body. "We will keep the bodies locked up, but tell Mr. Gifford that WAC protocol dictates I eventually cremate them here. He should have the memorial service, and I will get him the ashes when I can."

* * *

On the way back to the lobby, Scott asks what is on his mind.

"You said Dr. Wheaton gave you some useful information, and I don't think you were shooting nano up her ass."

I stop in the hallway. "Ah, ah, ah, I said what she told me was a big help. You need to be more precise. As a CEO, you deal mostly with actions, many times ignoring what is said and focusing on what people do. As an Investigator, both aspects are critical."

"Yes, ma'am."

"Ahem!"

"Yes, Nancy."

"Much better. You can figure this one out. What did she tell us that doesn't match up with what we think we know about the killer?"

Scott thinks.

"Nano."

I nod.

He goes into a lecture mode look, which is kind of cute. "If this is the same killer, from Alsace, deep in Union territory, why did he overkill spray? It was like he didn't know how it really worked."

"Yet I encountered the previous crime scene during the whole 'conquer and occupy' fiasco. There were years in the war left to go."

He grunts and we start walking.

"I don't like this," Scott says.

"I don't like this either. What is your first inclination?"

"Call for backup," he says without hesitation.

"Well, my MOF/B is a good start. But if necessary, we will use Ivan the Terrible, because we've already paid for his services."

"Roger that, Big Nancy."

I pause. "If you ever call me Big Nancy ever again, I will cry. Then punch you. Hard."

"Sorry. I meant that you're tall."

"Don't care. It implied that my butt isn't as heart shaped and tiny as Cyber Bambi."

He laughs. "You're wearing armor, you know, she's wearing a skirt."

"Pischt!"

We're in the lobby. A large, menacing and armored Military ATV with a rail gun and a missile launcher sits outside with a Fort Lewis MP logo. I don't recognize the model. In fact, it looks brand-new.

"Bah," I say, take a deep breath, and walk outside.

Cheerfully jumping down are two MPs.

During the three-way split after we adopted the Constitution, the Military was the one branch that got the short end of the stick. They got all the major equipment, land and orbital assets, but mainly staffed with burnt-out socialites. As the old Investigators and CEOs—during the rare times we meet up—like to say, "The smart ones quit."

Which is also a subtle self-depreciating dig, but it certainly applies to Military personnel.

Now, essentially, sorority girls and frat boys staff the ever starved-for-cash Military. Complete with the good looks, good service nature, and penchant for wild, debauched parties.

The two young women in front of me certainly fit the bill. They are wearing shorts, and their sleek, tan legs seemingly climb forever from their cute little Military boots. The first one, wearing corporal stripes, is a tall, stunning, brunette with vivid, hazel eyes. The other, a staff sergeant, is blonde, and not much shorter, but has a beautiful blue-eyed face that looks like an artist carved it from marble.

Despite their obvious workout routine (two hours a day, I hear), each has a pair of breasts that border on the downright perfect. Shapely. Perky. Generous.

This makes me jealous. I'm neither well-padded nor skinny. My Husbands call me curvy, and that's good. I do keep up with my PT by climbing Mt. Si to get to work most days, using hand-weights to keep the burn going in my arms. If I did the same workout these two did, my boobs would shrink. Losing weight for me means kissing my boobs goodbye.

That's so unfair. Moreover, I know they are real. You can't have cosmetic additions like fake boobs in the Military, even when I served, nor can you spend wads of cash and get a new pair in the regen tank.

Their thigh-holstered auto pistols and understated equipment harness over a skin-fitting ballistic cloth blouse, round out the package. I bet if they turned around, their ass…

What. The. Fuck.

It's then I realize it. I'm gay, or at least gayer, true to Arune's revelation. I should be nervous when confronted with MPs. Here, I just want to nibble on them, little tiny bites up and down their tan sleek bodies and…

No, no, no! This day sucks. What the fuck is wrong with me?

Well, my Libido Generator for one. Even if it were not malfunctioning, it would still be dumping desire into my body regardless of my mental health today. Or the fact I was, was—eugh.

They walk right over to me, stop in unison and throw up a snappy salute, which, before I can catch myself, I return.

"Lieutenant, this is Corporal Tiffany and I'm Sergeant Brittney."

It's all I can do not to groan. Tiffany and Brittney? Wow, that sure goes well with 'Bambi.'

I'm in Hell.

"Please, call me Investigator Toulouse, or better yet, just Nancy. This is CEO Scott."

They favor Scott with a guarded smile. I grin. At least they know how things work, and now I think I know how Scott felt when he first saw me several years ago at that seminar. They shake hands though, and Scott's eyes warm up, which in turn causes 'Tiff and Britt' to smile.

"What can I do for you Sergeant?"

"I'll get straight to the point: the MOF/B is making the higher-ups nervous and we would like to make sure Arune is being treated well. But more importantly, WAC protocols dictate we oversee any investigation to Union tech use." She nods, seriously.

I clue in to a patch on their uniform.

"Are you with the 42nd Military Police Brigade?"

"42nd, 504th Battalion, 170th MP Company, Manticore Platoon, Omega Squad, ma'am."

Manticore. My old platoon. The platoon I cheerfully led to their deaths, except for Vash and Juan, now Husbands Two and Three. We were the only Military survivors of Edinburgh. After that, they yanked me, plugged neural cyber gear in my body, and turned me loose behind the blasted and bleak enemy lines like a vengeful goddess of destruction. I went on a glorious slaughter-filled rampage wearing the very armor I have on now. It was so epic; they made a first person shooter after the mission. I know people still play it after all these years, because I get a royalty check every fiscal rollover. The fan base upgrades the graphics engine with each tech advance.

And that was before meeting Arune, when I really went to town. The sabotage mission was just a *warm-up*.

I'm staring at them.

My face is hot.

I can't breathe.

I can't breathe.

—High levels of anxiety detected. Normalization required.—

The two MPs startle as if I just shocked them.

Oh, they would certainly be on my armor channel, even if not wearing armor themselves. They are from my platoon, after all. Manticores.

Tiffany turns towards Brittney, hands on hips.

"Damn it, Brittney, I told you she would react this way! But nooooo, you had to go along with the brass's cockamamie scheme of 'welcome home.' Did you think for one second how she might feel?"

"Lieutenant, I'm so sorry!" the Sergeant wails, sounding like a distraught teen.

Like Layla.

Mommy I love you… Mommy…

I sink to one knee.

"Nancy!" Scott bends down to look at my face. He's not on my armor channel, so he doesn't know.

Enough of this shit.

—High levels of anxiety detected. Normalization required.—

I need out. I need out!

—Start shed-cycle immediately.—

—No combat detected. Cycle commencing now.—

"Help me out of this thing," I beg.

The two MPs push past Scott and peel me out of my armor, and I finally start to cry. They clean up my privates from the sealant goo, right there in the parking lot. I hate myself for crying again, hate myself for coming apart in front of my old platoon, hate myself just because maybe that's the only real emotion I have left.

Brittney bursts into tears and runs behind the building.

Yeah, this day sucks.

CHAPTER 8

TIFFANY GOES TO COLLECT Brittney, and I extract my cloth-based uniform from locker #2. Unfortunately, it's very similar to the MPs, shorts and all. I prefer to wear pants in the field but I usually can't after wearing armor. I don't want anything touching my receptors. That makes me cranky after heavy use.

Instead of an auto pistol like the MPs, I have a needler, a sidearm only made for Investigators and very deadly, the greatest handgun ever made. Without the backdrop of my armor, its shape is distinctive and intimidating as it rides my right thigh.

I also have a lazy green boonie hat on my bald head rather than a smart red barrette.

"Well, don't I now look like a dork," quips Scott.

"We can be, like, you know, like, your *harem.*"

"Stop."

I roll my eyes.

Tiffany comes back with Brittney, who has poufy eyes. She comes up to me and her quite kissable red lips actually start to quiver.

"I'm sorry, I never wanted to hurt you. I'm sorry."

Oh, damn. How can I steel myself against that? I can't.

I give her a hug. She startles but then hugs me back. I resist the urge to pat her nice little muscular bottom and, with a bit of reluctance, let her go.

It's not that I want her—okay, maybe just a little bit—but her hard-soft body is very comforting.

Now everyone is staring at me.

"Where to, Nancy? Back to Bacon?" Scott asks, but then, as if on cue, his stomach growls, loudly.

"Ah, no. We're done today. Let's get some chow and get a good night's sleep. We can start the interviews late tomorrow morning, since tomorrow is Sunday. Say, head out from the landing pad at 10:00."

I need to sleep. A lot.

"What about the tour bus?" Scott asks.

"Matches no profile, everyone accounted for. Fuck' em." I call Sam. The photographer probably is some minor creep, possibly involved in asset tracking from an insurance company, or something equally irrelevant to my job.

"Sam, we're done for today."

"Sure thing Investigator. Can I review your file from Dr. Wheaton?"

Sam, review the case file? Yeah, why the hell not? I have already purged Scott's and my talk on psionics, and the accident didn't make it to my official case file. Sam might even piece together something good. Sam's a good man, I decide right there.

"Of course. I'll send you the key now."

I whip out my PDA and send it to him.

I turn to Tiffany and Brittney. "Please, join us for dinner. I'll give you a brief on the tech we encountered afterwards."

"Uh, we brought our field rations with us," says Brittney.

"What? Don't be absurd."

"Sorry ma'am, we're on a tight budget," counters Tiffany.

Oh. I feel stupid.

"I'll buy. Husband Number Four is rich." Husband Number Four doesn't do micro expenses like that for the family, but still, we all like to say that, even Bill.

"Ah, sorry Lieut..., er, Lexus, er Nancy, that would be improper since we're here in an official capacity."

Shit, that means they are going to raid my files and follow me.

Sorry girls, I already erased the good parts. "Okay, Scott can buy you dinner."

"Oh, that would be worse!" Brittney looks like she's about to give birth to kittens. I actually have to work on not giggling.

I put my arms around her neck and stare into her (wow those are really nice) blue eyes. "Brittney, please. You're from my old platoon. The thought of you eating field rations while Scott and I are having a nice dinner breaks my heart. Please? For me?"

She nods and I give her another quick hug.

You're mine, I think.

How does that make me feel? Honestly, I just don't know. Men have been my forte for so long. But now, I think, since I'm swearing off men, I should make some effort in the other direction.

Tiffany looks so happy she could burst.

"Let's head to the middle of town," I say. We could walk, but leaving behind collectively millions of credits in equipment would be a bad idea.

Scott and I get in his SUV—followed by Tiffany and Brittney as they hop in the back seat. Scott and I turn to them in surprise.

"What about…"

"Oh, Roscoe? He'll follow us. He's really quite good at that," says Tiffany.

I look at Scott, and he shrugs, and off we go. The bigger vehicle, Roscoe, does indeed follow along. I should not be surprised but such casual use of advanced drone equipment used to be against regulations.

We find a steakhouse. Perfect. It's a family-like place, but it has a lively bar on one end. I elect to sit in the middle in a darkened booth that would be romantic if not for the fact I am falling to pieces.

* * *

With a bit of arguing I get Tiffany and Brittney to order what they want, and each orders the steak (rare) and lobster, with a loaded baked potato. With an appetizer. And a salad. It is not tenderloin and lobster, but a manly rib-eye. When I order a heady Washington Red Mountain wine, I thought they would have an orgasm right there. They have impeccable table manners (as all Military types do), but they are devouring their meal as if they have been on field rations for a month—or longer.

Scott looks at me. Scott is good. He picks up little social clues, better than I can, I think. I can see this one nags at him.

"So, how's budgeting this year?" he asks Brittney.

"Uh, okay, things are a little tight," she reluctantly admits.

"We're, ah, in the middle of a modernization cycle," Tiffany chimes in.

She's lying. Rather, she's lying by omission. She told me a little truth to push me away from a bigger one, and now I'm bothered. How could it get so bad that real food is an issue? Especially MPs? I suppress a frown. Let them enjoy their meal without two jaded old farts giving them shit.

I give Scott a look, and drink some wine. I will let it drop, but if these two little tarts, from my old unit at that, think they can dump cover smoke and have it work on me, they are going to be very surprised. I've switched girls for less.

The waitress brings the dessert tray, almost reluctantly, as if she's fearful the two young women will bite her arms. They order some chocolate cake thing that looks so good and on reflection, I change my order to that, which seems to please them.

Oh my gosh they are so cute, I could just eat them up nom, nom, nom, nom.

"Tell me about your ride. I have not seen that model before," I ask to keep my mind from sinking further.

Both women—faces flushed from drinking wine—perk up. They look very content, and I actually feel a little like a momma cat who just gave her cute little kittens a rabbit dinner.

"Roscoe is an AMU-FSV Mark I. Armored Multi-Utility, Field Service Vehicle. It's made by Honda and it's totally kick-ass," Brittney brags.

"We got him late last year. He even comes with a field maintenance bot and everything," Tiffany adds. "The accumulators on Roscoe are awesome. He has an enormous range. And the main gun, oh my gosh, I get wet just thinking about it."

Bwa!

"You MPs normally send out such an expensive vehicle to check up on Investigators?" asks Scott.

"Er," says Brittney.

"Um," says Tiffany.

Brittney gives me a weak grin. "Well, the PTB wanted to make an impression on Lexus. We were told to show the flag a little."

"Everyone in the 170th brags about you, ma'am, er, Lexus," adds Tiffany, and her face flushes redder than the wine can make it.

I close my eyes and lean back.

PTB. *Powers That Be.*

Powers

That

Be…

Blackness.

* * *

"*Lef*tenant, did the PTB send you out here?"

I look at the Scotsman, a young man with impressive sideburns and steel colored eyes. He wears hodge-podge armor, but his rifle is state of the art, well cared for and well used. He's insanely accurate with it, a true sharpshooter, bordering on the spooky. His name is Bruce. His accent is smooth but distinctive, and fits right into our impromptu base camp at Castle Edinburgh.

Despite his youth, Bruce looks like he's been around the block a few times, so I need to give him the straight up.

"Sorry Bruce. The PTBs are dead. My entire command structure is gone from General Williamson on down."

"What happened?"

"Nuke. Several actually, big fusion suckers. Iceland went bye-bye."

"How did they get nukes? How did they get past your defenses?"

These are good questions, for which I don't know the answers. We blasted off from Port Dis to head to Bermuda, and at the apex of our hop, Iceland exploded. Boom. Our forward base in the war, my home for the last year, gone, just like that. My Captain. The Lieutenant Colonel, the sister platoons, my friends on base, gone. All gone. All dead. And here I'm alive.

Alive for what?

My men, I keep reminding myself. My men.

"Don't know, Mr. Bruce."

"Ah fuck, here I thought you were the forward point to a rescue effort."

I give him a level look. "Look Bruce, I'll be straight with you. We got your call at the same time we decided that maybe touching down in Bermuda was not such a good idea. I only had seconds to make a decision."

Indeed, the sudden course change overloaded one of my hoppers, causing a hard landing and casualties. Unfortunately, all of my orbital hoppers are of the fling variety. They only use fuel landing, stranding us here. There is no launcher here; we were supposed to pick up two-way hoppers in Bermuda.

Now we can't get Bermuda on the BattleNet, the distributed anti-Union Military communication network. Nor anyone else for that matter.

"Ah Hell, *Left*enant, I don't care. Things went from bad to worse and your timing was perfect." He looks frightened. He looks relieved. He looks tired.

It *was* perfect. We slammed into the enemy from above with such force it broke all their fire teams apart. I lost two men, both in the hopper malfunction, but the violence of destruction we unleashed was impressive even to me.

My men are pissed.

Fully equipped pissed people in Heavy Power-Assisted Assault Armor tend to kill things, in great numbers. Angry cops. We have not done any policing in a while, but the mentality is still there.

Nelson, my comm tech, pipes up in my ear. "Ma'am, still no answer from anybody who knows what's going on, and attaching to a command tree is out because I can't find one. The mainland is intact, but there's a high-degree of panic since D.C. also took a hit. It makes talking to anybody who can do anything difficult. I think they also hit Beijing and Moscow, but info on that's sketchy."

He sounds worried.

Crap. The three capitals of the free world, gone.

"Thanks, Nelson."

"One other thing. Someone plugged themselves into the Base BattleNet—what is left of it anyway—but without an ID."

That gives me pause. What—oh, yeah. "You think it's a sub?" Subs have very particular communication protocols. They are paranoid, like Paranoid Plus Plus. Right now, the sub is probably in white-knuckle analysis trying to find what the hell is going on.

"I'll bet money on it, LT. Either that or the Union has figured out how to break our keys, and then we're just fucked, so I'll just pretend it's a sub."

"Well, alrighty then. I'll let you know how many civilians we need to evacuate shortly, then you can scream bloody specific murder over the comm, instead of just bloody murder."

"You got it, LT."

Shortly turned out to be thirty seconds.

Corporal Delcort looks grim. "234 irregulars, 16 with wounds. 23 children and babies with 4 caretakers. One old guy of about 90 clutching an old M4 and telling anyone who gets close to him to fuck off."

He nods and then sub-vocalizes.

—There were twenty-eight unmovable wounded, left behind in the hospital.—

"Thanks, Junior."

Two-hundred and sixty-two people. Out of thirteen thousand.

I turn to Bruce to ask him why the fuck did they wait so long before calling for help, but he's ashen, having heard Junior's report. I look north northwest to the multitude of burning boats in the water, and realize I don't need to ask.

"Bruce, did they hit you with stunners and sticky guns?"

"Yes."

Well, it seems Castle Edinburgh is going to be our graves.

"Why aren't they rushing, *Leftenant?*" he asks, timing his question with my dark thoughts.

"Well, their commanders are evaluating why you suddenly kicked their asses. A major part of it is we killed a huge number of them when we collapsed all the train tunnels near the castle. But the simple thing is it takes time for the Cocktail to work. Once they have everyone they took prisoner plugged in to the Union Net, they will be back, this time with assault rifles, supporting weapons and everything."

"Oh no. No. That's a rumor. It's supposed to take months for re-education."

Re-education. Ha, good one. He should know better, living on the doorstep to Hell for so long.

"No, it's not. Once 'upgraded,' your former friends and family don't need any combat training. Their new combat chip coupled with the intrinsic benefits of plugging into the Union Net actually makes them a more effective force than your trained militia."

What's left of his militia.

"Why! Why couldn't they just leave us alone? When we took back Edinburgh, we thought we made the point that we would…"

"Die to the last man before surrendering the Castle?"

He nods and finally big tears come streaming down his face.

"Bruce, we'll hold out and make them pay. We'll try to get everyone out, if we can find transport. What is going on here is a not so subtle hint that the Union claims this territory and will take it at any cost, no matter how high."

He nods and I mentally move on.

"Cheryl, what are you looking at?" I ask the lead of my Marine sniper team. Recently attached to my platoon, I feel I have won a lotto. It helps immensely that, at some point, one of the post-Collapse governments added a reinforced, tall tower to the center of the structure. It looms over the entire city, and now we have support drones hanging off of it for a 360 field of fire. And at the very top, Cheryl and her sniper squad have taken up residence. Perfect.

What's double funny is you can't even *see* the tower unless you have advanced sensors. We had a tanker truck filled with camo-LCD, and we just finished spraying the entire structure. Eventually the advantage of that will wear off, but for now, it's confusing as hell.

"Bunch of nothing, LT. About the only thing that's moving around out there is a fat cat sitting on the roof of that pink hotel."

"Shoot it."

"Excuse me?"

"Shoot it."

A shot goes out.

"Damn, LT, the cat was filled with green cyber goo. How did you know?"

"Cats in a war zone are skinny."

"And here I thought officers lost their brains at the Academy!"

"Ha, ha, ha. Shoot anything that moves, from as far away as possible. I don't care if it's a big bug. Shoot it. That includes adults, children, dogs, cats and large chipmunks."

"Roger that, LT. By the way, it's crowded up here. I love the vantage point, but we need the room since I have a three-sixty, and having extra bodies up here doesn't help with the cloaking. I'm sending Corporal Vash and Corporal Juan to stand at your elbow."

I laugh. "Sending muscle to babysit the Lieutenant so she doesn't do something stupid and get us all killed?" The squad has two snipers and their two spotters, which is, when it comes down to it, four snipers. They also have two riflemen who are responsible for their vantage safety. But since they are at the top of an invisible tower covered in automatic guns in a castle, the muscle is not really needed.

"Something like that." I can hear the grin on her face.

"Are they good looking?"

"Are you kidding? Vash is a chocolate god and Juan is a big Valentino. They are also super gay. But if you get them drunk enough, they will toss some mercy dick your way. And let me tell you, mercy dick from those two beats out most dick any day of the week."

I cackle in triumph. I also wonder if we have any booze around here.

At last, I stop putting off what I really should be doing.

"Dex, how's your load out?"

Dex answers in his normal gruff voice. "I have enough g-morts until the end of time, LT," and he squirts me his shell count.

Guided mortars are a particular nasty addition to my platoon's inventory: mortars assisted by micro thrusters and winglets. They are accurate as hell. We have what my supply guy would call 'a metric fuckpile' of the things.

"Beauty. Here's the plan. It's going to get very crowded. Try to hit something that looks like it's worth hitting, let the riflemen pick off clumps of people. And when the shit hits the fan, blow the crap out of any vantage point within five-hundred meters."

"Roger that, LT. You expecting armor?"

"No, but I do expect transport. Lots of trucks."

"Yum. I love me trucks full of euro trash!"

Ha, well, he's not going to love this.

"Dex, see the hospital on the tac-net?

"Yes."

"Hit it. Give it some HE, then a scrambler, then a FAM."

Dex is quiet, then, "Now, LT?"

"Yes, now."

Boom, boom, boom, crunch kerblam! The shockwave from the fuel-air-mortar almost knocks me off my feet, even from here. What is left of the hospital burns in the gray morning. The buildings around it burn, and in the breeze, I sometimes smell burnt flesh.

Bruce looks at me, pained.

"That's an obvious rally point for them. Anytime they find clumps of people they put guards around them as the Cocktail goes to work. Then, since they are social, others come by to talk in real-time, and sometimes they even engage in sex."

Killing Union while they are having sex is the highlight of any day. I take special delight in that. A woman on a mission, one could say.

"They 'Cocktail' wounded?"

"Always."

Poor Bruce. When his elders gathered the leftover Highlanders, they didn't go about it the right way. The Highlander insurgents should have stayed in the Highlands. Their victory in Edinburgh was no victory at all. Edinburgh is just a convenient collection point as far as the enemy is concerned.

Well, two can play at that game. We are going to kill many of them. *Many.*

Crack!

A Ham-scram M43 sniper rifle. I look at the tac-net floating in my right eye. A dead enemy, only 600 meters southwest.

"LT, they are trying to deploy snipers," says Cheryl.

Fuck.

"That one looked well fed, too."

Double fuck.

"Well, at least they have to shoot up hill," I casually say.

A snort in my comm channel.

Now two very big men are at my side, Marines in scout armor with M37 carbines and more grenades than a god.

"LT, I'm Vash and this is Juan."

Oh *my*. Yum, yum, yum!

"Vash, your voice is like, well, it's *pretty.*"

"I get that a lot," he says, showing perfect white teeth, "especially from women."

"*Señior* Vash, the ladies do love him," Juan says, holding out his hands a foot apart.

I laugh. Marines. I love them. Arrogant asses, but I love them.

"We're going on a tour, Gentlemen."

The tour sucked. Despite the now invisible reinforced tower, Edinburgh was a tourist spot. This was a terrible point to hold out against a modern fighting force. In fact, I'm now certain it was a trap. They let the Highlanders take the city on purpose. Classic.

"LT, we're going to die in here, aren't we?" asks Juan.

"Maybe."

Crack!

Another sniper kill. It will not be long now. Too late for transport.

"Okay, more than maybe."

I end my tour at the mech suit: one Mechanical Guardian, Mark II.

The mech suit is a twenty-ton hard shell that goes around armor. This one's weapon load outs broke in a hard landing, taking my Pilot with it, which is very unfortunate. It could actually make a great big jump for kilometers and kilometers, flying for a good distance before puttering out. It's still useful in that regard.

"Jason."

"LT, what's up?"

Jason is the new guy. He looks like he's scared shitless and trying not to show it, which is good enough for me. He's also the only other person, besides me, who knows how to use the damn thing. He isn't a combat Pilot, but his training lets him move the Guardian.

As the new guy, he also didn't have an established pre-combat hookup, so because Bermuda was still a hot zone, I fucked him royally and completely according to protocol. He had youth and an athletic body. Almost my favorite officer's perk. He was sweet, until I got him to relax. Then I got a wild pounding.

Yum. I'm even ovulating. New guy at my peak of wanting new guy.

Double yum.

"Okay, listen up. Jason, if I give you the order, blast out of here. Don't look back, just get the fuck away and try to last long enough for evac. Got that? That might sound bad, but if we make them bleed and get *one* guy out, I'll chalk that up to a victory in my book."

"I—yes, ma'am."

"Good man." I give him a peck on the cheek.

Crack!

I hit the all-channel.

"Okay, listen up. The bad guys want to take back their pretty castle, and we're going to make them pay for it. Pay hard. I know that losing Iceland was a terrible thing, but that's in the past. What lies in the future is all that concerns us.

"Our only mission here is blood. This is no longer a rescue mission. We can't get anyone in the BattleNet, and you can tell by listening to the snipers that things are picking up. So far, there isn't transport coming to rescue the people left. Or us. I know that's a harsh message, but there it is. Don't run around trying to save people. Shoot. Kill as many of them as possible, from as far away as possible.

"If by the Grace of the Old God we get our prayers answered, then we can play firemen and toss the girls and boys on our shoulders."

I close my eyes briefly. "I have never fought with such a brave and competent bunch of soldiers. You're all my brothers and sisters, and I love every one of you stinky assholes. What matters now, at this time, is killing the enemy in large numbers. They are going on the offensive, and we need to show them, we *have* to show them, that it will cost them dear. So if they try to come into our territory, our brothers and sisters will remember us, and protect our homes in our names."

Was it a good pep speech? I don't know. They all answer with a big hearty *"Hooah!"*

I look at Bruce.

"You're a crazy fucking bitch," he says, bitterly. He didn't like me tossing his people to the wolves.

Sorry Bruce, but I'm not the one who fucked the pooch, I want to say. Instead, I give him a level glance. "I'm not a particularly religious woman, but I get the distinct feeling we're supposed to be dead back there in

Port Dis."

"Yeah, it's what everybody is thinking, LT," says Vash, nodding grimly.

"Yup," says Juan.

"Sorry Bruce, I really am. But it could be we did die back there and this is Heaven."

"Heaven?" he asks, looking at me as if I have gone nuts.

"Yes, Heaven—Heaven for us is shooting Union fuckers until we run out of ammo. We have them right where we want them and I have a *lot* of ammo."

I walk away, chuckling to myself. Bruce is already dead, in my eyes.

I hear a mortar fly, followed by a distant boom.

"Scratch one truck full of cyber-pervs," says Dex.

Crack goes a sniper rifle.

"This is it. Button up, and don't just kick some ass, blow the ass to fuck!"

"Hooah!"

I look at my men.

Each one looks like they would follow me to Hell.

If I could cry, I would, but since I can't, I guess I will have to kill me some enemy.

Vash and Juan bump fists.

"The *Señorita* isn't so bad for an Army puke, eh Vash?"

"Kick ass, she actually talk-fucked this fag into a boner."

I chuckle again, and to my ears, it sounds grim.

* * *

"Jason! Lift! Jason, get the fuck out, now. Do it!"

I'm only alive because Vash and Juan are freaks of nature, fucking Bionic Marines, like from that ancient Clint Eastwood vid we watch every now and then while smoking pot. They are the reason I didn't tell Jason to lift earlier. For a moment there, I thought we would drive them back far enough to give us a pause.

Through the smoky haze from all the fires, my helmet auto-targets a lightly armored woman, carrying a mechanical spider on her back, running towards me. She's a recent Unionized civilian. The bot we call a

'Bartender.' Its sole function is to insert the 'Cocktail' into a person, which then Unionizes them.

I ignore her and whirl around my guess she's a feint is correct. My rifle sings out and obliterates two enemies, Union regulars in light armor, trying to rush me, their small-arms fire bouncing off my armor.

I continue to whirl around, but Vash has already shot her and Juan has shot the Bartender.

This is what makes the enemy so deadly. They can communicate as fast as they can think. And it's not a collective groupthink, but an instant sharing of thoughts to the exact person you want to share them with. They are very coordinated. And this speech has no limitations on distance.

Bartenders are everywhere, riding on recently Unionized civilians' backs or skittering here and there on their own. They are useless against suited infantry in shock troop configuration, but what they do to Bruce's people—I don't want to think about it. They will Cocktail up anything, especially children, all the way down to a newborn.

Bruce is actually still alive, but not for long.

A green laser paints across me—my suit screams a warning, and all four of us dive behind a stone pony wall.

The explosion rocks me back. This is how they have been taking us armored infantry out, one-by-one, with sabot RPGs, a rocket-propelled grenade with a big armored point. The point pierces your armor and then the grenade explodes, a shaped charge pointed right at the hole it just made.

Deadly and effective.

"Jason!"

"Jason's dead!" Cheryl says.

"Fuck."

So is everyone else. We've come back to the main courtyard, and there isn't anybody left to regroup with. A sniper, two Marines, Bruce and me.

I have killed all of my men.

But what a glorious way to die. I may have made fun of Castle Edinburgh earlier, but it was not a bad stand. We killed thousands of the enemy. So many, in fact, they stopped tossing simple Unionists at us and dropped in real soldiers. We killed those too, but the Union has decided this is a symbolic target, so they are just pouring in real troops faster than we can kill them. If they were smart, they would send in armor or bomb the place, but the castle is as emblematic to them as it is to Bruce.

We have only lasted this long because we were in shock-and-awe configuration.

I wonder how many I can kill before I go down.

Bruce is limping with an armor-piercing round in his leg.

"Bruce…"

Bruce flips me off, grins, draws his sidearm, flips up the helmet visor and shoots himself in the head.

Just like that.

Vash just shrugs his shoulders, always funny looking in armor and Juan picks up Bruce's rifle. "Well, LT, I guess…"

My suit beeps, indicating a new authenticated active communication channel. I'm finally in an active BattleNet. "This is the *SSBN Colorado*, Manticore, Manticore, are you still there? We're now in range for a long jump if you have the equipment. Our personnel capacity is limited!"

Fuck me sideways—a ballistic missile submarine. Why would one surface to save field troops?

I decide I don't care.

This is now a rescue mission. I can save somebody. I can save somebody!

Vash must have been thinking the same thing. "We'll cover you! Grab some kids!"

"The Guardian might not even be working!" I say, firing a burst where I see movement.

"I've got it covered! Go! Get some kids!" Cheryl screams over the comm. Her rifle is now a staccato, playing a cadence of destruction from her tower. It is obvious she is no longer conserving ammo, and any tarry will now waste her efforts.

We start running, firing as we go, and soon we're in a stone corridor. The mines turn off as we pass them. We don't have time for proper protocol. I just have to pray that they turn off as advertised, and then turn back on.

"*Colorado!* This is Lieutenant Lexus! Stand by!"

"Aye, aye, ma'am."

We're at a door. It's an old, old iron-shod door.

I sub-vocalize.

—Here's the plan. Give me two grenades. Then you both grab two toddlers each, one for each arm. Don't grab babies or older kids, or we're fucking dead. Then I'll cover you as we head to the Guardian.—

—We'll cover you, LT! You grab kids and blast off!—

—Look, you fucking jarhead, it's a fucking twenty-ton Mechanical with fucking rockets for legs! I can pick both you meatheads up like toys!—

They look at me, then they nod and hand me the grenades. Big boomers, and I snap them to hard points on my armor. Their hands are shaking. I see it in their eyes through their helmets. They both love me and hate me.

I think I will just appreciate the hate.

"Hurry the fuck up!" Cheryl screams.

I code the door. It beeps, and then opens.

A pistol shot pings off my armor.

"Stop! Those are Federation soldiers!"

Crying babies, children, and four young women looking oh so frightened fill the small room. How they could even breathe in here, I don't know.

I have to give Juan and Vash credit. They waste no time, and grab four toddlers in an eye blink. The children simultaneously scream like banshees and latch on like lampreys.

"Where are the…"

The woman doesn't finish her sentence, because I have shot her in the head, sparing her a task which she is unable to do.

The Marines are already out the door as my other three shots go out, killing the adults. They are just standing there, I'm moving so fast they are helpless.

I toss in the grenades.

I close the door and the lock engages.

I run. I run, run, run.

Boom! Kur-blam! The explosions ignite the mines and the secondary explosion almost knocks us off our feet, even in armor.

I overtake Vash and Juan. I'm firing in every direction, no need to conserve this magazine.

"Cheryl, get down here! You can ride my back!" My vision narrows, and everything is in super-sharp focus. I pull the trigger, and something dies. Run and pull, run and pull.

Her voice sounds pained, labored. "Ain't gonna be able to do that LT, hurry, there are so many, so many."

I'm not going to argue. It doesn't sound like she can make it. Normally I would be able to see her vitals but I lost that portion of the tacnet over an hour ago.

I'm at the Guardian. Jason is there, the victim of a sabot RPG. The explosion has popped his helmet off, and his body is literally running out of his armor.

Ah hell, Jason, I'm so sorry, I think to his corpse, pushing aside the memory of his kisses. His caresses. His lovemaking. Oh, my men. *My men.*

I drop my carbine and slam into the receptacle. It activates automatically, my armor fitting into it, the war machine enveloping me.

I stand up just in time to see Cheryl's tower explode in fire. Fire caused by a satchel charge—many satchel charges, actually, courtesy of the Marines—and as the tower crumples I actually hear Unionists scream in frustration at its destruction.

Shit.

"Fully charged, total weapons malfunction. Suggest evac," the Guardian tells me.

Oh ya Baby, I got your evac. Two gigantic hands go out and true to my training, I envelope my Marines without crushing them or their wards.

I deploy the winglets. *Shunk!*

"Hold on to those kids!"

Several green lasers paint me and I stab buttons on the joystick.

Fa-boom! I lift off, and three sabot grenades make contact with the Earth where I was standing not one second ago.

"*Colorado, Colorado*, give me a ping!"

A radar wave washes over me, indicated by my suit, and pinpoints the originating location better than any GPS could. They are northwest in the North Sea. The flight comp figures out what I'm trying to do and gives me a glowing path to watery freedom in my HUD.

Vash and Juan look like they are pissing themselves, and I pray no one freezes to death. Away from all the smoke, it's a lovely day, and the enhanced optics pick up the boat moving very fast on the surface. It's a big honker of a submarine. Actually, as I recall, it's one of the last nuclear missile subs ever made.

"*Colorado, Colorado*, stop moving. I'm not that good. I have fuel to spare."

"Aye, aye, ma'am, going stationary."

"ETA three minutes. Here's the plan, I'm going to use my wing brakes and drop two jarheads, and they have two children each. Stay away from the Mech. I will then push off and go for a swim. See if you can catch me before I drown."

"Copy that, Guardian. Divers tubed and standing by."

I can't reverse brake because I would cook my wards, but the winglets design lets me change angles and they have maneuvering thrusters. If I time it right, I can hover over the boat and simply drop them on the deck without using my main thrusters, which—over a ballistic missile submarine—would be a bad idea.

I've actually done this very rescue maneuver.

Once.

In a simulation.

And the boat was a ship, an aircraft carrier.

Glide!

Wing tilt!

Maneuver thrusters!

Drop!

Away!

I'm now free to use the primary thrusters, which is good, because the winglet thrusters are toasted. I hover over the water.

"Guardian, eject, eject, eject!" someone yells into the comm channel.

I contemplate sinking to the bottom of the sea. I almost do it, but then again, I need to see Vash and Juan and the toddlers on dry land to make sure they are safe.

"Full eject!" I scream at the Guardian comp. "Eject! Eject! Eject!"

SLAM! My suit peels back, and I'm violently unhooked from my plumbing, designed to come loose quickly, but it still hurts like hell.

But I don't have to worry about that because now I'm out and in the water.

Oh fuck, that's cold. I can't move. Luckily, I also can't breathe because now I'm frozen.

Then I'm yanked and pushed to the surface.

I live.

Yay me, I guess.

CHAPTER 9

I'M IN A CORNER, curled up into a ball. I blink and my eyes start working.

"Nancy, can you hear me?"

"No," I say.

"We got you, Nancy. Let me help you on your feet."

"No! Don't touch me! Go away!"

"You had an Uplink flashback. You need medical attention."

"Fuck off!"

"Okay, Nancy," I hear Brittney say, finally able to figure out who is talking, "we're going to help you to your feet, and if you put up a fight, we're going to stun you."

They help me to my feet. I blink again. "What, what? What happened?" The two MPs have me in a grip of steel, between them. What did they just say?

"You had an Uplink flashback."

"Oh, no. No."

I look around. The restaurant is completely empty. "Did I chase everyone away?"

Shit, I suck. I can't even go out to eat anymore.

"No, ma'am," says Tiffany. "They left out of respect."

I feel cold. I realize I have peed myself. It was like a vat of pee, it has soaked everything.

They help me out the door, and there is a crowd waiting. They press around us.

A man touches my arm.

"Thank you, ma'am, for saving us," he says.

Another person touches me. "Thank you," a woman whispers, tears in her eyes.

We press through the crowd, and tears fill my eyes and blind me.

"We love you, Pilot!"

Oh no, no, no, I'm not worthy of your love. You need to hate me. Please hate me.

Another person touches me, this man too choked up to talk.

A little girl puts a flower in my hand.

I choke out a sob.

"Make room, make some room," Scott finally says, but the crowd presses closer. It surges, and with a gentle yank, I leave the MPs grasp, hoisted up.

I'm on my back, and it feels like I'm floating in water. They pass me along to waiting hands, silently. People are touching me, patting me, and I'm at the edge of the crowd. Soon I'm at Scott's SUV. They gently lower me so I'm sitting on the back bumper. Tiffany and Brittney are there, and I'm relieved to see them crying too, even if they are silent about it. In moments, the crowd is gone, leaving me to my companions.

This has happened before. Several times, in fact, in different places from here to Tokyo. I want to hate them for it, but how can I hate a people I love so much? I love them so much, so damn much, and even when they prevent me from killing myself, I still love them.

I open the vice of my fingers and drop the flower, put my head in my hands, and continue sobbing.

Tiffany and Brittney try to stuff me in the SUV but I insist, in-between sobs in the removal of my pee-soaked clothes. They don't argue, and soon I'm naked. I'm in the back of the SUV, with my head on Tiffany's lap, lying lengthwise on the bench seat.

I feel terrible. I'm shaking slightly. I know the shakes will get worse. I could even have a seizure.

I can even die.

Is that what I want? I don't know. I need to catch the bad man first, though.

Layla would want me to.

Mommy I love you… Mommy…

"Arune. Get me to Arune," I whisper.

"Get her to her ship, Mr. Scott," Tiffany says in a cute little command voice.

I feel the SUV move. I can see emergency lights reflected off storefront windows back into the SUV, bathing everything in a surreal red and blue glow.

Tiffany is looking at me with concern and adoration in her hazel eyes, her fabulous hazel eyes. She's caressing my face, and it calms me. The shaking fades.

"Ssssh, it will be okay, it will be okay," she says in a soothing voice.

"I'm going to run a scanner over you," she says. I nod.

The medical scanner beeps angrily several times and she frowns.

"Lexus, listen, your receptors have caused your nervous system to go all wonky."

I wonder if wonky is a medical term.

"You need to Uplink," she says.

"Ship," I croak.

Brittney hands her something and Tiffany removes her Military watch. She shows me the back of her wrist.

She has a neural receptor!

She shows me the male-male cord that Brittney handed to her.

"We can Uplink. I've been trained for medical applications. It won't be like your ship but it will sooth you out."

I lick my lips. I want it—want it bad. Want to do it with her. But if I do it, she will own me, I will be hers, powerless against her will for the rest of my life. I will become addicted to her Uplink just as I'm addicted to sex and snorf and Investigations.

I shake my head. "Arune, get me to Arune." I deny my addictions, the need for instant gratification, and the tears start up again.

I want to hate them, the tears, but all I can see is Tiffany and her pretty face through the hot blur. She bends down, proving that she's very limber, and kisses my tears away.

"Okay, I had to offer. I understand," she whispers to me.

Where do people like her come from, I wonder? Is this what Layla would've grown up to be? How many Laylas will die before I catch the killer? I start to shake again.

Mommy I love you… Mommy…

"Lexus, calm down. You have to calm down. I can't Uplink with you against your will, so if you won't consent, we have to get you to Arune in time. We need time."

Oh but she doesn't know all she has to do is connect us with Brittney's magic cable and I will mentally spread for her like an eager snorfed out call girl with rent due in three days.

I don't tell her that.

I do look into her eyes, and nod. I close mine and part my lips.

She kisses me. A little kiss, a caressing kiss. I can feel tension leaving my body and I kiss her back, tasting her, savoring the connection, and I'm alive.

I'm still alive.

My men are dead.

But I'm alive.

"Drive faster," I hear Tiffany say through a long tunnel.

She squeezes my hand.

Because she wants me to, I hold on to life through her. She goes back to caressing my face, and the touch soothes me again. I stop trembling.

"Good girl," says Tiffany, her eyes dancing.

Okay, she will pay for that one.

The SUV comes to a halt, and we're in a shadow—must be Arune.

I listen to a one-way conversation.

"Uplink flashback. She needs to Uplink."

"Her armor is in the locker."

"Ten."

"Will do."

The door opens and Scott picks me up. He walks me towards Arune's passenger cabin, followed by Tiffney and Brittney dragging my lockers.

In the cabin, Arune says "Hey. You're naked."

I nod, weakly.

Now Scott is in the main cabin, and I almost giggle. It's a remodeled bedroom, a modern bedroom, complete with a queen-sized bed. I had no idea.

"Put her on the bed, and don't take this personally—get out. Now."

Then I'm alone with Arune. A tendril touches the back of my skull.

"Please..."

Without pausing, it clicks in.

—Uplink!—

—Stars, stars, I need to see stars; I need to float please, please...—

—Yes, of course, my Love. Lifting.—

Arune doesn't blast off with rockets. I imagine the outer airlock door sealing and *whoosh*, he's gone in a whisper.

—You need to pass out now. Twenty-minute Uplink nap.—

—Wait I want to see—

Blackness.

* * *

I slide out of Uplink as I wake. The covers on the bed keep me from floating about the cabin.

"How are you feeling?"

"Much better, my friend. Thank you."

"I thought you were over that Uplink flashback crap. This one was bad, Lexus. You almost died."

"This case is bad."

"Doesn't matter, there are physical..."

"There was an—accident. Involuntary Uplink to a Level Two AI."

"What? Who?"

"ICDA."

Arune is silent.

"Arune? I'm a little fucked up. Today has been monumentally shitty. Except for kissing a girl. And Uplinking to you."

"You kissed a girl?"

"Yeah."

"I'm going to access your armor recorder, Lexi."

Oh no. The armor recorder isn't my PDA linked to Bob. It's a true neural recorder. I could not erase its storage any more than I could erase my own memories. Only a Level One AI, like Arune, can read them.

"I don't recommend that. You will be mad at no one in particular."

Arune is silent, disregarding my warning. When he begins shouting a few seconds later, I'm not surprised. "That wasn't an accident! It was rape! Damn it!"

I can't describe the feeling of shame and sheer terribleness that washes over me, knowing that Arune saw what happened to Scott and me. I feel so stupid for it, so I curl up into a little ball and bury my face into my pillow.

"I'm sorry, crap, this shit has me unnerved. I'm sorry. What can I do? Tell me what to do and I will do it." He's pleading.

"I—I don't know. Do you know I haven't cried in what, ten years? Yet today that's all I seem to be doing." Even as I say it, I'm getting choked up again. "Ah hell, I know, I know, we're crazy…"

"Yup. So, what's next, crazy person?"

"Gonna use the head."

So I do. It's a cute girly bathroom, with girly stuff in it.

"You can talk to me while I sit here, it won't embarrass me," I tell him. He was always one for ship privacy protocol, but that training was before the bad times, the mad times.

"Maybe it will embarrass me."

I roll my eyes. Yeah, right.

I stand up, unseal a wet cleaning cloth and wash myself off, head to toe. It's not a hot shower, but it feels great anyway.

"You know, you're pretty good looking for a hairless old lady."

I laugh. "Thank you for waiting until I was off the vacu-potty to tell me that."

"Ha. Does your Lib-Gee keep you young?"

"Regen almost gave me back ten years off my life. You're right though, the Lib-Gee is a little marvel. It slows down the aging process," I admit. Only a few doctors in Japan know about that dirty little secret. And now Arune.

I float back to the main cabin. It's beautiful. Indeed, if I were to decorate it, this is exactly what it would look like.

"Arune, did you have this cabin decorated just for me?"

"I did. I knew you would be back."

"Oh, I'm sorry for leaving you. I just had to put my feet on the ground, I had to get out of Uplinking and become a person again, I had…"

"Lexi. I spent most of that time sleeping. Sure, I had the odd job of taking people to orbit and the moon and whatnot; but really, don't think of me using human time perspectives. AIs don't age and die like humans. I look at the outside world differently than you. You know that."

I nod. Still I feel bad. There he was, just waiting for me, and there I was, married and doing much of nothing. I snuffle.

"If you cry again, I will whip your ass and give you something to cry about!" A tendril waves angrily in the cabin, as if punctuating his statement.

"Sorry." I wonder if that threat is serious. I decide not to test him.

"That's better."

"Arune, I love you. I mean it."

He laughs. "I love you too, you silly human. You're a mess, a mental mess, so, now what?"

I frown and float around the room. Arune pulls no punches. He never did. I ignore him and explore the cabin.

In a recessed dresser and wardrobe, I find all manner of clothing, nothing I would buy.

"Arune, what's all of this?"

"I was buying you clothes, and quickly came to the conclusion your style sucks. So I said 'fuck it' and bought what you should be wearing."

I laugh. I never cared about fashion after I entered Basic. After Hell Week, clean and dry was about all I needed.

"Ha, ha. And this drawer full of lingerie?"

"That is for when we will have sex again. What can I say? I watch the vids and the girls on the vids wear that stuff."

"Those vids will rot your Think Goo brain, you big dope."

That's when I see it. I pull it out. A black slip. With shaking hands, I also pull out black stockings, and a garter belt.

"Look, Lexi, we can just space that."

"No."

I put on the slip.

"What are you doing? Are you out of—scratch that, you are. So back to my original question, what are you doing?"

"Conquering my fears. There isn't anything in the world I'm more afraid of right now than wearing these things."

"Look…"

"I can do this, please." My lip starts trembling again. It's all I can do to put the belt and stockings on, and I struggle with the snaps for a bit. Finally, I'm dressed.

Just like Jennifer.

Just like Layla.

Mommy I love you… Mommy…

"Your vitals are elevated," Arune warns.

I float over and haphazardly make the bed, hovering above it.

"Do the right calf, wind the tendril around before you insert it."

He does.

"Now the other one."

My left leg is now bound.

"Run out the cables so I can move my feet, yeah, like that."

I interlock my fingers, holding my hands out before me.

"Now tie my hands and then link, with both cables."

"Lexi…"

"Please."

I'm shaking in pure fright. This feels so terrible.

The tendrils snap into my receptors.

"Now wrap the last one around my upper torso, under my armpits. Now snap it in place."

"I don't like this," Arune says, but he does what I ask, and my skull receptor registers a link by sending a wave of pleasure down my spine.

"Shhhh, we're almost done. Now pull my hands down. Now tighter. Tighter. Right there."

"This is weird," he says. I know what he's thinking, he's thinking of when we first had sex. It was just like this, except my wrists, while tied, were not tied together, and I was floating on my back, relative to the cabin floor.

I shake my head. "No, this is real. What happened to me earlier was not real; it was a simulation. A very real one where I felt everything that poor Jennifer felt, but it was not the same. I didn't see his face. He didn't really put anything inside of me. And I lived. Here I am. With you. My Love, my first Adult Love."

"I love you, but you're one crazy bitch but I will admit it, it's a good crazy. You won: he tried to take everything from you, but you didn't let him."

It's a partial victory, I realize. "Still, I can close my eyes and feel it. I guess I have to conquer something else besides fear. Arune?"

"Yes?" He sounds shaken.

"When we make love again, and we will, you need to be very gentle with me. I don't know if I can ever let a human touch me that way again, but you can."

"Don't talk like that. You have loving Husbands. You will be okay."

He doesn't understand. As I lie here, I just can't imagine a world in which I would let a human male have intercourse with me. Not going to happen. No way, no how. The Pussy Is Closed. I used her in mercenary fashion during the war, and now she got back at me, giving me what I deserve. I also see a lot of drugs in my future. This self-therapy 'conquer my fears' thing is barely the tip of the iceberg of what I am going to need for a chance at recovery.

I decide to change the subject, pointedly.

"Uplink and take me to the beach, a nice warm beach. Let me sleep in your arms."

In an instant, I'm standing on a tropical beach, wearing the lingerie. There is a slight and warm breeze, and the whoosh and hiss of waves.

"Ohoooo!" I let out a sigh. It seems so real. I know he's using both our minds to conjure up what we think the beach should look like, but it feels so real.

It is real, I decide. As real as anything conceptual, like numbers or right and wrong; as real as anything I have experienced. Uplink is reality to me.

A tall man, Arune's human avatar, walks to me. He's muscular and exotic, with tawny skin and big dark-brown eyes. His black hair is long and curly. He smells faintly of the sea, and of sandalwood. He wears nothing but loose fitting, short beach pants.

It has been so long, so long.

"I'm a man here, Lexi," he says, pointing out the all too real.

He is indeed. Half of me is thinking 'yum'—the other half wants to run, screaming.

I grab his hand. "My body needs sleep. We can talk later."

He leads me to a hammock between palm trees and I have sand in my stockings. I laugh and take them and the silly belt off, leaving on the slip.

"How long do you want to be here?"

"A week."

"How many hours of sleep do you want?"

"Eight," I say. Time is mostly meaningless in the Uplink. All Arune has to do is slice the amount of time I want to spend here amongst the hours I will not be sleeping. A day, a week, a month, I could even go longer, but that's not advisable because of the harsh adjustment to the natural flow of time when I come out of Uplink. That's time when I am conscious. When I sleep, I sleep in real time.

Eight hours of sleep will still give me hours of non-sleep real-time in the Uplink, and those hours can be weeks until my real body gets tired again and I have to sleep for real.

We're in the hammock, and it's rocking a little bit, back and forth. It's very soothing, with the warmth and the ocean sounds.

And he feels so good. I'm lying on him, his arms around me, and oh it feels so good.

"I'm going to sleep," Once my body goes into a sleep state, it carries my Uplink avatar with it. It's like sleeping twice.

"I think you should."

I kiss him, and it's a nice kiss. I separate our lips and snuggle down. "I had a really, really bad day, but you made it better."

He's petting my hair. I notice I have hair. It's red and long. I giggle. Then I notice my skin is pale and soft

"Arune, in a couple of days, I might be ready, to get closer to you."

"Yes," he says simply. And that's all he needs to say, and it's perfect. He's perfect.

I sleep.

* * *

The stars are vivid, so very vivid. Indeed, I have never seen them like this, either inside or outside of Uplink. It's amazing. I feel like a small mote on a small mote floating through space.

Actually, that's what I am, I believe.

I'm on day three of my vacation, and reflective.

Arune gives me space, seemingly knowing exactly when to be here with me and when not. I guess it's not that surprising given that he's Uplinked to my mind, but I appreciate it nonetheless.

Who am I, really? Am I a Wife? Am I an Investigator?

Or is killing all that I'm really good at, my sole purpose?

When I closed that door in Edinburgh after tossing in the grenades, did I cease to be human? What the Union did to children was horrendously ghastly.

But isn't that a description of me?

My post-war therapist used to say a thin red line separated self-reflection and self-loathing. He was right, I think.

I lean back and Arune appears behind me, so I lean on him. He wraps strong arms around me.

He holds me forever, it seems.

Then he starts playing with my breasts. It's not a romantic caress, but a playful dance of fingers that almost tickles.

I squirm. This seems to spur him on.

"Arune…"

In answer, he sticks his tongue in my ear. It's just a simulation, but the action sends an electric jolt straight to my cunt.

I tense up in fear.

"Sorry."

"Nothing to be sorry for. Here, why don't you just lie back? I can warm up to this. I think."

"Lexi, making love should be desire, not simply PTSD therapy."

"I do, I do want you, to please you."

"To be pleased?"

"I—I don't know if I—yes, with you. Let me warm up to it, okay?"

"Anything for you."

He lies back on a suddenly appearing blanket. I take off his cute pants and kiss him. He's very much a man, and he's very hard.

People used to laugh at the idea of Uplink sex with an AI, but I can emphatically say that I can't tell the difference between Arune and say, Mitchel. Arune explained to me how it was a neurological feedback loop, so each experience is different. He also admitted, somewhat awkwardly (which was adorable) that he spent time as a woman making love to a man using the same learning process.

Arune, as I have always told him, is an exquisitely intense lover.

I run my fingers along his muscles. I kiss his nipples, and then lean up and kiss him slowly on that warm, spicy mouth, running my hands through his hair. It turns him on, and turning him on turns me on too.

I caress what he wants me to touch and he moans. He starts stroking my breasts but I grab his hand and gently push it away.

"So I'm just an avatar dildo to you?"

I feel like he just slapped me on the face. All my carefully built up desire rushes out of my body like the waves receding from the shore. I push him away, sit up and stare at the sea, trying to will myself to be something that I'm not.

He puts a gentle hand on my shoulder.

"Lexi, I'm sorry. That was mean of me, and I won't blame my relational interaction matrices either. It's just that you're such a desirable woman, and I want you so much. But I know you've gone through a traumatic event. I should be more sympathetic, instead of an asshole. You just light me on fire, Love."

I turn to him, and damn it all if I start crying again!

"Damn it, Arune, you're such a, such a—you're such a *male!*"

He laughs and I jump on him, and start pounding on his shoulders.

"Don't you laugh at me! I'm crying!"

"I win! I win AI maleness!" He's laughing and I can see that his eyes are getting damp too.

"I'm so going to kick your ass," I say and wind my fist back. I go to strike, but he latches onto my wrist and kisses me, a greedy kiss that takes my breath away.

I rip my lips off his. "Stop that! I'm supposed to be mad at you."

He smiles at me and then he leans back.

With my hand, I push down on his chest, hard. He makes a little 'oof' sound and obediently lies still while I shift down his body, put him in my mouth and proceed to torture him. The torture only lasts a little while, though—in no time he gives a mighty grunt and is spent.

Being in Uplink has its advantages. By the time I've crawled back up to face level, he's hard again. I don't wait; this needs to be fluid, one event leading smoothly into another. Nothing jarring, nothing to break the mood. I brace a hand against his chest, lift my hips and slowly, ever so slowly, begin to sink down on him.

The first hint of pressure brings panic, but I force my brain to realize that this feels different, that Arune is different. There are no terrible greedy thrusts, no sensory overload—no looking into Layla's dilated eyes, no binds on my wrists. I am in control. Me.

I try to live in the moment, with him just in me. I close my eyes and listen to the waves. With each crash and swoosh, each breath, the panic recedes. And then it's gone.

Low tide.

I look into his eyes and start to move slowly, ever so slowly.

Eventually, the sound of it all and the feel of it all and his hard body and his hand against me, and his smell his beautiful sweaty man smell and his big brown eyes and I forget and I'm crying and the waves are crashing I'm a crashing wave I'm a crashing wave I'm—

"Arune!"

I burst.

* * *

I'm a leaky mess. I have Arune in my fancy lush red hair, inside of me, running down my leg, just all over. Sometimes I wish I could program these little bits of inconvenience away. Last time I asked, Arune said, "Not a chance in Hell" followed by "reality is perception."

What is it with males and messy sex, anyway?

So I go out for a swim, and come back. Arune is sleeping so I stand over him, dripping, as the sun rises over the ocean. He doesn't wake up, so I stand closer to him and drip on his face.

"Hey!"

I pounce, but soon we're kissing. I snuggle close to him.

"That was perfect," I tell him. "Thank you."

"You're so beautiful," he says.

I melt.

"Arune?"

"Hmmm?"

"Relational interaction matrices?"

He sounds sheepish. "Sorry, when I get stressed I slip into cyber talk."

"You realize that every time you say stuff like that, all I hear is blah, blah, blah."

"I forgive you for being a Luddite."

"Pischt! I know how to cyber with the best of them. Well, no, not really. Fine. That's what subcontractors are for. But I'm not the worst, either!"

He snorts but goes back to lying there, holding me. I listen to his heartbeat with one ear, waves with the other.

"I want to get back together," he says, out of the blue.

Holy crap. "What? No."

"I want to get back together," he repeats. "Please."

I wrinkle my nose and sigh. "Listen, Arune, If I'm to be your girl, then we're just lovers. Got that? We can't be married; my Husbands would then think my marriage to *them* is a sham and I'm not too sure I would disagree with them. I also insist you take a Pilot. Another lover. I can't Pilot anymore. I'd leave the Earth and never come back."

"Deal." He says it immediately, and I can see how delighted I've made him. He looks at me with a look of equal parts love and lust, and a shiver goes down my spine.

—Make love to me, just as we used to. Make love to me my Arune, my wonderful Arune, be on top of me.—

—Yes.—

He holds me tight, and rolls over on top of me.

—You were always my girl.—

My body starts to sing.

Best. Vacation. Ever.

CHAPTER 10

SCOTT, TIFFANY AND BRITTNEY are there waiting for me as I come down the ramp from the main cabin.

"Whoa," says Tiffany.

I'm definitely not going to wear armor this morning, so to humor Arune, I dress the way he wants me to, and I even use *makeup.*

I have to admit, Arune knows what he's talking about: I have on brown boots with heels, white hose and, wonders of wonders, a forest green *skirt.* Over a tan blouse, I'm wearing a green vest, a deeper color than my skirt. To round it out, I even have a wig on, a high quality red affair that matched what he gave me in the Uplink. And a hat, with a brim.

And earrings.

With hoops.

Large hoops.

I simultaneously feel pretty and like an enormous dork.

My needler rides on my hip, and my PDA is in a little pouch attached to my belt. I just hope no one comments on my…

"Wait, is that a *purse?"* Scott's eyes are comically big.

"Shut up. Today, I'm pretty. Tomorrow, I might kick your ass."

"You *are* pretty," says Brittney, wistfully. "You look like a million credits, and here we are, all utilitarian."

"Bah, you breasted nubile hard-bodies outshine me any day."

"I don't think so, Lexus. How did you get your skin so silky smooth and creamy?" asks Tiffany.

"Nano."

They don't make the stuff that directly interfaces with a regulator any more, but Arune, as with many other naughty things, has a hidden supply. Maybe in a decade or two the company that produced the thing will come back from the ashes.

I look at Scott, who isn't wearing armor either. He's in a suit with not a single wrinkle, not looking too bad with cowboy boots and a Texas style hat, of all things.

"What are you looking at me like that for? No way am I going to be the odd guy out wearing armor."

How did he know I would not be wearing mine? Oh yeah, because he's *Scott.* "It's just that I've never seen you without your uniform."

"Well, I figured with my three angry bitches harem, I'm safe enough."

"Mr. Scott!" Brittney protests.

I chuckle as we get in the SUV. I put on designer sunglasses, yet another thing I found in 'my' cabin. I should put in contact lenses, but since I put on my neural watch, my PDA can talk to it and it can send telemetry right to my eyes.

I'm sitting next to Tiffany again, and she actually pouts at my glasses and sighs. "Now you're just showing off."

In reply, I hold her hand. She looks at me with wide eyes, and then squeezes my hand back.

"Where to, Nancy?" Scott asks.

"Let's harass the neighbors."

The SUV pulls out, and I hear Brittney in the front seat, humming.

"Well, you sound happy," I say.

"That's because she got laid this morning," quips Tiffany, sounding annoyed.

Brittney giggles. "You're just jealous that I got paid for it, too!"

Scott once again grips the wheel tighter to keep from driving into the ditch.

"Paid?" he asks.

"Paid?" I repeat, stupidly.

"Yup. Ten is excessively late for me—I was up at five. I was feeling a little stressed so I went for a swim in that nice lake during my cross-fit workout. Then this older man comes up and says I scared away his fish from around the bend, so I get out and apologize. He gets all flustered and then says he can't help it and that he must tell me I have great breasts. So I tell him for 300 credits he can have all the breast he wants. We did it right there in the park, and then he shared his fried fish breakfast with me, and because he was a big sweetie we did it again. He was a hottie, too. Perfect start to my day!"

"Uh, isn't that against regulations?" Scott asks, swallowing a worm.

Brittney looks at him, confused.

"What? Are you joking? Half of my take goes to my platoon. Where have you been for the last five years?"

"Uh, I didn't know about that stuff, either," I say, trying to save Scott.

Tiffany leans over and whispers in my ear. "I hear Husband Four is rich, and I would even give you a discount."

I push her back firmly because her whispering in my ear made me feel funny.

"I never had sex outside," I admit, trying to change the subject.

Everyone turns to look at me.

"What? I had a couple of offers, but the thought of chiggers and bugs in sensitive places kind of turned me off. Plus, I just like beds with soft sheets and fluffy pillows that could be placed under me at appropriate times."

"You could always drag a bed outside," Brittney says, snickering. "Hey, you could put one on top of your mountain!"

Tiffany laughs. "What's a chigger?"

"It's a bug," Scott says.

She looks puzzled. "So wouldn't that be 'bugs and bugs'?"

Kids these days.

Well, I guess I know how the Military could afford even to think of a modernization cycle, but I still wonder about a Corporal with Uplink receptors. *Follow the money* is so old it's beyond cliché, but I'm guessing that with these two it would lead me somewhere very interesting.

* * *

Unintentionally, we make an intimidating bunch. Fancy clothes aren't quite as good as armor, but they're a uniform of sorts, and people tend to sit up and pay attention to a real sharp dresser. I make sure Tiff and Britt understand they must wait outside. Actually, they should just go talk to Dr. Wheaton and then leave, but I think if they follow us around for a bit more, Scott eventually will get laid and I will feel a little less slutty and crazy for rutting around with Arune in the Uplink so soon after being abused by ICDA.

I always have a master plan.

It always goes to hell, but at least I try.

The first interview is a bust. On that day, those neighbors were out recruiting pickers for the upcoming harvest.

I do notice, and this irks me, my interviewing dynamic has changed. People are still respectful, but they are also more personable, and I can only think it's because I'm dressed differently, and made myself look attractive.

Harrumph.

As we're heading to the next neighbor, I'm reviewing Bob's take on the CSI Bot findings. I'll have to sort through the data later, but Bob is a smart Investigator comp, and his summaries are good.

"Hmmm."

"What?" Scott asks.

"I have a shit-pile of DNA and mounds of synthetic, non-organic compounds. That house was Grand Central."

I call the senior Gifford's residence.

"Paul, was there a party in the field house just recently?"

"Yes." He sounds awful. "We have one every year where we open a new wine for the first time, then the guys play poker and the girls play bunko."

Bah. "How many people?"

"It was one of those start it up in the afternoon and it just keeps going with people dropping in and leaving parties. About seventy-five?"

Bah!

"Can you email me a list of people who were there?"

"Of course." He pauses. "You don't think one of them did it, do you?"

"Not at this time. But I have to run the DNA through the Union Detectors. WAC Protocol."

He just grunts and disconnects.

I set up a forward for the information to Sam, Dr. Wheaton and the illustrious Cutie-Butt Bambi, the Cyber Tart.

* * *

The next neighbor, a young Mrs. Marshall, is so distraught she can barely speak.

"We slept in and didn't hear or see anything unusual, but they are almost a quarter of a mile away. I'm sorry, Investigator."

"Did Jennifer have another lover?"

"Not that I knew of, they were pretty smitten with each other. They talked about a poly, but really I think they did so they could say they talked about it."

"Do you know of anybody who might have wanted to harm Jennifer, or Layla?"

"No! Nobody. Everybody liked them. The Giffords are good folk. Were good folk." She starts to cry again.

I turn to the Husband.

"Do you know of anybody that stood to gain financially if Jennifer was killed?"

"No ma'am. I assume she has a will but everything would certainly go to Paul, since Layla is gone. If something happened to Paul then it would go to, um, his sister and she's just as wealthy. She's not a fan of the wine business, either, but she would never sell."

* * *

"Did you ever get a poser Investigation?" Scott asks on the way to neighbor number three.

I frown. That's such an unpleasant memory. "Yes, my very first murder case. It was one of the primary reasons I yanked my advertising for homicide."

"Did you get a lot of credits from the settlement?" asks Tiffany.

"Just over a million. I put it all back into the business."

"Wow," says Brittney.

There is a clause in the Constitution that says if someone hires an Investigator for a homicide case, and it turns out the Investigator can prove that person did the crime, their entire net worth is forfeit to the

Investigator.

The other penalty is Investigator Justice. In this particular case, I was very harsh. One of the witnesses fainted.

It took me and a few others to prove the point that if you're going to kill someone, don't hire an Investigator to try to look innocent after supposedly covering your tracks.

Yes, people are that stupid. It's one of the few times there's a jury trial of the defendant by five MPs—very competent MPs selected by OCE, one of the few ways the branches of the Government get together, all to assure the populous the Investigator isn't being greedy.

That is not the case here. Paul's car logs and the time of death reported by Dr. Wheaton give him an alibi. I have vid of him in his car, driving, vid normally recorded for insurance purposes and then erased about a week later. This requirement is very typical of a rich person's insurance company. It cuts down on the bogus claims of negligence. His car recording matches the anti-tamper key at the insurance company. It's legit.

His financials don't give him a motive, and the man is so grief stricken he's on the edge of insanity. This was not a crime of rage, either. It was a premeditated crime of sex and vileness.

No motive. No opportunity. No method.

Now, there's the stretch scenario where Paul just happens to be one of the best actors on the planet, and was fucking his daughter. Jennifer finds out, so he goes all wacko on both of them. I don't have any indication that's the case, and even if I did, he was still over two hundred kilometers away when the murders happened.

Then there is the fact that I have physical evidence Layla was a virgin. In the back of my mind, I know her being a virgin was important to the killer, just like the first murders.

But why?

Ugh, this case really sucks.

Hard.

***

The next neighbor lives behind a hill as far away from the murder scene as the crying woman. His house is nicer and bigger than the winery Gifford residence.

"Thank you, Mr. Purdue, for coming back from the fields for this. Did you notice anything early yesterday morning?"

"Didn't see or hear a damn thing. There were a few cars periodically on the road, but there always are. I was even outside, tending vines and tasting rows since I got up."

"Do you know anybody who may have wanted to harm Jennifer or Layla?"

"No, not at all."

"Did anyone stand to gain financially from Jennifer's death?"

"Well—yes, I guess so—but only if he sold the winery to one of us locals. The Gifford's winery buys in a lot of grapes, sure, but their estate vines are significant. The crappy soil and altitude produce some amazing grapes. We're talking premium stuff. But that doesn't make sense. Paul would sell his stake in the land to his sister if he was going to sell at all, but the thing is, Jennifer loved the wine business more than Paul did. I don't think he could sell it—ever. It would be dishonoring her memory."

That's exactly what I was thinking, and one of the reasons I keep scratching credits off my list as a motive. "Did his sister like Jennifer?"

"They were like blood sisters. She loved Jennifer."

He leans against a fence post. "This really sucks. I've offered to help coordinate Paul's harvest, hell I'll even help pick the damn grapes for him. What else could I do? I feel so Goddamn helpless. I've told my Wife that when she comes back from visiting her aunt, she isn't to go anywhere without her pistol."

He looks sad, suddenly pensive. "But that's just it. Jennifer was a good shot and Layla could outshoot both her parents put together. Layla moved like a snake from the draw; I saw her at competitions. If the killer could get them, he could get anybody."

Fuck, how's that for cold water on a lovely post-vacation day?

* * *

The last neighbor is a poly family: a Husband, his three Wives, and as near as I can count, six children. It is chaotic and wonderful, and I hate intruding. They grow grapes but only as a hobby. The make a house wine, and sell the majority of the grapes to surrounding wineries.

The kids descend *en masse* on poor Tiffany and Brittney, while the rest of the Adults get down to serious business. The sprawling house smells like baked bread, reminding me of home, and I repress a pang of hunger followed by a pang of nausea.

I question them all at once. Junior Investigators often make the mistake of trying to segment out a poly family. This doesn't work. I personally would be uncomfortable talking to anybody in an official capacity without my Husbands present. I probably would not agree to such an interview.

They are all holding hands, and the women are frightened. Part of that fright stems from the irrational, but completely understandable fear I will accuse their Husband, Cameron, of the deed. Cameron has a good alibi. He was having Saturday morning sex with Wife Three.

Now she could be lying, but lies in a poly are difficult, and lies about crimes more so. They will eventually surface, and someone will eventually call me. I usually find the lie first, but other Investigators have encountered the problem.

Cameron is trying very hard to play his part as the protector. I can see the thoughts in his head, and they are circular: *that could have been us.*

All four are armed.

Good.

"Anna, you were closest to Jennifer. Did she ever ask about your poly?"

Anna is the new Wife with a singular daughter.

"Yes. Yes, of course. Many people asked about it, mainly how it was going."

"Did she seem just curious, or do you think she might have been considering a poly herself?"

"I—I don't know." She blushes. "She liked to talk about the sex part, everyone always does, but it seemed to titillate her more than my other friends. She might have been."

"Do you know if she had a lover?"

"She never said anything, but, you know, I just don't know. I know one thing, though. She loved her Husband. She really did. They were a close family. She wanted a small family, but I think when she saw all the kids here, she might have started thinking about having another baby or two."

"Thank you, Anna. That's very helpful."

I decide to mix it up.

"May I ask how the financials of your family are?"

While some might consider that an inflammatory question, the innocents are more than eager to separate themselves from a murder investigation as fast as possible.

The Alpha Wife, Leslie, chimes in without hesitation. "Cameron is a tech broker, and I do programming analysis on mechanicals, mainly certification for insurance. Both are lucrative, Cameron's business more so."

"Do you know of any reason why someone might kill Jennifer? Perhaps for financial gain?"

Cameron shakes his head. "No. The simple fact is you can't murder your way into the wine business. All the wineries are heading into the old money bracket, with what, twenty years of post-war production? Anyway, it's a closed system here in Washington. Just about everyone wants to keep it in the family."

"Were any of your daughters in Layla's social circle?"

"No," says Leslie. "We're a new family—our oldest is nine, which might as well be five as far as Layla's peers were concerned."

"Are we safe here, Investigator?" asks Wife number two, almost looking ready to burst if she didn't get that question out.

"Get a dog. Actually, given the acreage, get three. One per Wife."

"Leslie is allergic to dogs," Anna says.

I turn to Leslie. "The new nano series has fewer side effects, but it's just as expensive. The upside is, with the new tech, you'll only need a singular booster ten years from now."

The room is quiet and still and then Leslie nods, tears starting down her face, the revelation that being safe and feeling safe are very different things weighing heavily on her soul.

* * *

Tiffany is the observant sort, but Brittney isn't shy. Not shy at all.

"Lexus, can I ask you if you think any of these neighbor interviews will pan out?" she asks.

"Running down my checklist," I say as I send the interviews in question to Bob, who will share them with Dr. Wheaton and Sam. "Basic data collection—none of these people fit a profile—none of these people had a motive. If I'm stuck, then interviews in such a short time after the murders will be worth all the effort. They are the shovel of a big dig."

She nods, and the SUV is quiet.

Tiffany pipes up.

"You seem really different today, and not because you've decided to girly it up. It's as if your center is anchored."

"Hey! I can do girl stuff! Kinda."

Almost in unison, the entire SUV snorts.

"Fine. I've just had a week's worth of therapy vacation, the last half of which was spent having sex so smoldering hot, it makes Brittney's local forays look like amateur hour."

"Hey!"

"Must be nice," snickers Tiffany.

"I don't get it," says Scott.

Tiffany decides to bail him out. "When you Uplink with an AI for an extended period, the perception of time you don't spend sleeping can be stretched out. Think about it. Your perception of the flow of time is dictated by the AI—a day, a week, even a month can happen in an hour."

"Wow, I never knew."

I look at Tiffany. She shakes her head.

"I've never Uplinked with an AI, only neural-interfaced with equipment or a direct person Uplink." She looks wistful.

"Sounds dangerous," says Scott. I can hear the frown, "you're at the mercy of the AI."

"To a certain extent, yes, but when it comes down to it, either party can pull out at any time," says Tiffany.

"Can you Uplink with more than one person? Who gets to determine the time flow?"

The SUV is silent, and the silence stretches out.

Scott realizes he has committed a social blunder, and sounds defensive. "What? It's a natural question."

"Scott," I say, "That *is* a natural question and I know it would not occur to you because all the neural equipment was out trying to kill the enemy or in space." I take a deep breath.

"It's not a violation of the Constitution, but nobody contemplates those things. It's like asking a dog breeder if they eat the leftover puppies."

"Oh. Unionization. I get it. Is it that similar?"

"Yes and no. It's similar enough to trigger a false-positive Union Scan. It's a good way to get killed on the spot by the Detectors."

"Holy fucking shit," Scott says.

—I have a priority call from Dr. Wheaton.—

—Thank you, Bob. Connect.—

"Bambi found some interesting things. Get down here. It's a break in the case."

"On the move," I answer.

CHAPTER 11

WE'RE IN A BRIEFING room and I again appreciate Dr. Wheaton's well-designed facility. The room is modest, but the equipment is good. I like all the plants; they're a nice touch, especially since Eastern Washington is nowhere near as green as the Western half.

Bambi looks like a dog turd warmed up in a flash oven and then refrozen. Her frown, poufy eyes, greasy unkempt hair and utility outfit make her look sad and old, completely smothering the youthful good looks and smiley nature that I know she has now buried.

Sam is here by my request. He's stoic.

Bambi may look like shit, but she sounds confident.

"I have the admin passwords to their comm gear and laptops. Standard stuff that fits all usage profiles and the low-level heuristic scan yielded no red flag words."

"Both laptops, however, contain encrypted key-based messaging chatter. Fortunately for us it's not a three-key system, otherwise the top key would obscure the key on the other side."

She pauses, looking for understanding. We all nod. Standard stuff so far. Even I get it.

"I can't tell you what these messages are, because I have neither key. The system, by default, logged the traffic. Neither erased their logs, so I can tell you that they were talking, but I can't tell you what they said.

"Let me list the facts, point by point.

"One, both mother and daughter were communicating with the same person starting almost a year ago.

"Two, a week before the murders, this traffic increases fourfold.

"Three, on the evening of the murders, there is another flurry of traffic.

"Four, on the morning of, both phones show records of voice communication with the unknown person, using the same encryption key their laptops used. This was a standard net call, not a cell call, so I can't give you the cell locations. The traffic could have been routed through Moscow for all we know."

She looks at us expectantly.

"They are talking to the killer," Scott says.

Bambi nods. "Yes. That's the only conclusion. But they created their encryption keys based on their own DNA—it's a dual system that many people like to use, because DNA encryption guarantees you are talking to a person who is actually who they say they are, rather than someone who just happens to know the key."

I abruptly stand up. "That's it!"

"I don't get it," says Scott.

I turn to him. "The uniqueness of the key is a weak point of the system."

"I still don't get it. An encryption key is an encryption key."

I turn to Bambi, hoping she can explain it. Me explaining cyber is stupid.

Bambi gives Scott a weak smile. I notice she looks at him differently now, and not in a good way.

"High-end cyber gear uses your DNA to authenticate who you are. So if you use *that* to encrypt your communications so that another person can trust that what you said came from you—that is the opposite of randomness. It's a built in vulnerability. Most people don't care because it's cheap and it works. You need the DNA keys of both the sender and the recipient to read the message."

Scott looks reflective. "It's still an encryption key though. It would take a quantum computer to have any chance—ah."

"ICDA," says Ivan.

"ICDA," I say. I got a quantum computer all right. You can say I have *the* quantum computer. "Bambi, this is awesome. Start banging on this right now." I turn to everyone else.

"I really don't need the actual message. I just need to know whose

DNA that is."

"Scott has a point," Bambi says. "It's still encryption. It will take me time to set up the cracker, and it will take time to run. I can run everything in parallel, but it could take up to a year to find the other half of the key."

I wrinkle my nose. "Well, that's not good news, but it is not terrible news either. Do it."

"This all means poop right now," says Sam, "at least to us, without the background. I know what a red flag on an Investigator request is."

I'm quiet. The room is quiet.

"You're going to have to tell us, anyway, Lieutenant," says Brittney. Her use of my rank leaves a bitter taste in my mouth.

"Tell us about the first murders," says Scott.

* * *

"There isn't much," I admit.

I take a deep breath. Whoa boy.

"Just before things went completely to Hell, we occupied Union territory. Back then, we didn't know the full communications aspect of Unionization, and had no idea that our 'occupation' meant very little tactically and nothing strategically. Indeed, it gave them time to breed, showing the full stupidity of the 'containment' doctrine."

And it was stupid. One Union citizen was two times more productive, on average, than a human was. Couple that with the fact that every single member of the Union contributes one-hundred percent, and then add on their use of robotics—it was a perfect storm of war preparations, right under our very noses.

At least the person who came up with the containment idea is dead.

We shot her.

"I was with the 42nd Military Police Brigade. Back then, we were performing our duties as assigned. My platoon's responsibility was the Alsace Agriculture Region. They grew a lot of hardy foodstuffs, and it was a nice place. We even drank a lot of German beer—they still made it back then.

"We had our share of Collaborators, too."

I let that sink in. Now they all look like they regretted asking, even

Sam.

"One day, we were called to a house by a distraught Unionist. I had never seen a Unionist so upset.

"What she showed me was bad. A Collaborator mother and a daughter from Israel, bound to a ring in the floor, dead, with pink scarves around their necks. After about ten minutes on the scene, I had an intense sexual response. Nano good enough to get through my crude regulator.

"At the time I thought this was a crime done by another Collaborator or one of my men. During the course of the investigation, I found three different nano squirts, the same kind used on Jennifer and Layla—a nullifier, the sex enhancer, and a DNA scrubber. On the daughter, I found a first-aid spray to prevent any bleeding from having intercourse for the first time."

I rub my temples. I have a headache.

"This crime didn't make sense. There was no motive except sex and violence. They were isolated—targeted because they were alone. All their possessions were Union goods, goods you could get simply by asking.

"Also, something you don't read about in the books is that Unionists were free with sex. With anybody. Each other, my platoon, Collaborators, visitors, anybody. All you had to do was ask. They *always* said yes."

I let that sink in.

"I thought it was free love, like in the Federation. We didn't know. We didn't know that sex was divorced from their gender relationships. It literally meant nothing to them; it was for fleeting pleasure only. Nobody got hurt because it meant nothing."

My voice cracks, so I take a deep breath and let it out slowly.

"So I concluded the crime was done by a deviant of the highest order. Either some Union member had malfunctioning personality construct or I had one sick fucker running around.

"That's it. All the evidence I collected was destroyed during the evac."

The evac in which I shot my Union lover.

I don't need to say that, however, they can read it on my face, hear it in my voice.

See it in my eyes.

Eyes which are now glossy, and blinking far too rapidly.

This meeting sucks.

Hard.

* * *

I'm alone in the room with Sam.

"You loved him," Sam says, not asking. "It meant nothing to him, but everything to you."

I shut my eyes.

"Not many people know they were so easy to love. It's the dirty little secret," he adds.

I open my eyes and look at Sam. Suddenly he looks old. His eyes have aged twenty-five years.

"Yes. I loved him. I loved his family. I loved his sister. Gretchen was like a little sister to me. She acted so good, so pure, she almost had me believing everything about the Union was right and we were the wrong ones."

"And then they tried to kill you."

"Yeah—yeah."

"Fuck' em. They duped me, too, and just like you, I got even. But fuck the war. They paid their price. Let's work on this problem."

He gives me a measured look. Sam sounds just like my commanding officer after Edinburgh.

"Detective, Portland PD," he says.

Sam is indeed older than he looks. One had to be experienced to be a pre-war detective. Regen, however, makes one look younger. Hell, just *makes* you younger. The enemy shot him up in the war, and we pieced him back together.

Just like me.

"Ah. I really would appreciate any help you can give me here Sam, I know offering money will piss you off, but I have to, it's Investigator culture."

"Credits, bah, buy me a coffee."

He pauses and frowns. "This case doesn't add up. You have two crimes with only the M.O. in common. But they are too far apart in both time and distance. Hell, let's pretend it is a Unionist. Why? What is the motive? What is the link?"

I slump in my chair. "I know, I know. It's giving me fits. During the time of the first murders, the Union kept strict watch over visitors. They claim, and I believed them, there were no visitors within several hundred kilometers."

He nods.

"As far as my men, my men are all dead except two, who joined my platoon *after* France but *before* Edinburgh."

Sam finishes, "And the Collaborators didn't come out."

They were the first to get the Cocktail, all at once, every single one.

He bites his lip. "None of this makes sense yet, but I'm certain now that you're the only one who can solve it. Nobody has your war experience." He shrugs. "By the way, we all watched that little horror film. It was nasty, pure nasty, but I see it in your eyes, you know it."

Oh don't I know it.

"Bambi isn't doing so well. If you want a future Investigator, you need to help her out. Mary is great, but in the end, she ain't you, Investigator.

"Nobody is."

As I leave the conference room, Sam's words haunt me.

What is the link?

* * *

Bambi's office/lab is a maze of tech, more of it and more advanced than even my workshop. Bambi, indications are, is both a hardware and software geek.

I find her sitting in a plush chair staring at a screen showing some type of list. She isn't looking at it; her gaze is far away.

"Are you okay, Bambi?"

She startles. She turns to me.

"Oh! Sorry. I was wool gathering."

"Are you okay?

She leans back and stares at the ceiling.

"No."

"You did really well today."

"Thank you."

"Better than I could do in the time you had to do it."

"Really?"

"Yeah."

I wait. She finally looks at me.

"I looked it up, you know, rape stats. The last rape in the county was five years ago. A Husband comes home drunk, and mistakes his sister-in-law for his Wife. Or so he claims. Two days ago, learning that would've been terrible. Now it seems so, *pedestrian.*

"Then my nasty little brain goes 'you know, there are worse things than being raped by your asshole brother-in-law. Much worse things.' Isn't that awful?"

"Bambi…"

"Then I looked up historic rape stats. Did you know in the ancient pre-Collapse societies, rape was common enough that large safety departments had entire detective units dedicated to the crime? Even some modern pre-Cyber War departments had them. I used to envy their societies' innocence from modern war, now I'm beginning to think they got what they deserved."

She looks at me and remembers that I come from a pre-war society. "No offense."

"You're not saying anything I…"

She bolts out of her chair and she's looking at me with her fists clenched.

"I want to kill him! Kill him. That's what I want to do! I thought I could be one of those Investigators in a large office, the kind that focuses on cyber, never Justice. No, I want. To. Fucking. Kill. Him. Slowly! With a knife! I want to…"

I grab her and pull her close.

"I want to…"

"Shhhhh, I know. I know." I hug her tight.

"How do you do it?" She's sobbing into my breasts. "How?"

"I'm not immune. I cry. But the difference between you and me?"

"What? What!"

"I can kill him. Slowly, with a knife."

She looks up at me, understanding sinking in.

She also looks like she wants to kiss me.

I'm really beginning to hate my malfunctioning Libido Generator. Hate, hate, hate.

* * *

On the way to Rachel Barrett's house, my last interview for today, MatchUp gets back to me with data on the photographer.

I should not have bothered. The photographer runs an active business and has an extensive bio page off his net landing, as artists are wont to do. I paid MatchUp mainly to surf the net. His pictures are nice, and the portraits are artistic and distinctive.

Fuck, what a waste of credits—an amateur mistake, one I made under stress.

Oh well. One little tidbit stands out:

Observed income inconstant with operating territory: indications are above initial projections.

Well, well, well. Mr. Jeffery Vanderhouse makes the cred, by about twenty-five percent above average.

I can't go trolling for official income records, because such records don't exist now. The post-war Government only collects usage fees and job payments, not taxes. MatchUp, however, will pull out every trick and observation to run financial heuristic analysis on Mr. Vanderhouse. They're good. Mainly used in industrial competition and thus expensive, they actually give me a small discount, hoping for a little *quid pro quo* if they ever needed an Investigator in my area. Enough business with them and I will feel obligated.

Well, I know boo about photography, so I call up my money guy.

That would be Husband Number Four.

"Lex, so nice of you to call. Even though you stood me up."

Bill has gone full video, and the PDA pipes it to my eyes through the neural link in my watch. He's lying on his bed with the most stunning raven-haired wonder of a woman I have ever seen. She's naked, perfect, on top of him, giving him a back rub.

Cazandra, the sex-bot. A Level Two AI, expensive as hell, at least one-hundred thousand credits. She can't learn beyond her programming, but she can improve her reactions to the outside world by experiencing it. This is quite clever, actually—it keeps a singular purpose bot, like Cazandra, from going crazy, yet it lets the bot adapt and become real to the people around it. Her, in this case. She would never take up painting, for example, but you could teach her a new sex trick and she would be able to extrapolate new ways of giving you pleasure from it. The longer one interacts with her, the more real she seems, especially if you avoid meta-life discussions and pretend she's real.

Arune is a full-fledged person, with rights recognized under the Constitution just like any other person—not programmed, but grown. Caz, at the end of the day, is a clever toaster with boobs that could learn the human-interaction equivalent that on Wednesday, you like your bagel toasted a few seconds longer and served with butter instead of cream cheese.

"You know the rules, Bill. I'm in the field on a case."

"You could have refused the case," he counters. He isn't argumentative, but Bill will always tell you what he's thinking. I love that in him. I find it refreshing—I always know where I stand with him.

"No, I could not."

He accepts this immediately. "Oh. Well, I'm glad you called. What do you need?"

"Can photographers make real money beyond their upkeep, like enough to have a swanky lifestyle?"

"Hell yes. First, you got the fashion photogs. They make good cred. For the really talented ones, the Uber-Rich will fly them everywhere based on their rep alone—for example, flying a photographer down to the Caribbean for a bit of the ultra-wedding. The good ones will ask for eight-K a day, and get it, and that's just the field fee."

"Wow!" I had no idea.

"Wow indeed." He gives me a look. "You want me to check someone out, financially?"

A chill goes right down my spine and I feel like throwing up. I gulp air and swallow. "No fucking way, Bill. This is bad shit going on here. You stay away, or you could wind up dead. No funny joke, Mister."

Bill's eyes get big.

"Yes, Wife of Mine. I hear and I obey."

I roll my eyes and Cazandra actually rolls hers too. I smile and remember my bot manners.

"Hey Caz—is everyone being nice to you?"

"Oh yes, Mistress Toulouse," she purrs. Her voice is about as sexy as one could imagine. "This morning I made love to Mitchel, and Bill here is almost ready. Two different men in one day make my fem parts go boom boom!"

I suppress a giggle. "Cazandra, could you please not call me Mistress?" If only she would stop that. It has been over a decade now.

"Yes, Mistress, I promise to cut back on your well-deserved title."

"Pischt!"

She grins at me over the video link, and for the first time ever I notice her breasts are so round, yet so perky. Then I notice that she notices I have noticed. She gives me a raised eyebrow.

Uh, time for a distraction.

"Bill, soooooooo, um, what's my surprise?"

"It's a surprise." He sounds wary.

"Tell me."

"No."

"Please? For your Wife?"

"No!" He looks adamant. What the hell?

"If you tell me now, I will, um, do you with Cazandra."

If I'm going to be fifty percent gay, even for a short time, I might as well take advantage of it. Plus, I bet I can get drunk or high enough to let him put his dick in me.

"WOO HOO!" Cazandra yells, pumping her first. It's her long stated bot desire to fuck me. She has even fucked Vash and Juan, but how she got them to do that, I have no idea.

"Oh man, that one hurts, it really does." He actually looks sad. "But, Lex, it's something I have to show you in person. It would be inappropriate to talk about it over vid, especially when you're working a case."

I frown. Damn it all, what is it?

If he got me a puppy or some touchy-feely shit like that, I will kill him.

"Okay. I will be home as soon as I can. Tell everyone at the house hello for me."

"You bet, Wife of Mine."

"Wife, Out."

* * *

At Rachel Barrett's house, I strike pay-dirt. It's a middle-class, modest home with a small view of the expansive grape fields.

"She doesn't want to see you, Investigator. She's very upset and doesn't know anything that could help you."

Sure she doesn't, Mr. Barrett, sure she doesn't.

"Sir, it's in your family's best interests if you let me talk to her. She will be a direct help in this murder Investigation."

"No. I think you should leave, now, Investigator."

Alrighty then—time for hardball.

"Mr. Scott, could you wait with our friends, please?"

"Yes, Investigator. Certainly."

We spend a few terse moments waiting for Scott to walk behind the corner.

I make it a point to look beyond Mr. Barrett's shoulder.

"Could I speak with you, outside, Mr. Barrett?" I look around. "Alone?"

He pauses, and looks behind him into the house.

"Yes."

I lead Mr. Barrett around where he can see Tiffany, Brittney and now Scott waiting with Roscoe. Mr. Barrett stops in his tracks when he sees the menacing Military vehicle.

"What…"

I pounce. I don't suffer fools gladly. "Mr. Scott isn't just my assistant. He's a Constitutional Enforcement Officer. One of the best."

"But…"

I'm a merciless bitch. "See those two young women? They are Military Police, from Fort Lewis. That impressive ATV is just their *ride.*"

He's silent.

I grab him and spin him around so he's looking at me. He flinches, but he doesn't resist. Spineless bastard.

"Now I want you to think, think good and hard, Mr. Barrett, just what type of murder case an Investigator, a CEO and two MPs would actually be working on together. Think hard and then tell me I can't speak to Rachel alone. I dare you."

* * *

I open Rachel's door and close it behind me in a heartbeat. I lock it.

Rachel is an attractive girl, for a fourteen-year-old. She is tall, like her father, but curvy, curvier than a fourteen-year old should be. When I was her age, I would've killed for her older looking body—breasts, legs, and a face with no baby fat. I just know she's a popular girl, certainly—a daddy's girl—the girl who has her father wrapped around her little pinkie.

She looks at me with frightened eyes. My mind whirls and makes a snap judgment, born of training and experience. Based on her good looks, the way the room looks, the way she's acting, I believe I know what I'm looking for.

"I told my father I didn't want to speak to you!"

I say nothing and look around her room. I key the closet door and it opens. There are all manner of clothes and girl things.

I may be a jaded old war vet, but once I was a girl, and I remember what it was like. I start rummaging around the back of the closet.

"Get out!" She says. Her hand moves towards her dresser and I stop what I'm doing, but I don't look at her.

"Touch your pistol and I will whip you with it." My voice is soft, but cold.

She freezes in place.

I find what I'm looking for—a big fancy box with a light floral scent.

"No! Don't touch that!"

In one swift motion, I have the box out of the closet. I tear off the lid, and dump the contents on the floor.

Lingerie. From the tasteful to the naughty, but absent any black stockings or garter belt.

Rachel sinks to the floor and sobs into her hands, and I feel dirty for exposing her innermost fantasy life. I feel mean and cruel, even though I had to act in the moment.

I go to the floor where she is, and lightly reach out to her. She flinches. "Go away, please, just go away." Her voice is small, and she sounds like a lost little girl.

I pull her to me and crush her in a tight embrace, yet she doesn't struggle.

"I've cried for Layla, too, Rachel. I've cried for her too."

God, did I ever cry.

Mommy I love you… Mommy…

The reassurance crashes into her as if I'd hit her. She clutches at me with all her strength, and cries into my shoulder.

Sometime later, her sobs turn into hiccups, and then silence.

"Did she say who she was going to meet?"

"No." She talks to my shoulder.

Of course not. That would be too easy. I try to repress a sigh.

"Do you know if it was a boy her age, or an older man?"

"No. I thought it was going to be a boy, but now I don't know. She didn't like any of the boys we knew. She said he wanted her not to tell, so it could be a surprise to her friends later."

The sheer evilness of that causes me to shudder.

"Rachel, look into my eyes, Honey, look at me."

She does, looking—broken.

Just like me.

"It's not your fault. Her killer stalked and seduced her. If you didn't give her those stockings and garter belt, this case may never have been solvable. But since you did, I feel I can figure it out. I feel I can catch the bad guy."

She looks at me, her lifeline back to the real world.

Now Rachel doesn't look like a teen contemplating declaring herself an Adult anymore. She looks like a girl—a young girl—unsure, sad and vulnerable.

She buries herself in my shoulder again, and my long red hair spills onto her, almost like a blanket.

"I miss my mommy," she whispers.

I did okay up until that point. Her confession, however, is a knife in my gut. My own tears well up, yet again, unbidden and raw, hated and despised, salty and stinging.

"I miss my mommy, too," I say. I clutch at Rachel, and rock her as she cries anew. I take comfort in her needful embrace. Moments before I was her lifeline, now she's mine.

A while later, she simply says, "I apologize for my inappropriate behavior."

"I'm sorry I was such a bitch," I reply.

She giggles, and all is right in the world.

"I'm going to go down and talk to your father a bit. I will call for you."

She nods. She has the look of a girl saved from drowning.

* * *

I was not there to save Layla from being raped and murdered, but I will be damned if I'm going to play Investigator while Rachel and her father become undone.

Henry Barrett is at the kitchen table, a bottle of red wine, sitting open, with an empty glass in front of him.

"Alcoholic?" I ask, as gently as possible. I hope he doesn't think I'm judging him. I'm a snorf girl, after all.

"No, but as I opened it, I came to understand why people go that way. I used to think they were weak. Now, I have a bit of homespun sympathy."

From a rack under a kitchen cabinet, I get out two additional glasses. I set them down on the table, but then I just look at him. I move next to him, and crouch down so we're looking eye-to-eye.

"Vet?"

He nods. "Field Officer."

I want to run from the house sobbing. Instead, I try to mentally disconnect my Investigator brain from my war brain.

"She killed herself?"

"The MPs told me it was an accident." He looks at me. "But nobody believes that. The happier our post-war existence got, the more I saw of her inner sadness. It was like a weight on her soul." He sighs at the memory.

"Mr. Barrett…"

"Call me Henry."

"Henry. I'm going to bring Rachel down and we can have a little chat. But I wanted to talk to you personally. I may look young, but we're a similar age, you and I. You can't think of post-war teens by what it was like when we were growing up. The Constitution gives humans past puberty the chance to reach out and define themselves on their own schedule, even if it's wrong."

He looks at me, knowing. He nods.

"Rachel is thinking about the Declaration, but she doesn't want it right now. She doesn't."

"Really?" He looks so hopeful he almost falls out of his chair.

"She might be thinking of sex and marriage, but Layla's death, and how she thinks she died, haunts her. She needs help. She needs you."

A single tear runs down his face. He looks at my eyes intently, my face.

"You've been crying."

I nod. I guess that's what I do now.

"I thought Investigators had tight reins on their empathy?"

"Your daughter, she, well, she reminds me too much of Layla. It hurts. It's too much, even for a person like me—maybe especially for a person like me."

I get up, afraid to show more of my weakness. I pour three glasses of wine, and call for Rachel.

She comes down, part girl and part woman, but all daughter.

She sits to my left with Henry to my right. We all sit and stare at the wine glasses, and I realize there is an odd tension in the room. I look at one, and then the other. I realize that they both want me to leave, and desperately want me to stay.

I can almost see the guilt in the air. A part of me bristles that the crime I am investigating has something to do with this guilt, but I know whatever it is, it is something deeply personal.

"Guys," I say, "I am the most non-judgmental person you will ever meet."

Boy howdy, am I non-judgmental. How could I blame others for their sins when mine are so great?

The words unlock some mental barrier in the two and as one we reach for the wine glasses. We gulp the wine, a local red blend. All three of us, gulp, gulp, gulp.

I grab each of their hands. "I want to say what I'm most afraid of. I'm afraid the killer has harmed this family. That he killed more than Layla and Jennifer, that he drove a stake into the heart of this one."

I look at Rachel. She takes a deep breath. "I'm afraid I'm next. But mostly, I'm afraid Dad will never look for love again." She looks at her father. "I can never be her, Daddy. I just can't. I thought about trying, but I can't."

Gah. I now understand the tension I felt before was *sexual* tension. The Wife was a Field Officer like me, a woman that used sex to bind her men to her. Such women have a vast capacity to damage the post-war people around her if she uses her training and conditioning for selfish ends. She has to be strong or her capacity to sexually damage the people around her is legion.

Does she ever have to be strong.

I hate the war. I fucking hate it.

Henry is quiet. "I'm afraid I'll blink and you will be gone," he whispers.

"Never," she replies.

"I'm sorry, Honey. You look just like her, just like her, and I know I have been looking at you the wrong way. But you're not like her. She left, but you didn't. Now I'm just glad you're my daughter. Will you ever forgive me?"

She rushes to his arms, and suddenly everything is okay. The tension melts until all that is left is a daddy and his little girl.

"Oh there's nothing to forgive! I know you never would hurt me, hurt anybody!"

I leave.

I may be an Investigator, but I'm also a woman, a whole woman in spirit but not body, who for all her sins did no sexual harm when she finally came home.

I'm also something *else*.

* * *

I'm outside in the heat and warm breeze.

I breathe the fresh air deeply, and my mind seethes with hatred, my body burns with it. I walk away from the ATV, gathering my dark thoughts. My hate is a fearful thing, an awful thing and I embrace it like a long-lost lover.

The enemy killed my parents.

They destroyed Port Dis, my home.

They killed all my friends.

They killed my platoon.

They killed my commander.

They turned me into a monster.

Their technology killed Jennifer and Layla.

They killed Rachel's mother by crushing her spirit.

Rachel—a fine daughter if there ever is one—she is a daughter I can never have, because the enemy took that from me, too.

Every single indication I have is someone local did this murder. If that's true, what does it have to do with Alsace?

I don't know. This non-knowing, I'm certain, will lead to more people dying. Another mother and daughter will be next, and I will be powerless to stop it.

No. Not powerless for something inside of me awakes. Something awful and terrible and righteous that has slept inside me for over twenty years.

I am the Goddess of War.

Mommy I love you… Mommy…

I stop walking.

"Bob, connect me with Dr. Ivan at Wheaton & Associates."

"Toulouse! It's good for you to call. Even if I know why you are calling. Is good."

Yeah, Ivan is the man.

"Ivan, I need a combat medic—briefing at 0530 tomorrow, at your briefing room. Get the good stuff out, Ivan."

He pauses.

"Sadly, I don't think you are talking about vodka."

The Goddess of War is pleased with Ivan.

CHAPTER 12

THE GODDESS OF WAR is in a foul mood, but I quickly kick it to the curb when I turn the corner around the back of Roscoe and startle the three squirts. They immediately look guilty.

I look at Tiffany. She's serene, a Corporal's guilty serenity and I have seen it a hundred times.

I look at Brittney. She's perfect, the perfect looking woman, vibrant and healthy.

Too perfect. Her makeup is fresh.

I look at Scott. His lips are swollen.

I turn to Brittney. "Sergeant! Have you been kissing my Assistant Investigator?"

She looks so guilty I almost laugh aloud. "It's Tiffany's fault!" she says.

"How is it—wait. Don't tell me. I don't want to know." I put my hands on my hips. "What do you have to say for yourself, Mr. Scott?"

"I confess…" he looks at Tiffany. He looks at Brittney. He looks embarrassed.

"I confess to needing kisses."

I open my mouth and shut it. It has been my master plan to get Scott laid—partly so I don't have to do it—but when faced with the reality, it makes me feel *jealous.*

Which is stupid of me but, hello, four Husbands and an AI lover—not exactly the brightest laser on the rail.

Obviously, I missed something, some social dynamic between the three. Part of me also wants to be pissed that I was crying my eyes out yet again while they were out here sucking face.

Which is unfair, considering Arune made hot Uplink monkey sex all over my virtual body, for virtual days.

"Okay. Let's, um, go back to the launch pad."

They all visibly relax.

Geeze, I'm not that intense, am I?

Okay, maybe I am.

I am the Goddess of War, after all. Intensity is my purview.

* * *

We're at the Bacon landing pad. Everyone is quiet, but they look to me. They are expecting me to issue *orders.*

Bleh. I want to feel sorry for myself and my long-gone solo Investigator status but, in actuality, as soon as Arune landed on my pad on Mt. Si, I knew those days were over.

They want orders, I'll give them orders!

I turn to Tiffany. "Will five-hundred cover an all-nighter? I have cash." Mitchel's five-hundred, in fact.

Tiffany actually jumps in her seat as if I shocked her.

"Uh, no need for that Lexus, a few drinks…"

"No, no, Corporal Tiffany. Your scrumptious athletic body will be put through its paces. You may even pass out."

She grins, and I return her grin, but I secretly chuckle to myself because I'm serious.

"Okay, yes. Certainly." She smiles and leans over, and kisses me on the cheek, her lips girl-soft and inviting.

* * *

I make sure our rucks are stored and Tiffany is in the small tactical station with the passenger seats that fold down from the wall. Arune has configured himself in the Pilot/tactical/galley/head/main cabin configuration, with storage beneath the first three.

Putting my foot on her chest, I pull on the harness to tighten it. Having her come loose during an abrupt maneuver and splatter all over the smaller forward-cabin would suck. Moreover, I think Brittney would gut me like a fish.

"Ever been in a MOF/B?"

"No. I have an A-Class Cert on zero-gee, though. I love it."

I look at her curiously. "Not enough to transfer to Orbital and Space?"

She laughs. "I like being a cop. The cop thing with big guns really gives me a hard on. The O&S MP slots are severely limited."

I totally understand. Certain people just love being MPs, and Tiffany matches the profile easily. Confident. Assured. Observant. No bullshit. Athletic.

And damn, she's pretty. Her eyes make me melt.

She crooks her finger at me with a *come-hither* gesture.

I come closer. She pulls me down and kisses me—a slow, hot, wet kiss, which reminds me of Mitchel. A soft Mitch.

I peel away breathlessly before I have a heart attack while my crotch bursts into flames.

"I can't wait to get in orbit," she says, voice low and sexy.

I take the five-hundred credits out of my pocket and stuff it down her shirt.

"I bet."

She giggles as I head to Pilot's access.

"Aren't you going to suit up?"

"No. It's been years since I've done a full manual lift, and it's an important skill to keep active."

She gives me another come-to-me finger crook.

I go back. I kneel down, and she puts her arms around my neck, just as I did with Brittney.

"Nancy. I may be younger than you, but I'm not stupid. Please don't lie to me. MP thing, remember?"

Damn it. I nod.

"It's okay to dislike the armor. You're allowed."

"I'm sorry."

She kisses me again.

Scorch!

The Goddess of War is pleased with kisses.

* * *

"Woo woo! I get to watch you have sex with a woman!"

"No, you don't," I tell him.

"Oh man, I suck."

"Believe me Arune—tonight, you're going to get to watch exactly what you deserve."

"Harrumph. So full manual eh?"

"Let's do it," I say.

"Would that be before or after you do Tiffany?"

"Pischt!"

"Fine. Let's go, Tiffany looks bored."

I put on an old-fashioned headset, and buckle in. Sitting in the chair without armor or a flight suit is weird.

"Accumulators," I say, looking at the readouts, trying to remember the visual indicator layouts. I repress a sigh. This is stupid.

"100%"

"Life Support."

"Green."

"Reactor."

"Green."

"Main Propulsion."

"Green."

"Thruster fuel."

"95%"

"Solar Collection."

"Green."

"Weapon Load Out."

"Green."

"Phased Radar Array."

"Green."

This goes on for several minutes. Finally:

"How do you feel?" I ask.

"Horny," he says with a pout in his voice.

Heh.

* * *

After rescuing Tiffany and serving a bland dinner, I show her the main cabin.

"Oooooo, swanky!" She floats over to the bed.

"Strip," I say.

She nods and does. I put her clothes and equipment in a drawer.

"So, Lexus, have you…"

"We're not having sex."

"What?" she says.

"What?" Arune repeats.

Hey! He's not supposed to be listening in.

"Arune, meet Tiffany. Tiffany, meet Arune."

"But…"

"Tiff, show him."

She catches on to my introduction. Tiffany pulls back her ponytail floating around her neck, and bends her neck down.

"Whoa," says Arune, spotting the neural interface.

"Tiffany, you're my present to Arune. If that's alright with both of you?"

She licks her lips. Flushed face, hard nipples—I can tell. She wants it. Wants it bad. AI Uplink Sex. Sex Plus Plus. She nods.

Arune can't talk to me privately because I'm not Uplinked, and not wearing my PDA. "You sure about this, Lexi?" He asks, sounding embarrassed, which is cute.

"Of course. It would be good for you. Good for you both. I just am not up to sex right now. I'm going to do some reading and then get some sleep. Have a good sleep and enjoy your vacation."

I bounce away for the cabin door.

"Arune, do you find me attractive?" asks Tiffany, sounding unsure.

"You're one of the most attractive women I have ever met."

"Oh, you're just saying that…"

I leave, smiling all the way.

* * *

I am in a sleep cocoon in tactical, tethered to the floor and ceiling. It's a great way to sleep, better than a bed if one is alone.

For some reason I am awake.

"Lexi," Arune whispers in my ear again.

"Mmmmm?"

"Can you help? She passed out."

"Well yeah, Arune, when you fuck all three holes the way you do, it tends to make one a bit brainless. I've told you before, neural receptors and the overlay makes humans sensitive to touch."

Okay, now I'm more than a little jealous.

"Please? It's, it's—it's a little scary when that happens. It's as if she died. Her vitals are fine, but it's as if a tessa harmonic that cascaded across her secondary nervous system."

I have no idea what that meant, but I recognize cyber when I hear it. Bah. "Sure, Babe. Just don't touch her receptors, okay?"

"Okay."

I unzip and float to the main cabin. I open the door and…

Splat! I get an eye full of Arune spunk floating around.

"Ewww! Arune! My eye!"

"What do you mean, 'ewww'? I've done the same to you!"

"Yes but it was for me, on me, caused by me."

"I don't get it."

I groan to myself because I will have to explain. It's only fair.

"When a human woman makes a human man come, another woman is probably not going to want to touch that unless she was intimately involved in causing him to ejaculate."

"Oh. Okay. Sorry. I really appreciate you telling me that. Those vids…"

"No problem, Babe, and I told you those vids would rot your cyber brain."

AIs like Arune use Think Goo. Unlike humans, they have backup systems because, well, because they can. They use tendrils to move the Goo around, if they need to. After a while, the backup Think Goo replicates itself from a nutrient reservoir and the older Goo needs disposal.

Arune, pervert that he is, created a system that imitates sex for disposal of the backup Goo and talked me (heh, heh, heh) into helping him hook it up. It was a long trip to the moon, we lifted when it was about as far away as it could get that year.

He has four tendrils in the main cabin that are thicker than the remotes that he uses to say, put a male Uplink connecter in my female receptor.

Yes, it's tentacle fucking. If the Japanese hentai fans only knew, a new era of bad anime would be born.

Tiffany is floating off the bed, her limbs loosely tied with the smaller tendrils. She passed out from neural overload. Even not connected to anything, the neural overlay provides the body with sensitivity to pleasure and touch. She was over-stimulated with sex, and her brain shutdown as a defense mechanism, rendering her unconscious. I envy the technique. Over-stimulation for me leads to other places.

All of them bad.

She has Goo on her breasts. On the corners of her mouth. Coming out her sex. Leaking out her ass. In her hair.

"Arune! Did you have to smother her in the stuff?"

Males! Human, AI, they are all the same!

"I couldn't help it! She felt so good! She liked it so much—the feedback loop, it was, it was, it was amazing. My autonomous systems actually took over my sensors. I had to replay them to see if I missed anything outside."

"Bah, now I *am* jealous. Well, unwind her, except one leg, and start collecting the stuff floating about."

It takes me a half hour to get everything—including Tiffany—cleaned up, bedding replaced, etc. Sex in zero-gee is messy, with Arune more so. I grumble, but it was, after all, my idea.

She's under the covers, sleeping serenely. I shrug and get in. I have never slept with another human in zero-gee, and I find it oddly comforting. I drift off, wrapped around the hard yet soft Tiffany. I tell Arune we need to be back on the pad at 0400.

* * *

I'm having a very naughty dream about Cazandra, the Husbands' sex-bot. She's in between my legs licking and licking and then I'm awake, my body tense, orgasm building.

Tiffany is looking into my eyes as she's rubbing me—down there.

"Tiff! What are you doing!?"

"Getting you off," she says sleepily.

I tense up. "I'm not ready to make love to a woman!"

"We're not making love. I'm just getting you off."

She kisses me and five minutes later, I shudder with an intense orgasm. I can feel the stress and tension leave my body. I melt.

"Mmmmm, thank you." I whisper.

"Thank you for cleaning me up," she says, looking embarrassed.

I drift.

"Lexus?"

"Mmmm?"

"You look at me as if you want me, but then look disgusted with yourself. It makes me feel bad."

"Oh Sweetie, I'm so sorry. I will stop that. As for my hang-ups, my malfunctioning Libido Generator is dealing with them for me just fine."

"Oh! Oh, I'm sorry. I didn't know you were sick."

"I'll be okay."

I drift again.

"Lexus?"

"Hmmmm?

"I'm scared."

I wrap myself around her again and hold her tight. "Shhhhh—sleep for you now. Scared is good. You're with me now, and I know what I'm doing."

She grabs an arm and pulls me tight, I press against her back and we laze under the covers.

The Goddess of War is pleased with your offering, Tiffany. No harm shall come to you now.

CHAPTER 13

ARUNE TOUCHES DOWN RIGHT before he wakes us up. The orbital decent is so gentle it disturbs neither one of us. Arune is a big sweetie.

It's another lovely summer dawn. I'm back in my Z armor, and Tiffany and I are outside after breakfast, scrubbing some dust off Arune, who insists that we're being silly. We ignore him, and use the pad's hose to rinse him off. It's well water and the pump is solar driven, so it's free. The pad, of course, is an orbital pad, the installation required and maintenance (what little there is) paid for by County Safety. They, in turn, charge their customers.

We watch the SUV followed by Roscoe wind its way up the hill, and out jumps a bouncy Brittney and a stoic Scott, back in uniform. I frown at his lack of expression, but then he winks at me.

You're welcome, Mr. Scott.

"Suit up," I tell the honeys. They pause for a moment, and then open the back of the ATV. They press a button and out pop two large lockers.

Then they look at me.

They look at themselves.

They look at me again.

Scott raises an eyebrow.

I march over there, glowering.

"Corporal. Sergeant. I'm going to make one thing clear. If those lockers open up and they contain Z armor, or some post-war shit like Z armor 'Mark Two,' I'm going to paddle both your nubile athletic behinds. It won't be right now, but I will switch you both, a good post-war parental switching for naughty little girls!"

They pout.

"Open it up."

Z armor. Soon, they are hairless and suited up. I look at Brittney's blonde hair on the ground, and wonder if they ever thought it would come to this.

Supposedly, they don't make Z armor anymore. The armor takes specific fitting and attunement. You can't wear someone else's suit. I was there when the factory burnt down—*to the ground.* Someone retooled a factory, or, my brain refuses to contemplate, built a new one.

Multi-walled carbon nanotube armor: fifteen *million* credits. Each! And that was back during the war. Who knows how much it cost now.

I narrow my eyes but say nothing more. What more could I say other than *war shit.*

The Goddess of War is angry.

* * *

I'm in Wheaton & Associates' conference room. Assembled is the usual crew, minus Sam, with Arune now plugged in live.

Ivan frowns at the two MPs. He isn't happy. He's wearing something arguably better than Z armor, crystalosnanoscale armor, stealth armor even I don't understand—a Russo-Sino invention of unparalleled sophistication. Like me, however, he got his in the war.

"We're going in. Alsace was the scene of the first crime, and there is something about it nagging at me. While I understand 'nagging at me' isn't the best excuse to head into former Union territory, not even three decades into its fallow cycle, it's significant. I left under hurried circumstances, both emotionally and professionally painful. Alsace was not the highlight of my career. Even though Bambi has sleuthed out the answer to finding the bad guy, there is additional data we can collect.

"On top of that, WAC Protocols dictate that we follow this lead to conclusion. We can't let Union technology fester in our society."

I let that sink in.

"I considered turning this over to the Military and advising an entire crash-team drop. However, I rejected this idea. Mainly because the best person to advise the crash-team would be me, and, well—if I'm going, I don't want to subject more people than necessary to whatever we find."

I look around the table. I press a virtual button, and a hologram of the damnable town pops up. It looks serene and pretty.

Looks are deceiving.

"Excursions into fallowed territory are nothing new. As long as one of the three branches of the Government has a need for it—in we go." I press another virtual button, and a red dot appears along with the words *Landing Zone.*

"Here are my three rules. Respect the chain of command. Most importantly, don't shoot me. Shoot anything that moves. If it's larger than a mouse, blow it away. Now everyone say 'yes ma'am'."

"Yes ma'am!"

"Good. The chain of command is me, Dr. Ivan, Arune, Brittney, Tiffany and Scott."

Scott doesn't even blink an eye about being low man on the totem pole.

"Stay buttoned up at all times; consider the area toxic, and any materials found a biohazard. Don't tense up, but don't relax either. We could be there for several hours, but I hope to be out by nightfall."

I look around the table. "Anybody want to back out? The stigma of the place is worse than the potential for harm. I won't lie to you though, towards the end of the war, many strange things happened. We need to be flexible, which is why I feel this mission is best suited with the personnel we have here.

"I can understand, completely, if you want to back out."

I look at Scott. "Scott?"

"I have a personal interest in catching this killer, Nancy. I'm in. This mission sucks, but I'm in."

Scott is a good man. He reminds me of my Husband Bill, whom I wish I could get a hug from right now.

"Tiffany?"

"Of course. It's my duty and my honor to be at your command, Investigator."

Her eyes are scared, but her chin is up and I can see a sparkle.

"Brittney?"

"This is what my squad trains for, ma'am. Daylight's burning."

Ha, already Brittney is playing the part of a Staff Sergeant with her blunt reminder of our timeline. I bump up my estimation of her worth a notch. But I am still going to switch her ass.

"Arune?"

"Can we just nuke the site from orbit?"

"Possibly. After I look around."

"Excellent. Let's do it."

"Ivan?"

Ivan is stoic. Finally, he says, "There isn't enough blood spilt to satisfy my craving to kill enemy. Is good you put me on your team. Yes, very good indeed."

"Thank you all. The mission is simple. Find the scene of the prior crime, look for clues, and get the fuck out. I don't expect to find any evidence, although the possibility exists. I just need to jog my memory and look for correlations. We swept the area for life forms—we didn't destroy it, like all intact regions, we neutron bombed it, repeatedly. Unless there was a battle in the house, it should still be there."

I look at everyone one last time. "Any questions?"

Nobody has any. They all look nervous, but not too much, and that's all I need.

"Grab your weapons. Lock and load, and hit the MP's fancy bus."

The Goddess of War is pleased with her devotees' willingness.

* * *

Fallow Sector FRA-ALS.15, according to Arune's radar map, is empty. Nothing is moving. Abandoned buildings and overgrown crop fields dot the landscape. I'm sure it looks depressing. It was so pretty when my men and I left, tails between our legs.

The sector is structurally intact because it's an agricultural region. Spared nukes, orbital kinetic torpedoes and moon-fired planetary bombardments, the region took it in the ass with Kill Squads after the obligatory neutron bomb party. Men and women with dead eyes and a grim purpose, leading squads of assassin bots. The squads left nothing alive but plants and bugs. Then we neutron bombed it again.

I'm strapped into Roscoe's command chair. The packed ATV is in the squad insertion configuration, attached to Arune. I didn't have to learn how to use the equipment, didn't have to ask any questions or study any manual. No, I just glared at Tiffany and Brittney and plugged myself in with a neural connection.

I have a holographic map of the small town. I can't remember which outlying house is the field house, which is pathetic, but some parts of my memory are missing or damaged.

I select a building on the tac-map.

"EMP slag it, please, Arune. Centered there."

"Aye. Launching."

Arune is firing a torpedo. It's a big sucker, a small fusion bomb designed to irradiate an area with a massive EMP burst without doing structural damage. Tiffany hunches her shoulders, and Brittney actually bites her lip. Technically, the torpedo is Arune's, but it cost upwards of 1.5 million credits. I have no idea if anyone makes them anymore. This particular one, and its twin, is over twenty years old.

The boards register the explosion.

We wait ten minutes.

"Hit it again."

"Aye. Launching."

Brittney actually turns towards me. I have no qualms about explaining myself. After all, I'm a mere Investigator. Technically, once on the ground, she could take over this little mission.

Since she's smart, she will not. My knowledge of the enemy is priceless.

I'm the Goddess of War, after all.

"We lost several Guardian Mark Ones in that region. If we encounter a refurbished one converted to a kill bot, we're fucked. Royally screwed. Boned. Dead. We can take one down, but someone will die, and it probably will not be me. I think your lives are worth more than three million credits. The bursts will take some of its sensors offline—and kill any of its friends."

She nods.

I don't need to tell them that in the Fallowed Regions, there are all sorts of haywire bots running around. They sometimes cannibalize other bots and turn into something nastier. They have to keep a low profile, however, or they get whacked from orbit. They mainly sit around and wait for the foolish.

I highlight several landing zones. "Give us a decent path please, Arune, and start a countdown."

Arune picks one. "Path locked."

"Go."

"Countdown on your HUDs."

"Go."

"Syncing re-insertion path."

"Go."

"Prepare for descent!"

"ATV green! Go!"

We don't just drop—Arune accelerates into a decent path and perversely applies only a small artificial gravity adjustment to make the coming envelope transition non-fatal. Even with this new constant nulling most of the g-force, it's like falling into a bottomless pit strapped with a rocket booster pointed down. If we were on the ground, it would look—as Scott described it—like the fiery Finger of God.

Without armor, it would be an 'interesting' ride. As it is, Scott is grimacing. Me, I'm the Goddess of War—I'm having the time of my life. I'm a Pilot. I feel alive, and if the pressure on my lungs weren't so intense, I would probably be laughing.

"Prepare for disengagement at two thousand meters!"

"ATV green! Go!"

The readouts have almost all of my focus. Dimly I hear Scott ask Ivan, "Two thousand meters?"

"New Military toy. Hold on to butt!"

"Disengagement!"

The ATV disengages from Arune as he swoops up to lose momentum. As soon as we leave his artificial gravity envelope, the plummeting maneuver feels as if it's going to squish me flat, and as the blood rushes from my head the darkness begins to cover my eyes. I let it happen, I don't fight. This feels as normal as blinking, even over twenty years after the fact. I'm only blacked out for a second before consciousness returns—not even long enough to lose control—and I feel us pick up speed as Roscoe plummets Earthward. This is where Tiffany takes over. It would be foolish for me to do this anywhere but a simulator. Having said it, though, I'm impressed that neither Scott nor Ivan have passed out cold yet. Their armor either is very good or they've had flight training.

"Engaging thrusters!" Tiffany says.

I can hear the thrusters scream from under the ATV.

"Engaging winglets!"

The ATV rattles back and forth.

"Air brakes engaged!"

Now, even with the sound damping, the noise is impressive. Tiffany is flying a brick. We still have a lot of momentum to kill.

"LZ imminent!"

"Parachutes engaged."

The jerk is painful. I relish it.

WHAM! We're on the ground, bouncing on six wheels, and we hit the ground running.

"Chutes disengaged. Winglets in."

The ATV rolls to an easy stop along an overgrown two-lane road.

"Holy crap, that was my first drop," says Scott. He sounds pretty faint, even if he is conscious.

"Me too," says Ivan.

"Glad we could pop your cherry," quips Brittney, staring intently at the sensor board.

Tiffany looks at me.

"Good work, Tiffany, right on the landing dot." Literally, the holographic ATV is sitting right on the holographic red landing dot.

Show off. I'm still going to switch, her, too. After she watches me beat Brittney.

She smiles. "Where to, ma'am?"

I pause.

Now that I think about it—that's a good question.

* * *

We're lost, and I feel like an idiot.

Imagine a serene landscape, with nothing in it but the echoes of ghosts and the houses of the dead. Houses with slumping roofs covered in ivy, streets of cobblestone and cracked cement running through the village of the damned. Weeds and tall grass are swishing back and forth, new trees mixed with the old, poles for power and fiber optics lines removed. I recognize the village, on top of this hill, but the houses are all a blank in my mind. I might as well have been driving around in Africa.

I can't even find Landis' house, which is just as well. I don't need reminders of Landis and his sweet smile and easy laugh. I would rather picture him as I left him, with the top of his head missing from a bullet in his left eye.

That was after I cut off his balls and stuffed them in his mouth.

Yeah, you could say I was a woman scorned. My real regret is that I didn't have time to look for his little sister and kill her, too. Slowly. With a knife.

The Goddess of War was not pleased that day.

"Sorry folks, but I need to get out and get to a vantage point so I can get my…"

"Turn left at the next street," says Scott, in a weird monotone voice.

Tiffany looks at me.

I shrug but then I nod.

"Go straight until you reach the T intersection, and then turn right."

Now we're all looking at Scott, because he has his eyes closed and looks vaguely purple.

Tiffany is swerving around abandoned cars. They make me somewhat nervous. "Down the hill and a left," Scott says without opening his eyes.

"Stop. Weeds and grass have grown over the dirt track. Turn thirty-seven degrees clockwise and then drive straight. Go over the small hill."

We do, and at the crest of the hill, I can see the house below, standing there looking much as it did when I left it, except for the abandonment and the untended, low-lying plants.

"That's it! That's it!" I look at Scott with wide eyes.

He merely shrugs.

"Let's go. Step lively and listen. This place will be quieter than a tomb, so if anything bigger than a bug makes noise, waste it."

The back door slams to the ground and we peel off, everyone except Tiffany. She will stay in the ATV, ready to blow away anything that needs blowing away.

Even before he steps out, Ivan disappears. He's gone from my passive sensors and my vision. That's some armor.

Looking around, I should feel nervous or disgusted or something, but as we circle the house, all I feel is curiosity. What is the connection between the crime here, so long ago, and the crime in Bacon, Washington?

I don't know if I will be able to answer that, but I have to try. Union technology in the hands of either a serial killer or a copycat killer is a menace almost unthinkable.

"Looks clear, Nancy. Nothing on my scanner," says Brittney.

"Looks good to me," says Scott. I imagine him putting mental quote marks around the word 'looks.'

Mr. Scott, I'm learning, is a very handy man.

CHAPTER 14

THE HOUSE, OF COURSE, is empty. Nothing but dust, moldy furniture, and the aura of desertion. Only the solar collector shingle roof has kept the house mostly intact. The shingles last forever. With the EMP bursts, however, any ability to restore power from the collectors is lost.

Everyone except Scott seems a bit creeped out by my CSI bots. For the MPs and Ivan, they must look suspiciously like Union bots, direct from their training. Or with Ivan, his experience. After a while, the other two wait outside.

This is well and good, because Scott and I are not doing very well.

The ring on the floor is still there. The Union abandoned the home and never went back. We stare at it.

"Nancy."

"Yeah?"

"This case blows."

"Yeah."

"Tell me this is the worst case you've ever been on."

True enough. "This is the worst case I have ever been on."

He frowns and we stand there longer, staring stupidly at the ring. We each know what it means.

Mommy I love you…

My bots are coming up with nothing. There's no more in the basement than there is on the first floor.

"How is this all connected?"

"I don't know," I admit.

"Let's get the fuck out of here, then."

Yeah. I tell the bots to pack themselves back up.

We walk out.

"Hey, want to drink on the roof?" I ask, remembering the last time.

He smiles. "Hazard protocol?"

"Fuck it."

The roof is slanted. It looks like it will last another fifty years. We test it carefully, but it seems designed to support snow weight, so we lean back on the incline, propped up with our boots, and look out at the shallow valley.

I get out my flask, and we pass it lazily back and forth. The air smells fresh and clean.

Other than the buzz of insects, and the soft purr of Roscoe the tank, it's silent.

"So, how was Brittney?"

"I can hear you, you know!" the Brittney in question says from below us.

Scott grins. "The best. Really. She's beautifully athletic. Gorgeous—and a bit mushy."

I grin in return and hear a faint giggle.

"And Tiffany?" he asks.

"Hello! I'm on the squad channel!" say Tiffany sounding pleased and annoyed.

"Tiffany is a great kisser. The first girl I have ever kissed."

"Really?"

"Yup."

"And how was she in bed?"

"I don't know, ask Arune."

"Ah-hem!" says Arune in the squad channel. Arune is a very private person. I guess if we want a ride out, we better be quiet.

"So, you went dry?" Scott asks me, cocking that eyebrow of his.

"No, she didn't. I fingered her so her bitchy level would drop a couple of notches," says Tiffany.

"Thank you, Corporal," says Brittney. I roll my eyes. I guess I was somewhat bitchy. Kind of. I reacted badly to interrupting a smooch fest. The Goddess, I guess, wanted some smooches of her own.

But wait until I paddle their asses over their armor. I will show them bitchy!

We lay there for a little while.

"Wonder if Ivan does Mary or Bambi?" Scott asks.

"Bambi is saving for marriage," says Ivan from, um, nowhere.

"Oh wow," Brittney says, "I didn't think anyone did that anymore."

"Notice Ivan the Terrible didn't deny any relations with Dr. Wheaton," I point out.

"Ha, ha!" says Ivan.

I look at a cloud lazily floating by.

It bothers me for some reason.

A floating cloud.

A cloud.

Oh no!

I grab Scott's arm. "Scott! Look at the landscape! Look!"

He looks. He gets up, walks to the top of the roof.

The shallow valley, with hills to one side, mountains off in the distance. Fields of old crops and orchard trees, overgrown now, but there is a hint of a pattern in how the Union farmers planted them.

"Gah," he says. "The landscape looks just like the hills in Bacon, especially the fields."

"Arune! What did they grow here, before Unionization?"

"Don't know, Lexi. The Union repurposed all of their agricultural lands for maximum productivity and you know all about the Cyber War and the fragged online databases."

"Ivan, do you know what they grew in Alsace? Was it grapes?"

"Nyet. I don't know."

"Arune, can you please patch me to Bob?"

"Bob here."

"Call Chen."

"One moment."

I have no idea what time it is on the eastern coast of China, but Chen answers. Chen is a wine collector.

"Lexus, what's up?"

"Chen, sorry to bother you, but I need some of your wine expertise. I'm in the middle of an op. What did the Alsace region of pre-Union France grow?"

"Grapes. For wine. It was a real downer to drinkers and collectors outside the Union when they repurposed all of their wine territory."

Shit. I thought so. You can look at the landscape and imagine it.

"Thank you, I'll call you later. Lexus, out."

I jump down from the roof. Grass crunches beneath my armor and a cloud of dust flies up around my feet.

"I don't understand," says Brittney.

"It's the same killer. He grew up with wine, or what was wine, here, and so went with wine in a similar area: Bacon," I tell her.

"So it's an older gentleman in the wine business?"

"Don't get hung up on the physical age, but the business portion could be correct," Scott says.

True. A Collaborator could have used advanced regen. The Unionists were good at it. It was expensive in resources for them to use it, but it was available to them.

Scott continues. "This isn't a copycat killer. This is the same killer, and the killer knew his victims. Since Gifford invited everyone in the wine business at Bacon to the party in the field house, we now are certain one of them is the killer, that they were at the party, that they did indeed know their victims, and that he murdered them using the same M.O. in his twisted way to get his rocks off."

"Correct," I say, "but we're missing the link. Sure, Bacon is similar, but there must be some other draw. Some other factor. There are places in California that are similar, same for Russia, Peru and China. Australia, too."

I would twirl a lock of my hair around my finger if I were not in armor, or actually, had hair. "We can't simply let Bambi take her investigation to the conclusion. We have to investigate in parallel incase…"

"I have an SK-Mark Three heading this way from southeast, very fast," says Ivan.

My helmet forms back, and I try not to moan as my suit sends a euphoric squirt of battle enhancement drugs up my butt.

SK. Seeker-Killer, a late model Federation robot that rooted out all animal life forms in its area of operation, and killed them. The prior models detected Unionization. The third model eschewed such subtleties.

It just killed anything not carrying a Federal ID code.

We have the FF codes, but the war was long ago. With the bots' cyber as deteriorated as it is now, the codes are no guarantee.

My neural linked armor sends images to my eye as if my brain itself came up with the visuals. In my eye, I get an image of the bot through Ivan's sniper scope. It's dirty, patched, but oh so deadly.

I open the bot broadcast frequency.

—Lt. Lexus: SK Three, stand down, authorization code follows, stand-by for Code Omega key.—

—SK30032424e: Must kill, must kill! I kill the rabbits, but they always come back!—

The bot, wonders of wonders, stops when I transmit it my identification. It hovers in place. My Omega codes do come in handy sometimes, it seems.

—Lt. Lexus: SK30032424e, status.—

—SK30032424e: The rabbits keep coming back! Always with the rabbits! But I have help now! The Master helps me with the rabbits!—

I really, really hope the bot is talking about me.

—Lt. Lexus: Who is the master?—

—SK30032424e: The Guardian, he who sleeps, he who waits to feast on your bones and suck out—

Boom!

Ivan has shot the bot. Parts and pieces scatter everywhere, his recoilless rifle showing the visual through its scope.

—Okaaaay, please to not talk with crazy killer bot while it attempts to pinpoint our position.—

"That was me, Mr. Scott," Ivan says, speaking on the squad channel.

Everyone except Scott 'heard' the Active Thought exchange. This is why Scott is last in line for command. He has no neural interface receptors. He can't communicate via Active Thought like the rest of us.

"Okay, let me go look for my balls, because I think they shriveled up and ran off," says Scott.

"Hey, I didn't give them permission to do that," Brittney quips.

"Cut the chatter, birds," I say. "Ivan, what do you mean?

"Play video back."

I do. This time, I notice the radar probe the bot had extended while we were talking. It was getting ready to ping us, revealing our exact rather than general location.

"Timely shot, Ivan. Do you think it went nuts? Or was it Unionized?"

"A betting man would say both," he says.

"You don't think the 'Guardian' is an, um Guardian, do you?" asks Tiffany.

I look at Brittney.

"We can't leave a Guardian running loose. Maybe Arune slagged it enough where we can deactivate it?" Brittney asks sounding hopeful.

"I hope so." I repress a shudder. I'm intimately familiar with the carnage a Guardian can bring. I'm dreading the possibility of bringing in Britt's platoon.

"My shot took out its power core. Its little ugly brain should still be intact," says Ivan.

"Daylight's burning, let's poke it," I say. Indeed, the shadows are now long. "If the trail leads out of the EMP area, we're out of here."

We trot out to where the bot went down. I draw my combat knife and in short order, I have it disassembled and its cyber brain exposed. I get out my PDA, and make a wired connection using an omni-cable.

"Whoa," I say. "This little fucker is trying to hack my PDA. It's Unionized up to its little cyber eyeballs."

Luckily, my modern PDA is laughing at its twenty-year-old plus antiquated hacking routines, but it can't counter either. The PDA is not made for hacking, after all.

"Arune, we don't have time to dick around here. You're going to have to gank it."

"Oooo! Cyber brains, nom, nom, nom! Give me a channel."

Hack, hack, hack, hack. Arune, in short order, has possessed the memory of the freaky little killer bot.

"Okay, this personality is gross. Bye-bye, time for oblivion." he says.

I wrinkle my nose. Someday, I will go back to school and take a few cyber classes.

Considering I'm swearing off real-time sex, I may have time for that now.

"I have good news, bad news and then good news. The good news is the location of the 'Master' is well within range of the EMP bursts, which most likely fried all of his creepy minions. Only the ones on patrol seem to have escaped it. The bad news is it's almost a klick underground. The good news is the 'Master' is without any weapons. The SK bot has a secondary routine for scavenging them up to make a 'sacrifice' for the 'weaponless Master'."

"Would being underground shield them from EMP?" Tiffany asks.

"No," says Arune. "There is a large shaft leading directly down. It was an EMP highway right into their little black hearts. Only organics would be down there alive, or hardcore cyber."

"Organics we can kill." Ivan says.

"Isn't the Guardian shielded?" asks Scott.

I give Scott a look. "We built them shielded, but it's hard to modify one because doing so creates exposure in its armor. The most likely scenario is someone modified it and then we subsequently slagged it in Arune's EMP attack. Now that I know where it is, without its cyber buddies and weaponless, I feel better about going after it. Assuming it's still active."

I give him a thin smile.

"What?" Scott asks, looking hesitant.

"You jump certified?" I ask.

"Hell no."

"Heavy weapons? Like, big guns that go boom?"

"You mean, like his penis?" asks Brittney.

"Can it, Sergeant."

"Yes, sir!" She throws me a salute.

Memo to self: Sergeant Brittney gets punchy when laid—must put in place soon.

"I've used every handheld weapon to come out of Idaho," Scott says, sounding like he wants to change the subject away from his penis.

I wonder what his penis looks like. He saw me in the buff—it's only fair—uh, my Lib-Gee. "Tiffany, you got any fancy Idaho toys in your car?" I'm as eager to change the subject as Scott, now.

"I got a SIB-Gee."

Standard Issue Big Gun.

Awesome.

"You got an extra jump pack?"

"Two."

Scott eyes me. "I told you I wasn't certified."

"You said you were not certified, not that you've never done it. Have you used a jump pack?"

He sighs. "Yes."

"And you didn't like it."

"No. No I didn't."

Not many people do, especially those without NI receptors. It's an out-of-control feeling where one small mistake can equate to *splat.*

"Hit the car and let's ride. Sorry Mr. Scott, but it's a klick underground. You'll need all the oomph you can get if we have to bug out in a hurry."

* * *

The house is on a flat part of town. We open the door, and the entire inside of the house is gone; there isn't anything but a big house-shaped shaft going all the way down.

We're all wearing jump packs. Some call them ghost wings, others, devil flaps. It's a jump-flight system. It hooks to your back, and adds stiffness to your armor. On command, winglets will extend a short distance for jumps, full length for flight. It's a sophisticated and hideously expensive armor modification, because you can actually wear it on power-unassisted armor. It's that light.

It has its drawbacks. Mainly, it packs so much energy in such a small, light package, that a direct hit in the right place can make it explode.

Exploding is bad.

The other problem is, as Scott knows all too well, that it's difficult to fly, especially for someone without neural receptors.

All of our armor is power assisted, although—funny enough—Scott's armor more so. Looking at my almost skin-tight armor, one would think there are no power enhancements—but there are plenty. Even the gloves are a technological marvel. They will stiffen when I put power into a swing, least I break my own fingers. Yet, if skilled enough,

I could perform surgery with them if I turned up their sensitivity gain.

I wonder if I'm going to punch something today. Looking at the hollowed out house and the resultant shaft going down, I would like to. Obviously, some monkey business is—or was, since the EMP bursts—afoot.

It takes engineering and effort to do what I see here. Digging below the water table, hiding the activity from the orbitals, it all adds up to war shit.

"Everybody go full active."

As one, everyone activates his or her sensors.

I look at Tiffany.

"Roscoe going to be okay up there?"

"Yeah, he's mean."

"Everyone, remember my cardinal rule: don't shoot me. Let's go." With that, I activate my winglets and jump into the shaft.

Since my sensors are screaming, I'm not particularly worried about stealth. I paint the shaft with multi-band radar. I turn on every light as I descend. Once on, I pick up speed.

The Goddess of War is coming for you!

"Lexi, you're giggling," Arune says in my ear.

Whoops.

CHAPTER 15

IN MY MIND, I expected a nasty bit of business crawling through tunnels, destroying shielded kill bots one-by-one—like a jumpy horror vid with aliens bursting forth out of dark recesses to impregnate Brittney and Tiffany with devil spawns after wiping their personality from their brains, turning them into mindless demon-baby factories.

Actually, that pretty much describes the last years of the war.

My thoughts betrayed me. Must be the rust brought about by over twenty years of downtime. The Union was nothing if not efficient: everything clicking in place at the exact right time for the maximum amount of—whatever. I should have expected simplicity.

As we drop, my sensors detect motion, and then a big honker of a blip appears in the wire-frame of the large cavern we are falling towards at combat speed.

It is the Guardian, and it is moving directly below us!

Kerblam, kerblam—sounds muffled through my helmet indicate Scott's SIB-Gee, his rifle sending armor-piercing rounds directly at the Guardian. As one, the rest of us peel to the sides of the shaft, giving him as much room as possible.

In my hands, I have a Hamilton NI Carbine, a nasty little fucker that shoots 6mm rounds from a clip that consumes itself while firing. Wired directly into my nervous system through the neural receptor on my right wrist, my suit's battle computer gives me a targeting interface with data piped directly into my optic nerves for visual input. It doesn't project a HUD; it interfaces with my eyes directly. The display is in my eyes because it *is* my eyes.

My needler is a lethal weapon, but it's not NI technology. With the Ham-nCee, as we call it, I'm one of the fastest and most accurate shooters on the planet. No one un-augmented could come close to my scores.

Corporal Tiffany is proving today that the world belongs to the young, because the little skank is outshooting me!

Firing the SIB-Gee might have been impromptu reflexes on Scott's part *(big blip, kill it now!)*, but the next step for our squad, even untrained as a unit, is to exploit the holes he is making in the Guardian's armor.

Underneath my Ham-nCee is a 15mm grenade launcher, holding ten rounds of pure Hell Fire (the HF-nGL). The grenade is a ball of plasma in a shaped magnetic containment system inside of a composite shell. Once activated through my battle computer, the grenade's magnetic field propels itself down the scram rails of the launcher. The mag bubble degrades at the apex of its flight maneuvers, and then the plasma uses the rest of the shell as fuel. The resulting confabulation smacks into the target, and burns.

And *burns.* It will burn anything for a brief time. Metal, rock, people.

What makes a Guardian so fearsome is its armor—composite armor constructed of multiwall carbon nanotubes, similar to the armor I'm wearing. Everything on the inside has armor too. The fiber-optic from a control node? Armored. The hydraulic lines? Armored. The relay for the accumulator/reactor switchover? Armored. Every component, no matter how small, is unbreakable through conventional means. You need to expend a lot of effort, and a lot of tech, to damage a Guardian and take it out of battle. The enemy hated them.

Scott poking holes in it with his SIB-Gee is just the first step in taking down this one. The next step is tossing munitions, like a grenade, at the opportunity holes.

That's exactly what Tiffany does right before me like the little snake she is, with Brittney bringing up the rear. Shooting a Guardian from the top is never the best way to take one out, but since it is weaponless, we might be simply able to hover while...

Whoosh, whoosh, whoosh, whoosh, plasma fire fills the bottom of the cavern in righteous brightness. The unarmed Guardian, now in my optics and burning merrily from within, bends over, picks up a big rock and tosses it at Scott.

Scott dodges, but not fast enough. It slams into him.

"Scott!" I use full breaking thrust and angle my way to his position, then accelerate, hard. He slams into the rock wall, and as he starts to plummet, I latch onto his armor from the back. The momentum throws us against the shaft again, with Scott between the wall and me. Now we both plummet.

I crashed into him hard, the kinetic overlay in my armor not able to absorb the entire blow. A brief thought flashes through my mind: I have squished Scott! I banish it because somehow I have to stabilize us both, even when both his thrusters are working independently of mine and I can't interface with his armor.

Then I spin around dizzily and, just like that, I'm slowly lowering Scott to the ground.

—Attempted rescue maneuver ineffective. Automatic stabilization engaged. Suggestion: discontinue squad use of dissimilar armor systems.—

My armor tells me it saved our asses because I'm lame and gave me a lecture, all in a split second.

Thank you.

Bitch.

My eyes are straining for visual indication of the Guardian most likely about to snatch us from the air and stomp on us like bugs (I have seen a Guardian do just that to the enemy). But I have nothing. My brain catches up with my readouts. The Guardian has zero energy emissions, zero movement.

My squad has killed it.

I look to Scott's telemetry as we touchdown.

Everything green.

I start to breathe normally. Scott's thrusters disengage. His winglets deform.

"Geeze Nancy, if you wanted a hug, you could have asked," Scott says weakly.

I burst out laughing, and peel myself off his back

Then I turn away from everyone, deform my helmet, and puke my guts out.

The Goddess of War isn't feeling so hot right now. I almost pass out from the nausea, but my suit squirts medication up my butt again, and then I feel better.

Drugs! Yum.

* * *

There are fried bots everywhere. Hundreds, all slagged in the EMP bursts, all of them armed and all of them deadly. A few try to move, backup systems struggling to become mobile, but we quickly cut them down by carbine bursts.

Down this far there is ventilation, and I can see Tiffany, Brittney and Scott wrestle with this factoid. The bots were building underground living quarters.

For organics. There are even lights. A hydroponic garden under construction.

I can't see Ivan, but I don't need to. I know what he's thinking. I know it.

"Lieutenant," Brittney says over the comm, for Scott's benefit. "I found—I found—something."

Oh, I know what you found, Brittney. I make my way over to her position.

On the cavern floor is a cyborg. It's a bot with organic parts, rather than an organic with robot parts.

As the war began to conclude, the Unionists got desperate—really, really, desperate. They couldn't bring themselves to use cybertech beyond what they carefully evolved from a strict evolutionary program. We speculated the Union Net was persnickety. Deviations or AIs were a gross anomaly, and subsequently purged.

Nevertheless, they were not above creating abominations as slaves. Since they were running out of manufacturing capabilities, they turned to growing parts for their bots.

From clones. Purposely mutated.

Prenatally.

It was bad.

Or is bad, because here is one of the little perverted cyberdemons now. It resembled a large mechanical spider, somewhat like a Bartender, but with chicken feet. It also has a muzzle, with a nose and a mouth, with fangs.

It lies there, on its side, weakly trying to drag itself along the ground.

The cyber parts are all fried, but the organic parts still live. The squad is staring at it in horror. It makes little suckling and mewing sounds. It whimpers.

"What should…"

I shoot it, interrupting Brittney's question, or rather, answering it.

Then I move along the direction it was crawling. I come to a stone wall, smooth and clean. I talk to my suit.

—Run ECM package three, transmit frequency sixteen-delta-four.—

—Sixteen-delta-four restricted frequency.—

—Override, authorization Omega-12.—

—Acknowledged. Transmitting.—

Ivan is there standing next to me.

—I am sad, Borislava, much sadness. This should not be here.—

I giggle, actually giggle, at Ivan's use of my given Russian name. My reputation with Russian soldiers precedes me.

—Sorry, Ivan, I'm beyond sad. I'm…—

—Broken.—

I look at him, lips pursed as tears prickle and threaten behind my eyes. I nod.

—ECM package three in second cycle. Hacking program now running. Please stand by.—

"Nancy? Are you okay?"

No, I'm not.

"Nancy?"

—Lock penetrated. Cycle door?—

—Stand by.—

The previously camouflaged outline of the door appears, and in the door's center is a glowing symbol.

"Ma'am, what is that?" Tiffany asks.

I find my voice. "It's a door."

"Door to what?" Brittney jumps in.

"A crèche."

"What the hell is a crèche?" Scott asks.

I turn to them.

"Sergeant, Corporal? Please escort Mr. Scott to the surface. I don't trust his jump harness after that large rock."

Not to mention I smushed him.

"Nancy…"

Smush being a technical term.

"Please leave behind your satchel charges."

"Lieutenant, what…"

"Ivan and I will be about forty minutes."

"Lexus Nancy Toulouse!"

Brittney, it seems, has had enough. She actually spins me around.

"I'm not a Child! I know what is beyond that door, that's why we're here, damn it!"

I look at her. Fresh, wholesome, young Brittney. Previously blonde. Nubile and pretty, even when I can only see her face.

"No dishonor intended, Brittney. It's just not something you should see. Not anybody."

"Damn it Lieutenant, Tiff and I trained all our lives for problems like this."

I'm undone. The thought of exposing Brittney, Tiffany, and Scott to an end-stage war crèche is unbearable.

Please Brittney, please. Don't go in. Please don't go in. It's why Ivan and I fought the war. So good girls like you don't have to see this. Please.

Please.

I'm begging you.

Please.

The thought is unbearable. It will kill me.

Please.

Then I realize Brittney is looking down at me. I'm on my knees, my arms wrapped around her thighs.

I realize I have been talking aloud.

Whoops.

She pulls me up.

"Lexus, you're not supposed to cry in armor." Her voice is soft and easy.

"Crying is what I do now."

Her helmet deforms. She holds me close.

"Okay, we won't go in," Brittney whispers in my ear. "But on one condition."

"Anything."

"Promise me you won't switch me about—earlier."

I giggle. It sounds mad, high pitched.

"Deal."

She holds out her pinky.

"Pinky swear."

I smile weakly and clasp her armored pinky. She gives me a quick kiss, along with her satchel pouch. Tiffany does the same.

"What the hell is a crèche?" Scott asks again.

"Shut up," Brittney says curtly.

"Let's just nuke it from orbit," Scott counters. He might not know exactly what it is, but he knows it's bad. He looks frightened, far from his normal, armor-backed, stoic look.

"You can't just nuke it. You need samples for the Union detectors," Brittney tells him, her look softening. "WAC Protocol."

He pales as understanding washes over him.

"We're leaving," Tiffany says. Her voice is husky, sad. They grab Scott at each armpit and *zoom* they are gone.

I turn toward Ivan.

He nods.

I draw my combat knife. Ivan pulls out a medical probe from a pouch and attaches a long, thick needle to the end of it.

I could use my carbine, and he could use his rifle.

But we don't have nearly enough ammo for that.

The Goddess of War doesn't need ammunition. A sharp blade will do.

—Cycle door.—

—Engaged.—

CHAPTER 16

"SCKQREEEEEEEEEE!"

Ivan and I step neatly to each side of the door, and as it opens, some awful cybernetic cross between a monkey and a bat twists in mid-air and flies straight for my head.

—Threat level increase!—

"No shit," I whisper to my Battle Comp and pivot on my heel. The hand not holding my combat knife strikes out, grabbing the tail of the creature as it flies past.

Zap! An arc of electricity cages the little monster, and it convulses.

My other hand lashes out, and I stab the fucker with my knife. If it wasn't convulsing I am sure it would be screeching like a banshee, but it is silent as I complete the swing and pin it to the wall. One second later, cyber goo spurts everywhere as Ivan stabs it in the head with the medical probe needle. The needle crunches past bone and inserts right into the middle of its brain.

The cyborg goes limp.

—Probe telemetry inbound.—

Medical data fill my vision but I shunt it off to one side with an Active Thought command to alert me if there are any Class 1 red flags. I don't need to go over the summary, that's what I brought Ivan here for.

"Data is—interesting," said Ivan.

Interesting is bad. I repress an urge to chew on my lower lip.

Ivan looks at me. "Got it. This is only a second-generation mutant. No traces of XY, it's a straight-line mutation from XX to ZW."

I sigh. "Ivan. I don't know what that means. While your sniper team was pushing into Europe from the east I was a Pilot, remember? I flew CAS for you. Close Air Support. Space Girl. Death from Above."

"Yes, yes, un-pucker your athletic ass, LT. Human female after puberty, da? Three-hundred-thousand eggs, yes? This little fucker one generation from a human's eggs, but no viable Y chromosome available, so eggs XX birth mutated into, um, different chromosome track. Get it?"

I jerk my blade free and the little demon plops to the ground.

I get it. A Unionist found a female human, couldn't rape her and make Union babies because he was sterile—so he put her into the cyborg-breeding tank.

I burn. It as if a nova has gone off in my gut.

Ivan steps back and looks at me.

"Easy there, LT. This Ivan, right?"

I notice I am shaking and I am gripping my knife too hard.

"Aye, Comrade. Aye." I take a deep breath and move to the point position.

I pause and let the active sensors go to work. In front of me is a corridor where the walls slope inwards to form a flat 'A'—typical Union architecture. Several yards away the corridor splits off left and right and, by the indication of my main sensors, a host of cyborgs awaits us in the room where they meet up.

My experience with previous crèches leads me to think they won't be a threat, and the view that greets me when I turn the last corner validates it.

Incubators on an assembly line—that's an accurate description of a crèche. The fetus is grown and mutated in a vat, and then slowly moved down an assembly line over the course of a month. Cyborgs run the crèche, assembling the later monstrosities. It all starts up from a tank containing the host. The first egg manually extracted by a Unionist grows up as a helper cyborg, which extracts another egg and makes its own helper, and so on until the perverted bio-assembly line comes on line.

Then the real cyborg production starts.

It's grossly obscene and terribly efficient.

The first cyborg we come to mews at me. It's a scout, and almost finished. It looks like a spider with a monkey head on top. It does have weapons, but they are not online; it was in the process of having circuitry added to its limbs.

It turns to look at me. Its eyes are vivid blue, full of pain and sadness.

"Hun-gry. Hun-gry," it says, in a metallic, hissing voice. It sounds like a pre-pubescent girl with a sore throat.

"Gah!" Ivan says. "Hate when they talk."

"Me too."

"Thirs-ty. Please. Help. Help meeeeee…" It struggles weakly, trying to unhook itself from the gear holding it in place.

I stab it in the head with my knife, my blade sinking into its skull all the way to the hilt. It convulses and then is still. It's Unionized and an evil thing, but I feel sorry for it. To the Union, cyborgs were worse than slaves were. Despite their capacity for learning, for free will, they were considered to be tools and nothing more. The Union cared not one bit for their suffering.

Things like this were fuel to my genocidal fire. Killing Unionists with me, and it seems, with Ivan, became personal—a vendetta.

Ivan and I walk down the high-tech bio-line and kill all the cyborgs. I stab them with my knife and Ivan simply uses his medical probe. He samples everything, and we'll upload the DNA into Zero Net for the Union detectors.

In no time, blood and cyber goo runs down our armor; it coats Ivan and I'm sure I don't look any better.

Soon we come to the beginning of the line. A large tank of green semi-transparent goo is before us, but it's not what I expect. I expected to see a human woman in the tank, bound with tubes in every orifice, eyes mad and pleading for a quick death.

But what is in the tank is something else. It's not a woman, but a woman's reproductive system floating in the goo: a pair of ovaries, the fallopian tubes and a uterus. Where the cervix and vagina would be is a cybernetic tube.

Ivan and I stare at it for the longest time.

"Never seen that before," I say to break the silence.

Ivan turns to me and gives me an impish grin. "Eh. Well, Lieutenant, your parts are cyber, yes? You could use these. All packaged up and ready to go."

I burst out laughing.

"In Soviet Russia, ovaries have you!"

I cackle louder, and start to cough. "Stop! You're so bad."

Ivan stabs an ovary and takes a sample. Then he frowns, and I can guess what he is thinking because I'm thinking it too.

"Only reason to separate from woman is if they need woman," he says.

"Alive," I add. "The killer has her. Alive. I know it."

Ivan stares at it all. Then he starts to shake, actually shake, in his armor.

"Easy Ivan, dial it down," it's my turn to say and I take a cautious step back.

He shakes his head to clear it.

"Lexus…" he whispers.

"This case just got very, very serious," I finish for him. We may never find the woman, but if we don't find the Unionists, they will just keep doing this, over and over again until they are caught.

* * *

"Space Station Matachi, this Zebra-Zero-Zero-One-Two. Verbal confirmation of WMD request."

"Zebra-Zero-Zero-One-Two, WMD confirmation—go ahead."

"Orbital torpedo strike requested. Data uploaded. Target lit. Launcher re-task course uploaded. You are green for launch."

"Zebra-Zero-Zero-One-Two, data received. Launch authorized. We are green. Re-task in progress. Set. Two keys in the launch board. Arming. Armed. Kinetic torpedoes locked. Launching. FA torpedo locked. Launching."

"Space Station Matachi, visual confirmation Fallow Sector FRA-ALS.15 destroyed. Sensor telemetry uploaded."

"Zebra-Zero-Zero-One-Two, data received."

CHAPTER 17

I'M BACK IN THE cockpit and Arune is heading back to the orbital landing pad in Bacon, Washington. The rest of the squad is in Roscoe, the fancy ATV. I'm not Uplinked. I need downtime, and Arune is giving it to me. Right now, I can barely tolerate my armor; the dull, itchy ache is all over my body.

"You're all fucked up," Arune says unceremoniously.

"Gee, thanks."

"Look, Lexus—that little horror show of the squad taking you to the river so you and Ivan could get washed off told me everything I need to know about your mental state. But, we've seen worse."

I sigh. We've done worse too.

"Yeah, we have."

"So I'm not really talking about your mental issues."

"Oh?" I wonder if Arune knows I'm falling apart. Literally, I can feel myself on the razor's edge. On one side, I can see the Goddess. She's a frightful presence, demanding, angry. On the other side, I can see Lexus. Hairless, scared, surrounded by love, yet alone.

If you can actually feel yourself going insane, you know you're on the edge. I guess he will get all that when we Uplink next. If we Uplink. He could always refuse. In his place, I would.

"I've reviewed your armor data. Your Lib-Gee is now worse. It's dumping crap into your body. Have you felt nauseous?"

"Yeah, I barfed. I thought it was PTSD from playing Military again."

"Well, you do have PTSD for that very reason, but you're also at the edge of acceptable parameters for hormone levels. The bad Lib-Gee is also having a cascading effect. For example, your artificial thyroid is off."

Ah, crap. Shrapnel damaged my thyroid in the war, but it mainly had to come out because my body needed a cyber-system to interact with my Lib-Gee.

"It's not in the red either, but a lesser person would've been admitted by now. Your suit isn't screaming because it thinks it's the old you, not the fucked up twenty-year older you."

"Ugh."

"I'm taking you to your GYN."

The way he said it left no room for argument. When it came to my health, Arune owned me, and he knew it.

"Okay. Let me get some sleep and check in with my Husbands first. Then I will go."

"Promise?"

"I promise."

"Okay then. Landing cycle started. Standby."

"I have the path, looks good."

"Lexi?"

"Yeah?"

"I'm worried about you."

"I'll go see Dr. Takayasu. You're right. I'll take care of myself, I hate feeling this way. I just need rest, Arune, and I need to make sure my Husbands aren't going to track me down and start shooting people."

Especially Vash and Juan.

"Roger that. Lexi?"

"Yes, my Love?"

"I saw you take a branch from a linden tree. What's it for?"

"It's for a very naughty girl."

"Eep."

"Arune—don't interfere. I mean it. This is important."

"Aye, Lexi."

* * *

We're at the landing pad, and the girls are stripping. They stripped

Scott first, and he's a bruised mess, but he doesn't need medical attention. If there were any internal injuries, his armor, crappy as it is, would still tell us he needed fixing. It was good enough to prevent serious injury.

And—oh my. No wonder Brittney likes him. He's muscular-manly and no slouch in the *oomph* department either.

I look at Ivan. By protocol, as the squad leader and with him not paired with anybody right now, I should be taking Ivan back to his place and fucking him silly, relieving his combat stress, and he of mine. But I can't do it. I just can't, and I'm too embarrassed to admit it.

He looks at me and winks. He knows exactly what I'm thinking.

—Borislava, I'm good. I have a companion I can call. She charges a good credit, but she's very worth it. You would like her, tall and curvy, like you. I charge your account.—

—I'm so embarrassed, Ivan. It's not you. I have…—

—I saw the recreation, Borislava. No need to explain. You made mistake if you plugged into it. But that's not my business.—

—You're a good man, Ivan. You're also one tough son of a bitch.—

—Ha! I think the same of you! I take, how you say, rain check. Yes, later, when you're feeling better.—

—I look forward to it.—

Ivan jumps into the driver's seat of Scott's SUV, and presses the start button.

Now the rest of the squad is looking at me, the girls have their armor squared away in Roscoe, back to wearing the cuteness uniform.

Scott and Brittney are holding hands.

"Uh, if you can take Roscoe, Brittney, I will take Tiff up in orbit. Arune and I will take care of her. I'll drop her off at Fort Lewis tomorrow."

Brittney grins weakly. I feel proud that I extracted that much.

They leave, with the ATV following dutifully behind.

"Tiff, can you help me out of this damn armor? I'll help you out of yours."

"Of course."

We strip and lock the armor away in their trunks.

"Arune, you mind if I just hit the main cabin?"

"Kindly don't be a silly shit," he quips.

"Yes, Major."

He makes a snorting sound.

I don't even bother putting on any clothes. Arune ties us to the bed, and soon we're weightless.

I look at Tiffany, a nude and nubile ball of post-stress. She's got a perpetual sad face that I'm pretty sure she's not aware of, and I can see the day has weighed heavily on her. But she was good—she really was—in combat, anyway.

After Arune uncoils us, I drift to her and latch on fiercely.

"You did a good job today. I'm very proud to have been in the same platoon as you. You're a Manticore."

She hugs me tight. "You're going to make me cry!" She nuzzles my neck. She wants me. I can feel it. Can feel her heat, her need. I can even smell it, the musky tangy smell of a hairless female soldier wanting sex after combat.

Ha. She has no idea. Better to get this over with right now.

"Tiffany," I say sweetly after I disengage from her embrace and look her right in the eye, "I want you to go to the small locker right before the cockpit. You'll find a switch there. Bring it here."

Her eyes get big. "But…"

"Don't make me get it myself. You will regret it." I push her off the bed, none to gently, and she drifts. She rights herself and gives me a dirty look. But it soon turns to worry.

She goes.

Brittney, the smart one, has negotiated her behind to safety. Tiffany, it seems, isn't as quick on the uptake.

She comes back.

She's shaking, holding the switch.

"Nancy, I know I deserve this, but I ask you please not to do so," she says as she hands it to me. I look into her eyes and see an ocean of guilt. It is then I know for sure.

"Oh? You think I should forgive you and Brittney? For coming out here to kill me?"

To her credit, she stops shaking and grows calm. I repress a smile. Oh, how lying eats at the young today. She even looks relieved at not carrying the secret anymore.

"How did you know?" she asks with resignation. She can't meet my eyes, and that adds to my general pissed off state.

"Brittney bursting into tears when we first met, once I thought about it, was too much, even for little fluffy socialites. When I went over the scene in my mind, self-doubt and guilt painted her face. The fact that Scott never left my side gave both you two squirts a lot of pause, didn't it?"

"I'm sorry."

"And give me a break. A *tank?* NI gear? A little over the top, don't you think? If the brass was really worried about Union tech, they would have sent a bio-team, not someone from my old platoon."

"We just didn't know. Psyche-Comp put a red flag on you and Arune investigating Union tech. The thought of you losing it and taking Arune with you was too much for the squad to contemplate. Everybody in Omega drew straws. Britt and I lost."

Instead of lashing out, I think about that.

"Well, on one hand, that's actually sweet. I'll honor your request."

I drop the switch and it floats in place.

Then I lash out with both my hands. My left grabs her with unerring aim between the thighs. The other has my combat knife right under her jaw, the tip resting against her skin.

"On the other, I should slit your throat and push you out the air-lock."

Her eyes take on a sadness and hurt that only the young can have when someone they respect voices her displeasure. She is very still.

"Tiffany, you came up here to fuck me and I came up here to beat you until your implants switched the pain to pleasure. But I have a better idea."

My hand, I notice, is wet. I pinch her folds none too kindly, and pain fills her eyes.

"You forget I am an unholy bitch of vengeance and destruction. My honor is a thin thing, repeatedly stripped away during the war and reapplied in a vain attempt to keep me sane."

I put my lips to her ear and give her another pinch. She whimpers. "But I tell you this," I whisper, "I am an Investigator working to catch a serial killer who started murdering before you were born. If you interfere in the execution of my duties in this case, I will fucking gut you and use your spine to bludgeon Brittney to death."

I push her and float backwards. Eventually we bump against opposite walls in the cabin.

I sheathe my knife in its thigh holster. "Gather your things and go sleep in the cargo hold. I don't want to see you again until you have an appreciation that this case is not about me and certainly not about you. I want you to grow up."

She starts to sob then, but leaves.

As I put the switch away, I notice little drops of water floating in the air. I touch one on my finger and put it in my mouth.

Salty.

I now feel guilt, but I push it away. I would extract a bittersweet lake of tears to catch the killer.

* * *

I wake up on the hammock by the ocean with Arune wrapped around me, and I smile. Arune and I are so attuned to each other, he can Uplink to me while I am sleeping without waking me up.

"Mmmmm…" I snuggle close. This is nice.

"I am confused," Arune says.

I look up to him. "About what?"

"Tiffany."

"I told you to butt out. So, butt out."

"Quiet, Woman, this is about me."

I try not to, but wind up giggling anyway.

"I thought you were pushing me to consider her my Pilot," he says.

"I am. She's quick, she's young and she's—something. Your type? I dunno."

"But…" He trails off, hesitates and then sighs.

"So, is this one of those things that even if I was a male human I would be scratching my head?"

"Exactly. Now let me sleep, Male Pillow."

"Yes ma'am."

CHAPTER 18

FORT LEWIS.

We're in a crowded, busy landing facility. If I didn't know better, I would say they were on alert.

Alert for what?

Certainly not Arune and me. We sit on the pad, awaiting our departure time after Tiffany practically ran down the gangplank and it's as if we don't even exist. Two hundred meters to our five o'clock is something I can only describe as a *space*ship. Like, a warship built for space combat, not for blowing up planet-side things like a MOF/B.

I watch the busy bees go back and forth, almost like a dance, and Fort Lewis isn't even a port. It's the North Pacific Armored Division Hub, not a Starport like SeaTac just to the north. It should not have so much traffic, nor a spaceship simply sitting there.

—Arune?—

—Yes?—

—Remember when you said I would regret turning down the promotions because my need-to-know nature would someday clash with my independent combat streak?—

—Yes?—

—Fuck you.—

—Snicker. I rule on so many different levels.—

"Zebra-Zero-Zero-One-Two, you now have a countdown. Please don't deviate from your path out of restricted space. MTC, out."

"Acknowledged, MTC."

—Wow, Major, they hate me.—

—They don't hate you.—

—Who knows what we backed up by taking this pad. They hate me for our unscheduled arrival.—

—Okay, maybe a little.—

—Next time just land on the lawn.—

—Lexi…—

—The General's lawn…—

—Quiet. Lifting.—

—Aye.—

Soon we're lazily floating over to Mt. Si.

—Arune, let's go into orbit for a bit and have wild monkey sex.—

—No.—

—No!?—

—I'm not having any type of sex with you until you see your GYN. And before you get all pissy, I suggest you don't have sex with your Husbands either. Your Lib-Gee is running you, not the other way around.—

—It's been running me since they installed it!—

—This is different. It's broken.—

—I know that!—

—It's making you grouchy.—

—I know…—

—…—

—Fine. Can you wait for me until tomorrow? I have a big family.—

—Of course. I'll be right there on the pad on top of your mountain, looking at your house. Glowering, actually.—

—I love you.—

—I love you too, you silly broken human.—

* * *

I leave my suit in Arune, deciding my girly uniform, minus the wig, will work just fine. No sooner do I walk down into my office than I run into Bambi, Dr. Ivan, and Scott.

What. The. Fuck.

"How did you get in here?"

"Your security sucks," Bambi says, unerringly smug. "You haven't upgraded it in a while."

I put my hand on my needler. "That's because there are severe consequences to breaking into an Investigator's office!"

"Kindly un-bunch your panties, Borislava," Ivan says sternly.

"What are you three doing here!?"

"I retired," says Scott.

"I was fired," says Bambi.

"I quit," says Dr. Ivan. He grins.

I just glare.

Bambi melts first. "It was Ivan's idea!"

I narrow the glare. Finally, it seems to have gotten to him.

"Your Seattle Investigator friends have been bugging me long time to set up a Coroner's Office on the eastside of their pretty Lake Washington. What better way to do so than to attach to an already established office?" Ivan says.

No!

"I don't do dead bodies! Especially homicides!" Can't they see what this one is doing to me?

"I'll handle that part," says Scott.

"You shouldn't do homicides either!"

"Nancy, you're the one who turned me into an Investigator!"

Fuck!

I switch my glare to Bambi. She withers.

"I, uh, was really fired. I watched the re-creation again after Mary said it was forbidden."

"Why? Are you crazy!?"

"I have to know. I have to know everything about this crime. Everything. We have to solve it, and for me to help, I have to know every detail. Every single one."

"I..."

I'm speechless. My mind whirls.

"I don't have the funds to expand!"

"We came with our life savings," Scott says. "We'll make capital investments. We all have Investigative experience, Ivan is a certified Coroner, and we three would like training. We all want to be Investigators. Real Investigators, not just your lackeys."

I grab a chair and sit. I put my head in my hands.

Fuck. They all would make great Investigators, and for the first time I need to think beyond my desires and wants and think about my place in the community. Something I have been trying to avoid for twenty years.

I look at Ivan. I realize I have pushed Ivan too far. There is no turning back for him. The moment we stepped into that crèche, I bound myself to him, and him to me. It's more than a marriage. We're now soldiers on a mission for a war that is supposed to be over but no one can forget.

"Fine," I say from my hands, "congratulations, you little snots have beaten me down."

"Really?" Scott asks.

"I can't argue with such a well thought out Evil Plot." I look up at them.

"Awesome!" Bambi says. "That goes well with your Evil Underground Lair! This place is huge, like even for an office of four."

Ivan cackles.

I stand up.

"Bob, please log Ivan, Scott and Bambi as my apprentices."

My worthless office comp. Did I really neglect his security program? I feel somewhat guilty about it, and that's silly.

"Acknowledged."

Bambi starts jumping up and down and then kisses Scott.

Kids these days.

"So, Borislava, Mary never said how you go from Apprentice to full-fledged Investigator."

I get up and leave. At the door, I turn to them.

"That's because you have to find out yourselves. Otherwise, you wouldn't be much of an Investigator, now would you?"

I let that sink in for a minute. They nod.

"My equipment lockers are still in Arune. Bambi, get them out, clean and charge the equipment, and put it away. I need to go home and schedule a doctor visit. Scott, you can drive me home. I assume your SUV is parked in my garage next to my beater."

"I still have it until the end of the month."

"What about Ivan?" Bambi asks.

Already I'm getting lip. I sigh.

"*Doctor* Ivan has to set up a forensic medical facility, which will take twice as long as for you to molest my computers and install your own lab. You, my little tart, are Junior Squirt, so you'll be doing most of the grunt work."

She stands there, staring at me.

I glare.

"Yes, Nancy, of course."

* * *

It's a short drive to my house in North Bend from Mt. Si. It's on top of a hill overlooking the Snoqualmie River.

"Nice house," Scott says.

It is a nice house. It's a sprawling two-story home in two wings and a furnished basement. There's plenty of room for five married people and a cybernetic maid. More so than that, it's made of steel with composite siding that looks like wood. And the gorgeous, armored windows. They are big and generous and have a great view of the river on one side, a territorial view of a forest on the other, and then to cap it off, a view of my Mt. Si on yet another.

We're in my driveway. I can hear dogs barking inside.

"Nancy, are you okay?"

"I feel bad."

"Like, guilty bad, hurt feelings bad, or gonna puke bad?"

Mommy I love you…

"Yes."

He holds my hand.

I sigh and look at him. "Don't think because you're my apprentice, I'm going to let you kiss me."

"How do you know I want to kiss you?"

"Because you're kissy. But I have a complicated home life, and an AI lover." I look at him. "I would like to kiss you, but I need a friend. A male friend. One I'm not kissing. I really, really, like being your friend."

Scott smiles and I punch him on the shoulder. He winces.

"Ah, oops, sorry. Heh. I take it Brittney didn't give you time to heal."

"Ah, no. But I rose to the occasion."

I groan.

"Hold down the fort, Scott. I will be gone for at least two days." I waggle my finger at him. "No new cases. Take it easy. Seattle has been screaming at me to expand for years—they handle Bellevue and the Bellevue market is bigger than Seattle. I don't care what Walker in his snobby office with a killer view of the sound tells you, tell him we're not open quite yet."

"Got it."

I give him a look.

"It really was Ivan's idea."

"Harrumph."

I kiss him on the cheek, take a deep breath, and get out. I watch as he drives away and it actually hurts to see him go.

I'm a dork. Four Husbands, Arune and I want more, but I don't even know if I can have sex with a human ever again.

Humans, it seems to me, are bad. They can do such horrible things if pushed too far.

I, the Goddess, do even more horrible things, but I think after I left the Military patched up with cyber, I wasn't much of a human. Looks are deceiving.

For example, Scott looks normal, but he's so very not.

Mommy I love you… Mommy…

I walk to the door.

The Goddess of War is home.

CHAPTER 19

BEDLAM.

Normally all of my Husbands home at the same time would be sweet, sweet chaos. Now, the noise is confusing, almost otherworldly, as if I walked into someone else's house.

The two dogs are barking, wagging their tails. Mitchel's cat is even meowing at me from the kitty condo. Cazandra is at the foot of the stairs in her French maid outfit smiling and—and my Husbands surround me.

Juan picks me up, literally lifts me off the ground, and twirls me around.

"*Señorita!* Who was that rugged man in the expensive truck you kissed on the cheek? Eh? Is he a new lover, are you going to share?"

Vash grabs me, yanks me from Juan's grasp. "Juan, quit being a fag for five minutes, my God." He gives me a big kiss.

Normally a kiss from Vash is like sweet flavored butter melting in the mouth.

Now, I'm terrified.

He sets me down and frowns. He senses something is wrong.

"Uh guys, she doesn't…" Caz is cut off.

"Are you okay Lex?" Bill is there, and takes a step towards me.

I take a step back.

"Guys, I think you should give her some space."

Mitchel approaches, looking concerned. "Hon, you're sweating."

I back up even further towards the formal living room off the foyer.

"Guys…"

"Scream all you want, Jennifer," Bill says.

"No one can hear you," says Mitchel, coming closer.

"Please, please, don't hurt my daughter," I plead.

Vash laughs.

"Guys, back the fuck off!" says Layla, as Juan reaches for her, an evil leer on his face, pink scarf in his hands.

"Layla, run!"

I bump into the loveseat, and scream.

Blackness.

* * *

"Lieutenant, you're wanted on the bridge."

I'm in the captain's cabin, wrapped up in a thermal blanket. I had just gotten dry, and now I'm getting warm. I'm wearing nothing except my dog tags and a combat knife strapped to my thigh. I thought about leaving the knife off, but old habits die hard. I sleep better wearing it.

They dumped me here because the infirmary contains Vash, Juan and four kids, whom I'm sure make the small medical room crowded. They even left me alone. Sweet, sweet alone time.

So much for sleeping. I'm exhausted. I nod and just wrap the blanket around my shoulders. I may be wanted on the bridge, but I don't have the energy to get dressed.

The yeoman gives me a strange look that I can't parse. "Watch your step ma'am. It's easy to bang your shins."

Or your head. I'm somewhat tall for a woman, and there doesn't seem to be an inch of wasted space on the sub. I notice I'm walking on a runner over vac-cans of food, making the ceiling even shorter.

The bridge is a modern marvel: intimate and efficient, sleek and quiet. The captain is at a little nook, illuminated by red lights and a strategic map of Europe and the Middle East

He's an older gentleman, handsome and bookish in his old-fashioned glasses.

"Lieutenant Lexus, sir, reporting as ordered."

"At ease, Lieutenant." He sticks out his hand. We shake, and he's warm.

"I'm sorry about Port Dis and your platoon. We got snippets from your marines, and what we got was a horror tale."

He's talking to me, but I'm not listening. I recognize what this is. I'm no expert in submarines, but this is obviously a launch board.

For missiles.

Intercontinental, nuclear, ballistic missiles.

I look at the board. A dog tag is stuck in a slot.

The entire bridge is silent. The people make no noise. The equipment makes less. Everyone is looking at me, and some are actually shaking. A chill goes down my spine.

I shake my head.

"Sir, I have a tag key, but it's for artillery. The small stuff. Armor busters, all tactical. Even then, I'm just backup due to my rank."

He simply nods.

I wave my hand at the board. "Just get your final key from CIC."

"Cheyenne is offline, Lieutenant. They've buttoned up and are not answering the phone. They might have got a false signal that the sub fleet, what's left of us anyway, was destroyed, so they are probably running some go-to-ground protocol."

Bah. "Looking Glass, then."

"Shot down. They thought it through, but they didn't have complete intel about our launch protocols. Now they are demanding an armistice, and some people in the BattleNet are saying that may be a good idea."

I look at him blankly. It's the end of the world. Just like that. Armistice is just a ploy, just as the first surrender and occupation was just a ploy. All the Union needs is time. Given enough time, we will all disappear into their Union.

I'm thinking some people might think it would be better than this endless war. Even after everything I have been through, all the crimes against being human I have committed, I'm not sure I disagree with them.

"Sir, it's not going to turn."

"There's a Whisper Net, see? It's an ancient backup to our backup, hush-hush, put together by the old US Naval intel-skunk works guys, that's how monumentally old it is."

"It's not going to turn!"

"You're the only officer alive from Port Dis. In case of total CIC failure, we can launch when authorized from other sources, if we have two authenticated nuke officers who agree. Somebody popped an authorization into the Sneaker Net, which matches the code stored in the safe. Now all we need is two keys and two officers from two different chains of command. Normally subs are outside of this fail-safe without planning, but we found you, so here you are."

"It's not going to turn," I whisper.

"I can't order you to do this, Lieutenant, no one can. But I think it's a really good idea. The longer we wait, the harder it's going to be to launch. The enemy knows this. They are betting on time and a lack of conviction. Every minute that goes by without a response eats at our will to survive."

A calmness descends on me. I nod. I will humor him, because I'm a Lieutenant and he's a Captain, and that's what Lieutenants do.

I let the blanket drop, and I do not feel cold anymore. I take my dog tags off. I put one in the waiting slot at the other end of the board. I twist it clockwise.

Click, it turns.

It turned.

Oh no, it turned.

I stare at the board as it glows from mere red to blood red.

The board talks to me, sub-vocally.

—Lieutenant, do you authorize a launch of your own free will?—

I can't feel my fingers. I realize some sort of electric pulse is running from the board through my fingers, debugging my identity.

—Lieutenant, do you authorize a launch of your own free will?—

Do I even have a free will?

—Lieutenant?—

After Alsace—after I led my platoon to safety from deep in enemy territory against all odds—my men started calling me the Goddess of War.

Now they are all dead. I guess that's what I really am. And the Goddess needs blood to fuel her desire for vengeance. Lots and lots of blood. All of it, in fact.

—Yes. Launch authorized.—

A small chime sounds. The map glows brighter. The Captain presses a button.

Dots move on the screen from Military targets to cities. "FULL DEAL" splashes across the top of the screen. "TARGETS ACQUIRED AND PROGRAMMED."

The Captain doesn't hesitate. He presses the big button. "Commence launching," he says to the board.

The boat shudders.

And shudders.

And shudders.

He looks at me, his voice academic. "Twenty-four birds in all. Each with twelve MRVs, each MRV a four-hundred and seventy-five kiloton warhead. The birds have a ten thousand nautical mile range."

The shuddering continues.

"Any decoys?" I'm curious. On the board, lines appear, representing the flight path and the missiles. They are fast, and we're at Europe's doorstep.

Shudder.

"Negative. But they're fast enough."

Shudder.

Two-hundred and eighty-eight warheads.

The shuddering finally stops.

"Helm, evasion course Tango-Two."

"Aye, aye, Skipper, evasion course Tango-Two."

I can feel movement, and the boat dives.

I stare at the screen. Twenty-four lines split into two-hundred and eighty-eight lines, and they are falling impossibly fast towards the waiting dots. Some angle towards the same dots.

Only they aren't dots, not really.

When the first one registers a hit, on London, I grab the Captain's hand. Two more follow the first.

I watch Europe die. I have killed Europe, along with a good portion of the Middle East. My butcher's bill is now many, many times longer than it was when I left Edinburgh.

As the last warhead registers an impact and the dot disappears, the Captain grabs me and spins me to him. I clutch him fiercely and I kiss him, kiss him hard and passionately. He runs his hands down my naked back, cups my ass, and pulls me into his hardness. I hold him tight and the kiss goes on forever.

He's whispering in my ear. "If there is an ounce of honor in you, Lexus, you'd do it. Please."

I nod. "What's your name?" I whisper back.

"James."

"James, kiss me again."

He does.

And then, in a flash, I draw my knife, and plunge it between his ribs, into his heart and he moans.

"Thank you," he whispers, and his eyes roll back in his head. He goes limp.

The yeoman is rushing the nook. I grasp the hilt of my knife in one hand, and in one smooth motion, push the Captain's body into the yeoman with my foot. He falls to the ground, and now there is shouting.

I flick the knife into the air. It lands in my right hand, with the edge pointed towards me. I swing my hand out, and it comes back towards my own heart.

I see movement out of the corner of my eye. Then I feel like someone hit me in the head with a sledgehammer.

Blackness.

* * *

I wake in my bed. I feel fine. I'm alone, blessedly, and it's night.

Obviously, I have had another Uplink flashback, one I richly deserve to relive repeatedly until I die and go to Hell.

But I feel fine. Odd.

I even managed not to pee myself, because my bladder is about to burst. I go silently and eschew flushing, no need to wake anybody else up.

As I go back to get into bed, I hear arguing. I look at the clock. It's barely nightfall.

I open my door and sneak to the top of the stairs.

"That's out of line!" Bill says.

"I agree," says Mitchel.

"Oh? Is it? Is it? Tell me, William, since when is it out of line to call you all on the carpet when you were such assholes?"

Oh my God. Cazandra, the sex bot, is giving my Husbands what for.

Woo hoo!

"We didn't know she was traumatized, Caz."

"How could you not? It was all over her face! As soon as Juan touched her, she looked completely terrified. Yet you yahoos persisted even after I pointed out the complete obvious to you *four fucking times.*"

"Oh man, I feel like shit," says Vash.

"That's because you are a shit! She even peed herself!"

Ah, crap, so much for bladder control.

Wow. Caz isn't just mad, she's righteously pissed. I had no idea her programming was even capable of that, but it makes sense. She's very kind and protective of me. I have never heard her talk to anyone this way, much less my Husbands.

Then again, I don't even talk to them that way. Maybe I'm just a Junior Wife to the house sex-bot. The thought makes me want to giggle.

"You're overreacting," Bill says, but now he sounds defensive.

"And then I had to yell at you four to respect her long-standing wishes and not take her to the emergency room if the medical scanner came up green! I am very upset by your disrespectful behavior towards your Wife!"

"Sorry to interrupt our ass-chewing," says Mitchel, "but we need to find out what happened. I'll ask her in the morning."

"No! You will not! I'll take care of it. If any one of you poopy-heads says one word to her about whatever happened to make her react that way, I swear to your nebulous God concept I'll cut off your balls while you're sleeping and use them as fish bait in the river!"

"Caz..."

"And that might get me deactivated and thrown into the trash, but at least I'll hit the recycle furnace with a smile on my face!"

I'm biting my hand to keep from laughing.

"Well..."

My Husbands. They are all smart. But they are males, and sometimes they just don't know when to shut up. Now they are learning what it means when they have angered the *faux female.* Her adaptive Level

Two AI program must be very impressive—programming that sacrifices short-term household bliss for long-term gain. Wow.

"Well nothing! I'm going to bed, and don't even think of summoning me for a bit of play, unless that's exclusively me beating your fat asses with a switch! And you two jarheads can do your own chores!"

"Until when?"

Juan, shut up before she kills you!

"Until Lexus gives me the green light! In writing! Good night!"

Slam!

I hear stomping down the basement stairs.

"Well, my ears are ringing. Juan and I are going to turn in early. We'll, uh, do dishes in the morning," I hear a chair pushing back across the hardwood.

"Si."

Their bedroom is in a separate wing with its own staircase, so I stay at my little snoop spot.

Moments later, a heavy sigh. "You know, Mitch, sometimes not being gay has a distinct disadvantage in this family."

"Tell me about it." A pause. "We'd just fight over who would be on top anyway."

"Ha, and here I thought you would just automatically be the bitch!"

Mitch laughs heartedly. "Who are we kidding? Vash would bend us over the kitchen table faster than either of us could say *does that thing have lube on it?*"

Now it's Bill's turn to laugh.

"Caz will get mad if she sees a dirty dish. More mad."

"Yeah."

"Let's do them, then drink beer and play some vids."

"Now that's a good idea."

Another stretch of silence as I hear dishes going into the dishwasher.

Mitch speaks. "Do you think we should talk to Arune? He's sitting up there on her mountain."

"Are you kidding? No. Arune is very protective of her. Don't ever get Arune mad. And not because he's a flying killing machine. Arune can fuck with the unfuckable in cyber ways we can't imagine. And we fucked up." Bill sighs. "Caz is right. We acted like a bunch of selfish little boys when she came home. We're lucky she didn't draw her needler and plug us all."

"Ugh, I feel like shit. I've never seen her like that. I can't live without her, Bill, I can't."

This time the silence is unnerving and I feel bad for snooping. But I'm glued to my spot. Snooping is what I do.

"I can't either. I can't either."

"I also can't stand the thought of Caz being so mad at me. I know she's a bot, and I'm dancing to some programmers strings, but I love her. She's been making me happy for ten years."

"Yeah, I love her too."

"So what do we do? Meathead and Meathead aren't going to fix this."

"Chocolate and jewelry, Mitch my man, chocolate and jewelry. And copious amounts of groveling. Plus, I think my present will go a long, long way at banking Lex Credit."

The fridge opens. I can imagine Mitch grinning at the Bill Wisdom. I hear the snick-hiss of bottle caps coming off, their little tink-tinks on the counter.

"Here's to our women feeling better," says Mitch.

Clink.

I pad my way back to my bed and stare at the ceiling.

I never knew Mitch and Bill were so close.

I never knew Cazandra was so fiercely loyal to me.

I never knew I could have an Uplink flashback without needing to Uplink afterwards. Uplinking to myself causes my nervous system to go out of sync. If it's a bad episode, and that one was a doozy, the only way to fix me is to Uplink with an AI or another person to bring my system back into its own rhythm by interrupting the neural overload.

Yet somehow, I escaped that.

Arune is right. I'm sick, and need to go to the doctor. I'm just glad I'm not in a hospital right now. I left explicit instructions that if something happened to me and I did not look injured, they were to wave my first-aid scanner over me. If I needed to go to the hospital, it would call in for them. Otherwise, they were to leave me alone. Or else.

A NI soldier waking up in a different place is bad. It seems only Caz remembered that.

But right now, I'm going to go to sleep.

What is the present Bill got me, anyway?

I close my eyes.

—Please, my God, no dreams.—

—Sleep tight, my Goddess of War.—

—Okay.—

Oh man, I'm so losing it.

Blackness.

* * *

I wake up and look at the clock. Three AM. I'm not on Pacific Time, it seems. That happens when the body attunes to Uplink.

I pee, wash up, and brush my teeth. I put on my best long silk robe and wind a fancy silk scarf Caz gave me for my birthday several years ago around my head. I put on my pink fuzzy slippers, and head downstairs and into the basement.

It's a finished basement, but it's cold. I walk silently to Caz's room, and the door slides open on quiet gliders.

Her room is small and sparse. It has pictures and holos of the family, and she's lying on her small bed with a thin blanket.

I know it's silly but I feel guilty. She's a bot, but now it seems I have taken her for granted, and I feel bad.

I pad over to her bed and look at her feminine form.

"Caz, I know you woke up when I came into the room." She sleeps very lightly. A Level Two AI even dreams, I've heard, but Caz as a domestic sex-bot is used to infrequent downtime.

She giggles. "Busted."

I sit on her bed and she sits up.

"Mis—uh, Lexus, what can I do for you? You look a lot better."

I look her right in the eye. "Can you sleep with me, in my room?"

"Yes, of course, don't be silly." She hugs me, and all is right in the world again.

* * *

I'm lying in bed with a naked Caz around me, luscious black hair spilling on to my shoulder. I stroke the softer-than-soft skin on her arm and she sighs, and snuggles closer.

I want her. I want to kiss her and have her kiss me and lick me and I want to taste her.

But I need something else. Desperately.

I turn and face her. "Caz, I..."

She looks at me, expectant.

"I..."

I can't say it. I feel so, so stupid. It was a stupid simulation! It wasn't real!

"I was..."

But it sure seemed real at the time. I can close my eyes and feel him in me, thrusting and how *good* it felt.

Now I feel nauseous just thinking about it. Instead of talking, I start to cry again. Why can't I stop crying? Why?

"Oh Lexus, what happened? What happened to you?" she whispers. "You're pale as a ghost."

Mommy I love you... Mommy...

"I—oh Caz, I'm so ashamed and I know that's stupid but that's what I feel!"

Caz looks at me in utter horror.

"No! No! Not you!"

She latches onto me, squeezes me impossibly tight. I hug her back fiercely and cry into her hair.

"Oh no, my Love, no. Not you, not you. That's not fair! That's not fair!"

I sob and she holds me, and rocks me, and she's kissing my tears and caressing my face. Surprisingly soon, I'm calm.

She looks me right in the eye, and I'm not too sure I like what I'm seeing in hers. It is frightening.

"Who did this to you?"

I was not going to tell her because as a bot I didn't think she would be able to parse it. But her eyes have me, are drinking me.

"It was an accident, an Investigation accident. It was real but not real."

She tilts her head, and looks curious.

"Explain."

I'm powerless. My mouth opens and I talk. I talk and talk and cry and cry, and she cries with me, and we both clutch each other, afraid to let go.

The Goddess prefers loneliness, but that's her. I can't be alone. I cannot.

I cannot.

—Sleep.—

—Okay.—

Warm, blessed blackness.

CHAPTER 20

I MAKE EVERYBODY BREAKFAST. Everyone apologizes to me, and then I glare, and each apologizes to Cazandra too.

"Why do I have to apologize to Caz?" Vash is confused.

"For arguing with her!"

"Oh man, the double-teaming is finally here," bemoans Mitchel.

"A dark day in the Toulouse household," says Juan, "ten years in the making."

"We all knew this day would come," says Bill, hanging his head.

"Ha, ha, ha. Not," I say.

Cazandra glares at them and I swear the room temperature drops several degrees. I guess even joking to ease the tension isn't going down well with her.

I wait until everyone is done with breakfast and insist Caz does not do the dishes. I gather everyone back to the table.

"I want to apologize for not calling ahead of time. I have some cyber systems on the fritz, and I need to go to Tokyo today to get it all straightened out. I…"

I swallow, and Caz grabs my hand and gives it a little squeeze.

"This case is bad. Really bad. It brought out all the bad memories and I've had Uplink flashbacks."

My Husbands look concerned.

"Anyway, I just need some time. I feel bad, but just give me some time before I can be a proper Wife."

They all nod, agree, and tell me *of course.*

I look at Caz. I have sworn her to secrecy. I can't tell any of my

Husbands right now. I can't.

She kisses me.

I kiss her back.

"Oh wow, that's hot," say Bill.

"I'm getting my hi-res vid cam," says Mitch as he gets up.

"Shut up!" says Caz, but she's laughing.

I turn to Bill.

"What is it that you planned?"

He practically jumps out of his chair.

"Uh, I will show you when you get back from Tokyo."

"Show me what?"

"It's a present."

"I know that! What is it?"

"Come back to us and you'll find out."

"Grrrr!"

One of the dogs growls back at me, and everyone laughs.

And I'm home.

* * *

I ride my bike up Mt. Si and the physical challenge is exhilarating. I may be physically in my forties but I certainly don't feel old and I don't certainly feel my actual getting-a-little-to-close-to-halfway-to-sixty. I don't feel like I'm twenty-two, but still, the bike ride all the way to the top of the mountain gets my blood flowing.

If I can't have sex, I can at least work out.

"Morning, Investigator," says Bambi, covered in dust and grime. She must have been rooting around the unfinished, closed off rooms, but right now she is in the reception area. Duster in hand, she's glued to the historical photos on the wall.

She's in front of the most provocative one. It's a photo of the road to the summit, with heads on pikes that alternate on either side until they fade into the distance.

"I had no idea," said Bambi.

"That was Fredric Day, a post-Collapse warlord. He ruled all the way to Seattle."

Bambi wrinkles her nose. "Quite the tyrant, I see."

I shake my head. "Draconian, more like it. He didn't have the resources to maintain a large criminal population in prisons, so he took everyone convicted of murder and rape and stuck them up here. Then he took everyone convicted of assault more than once and did the same thing. Then he let everyone else go."

"Ah." She dusts the picture. "Did it work?"

"It did indeed. That's why nobody complained when I claimed this place. After Day was assassinated, Mt. Si got a reputation as a place of ill-omen."

"Goodness," she whispers. "This place really is an evil underground lair."

She looks at me. She looks like she wants a hug to banish the bad thoughts, so I give her one.

"Oh, you'll get all dirty!"

"Gotta shower, anyway," I say, and head off to do that, smiling.

* * *

The holo call with Paul Gifford is not going well.

"I need you here, working this case like I paid you to, not off in Tokyo."

"If I don't go to Tokyo, I'm not going to be working anything," I snap.

I am in no mood to argue. I have not told him about France. I'm not about to tell him Justice is now a lower priority for me. I have a missing woman to find. I don't think laying waste to Alsace put her out of her misery, either. I can feel it in my bones.

He looks angry and opens his mouth to yell at me but then he just—slumps. It's like a soul-sucking vampire drained away his energy. My heart goes out to him. I get the feeling I am the only reason he's alive.

"You're that sick?"

"I'm that sick." I hate to admit my weakness, but there it is. He looks dubious, so I turn into a total ass and play the card I've been keeping close to my chest.

"It's a war injury, Paul. It follows me around like a shadow and if I don't deal with it, because the MPs are *literally* following me around, they will yank my Investigator certs."

He flinches. He puts his head in his hands.

"Sorry."

"Don't be. Paul?"

He looks up at me.

"There isn't a place for this murderer to hide. I'll chase him to the end of time itself."

He nods. "Aye, Investigator, aye."

* * *

To: My Evil Minions

From: Your Evil Overlord

I'm going to Tokyo. Don't take any cases. Don't take any referrals. Don't talk to the Investigator office in Seattle. Go house/apartment shopping, whatever. Get setup. I will be back soon. I will come back cranky. If a speculum were shoved up your vagina and dialed open for several hours (not minutes), you would be cranky too. Don't give me an excuse to beat your asses when I get back.

Love,

Nancy

* * *

Arune and I are on our merry way to Tokyo, and this time I wear a flight suit and nothing more. No plumbing. My armor can stay right where it is. I'm sure after the appointment I will not want *things* in me.

—Arune?—

—Yes.—

—How come you were able to make love to me, and I didn't lose my shit?—

I love that phrase Caz used. I now claim it as my own.

—I cheated.—

—What?—

—I cheated.—

—How do you cheat at sex?—

—We've talked about this before. When an AI and a human engage in Uplink sex it's a feedback loop process tied to the manifestations of our avatars in cyber, right?—

—Yes, of course. I'm an expert in Uplink woohoo. That's not answering my question.—

—Lexi, it's a *feedback* loop. I control the gain. I just turned it up until you didn't have any resistance to it.—

—But that's manipulative.—

—Yes, it is.—

—But you didn't get hardly any pleasure, then!—

—It made me happy to make you happy.—

—So, basically, I masturbated.—

—Pretty much.—

—Well, that was mean. It caused a big stink. I thought I could go home and as soon as one of my Husbands touched me, I lost my shit.—

—That was a possibility.—

—But you felt it necessary to, to…—

—To what?—

—To soothe me, I guess.—

—You're not you. Does this make sense? You're all fucked up, mentally and physically. When Tiffany fingered you, she knew exactly what she was doing. I just did the same. If you lost it with your Husbands, after I took care of you, you would've *really* lost it if I didn't.—

—You still manipulated me.—

—I know. I know. I'm sorry.—

—And I feel bad, because I didn't please you like I wanted to please you.—

—Don't feel bad. Since you didn't switch Tiffany, she asked me to spank her in Uplink.—

—Ewww!—

—Want to go somewhere and have me spank you?—

—No.—

—How about I look like Tiffany and you can switch me?—

—What? No!—

—Fine.—

—Fine. Arune, what if I lose it in the doctor's office?—

—Ask for drugs.—

—You know, you're not being a big help.—

—You mean I'm not coddling you?—

—Ptthhhht!—

—Still as mature as ever.—

—Arune?—

—Yeah?—

—Am I still your girl?—

—Always.—

CHAPTER 21

JAPAN.

The borderless nation. There are no borders anywhere except those that define settled areas from fallowed, forbidden, former enemy territory. Yet Japan still exists. On a world map that just contains cities, as they all do, any child can point to where Japan is with pride and explain how in all the madness, the people living there stayed the same.

New York City may be the *de facto* capital of our hyper-capitalistic planet, but if you were to poll random people anywhere and ask them where the real power is, they would say Japan.

And that's a little marvel that a nation exists where there ought to be none.

I love Japan. People are polite and kind. And if you respect their traditions, they are more than polite they are instantly your friend, for life. You may never be Japanese, but you certainly know you're an honored friend.

—You should move to Japan.—

That's an interesting opinion from Arune.

—Why?—

—Nothing bad ever happens to you here.—

—True.—

—And man, if those women knew what I could do with a tendril.—

He waves one around at me and I swat at it.

—Stop that, naughty boy!—

* * *

At the landing pad is a car and "my" driver.

I think he's a bot. He's tall, blonde and looks vaguely native Alaskan, and has not aged a day. When I first visited Japan after the war, he was waiting for me at the gate with a little sign that said "Lieutenant Lexus Toulouse."

I asked him whom he worked for, and he just smiled and said that such things don't concern me. Every time I have visited Japan, no matter how remote the airport, he has been there. And I have flown into some remote airports.

I think he's a Military bot, based on the way he talks. The Military is very fond of Japan, and my current theory is he's here to make sure I don't fuck up anything for them.

He will drive me anywhere I ask, and he doesn't follow me, just stays with the car. Literally, he is simply a driver.

He said his name was 'Thor,' but I don't believe that.

And here I am, on a Military restricted area pad, and there is the car. 'Someone' upgrades it every now and then.

"Hello, Thor, my friend."

"Off to a doctor's appointment, Lieutenant?"

"Yes. I'm going to have my artificial cervix poked at, and my cyber gear tinkered with."

"Sounds mildly unpleasant, ma'am."

"To be honest, it's not bad at all. As long as I don't lose my shit."

"I suggest drugs, Lieutenant."

I laugh.

* * *

I'm in my gynecologist's office, and I'm losing my shit.

I'm waiting; I have never had to wait before, because I've always scheduled my appointments here well in advance until today. And there is someone here with me waiting. I have been seeing Dr. Takayasu since I was a civilian, which is almost twenty-one years now.

I see him because he's the best. Literally, the best GYN on the planet. He's so good, he doesn't even do babies. Babies are beneath him. You want some OB, you go slum somewhere else.

He also refuses to take any money from me. The first time I tried to pay him, he slapped my hand with a piece of bamboo and told me never to insult him again.

That was a lesson learned. I get that sometimes, with people who know my story beyond the limited wiki page devoted to me.

But now I'm losing it, and wishing I had drugs. He has no receptionist, so I can't ask for any.

The young Japanese woman waiting with me must be twenty years old, max. That makes me wary, as it is my experience women of that age have an unhealthy hero-worship of me. I do not understand this post-war fascination. Would it have been the same if I were a man? I don't get it, and so I avoid young women her age.

No one should worship the Goddess of War. Especially a woman.

I am also wary because she is, quite possibly, the most beautiful woman I have ever seen, with large eyes and a firm, soft, feminine build. She makes Brittney look like a bag of shit. She is even tall. In the right shoes, she could be taller than I am.

Her dress takes my breath away—blue and gold silk interlaced with some type of thread that changes color when she moves or I look from a different angle. I also had no idea Japanese women could be so, um, perky. She looks somewhat familiar, but I can't put my finger on it.

I can't put my finger on it because I'm losing my shit.

She's intently studying a reader, poised, reading the words like a beautiful model ready to be painted.

It's odd, seeing her here. The exit to the office is through a different door to a different elevator. And even Dr. Takayasu's office is sixty-three stories up—the view, for that matter, is marvelous. I don't recall ever seeing another patient.

Finally, I can't keep quiet any longer. To remain silent is to invite the screaming, or worse, tears. I get up to introduce myself, wishing the Doctor allowed cyber tags in his office. Then I wouldn't need to guess who she is, I would know.

She stands, revealing that she is indeed taller than I am, and I bow low. "Forgive me for not introducing myself earlier. I'm Lexus. I'm very pleased to meet you."

She bows in return, not as deep as mine, but almost. An interesting social dynamic, and I wrack my brain trying to remember what it means. "No need to apologize, Lexus-san." She holds out her hand, and we shake warmly. "I'm Kori. I was going to introduce myself but you looked so occupied in your thoughts." She sits down and pats the spot next to her on the couch.

I sit. "Yes, I admit to being somewhat nervous."

"I must say, you look very fetching, Lexus-san, in your dress."

I'm wearing an Arune special—it's slinky without being too slinky, and a deep green, to go with that red wig that he seems so found of me wearing.

"Why thank you. It's not nearly as fetching as yours, though."

"You are too kind. Here I'm looking typical, and you are very exotic-looking. But is it not funny, dressing up to see our gynecologist? I even spent longer on my makeup than usual!"

I laugh because I did the same.

"Yes, we're silly."

I look at her. I wish my brain would work and I could place her. "I hope you have the appointment before me. Mine can go for quite a long time."

"Ah, I don't think so. His calling service called me and said a patient had an emergency. I had the choice of rescheduling for a different day, or waiting, and she warned it could be a long wait. I'm not worried; I brought a marvelous book, and the next two in the series." She gives me a beaming smile. "I confess I'm hiding. No one would dare bother me here."

"Oh, Kori-san. I'm so embarrassed. That patient is me."

"Oh! What is wrong? You seem fine!"

"I—I…"

My eyes start to sting.

Oh no!

"What's wrong?" She looks so concerned it almost takes my breath away. Yet another outstanding young woman, made possible by people like me selling their souls.

I stand up.

"You take your appointment back. I can't do this."

I turn to leave, but she latches onto my arm.

"But the service said it was an emergency! If you're unwell, you have to stay."

"I can't!"

Please, Kori, my new friend, just let me be, please.

"Why? I don't understand."

The panic hits me like a fist. My ears roar and the room actually darkens. I see spots in front of my eyes. I'm sitting back down, and realize she pulled me back to the couch.

"I can't! I feel so ashamed! I don't want to insult him, but I can't have him touch me, put things in me! It's as if I'm trapped! I feel so dirty!"

"Ashamed? Dirty? Why, surely you must have…"

She stops talking and actually turns pale.

"No! Tell me this isn't so!"

Oh no, this is too familiar. I'm in Hell. I'm in Hell.

"No! Not you! Not you! Anybody but you, anybody!"

I lower my head. I can't look at her. She really does know who I am and I've shattered her illusions. She was just being polite earlier.

Mommy I love you…

She grabs me. Her voice takes on a commanding quality, a demanding tone.

"Who did this to you? Tell me, who!"

I wail. She's now shaking me. Her strength is ferocious; I'm like a ragdoll in her hands.

"Who!? I must know! *Tell me now!*"

I lose it—really lose it. I latch onto her as if she's the only thing keeping me afloat in a sea of despair. I sob into her fancy dress.

"Oh Lexus-san, I'm sorry, I'm so sorry. Forgive me—forgive my awful temper. I'm sorry." She strokes my back. "Shhhhh—shhhhh—you can tell me later. Yes, later. You're safe with me. I will not let anybody harm you. Not anybody. You're safe now. Yes, safe with me."

Here I am crying yet again, embarrassing myself, this time in front of a stranger.

But she doesn't sound like a stranger.

Who is she?

A serene voice comes from the ceiling, the Doctor's office comp.

"Toulouse-san, the Doctor will see you now."

I tense.

Kori looks at me. "Stay here. I will go and speak to the Doctor on your behalf."

"No! You can't tell him!"

"Lexus-san! He's your gynecologist. He must know. But we will think of something. A drug, perhaps. Just stay here."

She goes into the examination room and I'm alone.

"Screw this," I say aloud. I get up and head briskly to the door.

Bonk.

The door doesn't open for me. I actually bang my nose.

"Ow!"

I sigh and fling myself onto the couch.

After an eternity, the examination room door opens and Kori the beautiful comes out.

"Lexus-san, I have talked to the Doctor. He understands your reluctance. So I will be doing your exam today and any corrective outpatient surgery."

My mouth opens, and then I close it.

"You?"

"I don't have a medical certification, but I did have four years of formal pre-med instruction. I can work most of his automated equipment. He can remotely walk me through everything except invasive surgery. You won't even have to hear his voice."

"I—I…"

I can't refuse. To do so would be a big insult to her. And to my doctor. I might as well jump out the window right now and save myself the shame and dishonor.

"Yes, Kori-san."

She holds out her hand.

* * *

I'm lying on my back and my feet are in stirrups. I have a beautiful woman not even half my age, who I have just met, putting her fingers up my twat and poking my augmented cervix, amongst other things.

No matter, because I'm high, high, high. I'm on some gooooood drugs, and I would know.

I admit it. I'm an occasional snorf user. I even, on occasion, use snorf plus—a little pill, expensive as shit, which you take after getting drunk. Once you take it, the pill starts a process in the bloodstream where it converts the alcohol into snorf. How cool is that?

It's very cool, and there is no hangover.

Whatever she gave me—and she just shot me up without asking—now I'm like all weeeee! *Way* better than snorf plus.

"Lexus-san, we're going to send a small bot up your vagina, past your cervix, and make adjustments to your Lib-Gee. You won't feel a thing. Okay?"

"Okay!"

She grins. We're in a sterile field, of course, she could sneeze on my eyes and I would not get sick. It's nice because I can see her pretty mouth with her perfect teeth.

Mmmmmm.

A very small little bot trailing an even smaller wire heads into my pookie. I know because I can turn my head and look at the telemetry on a monitor, which includes video.

It comes to my cervix, which is mostly cyber with organic connections to my flesh. It's not guarding a uterus, as I don't have one, but it's there to prevent things from going into my body that should not.

I envision the little bot knocking at a door, and barely suppress a giggle. The monitor is boring so I stare at the ceiling, which at least has a soothing mural. Soon melodic music fills my ears, and I drift.

—Knock, knock.—

—Who's there?—

—It's the plumber! I've come to fix the sink!—

I snicker.

—That's a terrible joke.—

—Sorry. Sleep now.—

—Okay.—

Blackness.

* * *

I wake up in a room I have not been in before. It's small and dim, one side of it is smart glass set to restrict light. I'm on a futon, thick and plush, and Kori is sitting in a chair off to one side, glued to her reader. Her hair is a mess; she looks like she was sleeping. She's wearing a simple robe. She notices I'm awake.

"How are you feeling?"

"A little fuzzy. I really gotta pee."

She points and I go freshen up.

I notice I am wearing a medical bracer so unobtrusive, I didn't notice it until now. I'm also wearing cute little undies with a cute little pad, which I guess makes sense as she stuffed all manner of things in me. I seem no worse for the wear, and I actually feel different. I'm not even sore. I'm hungry and must have been sleeping for quite some time.

I drink a lot of water, and I feel much better. Now that my system isn't being flooded with a bunch of random Lib-Gee crap, I feel fine. Good even. Clean inside: detoxified.

I come out of the head. For some reason, I feel embarrassed that I'm bald more than anything else, which is silly.

I still feel tired, though, so I lie down. Kori sits next to me.

"Lexus-san, the Doctor and I fixed all of your systems. The Lib-Gee we left at fifty-fifty, because it's broken. We calibrated it as much as possible and adjusted your thyroid too."

"Thank you, thank you. I feel a lot better."

"Unfortunately the calibration will last only a short while, two months at the most. You must schedule a replacement."

"Damn that EMP attack."

She cocks her head and is silent. I realize she's having a sub-vocal conversation with the Doctor.

"Lexus-san, your cybernetic systems are immune to EMP."

Ah—oh. I assumed since my contact lenses fried right up, that other parts of me did likewise. But they were civilian contact lenses. I'm a dork. No wonder nobody asked me what my cyber gear should be set at.

Yeah, doing snorf after the attack—not my best idea.

"Your Lib-Gee simply broke. It was the very first one. It's supposed to last a lifetime, but, well, don't take this the wrong way; you are not a normal person. It was always possible it could degrade, and it has now done so."

"I can't begin to tell you how much I appreciate all you've done for me, Kori. Thank you. Thank you. And thank you, Doctor." I know he's listening. "I love you both. I'm working on a very stressful case, and this health issue almost undid me. Thank you."

I'm getting tearful again, but in a good way. Now how about that.

She smiles and pats my hand.

"So, Lexus-san, we, um, need to talk about George."

George. Ugh. George is a male sex bot. A very good male sex bot. I have had my Lib-Gee re-calibrated before—something I have to do every few years. To see if the system works, I have to have sex (oh, if I must!), and then I need to be reexamined. One time, a few years ago, George had to fuck me three times before the doctor was satisfied with his adjustments.

And George is very, very good at fucking me.

But he's a male. The thought of it all makes me want to hurl anew.

"Uh, Kori-san, if I even *see* George I'm going to shoot him in the head with my needler, and possibly go on a murderous rampage that will continue well after my ammo is gone."

She smiles thinly.

She cocks her head. She looks like an elegant, curious cat, waiting for the right moment to make a move.

She stands up, and her robe falls to the floor. She's naked, painfully exquisite. I cannot help but stare because I have never seen anything so beautiful.

I shake my head to break my gaze. I sit up. "No, Kori-san, I could not impose on such a personal level."

"Shhhhh."

Did she just shush me? She sits next to me.

"Kori...

She puts a finger to my lips.

"Lexus, I have never been with a woman. But I can give you a quick orgasm. Just a little one, that's all the Doctor needs. Just promise not to post your experience. It will be our secret—our naughty little secret between you, me, and the honored Doctor."

I just nod.

She pushes me down, and unties my robe.

She proceeds to give me the best full-body massage I have ever gotten, and it's a little slice of heaven. She works her way down, pulls my panties off and then immediately reaches up to play with my breasts instead.

Oh.

Her hands tremble, and she looks, she looks *feral.*

She grabs all the pillows and props me up, and spreads my legs out while I'm sitting.

This is naughty. I feel very naughty. Each breath makes me tingle.

She's in front of me now, and looks me right in the eye. Then, all confidence and self-assurance, she licks her thumb wetly and rubs it over my clitoris.

It's too much, and I moan and squirm sharply. In response, her touch gets lighter and gentler.

I moan louder. I'm wet. She has bright, predatorily eyes, and she carefully slides two slender fingers inside me. She just leaves them there, and continues to stroke with her thumb, and I can see her do everything.

Oh.

Oh!

Yesssssssssss!

Then, somehow, she does it again, looking ravenous, using a much lighter touch. I have no idea how she made it happen so fast. The hungry look does something to me, makes me *want* her.

"Ah!"

And then again!

How many times can she make me come? I decided not find out, so I push her away, and then I pull her close and kiss her. She kisses me back, hard.

"Kori-san," I whisper, "do you…"

"Not now, Lexus. Not in this setting. Promise you will come to me later. Promise me."

"I promise."

"The Doctor says you are all fixed." She takes off my medical bracer.

"Yes. Yes, I am," I purr.

* * *

We're now in the room familiar to me, the exit room. We're both back to our impeccable selves.

I bow all the way down, and kiss her dainty feet. She laughs and picks me up and hugs me.

I hand her my card. "I owe a debt I can never repay. You're the nicest person I have ever met, Kori-san, and I have met many nice ones. If you need anything, anything at all, call me. I'm forever at your disposal."

She gives me a deep bow, a little deeper than her first, and hands me her card. I go to look at it in the traditional way, but she grabs my wrist, and I look at her.

"Lexus-san. I will take you up on your offer someday, I'm sure, but not because of all this. You and I were destined to meet. I don't believe in luck." She pulls me close.

"But I believe in you," she whispers, "I believe in you. And someday, you must tell me who needs killing for what he did to you." She kisses me for what seems like eternity, and then is gone before I know it, the elevator door closing.

I feel silly, flustered, and then silly again, but I bow low towards the Doctor's office—and, with a confident stride born of rest (of how long I don't know) and orgasms (three!), I leave.

Thor is waiting for me. I go up and give him a hug. He stiffens but then laughs, pats my shoulder, and shoves me in the car.

"Back to the landing pad, Lieutenant?"

"Uh."

Don't I sound smart. There is something I'm forgetting, though—oh, right—Bill!

"I need to go shopping!" My stomach growls. "And I need to eat!"

"Shopping for yourself or one of your Husbands?"

"Husband Four."

"I'll start driving and you can start telling me about your Husband. We can get him a nice gift. This is, after all, the shopping capital of the known universe for thoughtful gifts. First, let's get some food in you. Noodles?"

"Yakisoba, please! With chicken! And shrimp!"

Thor chuckles.

Then I remember the card. I look at it—it looks hand-written in delicate, beautiful script, and then brushed with a very thin laminate. On one side is a yellow flower with black outlines and background. The central disk has a front set of sixteen petals, and a rear set of sixteen petals are half staggered in relation to the front set, visible at the edges of the flower. Oh, a chrysanthemum! I think that means something in Japan. I flip the card over.

Kori Suiko
推古天皇 | *Suiko-tennō*
Empress of Japan
女性天皇 | *joseitennō*
Tokyo Imperial Palace
皇居 | *kōkyo*

I stare at the card for a long time.

I'm a dork.

* * *

—You're a dork.—

—Thank you, I know that!—

I had to tell Arune, of course. He would find out anyway. There are no secrets from your AI partner. None.

—No, this dorkage is epic in nature. Only you can obtain this sheer utter dorkiness. This is like the dork maneuver of the century. Bards will be singing your dorkitude for ages.—

—Shut up!—

—Let me see if I have this straight. So you were given a GYN exam, given outpatient surgery, and then finger fucked, three times, by the Empress of Japan, the *de facto* leader of the entire planet. Did I get that right? Be accurate, I'm writing this down for prosperity.—

—You forgot about the part where I stole her appointment, she shook me like a ragdoll, shot me up with outstanding drugs, and then I promised to call on her later so I could return the favor.—

—You just can't make this shit up. That's, that's, that's *awesome*. I can't even tell anyone this, because nobody will believe me.—

—Just so you know, we're never having sex again.—

—Why do you need sex from me when you can go to Japan and get fucked by your Japanese Empress luvah?—

—Who said I was the one that needed sex!?—

CHAPTER 22

"I GOT YOU A present."

Bill looks at the fancy wrapped box, and smiles. He's not a material man, my Bill, but he's fond of thoughtful gifts. He unwraps the paper to reveal a beautiful, hand-carved wooden box, and opens it.

Inside is a pen and calligraphy set. The fountain pens are old fashioned, and come with special ink. The paintbrushes are the best with minute carved *kanji* characters on them, and the paper is unique and hand manufactured.

Bill has impeccable, artistic handwriting.

"Oh Lex, this is beautiful. And very thoughtful. Thank you, thank you very much."

He wants to kiss me but doesn't, so I lightly kiss him instead, and I manage not to lose it. So far, so good.

Then I grab his balls through his jeans.

"Now what is my present?" I give them a tiny little squeeze.

He squeaks, and then laughs. "Down girl!" He pushes me away.

"You're a monumental tease. *You* have singled handily turned me from a spartan soldier to a woman who likes presents. You're the best; you're also the Devil incarnate."

He laughs. "Well, that's good because I have totally and completely outdone myself. Come," he says. I take his hand and he leads me to his bedroom.

For a moment, I think this is some ploy to get me in bed, and I tense. I push the thought away. Bill is better than that, and I feel guilty for even thinking such a thing. Boy am I paranoid now.

The door slides open and he guides me to his love seat with his view overlooking Mt. Si.

I sit and put my hands in my lap. He sits beside me, and after a moment's hesitation he puts a small case in my hands. It's an exquisitely artistic and feminine box carved out composite synth-wood. It's beautiful.

I open it.

Silver polished to an almost painful shine greets me. It's a flute, a sterling silver flute. It is striking and beautiful, almost like my old…

I catch my breath. It's just not any flute, it has my initials engraved on the mouthpiece. It's my old flute, from high school. The flute Mitchel gave me to replace my broken one—his grandmother's flute. A gesture so touching that I gave him my virtue the very next day.

I pick up the middle joint with shaky hands.

"How?" I whisper. The Seattle Firebombing should have melted it to slag.

Like my parents.

"You went off to war and your parents didn't tell you, but they were broke. Someone was looking for this specific model and they sold it to her on the condition that they could buy it back when the war was over."

The middle joint goes blurry and I realize I'm crying.

Bill rubs my back.

"Mitchel mentioned the flute one day, and I went looking for the same model a while ago. I finally crossed paths with the woman who was trying to find a living relative of the couple who sold her the flute. She didn't know their daughter's name."

Bill looks at me. "She says thank you for the use of your flute. She made lots of people happy with it over the years."

I clutch the middle joint to my chest and start to sob. Bill pulls me into an embrace.

"I miss my mommy," I whisper. "I miss her so, so much."

Mommy, Daddy, oh, how I miss you. I'm sorry. I'm sorry. I'm so, so sorry.

Bill takes me to bed. I clutch at him until I fall asleep.

* * *

In the middle of the night, I try my best to snuggle into him.

"Bill, I'm sick. My Lib-Gee is broke and I'll need another one," I whisper.

As a bonus, I've been raped, I mentally add. I try to say it out loud, but it won't come out.

"I know half of you doesn't want it," Bill whispers back.

The Federation, as we were calling ourselves, were experts at tanking the non-walking wounded. Our survival rate was extraordinary, even for grievous wounds, because trauma teams could be assembled in an organized fashion, the tank sent to just the right people to fix you up. Once fixed up, they put your blood back in and there you were.

The enemy figured this out and started shooting us with radioactive bullets. The medics can't tank a person shot with radioactive bullets, because they sit there and irradiate the tissue around them. Stay in there long enough, and the dose is lethal: if brought out of medical stasis, the patient dies.

Yes, they were evil fuckers.

I took many bullets to my middle, and they tanked me anyway, they had no choice. By the time the trauma surgeons got to me, bye-bye woman parts. Everything regenerated except those.

Hence, the Lib-Gee.

"You should check to see if regen can do reproductive systems now. It's been over twenty-five years."

I wrinkle my nose.

"I wish, but I doubt it." The person who invented tank regeneration, Dr. Sharon Hershel was a close friend of mine. We saved each other's asses in the war on numerous occasions. She was still working on improving the process when she died of old age ten years ago. I suspect she was trying to fix me, but she was an old, very war-weary lady. I'm not too sure she was all there at the end.

"I can look into it for you," Bill says, interrupting my thoughts. "Just check back with me before replacing your Lib-Gee."

"You bet, Husband Four," I say to humor him. He's a sweetie and the most romantic alpha ever to walk the Earth.

Then I feel like a total liar because I can't tell him. I just can't. I have to, but I can't.

I roll over and look out the window at the night sky until the sun comes up.

I get out of bed. I know I must conquer this fear, but I need time.

CHAPTER 23

I NEED TO GO back to Bacon, but the first order of business is my apprentices. And frankly, they are a monumental disappointment. Perhaps, collectively, they lower their IQ when they are together.

Scott is in my office, telling me how "clever" they are, how they found the landing page where I type in their names and make them Investigators.

"And all you do is put in your code, and there we go. As near as we can tell, this landing page is the only way one goes from an apprentice Investigator to a full-fledged one."

"Okay."

"So, what is the code?"

"You tell me, Mr. Scott."

"What do you mean?"

I roll my eyes. "Did you think it would be this easy? That's all there was to it? Well, there are several ways for you to get the code, and simply asking nicely isn't one of them."

Are they really as bad as this?

"Yeah, we thought of that."

I startle as hands of iron grip me and hold me tight in my chair. I can't see the hands, but I can certainly feel them.

"Ivan! Let go of me this instant!"

Now the armored hands flicker into view, wrapped around my unarmored arms.

"Nyet."

I glare at Scott. "Did you think you could coerce the code from me?

Are you two out of your minds?"

"Oh, we think we can get the code from you," says Scott grinning. The door opens, and Bambi comes in.

"Nancy, I need to know where the secondary accumulator…"

She stops when she sees the scene.

"What the hell is going on here?" she asks, and puts her hands on her hips. Good! At least I have one smart apprentice!

"She thinks we can't get the code from her."

Bambi looks dead at me. "That won't do. Tell us, Nancy, and things will go easier for you."

You've got to be kidding me.

"Go fuck yourselves, you stupids. This isn't how it's done."

"Yeah, we figured that. But we all have too much experience, minus Bambi here, to pussy-foot around."

He has a point, but this isn't how we do it.

Scott nods to Bambi.

She takes out a funny looking tool I don't recognize, somewhat like a wand.

"Sorry it came to this, Nancy, but I did ask, nicely."

She walks towards me, and I just can't believe this! I should sub-vocalize a call to County Safety but I'm frozen in place.

She points the tool at my desk, and presses a button on the handle. It bleeps and hums, and my locked drawer comes open.

"Stay out of there!"

"Oh, hello, what's this?"

She reaches in, and pulls out…

She pulls out my dildo.

"Goodness, Girlfriend, this thing is huge," she says.

"Uh, that's because its, uh, a model of my Husband Vash's penis he made for our tenth anniversary."

"Mmmm," says Bambi, she examines it, and then presses the switch. It starts vibrating.

"Put that down!"

"Oh, this is good." She rubs it across her chest. "But who the hell needs a dildo with four Husbands?"

"Bambi!"

She starts to molest my dildo, but I turn away.

"I believe, my friends, we need to take an alternate track," says Ivan.

Finally!

Bambi turns off the vibration, and hands it to Scott.

In a flash, he has his combat knife out with the dildo on the desk.

"Tell us the code, or Vash here gets it."

"No!"

"Code please."

I scrunch my eyes and turn away.

"One for the money," Scott says.

"Two for the show!" says Ivan.

"Three to get ready," says Bambi.

Scott chuckles evilly. "Four to…"

I open my eyes. "Oh, come on! Fine. I'll tell."

Ivan actually lets me go, but Scott sits poised to kill Vash's penis.

I'm very fond of that dildo, damn them! It's the only way I can orgasm outside of Husband Sex. Well, and Tiffany's and Kori's fingers.

I type in the code.

Bleep. Dr. Ivan, Investigator. Needler SN: TOUL002.

Bleep. Mr. Scott, Investigator. Needler SN: TOUL003.

Bleep. Ms. Bambi, Investigator. Needler SN: TOUL004.

"Congratulations," says Bob, "I have logged three new investigators to Toulouse Eastside Investigations."

Scott hands me Vash. I look him over, but he's no worse for the wear except for some slobber from Bambi.

"Yes, congratulations, Investigators," I say with a sneer.

And now, Bambi, I have decided, will pay the price for her insolence. At the comp, I select my way deep into the bowels of the agency declaration I made so long ago. Almost twenty-one years ago.

Agency Reconfiguration:

Bambi: 26%

Ivan: 25%

Scott: 25%

Lexus: 24%

Name change: Bambi & Associates

Agency Status: Full Service

Engage.

Associate Reconfiguration can't be changed for another year, and will result in majority of agency owner from Lexus (100%) to Bambi (26%). Please confirm.

Confirmed. Engage.

"Congratulations on your new majority stake, Investigator Bambi!" says Bob.

Bambi looks at me confused. "Wait—what?"

I flip the screen over.

"No! I don't know anything about running an agency. I've only been an Adult for three years! If you don't want it, have Scott do it!"

Scott laughs. "Don't look at me. You actually know more about formal Investigator culture than I do."

She turns to Ivan.

"Nyet, my little Bambi. As the agency's Coroner, I will be too busy to engage in administrative minutia."

"Fine, I will just change it back!"

"You can't," I say hoping I look as smug as I feel, "to prevent community destabilization, you can only change the ownership stake once a year. Unless, of course, one of us dies."

I grin.

"But—bu—"

"Lexus, I have an audio call from Investigator Walker."

Oh, this is too perfect. "Speaker it, Bob."

"Lexus!"

"Neal!"

"Am I reading this right? You've sold out to some new tart named 'Bambi' and now your new agency is full service?"

"Yup."

"Hot damn! I get a vacation! I don't know who this Bambi is, but I love her already! Gotta go, bye!"

Five, four, three, two…

"Bambi," announces Bob, "I have four referrals from Seattle for review."

"Referrals? I don't even know what that means!"

I stand up, taking Vash Jr. with me, and make my way to the door.

"Ma'am, I'm going to Bacon. I need to think. I want to take Scott, and I suggest you and Ivan stay here and work on your labs. Let's hold a daily scrum at, say 10:00 AM?"

She opens her mouth, and then closes it.

Ivan and Scott snicker. I leave, and I can *feel* her glaring at them as I go.

* * *

Wow that felt good. For the first time since Scott called me, I feel like I'm in control of my life. Part of my losing it, I realize, is I was out of my groove. But I'm back now.

Life doesn't run Lexus, Lexus runs life.

I say this to myself, repeatedly.

I ride my bike home, and get all sweaty again. I shower, and pull Bill into his bedroom.

"Can you write a letter for me, in fancy handwriting? It will be a bit long."

"Sure!" He sits at his desk. "Who is this letter to?"

"Kori Suiko."

"Ha! She has the same name as the Empress."

I look at him.

He looks at me.

"Oh." He shrugs, and I want to grin, but I can't.

"My Dearest Kori-san," I start. I speak slowly, and Bill's writing is beautiful. I tell her, without saying anything about Scott's psionics, how the ICDA accident occurred.

That I lost my identity and didn't know who I was, only that I was a mother and the girl was my daughter. How, because I was Uplinked, it was as real as if it actually happened to me. That I was raped under the influence of a simulated sex enhancer for half an hour, then got to watch Layla, a Child, barely a teen, raped for another half hour—how I knew what she was feeling.

The worst was the artificial hate for her for the attention she was getting because the simulation *made me want it that bad.*

That I watched her die, felt her hands bound to my wrists go slack, watched the life go out of her eyes, seeing her slump over, seeing her dead eyes, her terrible dead eyes.

That this fucked me up in ways I still don't understand. That I know I'm being stupid, but I feel so dirty, so ashamed. That I think of killing myself because I'm afraid of my own Husbands, afraid that they will hate me. That I'm very sorry I told her all of this in a letter, but I just can't say it out loud. That I love her and hope someday to see her soon, when I'm less broken, and I'm a real woman without a broken Lib-Gee.

I'm finished.

Bill puts down his pen.

The room is silent.

He turns to me, and he starts to cry.

"Oh Baby, I'm so, so sorry," he whispers. "I'm sorry I wasn't there for you." He holds out his arms for me, and I cry along with him as he holds me tightly. This time, I want to cry. I don't hate these tears.

Because, I'm home.

He pulls me to the bed and holds me, head tucked beneath his chin, breathing against his throat. Oh, it feels so good. He feels so good.

I sleep.

* * *

"Since the war ended, I have never had such a strong desire to kill somebody," Vash announces at dinner. He's a bundle of tension, and tension in Vash usually leads to people shot, run over, or blown up. Sometimes all three.

"Yup," Juan says.

I grab his hand over the table.

"I'll catch him," I say, "but it won't be me who deals with him."

Mitch looks confused. "What do you mean?"

"The Goddess of War is loose, and the blood price has already been paid. When she catches the bad guy, there will be revenge."

My words startle my family, especially Caz—but not Vash and Juan, who merely nod, understanding.

I look around the table at my men.

It is then I know it has to be Mitchel.

* * *

Mitch and the boys are playing poker. He's winning. Mitch has an excellent poker face, and it drives everyone nuts. How can someone so honest be so—blank—while playing cards?

It doesn't matter. I'm wearing a short, white, silk robe, which is my married woman signal for 'I want to make love.' I have put a synth-silk scarf on my head.

I stand behind Mitch, and he looks up to the rest who are looking past him. "What?"

He turns around, and I place a hand on his shoulder.

"I fold."

He picks me up, right off the floor, and I laugh.

* * *

He's in me and I'm not crying.

He's in me.

He is on top of me.

Mommy I love you…

Not now, Baby, Mommy is busy.

Okay. Can you tuck me in later?

Yes, of course.

"Oh, Mitch, oh, oh mmmmmmmm…"

* * *

I am back in the crèche and my father is standing in the tank with the woman's reproductive system floating by his feet.

"You're a nasty girl, Lexi, but I love you," he says as he picks up the parts and holds them out to me, viscera and blood and green goo dripping from his hands. "You don't deserve these, but it will make you feel better," he says and his face goes featureless blank, "But first," he says, sounding just like the killer, "you'll have to take off the scarf."

That's when the pink scarf around my neck starts choking me. I reach up to claw at it and then I am awake, my fingers at my throat.

Mommy I love you… Mommy…

I grab Mitchel, feeling as low as I have ever felt. He wakes up and I sob into his shoulder for the longest time.

Mitchel holds me, thinking I'm crying for me.

Oh how I wish I were.

CHAPTER 24

SCOTT AND I ARE tooling down Scenic Highway 2 over the Cascade Mountains. We'd leave Scott's brand new Investigator SUV (Ford E14 Mark 3) to drive to Bacon by itself, and just take the I-90 train ourselves, but the truck is packed with equipment of a very sensitive nature, so that would be a bad idea.

SH2 Corporation doesn't allow automatic trucks on their road, which is why we're driving on it. The cargo goes on the train, and the highway is for people in cars, unlike the I-90 and I-5 corporations' business model: for safety reasons due to the high speeds, those freeways are for drone equipment and empty auto cars only, and people take the train. Your car meets you at the train station.

I never understood why people call I-90 and I-5 a f*ree*way, when it is a toll road just like all the other major roadways. While I was studying for my Masters' cert, one of my fellow students conjectured that at one point, it was actually free to drive on—which seems strange, but after the Collapse records got sketchy and then when the Cyber War ate all the electronic records things got *really* sketchy.

Scenic Highway 2 is quaint and touristy, and Scott seems to relish driving his new ride on manual. We even have the windows down.

My eyes eventually wander away from the beautiful, temperate forest at either side of the mountain highway and settle on Scott. He's looking good. I get the feeling he was bored as a CEO.

"What?" says Scott, and I realize I've been staring.

I quickly look back at the road, my face heating up.

"You remind me of my dad," I say, and then wonder why the hell I said that, regardless of it being true.

He smiles at me but goes back to looking at the road.

"I hope that's good."

"Yes, of course. Daddy was the best. I mean it. I was the only child, and I was his baby girl. He thought I was the best thing in his life besides mom. I'm like him more than my mother liked to admit."

I realize I've now equated this to Scott and my face just *burns.*

"Anyway, he was inquisitive and didn't like to waste anybody's time," I hastily add.

"He sounds like a great guy."

"He was. Other than the part where he smacked Mitchel around for—son of a bitch!"

Scott hits the brakes.

Brittney is on the side of the road standing next to her armor trunk, wearing her summer MP outfit. She has her thumb out.

"Well my evening just started looking up," Scott says.

"Harrumph."

We pull on to the shoulder. Scott gets out and stacks Brittney's trunk and rucksack in back. They fit, but barely. I do not vacate my shotgun seat for Brittney.

"Hey, Britt," Scott says.

"Hey Scott."

I am quiet.

"Nancy."

"Brittney."

I cross my arms and look out the window.

"I do not appreciate what you said and did to Tiffany, Investigator," she says. "And getting Arune to remove her from my order segment…"

Brittney stops talking because in an eye blink I have my needler drawn and pointed at her head. She startles but then stays very still.

"Shut up and listen to me. If you ever consider fucking with an Investigator murder case again, I will fucking kill you. And this needler will slice right through the faceplate of your fancy Z armor. If you're lucky, I'll use that. If you're not, I'll use my knife."

I stare into her eyes. I stare into her eyes as the Goddess of War. A part of me thirsts for her blood. A part of me wants to pull the trigger and bathe in it.

She blanches.

"Yes, Nancy," she whispers.

Then she pees herself.

Scott sighs and pulls the SUV over again.

* * *

Scott is driving and I'm in the back seat with Brittney's head in my lap. I am stroking her hair.

"I'm sorry," I say. I am.

"No, I'm the one who's sorry."

"Still…"

"You two should sort out your post-war female dominance issues sub-vocally," Scott says from the driver's seat.

"Shut up!" I say.

"You're not a CEO anymore," Brittney huffs. *"Investigator."*

"That will make the sex so much naughtier," he says. I could swear I can hear his asshole man-grin from back here.

"Mr. Scott, you are a bad man," she says.

"You know it!"

Harrumph.

* * *

Bacon, Washington—the guide books will tell you—is a picturesque tourist town of over two thousand people who split their time working the wine business and serving tourists who tour the ancient Grand Coulee Dam and come back to Bacon for wine tasting. It's a beautiful town on a hill with two lakes at the bottom of it.

What the books won't mention is that when you look out at the ordered rows of grapes that roll out for miles around, you might as well be in France.

"Okay, not liking Bacon so much anymore," says Brittney.

"I'm with you there," says Scott.

"Let's find an inn without a view," I say.

* * *

We deposit our armor lockers at the Grant County Safety Bacon Branch (which sounds like a salad dressing) and make our way to a modern inn with an emphasis on serving the wine businessmen and women rather than the Seattleites who come here to drink and have romantic wine country sex.

"We'd like two rooms overlooking the pool, please," I tell the receptionist, a large woman who looks like she really enjoys drinking wine. She smiles warmly.

"Certainly, Investigators."

"Two?" asks Scott.

"One for you and Ms. Easy Money, and one for me."

"Hey!" Now it is Brittney's turn to fold her arms across her chest, which makes the athletic blonde look ridiculous. "That's awful presumptuous of you, Nancy."

"Yes," says Scott, sounding all prim and proper. "Perchance Brittney would like to sleep with you?"

I snort. "Like anyone wants to take me out for a spin for the first time with a broken Lib-Gee."

"Or," Scott offers, "You could both share my bed."

"We have a King sized bed just for that," the innkeeper says.

"Not helping," I say good-naturedly. I slide over the new Bambi & Associates credit chit and she hands us two keys after scanning it. Our PDAs all beep at the same time.

"I've sent you all both keys to each room. They connect. Keep in mind we sometimes get kids walking to and from the pool, so use the connecting door if yer nakkie."

She winks.

Harrumph.

I turn to them both. "Senior prerogative. I get my own room. Scott, I get to boss you around because I'm going to take the hit and talk to Mr. Gifford tonight, and Brittney here is a tag-a-long. Everyone's on their own for dinner. Don't forget about the scrum meeting at 10:00 AM."

Both Brittney and Scott stick out their tongues, although I catch, as we head to our rooms, Scott staring at Brittney's perfectly toned Military ass.

Men.

* * *

Mr. Gifford, I think, is cycling through the five stages of grief. He was happy to see me, but now he's asking questions he shouldn't be asking.

"Paul, I'm not going to answer any of these questions. Both for safety reasons, yours and mine—but also because I don't want anything getting in the way of my extracting the information I need to solve this case."

He looks at me.

"Okay," he says.

"We need to run the decryption program to its conclusion, no matter how long it takes."

"Okay," he says again.

At least he's learned not to argue with me. In general, arguing with a post-war woman is not a recommended course of action for a male. He is an alpha, though, and his Wife and daughter are dead.

But he can see it in my eyes, I think, and I can see it in his. If I don't find the killer, he will die, his body going the way of his dead heart.

I finish the call. I'm not too sure that would be a bad thing if it happened. Paul deserves vengeance and Justice, and if he can't have that, he at least deserves mercy.

Maybe that's the real reason he hired me.

He knows I'll do it if he asks.

* * *

I am sitting in the same chair Jeffery Vanderhouse sat in, but unfortunately, it brings no revelations other than that it's a place I also would sit to drink coffee and read a book.

I'm back in my green skirt and tan blouse with the vest, and I have the wig on beneath my ranger hat. I look mildly fashion-conscious and official in a feminine kind of way.

"Can I bring you something else to drink, Investigator?" asks the barista as she takes my sandwich plate and coffee mug. Her dress is slinky and black, although she'd need to eat a few more cookies every day to be my type.

My new type.

Bah!

"I'll take a beer please—something crisp and girly."

She smiles and heads off.

I sit there and go over the facts of the case, or, rather, the differences.

I can see in my mind the poor Israeli mother and daughter. I had met them previously, of course, as they were living in my area of operation. They were trying to talk themselves into joining the Net and the Union loved free converts more than anything else.

I sip my newly arrived beer and frown. I can't remember much else, of course, because I was there to do a job, and all the time not spent doing that job revolved around Landis and his sweet, sweet lovemaking.

Gah—here I am feeling sorry for myself. I hate that as much as I hate crying.

The first two victims, though, were nude.

And the next two were wearing lingerie.

Yet all indications I have the killer is the same person.

So why the difference?

I get out my PDA and make a few queries. Up pops an answer from my search agent:

Good Kitty/Bad Kitty Lingerie
Proceed 2 blocks west down Grand View, right on Well Lane NE
One mile to the old B&B we've repurposed!
We have all major brands and local made pieces
for that extra wine country flair!
(Come visit us in the morning, Lexus! Government servants receive
5% off our already fabulous prices!
We open at 9:00 AM tomorrow just for you!)

Now there's an idea. I can buy something slinky to make up for the fact it's going to take me a while to get back into the sack on a regular basis, and work the case at the same time. I can then have our short check-in meeting and then go to County Safety to suit up for a day's work.

I need to remember, however, not to let Arune know his lingerie-shopping spree put ideas in my head. That male already has an overblown ego.

* * *

After turning on the virtual fence, I snap off my NI watch and snuggle under the softer than soft sheets in my hotel room. I'm tired but I'm not ready to sleep, so I look out of the window through the sheers, and think about my personal life.

"Bob—connect Arune."

"Oh, blessing me with your sexy voice," Arune says.

"Just checking in. How goes Pilot training and acclimation?"

"I forgot how tedious this is for an AI. Tiffany, however, thinks this is all rather awesome."

I grin. It is fun, in a terrifying difficult way.

"Thanks for checking in. Love it when you stick to protocol. We'll be up there tomorrow afternoon to practice CAS shadowing. Not really comfortable with you on this case, but I hear Brittney is there to lend some support."

"Harrumph."

"Not my idea."

"Roger that. Be nice to Tiff. Love you. Lexus, out."

"Love you, too. Arune, out."

Taking an AI lover isn't the smartest thing in the world, but Arune is good for me. I love my Husbands more than an old soldier likes to admit, but none of them can Uplink with me. I need it, and I wonder how I could have gone so long without it.

I stretch like a cat and try not to think of manly Scott and sensual Brittney getting it on. I want to be angry with Scott for bouncing back so quickly from his simulated abuse, but I know that's unfair. Despite my attempts to guilt him into therapy, the fact is that he's a man, and he suffered the abuse as a woman. Closing your eyes and feeling yourself violated in a body that doesn't feel like your own is significantly less stressful. Psychologically painful, I'm sure, but he can only relate to memories of a female body so much. It wasn't nearly as personal for him. Unfortunately, being a woman myself, I get none of the benefits of that kind of dysmorphia.

Arune opened the door for me in that regard, and Mitch was the one to grab my hand, but I'm laying here alone and I love the solitude, knowing that no one will make any demands of me. Touch me. Put things in me.

I'm fucked up, I admit to myself.

"You have a conference call request," Bob says as I start drifting.

I sit up to try to clear my head.

"Who's calling?"

"Your Husband Bill, Dr. Takayasu and a Dr. Kaitlin Hershel."

I grunt. My Husband, my GYN and the daughter of my best friend who died ten years ago.

I don't know if I can face Hershel right now. Long ago, Sharon, the surgeon who repeatedly fixed me in the war, had some of her eggs removed, as did all women soldiers. After the war, she was too old to have children, but she took an egg out of stasis, had it fertilized and planted in a birth donor, who gave birth to her daughter.

And all without telling me—I only found out when Sharon died ten years later and I held the ten-year-old in a lovely black dress that cried and cried on me. My thoughts were full of unbearable grief and anger that Sharon never told me about her daughter. But I suspect the war drove Sharon mad, and, in the end, how can I fault a mother who didn't want her child around a vengeful soldier and professional dealer in death?

When her host mother extracted her from my arms, the look of longing and sadness Kaitlin gave me almost drove me to ruin. I discreetly asked about adopting her, but her Guardian in so many words told me to go fuck myself.

That was my major post-war social failure, and a painful reminder that my own set-aside eggs are ashes in Seattle along with my parents.

"Lexus?"

"Sorry Bob, one moment."

I head to the closet and put on a robe. I go to the desk and sit in the chair after turning it to face the little lounge area.

"Connect."

Three life-size holograms appear in high-res. Dr. Takayasu looks his healthy, studious older Japanese gentleman self. Bill is wearing casual clothing and I think he's actually lost some weight, but I only briefly take them in to look at Kaitlin.

That distraught ten-year-old is now a stunning, tall and slender blonde barely out of her teens. As I look at her tag, it expands to show her certs. She has advanced certification in human regeneration and a full surgical medical cert from Harvard Medical School.

And she's only twenty. Impressive. She looks at me without a hint of anger or accusation. In fact, she looks happy to see me, her blue eyes warm and inviting.

"Sensei. Doctor. Bill." I can see where this is going and I don't want to have this conversation now, but I can be polite. "What do I owe this pleasure?"

"Lexus-san." Dr. Takayasu speaks first. "I received three calls about your health. Your Husband, the Empress and Arune."

I purse my lips. Okay, *that's* funny.

"Hershel-sensei believes she can regenerate your reproductive system. It will take some time, but her Medical Action Plan is valid."

The young Kaitlin nods. "I picked up where my mother left off, and I now believe we can take out your cyber-gear and sync your mil-grade nano-regulator to the regen sequence. It'll give you back everything but your eggs—your thyroid, cervix, uterus, even your ovaries."

"Wow!" That is amazing. But…

"Lex, you don't need to go into menopause just yet," Bill says.

I sigh. Regen is expensive as hell and slows down the aging process. It can even back you up a bit—make a person younger. I am sure the procedure they are talking about will cost millions of credits.

I'm not worth it. I may have cheated menopause for now, but that won't last much longer. Five years, ten at the most.

Kaitlin sees something in my eyes. "Let me be clear: I have not proved this technique. It will use much of Mr. Toulouse's money, and there is still a chance that it will not work, necessitating a new Lib-Gee or menopause anyway."

She gives me a haughty look, just like her mother used to give me when we were arguing. "But I think we should try. You have nothing to lose except credits and six months."

I sigh. I am, actually, in no mood to argue. I don't like the idea of leaving broken equipment inside me, and besides, my Husbands aren't going to complain about my having a younger woman's sex drive. If someone gets to enjoy it, I'll chalk that up to a win. After all, I used it mercilessly in the war to keep my platoon in shape and in line.

And having sex with Mitch proves that I can get over what happened to me.

"Alright. Are there any major side effects?"

"No, only the normal ones for massive regen. You'll look younger."

I sigh again. "I'm on a case. When I solve the case, sure. Why not?"

"That will be fine, I still need to tick-and-tie the MAP to my research," she says.

Everyone looks relieved they don't have to argue with me.

"Can I talk to Dr. Hershel privately, please?"

Both men say their good-byes and drop from the call.

And all at once I crumple and begin to cry.

Fuck. Fuck—just, fuck!

"Oh, oh, don't cry, don't cry, it will be okay." She looks distraught.

"I'm sorry. I'm an emotional wreck. I'm sorry I didn't try to contact you, but I didn't even know you Declared yourself an Adult."

"It's okay, Lexus." Her voice sounds young, but her words and demeanor are mature. Oh, she's just like her mom!

"No, it's not. I loved your mother, I really did. When she died, I even tried to adopt you."

She looks taken aback.

"You did?"

"I did. Your Guardian told me no and that it would be a good idea if I didn't contact you again."

She lowers her head. "Olivia was a harsh woman, but she was also very protective of me. I am sorry. I don't know why my mom didn't tell you about me. Maybe it was guilt. Her eggs were stored in Australia, not Seattle."

I nod and wipe my eyes. Not stored in Seattle.

Like mine.

"Holographic hug?" says Kaitlin.

I laugh and we do.

My face is right next to hers. I have a stupid desire to kiss her and I am glad she is only a hologram because *that* is fucked up.

"Are you as smart as your mom was?"

"Smarter," she says, with a twinkle in her eye.

CHAPTER 25

GOOD KITTY-BAD KITTY Lingerie turns out to be an old-fashioned farmhouse on about ten acres, in the middle of a beautiful garden of vegetables and flowers. Not exactly what I was expecting. I look at the house and my PDA sends information to my watch, which makes tags pop up in my vision. I already like my watch much better than standard Investigator contact lenses, which is what my PDA talked to before I took the watch out of the locker. Not only are the tags in higher definition, they don't have that odd lag contact lenses do that only someone with a neural lattice can detect.

One of tags tells me this used to be a bordello. Heh! The historian in me perks right up.

I am at the door right at 9:00AM and, true to the agent's message, it opens as I approach. Greeting me is a pretty woman of dark brown hair wearing a corset, black lacy panties, lacy stockings and a garter belt. "Lexus Toulouse! I am so glad you followed my return agent! My name is Ms. Kitty!" she says, in a bubbly voice. She holds out her hand and we shake.

I grin. Bad Kitty indeed.

"The optic scanner says 36D-24-36—enticing brown eyes, a great complexion, an athletic build, and your breasts are epic. Lady, you've got a body!"

"Thank you." I look around. As her agent said, she has all the major brands.

"Oh, one of your tags says you have a double Masters in history. Let me give you the tour, this is a pre-Cyber War house," Kitty says.

"Wow! Please do. I would love to see some pre-Cyber War printed paperwork, if you have any."

"It's pretty boring, but we do have some, which is more than a lot of other old networked houses can say."

I get the grand tour. Upstairs there is a sewing shop. Several mannequins stand around showing off some really elegant, yet naughty, stuff.

"This is really good," I say, stopping at a silk blue body suit. This one is long, like a gown, but with a slit up each leg to the hip. And it has a hood, which would go well with my bald head.

She smiles at my interest. "My son made that and it's not a printer pattern, either. I told him the likelihood of a tall woman with real curves coming in here was low, but shows you what I know."

I look around for the son in question.

"He's eighteen, but don't worry, he's in Alaska with his dad on a hunting trip."

I give her a smile. She doesn't look old enough to have a hunting son, much less one that is eighteen.

She sees my look. "Hubby knocked me up when I lied to him and told him I Declared. It was quite the scandal—in fact, that's where Bad Kitty came from," she says with a sly look. "Strip to your panties, Investigator, including the wig. I know the price tag is outrageous, but *it* is an original."

I put my knife, PDA and needler with its holster on a table and strip, although I leave on my NI watch. I turn, naked, and catch an appreciative glance. She doesn't even pretend to be demure.

"Damn, Investigator, your legs go on forever. Totally jealous."

I put on the silk one piece. It pushes my breasts out, flashes my butt, and highlights the long legs in question. And I love the hood. Frankly, I am amazed I feel sexy again. I thought I never would, and I can feel the goofy grin on my face.

"Yummy!" she says. "Your man will love it. Say you'll buy it so I'm not compelled to start dickering."

I laugh. "Men, and I am so buying this, but let's haggle any…"

—Lexus! Vampire! Vampire! Vampire!—

The Active Thought from Arune is sudden, but I have my needler in hand in a heartbeat.

I turn to Kitty. "Get out! Run!"

She looks frightened and confused. "What..."

I raise my needler to the roof. A Targeting HUD fills my vision and I see the missile streaking through the sky in holographic detail.

"No time," I scream as I aim the needler, pull the trigger, and leave it down. The supersonic crack-crack-crack fills the air and turns into a scream of compressed air, shots slicing through the ceiling and roof of the house. "Get out! Get out! Get out!" I scream.

In my peripheral vision, I see her turn and run, but my thoughts narrow at the HUD in my eyes.

A normal person would think trying to shoot down a missile with a sidearm is impossible.

But I am not a normal person. The satellites that Arune and I turned on detected the launch and Arune, with his AI like mental reflexes, sent me a warning. My PDA uploaded the telemetry to my neural watch and the combat heads-up-display gives me the target.

The wood and composite building material is no match for the needles, and needle after needle shrieks to the missile. In flight, they relay course corrections to each other based on the telemetry, and I only have to make the slightest adjustment to my aim.

In mere seconds, a cloud of nano bullets fills the air in front of the missile and when they meet, the missile explodes quite spectacularly.

Ka-boom! The shockwave drives me to my knees, but the house is still intact.

And in my HUD, I see pieces of the missile go everywhere, the largest falling towards the house at great speed.

Ah, man, that's going to

CHAPTER 26

SOFT TOWELS START REMOVING the goo. Well, crap, so much for postponing regeneration until after my case. I sigh.

The bench folds and sits me up, and someone is drying my hair. I am in a tank room. The sign on the door says "Evergreen Hospital Max Security Tank Room J-4."

Oh hey, I have hair!

Now I can see hands, faces. Dr. Takayasu, Kaitlin, and Bill. The lights come up, slowly, but stop at dim, and for that, I'm thankful. Without asking, I wiggle my toes and fingers. Then I wiggle my hands in front of my face.

Wait a sec. I bring my hands closer. They are small and dainty, girl-ish, without a single blemish. These are not my hands. These are a young woman's hands. Like, really young.

"What the fuck?" My voice is pitched higher than I remember it, too.

Dr. Takayasu and Bill stop wiping me off and pause. Dr. Takayasu looks at Bill.

Bill looks at Dr. Takayasu.

Dr. Takayasu looks at Kaitlin.

Kaitlin looks at Bill.

"Enough!" I screech. "Spill! Now!"

"Uh, Lex, there was, well, I'm just gonna come out and say it," says Bill. "You've come out younger. Really young."

"How young?"

"Young."

"Age!"

"Well the good news is you have your reproductive system back," says Kaitlin.

"Age!"

"Seventeen?" she says. Hesitantly.

No!

"Take me to the mirror in the bathroom."

"Lex…"

"Now!"

They help me stand. I can barely walk. I have strength, but my coordination is off. The simple act of putting one foot in front of the other makes me want to fall on my face.

Soon I'm in the bathroom.

I look in the mirror.

I am fifty-three years old.

Thanks to the wartime regen sessions and the Lib-Gee, I got to wear those fifty-three years well. The forty-five year old body I had before was muscular, fit and strong, but I had the lines, the thinner lips, the cheekbones, the *maturity* that any forty-five year old would have.

Now, staring at me in the mirror, with quite the surprised expression on her face, is a teenager.

A fucking teenager!

I'm seventeen! Maybe!

I flip my wrists over. My neural implants are still there, at least.

"How?" I squeak out. Literally.

"The damage to you was extensive. We decided to go for the full regen according to your wishes. There were several problems and we had to start over," Kaitlin says.

I'm furious. I feel elated that I'm alive. I want to choke them all. I have my woman parts back. But this is stupid!

"It was the only way. When we saw what was happening it was too late," said Dr. Takayasu.

"No! I'm not just young. This is barely my face! I didn't look like this! Sound like this! This isn't my body when I was seventeen! I'm *short!*"

Kaitlin shakes her head. "Massive regeneration doesn't literally turn back time. It's really a re-sequence. You reverted back to when your brain stopped growing. Nobody has gone that far, but if she did, the chance she would look like a sister instead of herself is certainly plausible. I am sorry, Lexus, I know you're mad, but you must understand we tried to follow your wishes the best we could. The damage was extensive. We could not wake you up and ask. You had no vocal cords. Or fingers."

I wince. Fuck. I sit still and try my best to calm down, taking a deep breath and letting it out slowly.

"Sorry. I was never fond of being younger than my Husbands as it was, and this is extremely sudden."

I pause, and give myself a little shake. "Ms. Kitty?"

"She is fine. Arune took her someplace, where he is not saying," says Bill.

I look at all three. "I want to give you all a hug. Then I want Bill to take me home." I pause and look both of the doctors in the eye. "Please do not take this as ingratitude, but I want to go home, and I want to be with my family."

The doctors nod. I give them a hug, and somehow manage not to cry nor kill them with my bare little girl hands.

But I came close to both.

* * *

I am outside waiting for Bill's sedan to pull up. My clothes didn't fit. I'm wearing a borrowed dress, and I'm fucking cold because even my fucking undies didn't fit and it's fucking January.

Literally, beneath Bill's coat I'm wearing only the dress and my combat knife on my thigh, and even the five-minute wait for the car to pull up had me shivering. If it was not for the coat, I'm sure I would've turned blue. Bill looks horribly embarrassed that he didn't realize I would not be able to wear my old clothing they brought for me. He also looks like he has aged a couple of years.

My needler is in a locked case, because the belt for my holster doesn't attach over the dress. I'm barefoot. My shoes didn't fit. I'm fucking *skinny*. I've gone from a curvy, muscular woman proud of her strong body to a lithe and immature teenage girl. I have traded half my muscle mass for a petite frame and gravity defying boobs. I'm not even tall any more.

* * *

In the car, I pull out my Investigator PDA and activate it.

"Bio-key error," it says. "Unauthorized use of Investigator technology is prohibited by Constitutional protocol. Bambi & Associate notified of your attempt at using this PDA."

"Oh, for fuck's sake!"

I glance at Bill, and he looks guilty again.

"Bill, stop it. I'm just being my ornery self. I am happy to be alive."

Mostly.

"I'm happy too," he says. Then he starts crying.

Oh, for fuck's *sake!*

He puts the car on auto, and I give him a hug. For me no time has passed, and all I endured was a few seconds of foreboding blackness before they pulled me out of the tank. But for him, his Wife was hurt—badly—and he had to stand by all that time waiting and hoping that I would be safe. He holds me as if he never wants to let me go.

* * *

It's raining, of course, and as we pull into the driveway, I tell Bill to stop the car. He does as he's told and looks at me.

"I need to feel *something.* I need air," I say and get out and walk to the house.

I feel something all right—wet and cold. But it's better than that different feeling. It is as if I can feel my blood flowing through my veins.

I get to the house and use the front hose to clean off my feet. I head into the open garage to the door there, I'm not sure the front door is going to open for me. I enter the mudroom, and my borrowed cotton dress is soaked.

Percy, our dog, barks at me none too kindly. In rushes Maggie, the other dog. They growl.

I raise my hand. "Bad dogs! Bad! Now get!" I take a step towards them.

They run.

I emerge from the mudroom and there is the Toulouse family

household.

"Welcome home, Lexus," Cazandra says and then she bursts into hysterical sobs and latches onto me. Now I'm not feeling sorry for myself. I work at calming her down. Mitch looks guarded, Vash and Juan are grinning like idiots, and Bill still looks guilty.

I suck.

* * *

We're in the living room. Everyone wants to know what happened and how do I feel and if I am okay and blah, blah, blah.

But they are not listening to my answers. They are just staring at me and my wet dress plastered to my nubile (damn it!) body.

I stand up.

"Okay, obviously, I need to take a different track. I'm going to start by kicking all your asses. Mitch, you're first, because, because—Mitchel Jameson Toulouse! Look at my eyes when I'm talking to you! Not my breasts!"

He *blushes.* "Sorry, Lexus. I'm just kind of, um, I mean, you're really young. Kind of too young, almost, except that I know you and I love you so I'm not too weirded out or anything, and, just, well, I'll just come out and say it. You were never that hot. And now you're just smoking."

Bill lets out a long breath as if he's relieved he doesn't have to admit it first. "Goddamn, Lex, you're just freakin' smoldering, like high-clique love bunny smoldering."

"I am *not* a bunny!"

"She's not *that* attractive," Vash says.

What? I turn to him. It's not my body but I do have to admit, it's a sexy number. Lots of potential. "Hey now."

"You look so *young*, and your bubble bootie and Earth mama breasts are gone," Juan says, sadly.

"Hey! I had curves, damn it, not a bubble butt! And my breasts were just fine. My bra size hadn't changed in nineteen years!"

Vash looks depressed. "And now look at you; you don't need a bra at all."

"I—you—but—ahhhhh!"

I'm going to just fucking lose it with these males.

"I'm going to bed," I say. I stomp up the stairs, pissed that now when I stomp, I come off as a teenage drama queen instead of a righteously pissed woman. I was never a drama queen.

I take a superhot shower and climb into bed.

"Fuck this shit," I whisper to nobody in particular.

* * *

Dr. Takayasu comes to examine me first thing in the morning. He's made a house call. I appreciate it, but I also feel honored by it to the point of nervousness. There are many people I don't care about fucking with, but Dr. Takayasu is not one of them, and I feel like I am imposing on him. Nonetheless he is careful, caring—his bedside manner goes above and beyond. I have never felt in better hands; never safer.

Finally, he is done, and removes the medical bracers from my arms.

"Well, you are in perfect health."

I just stare at him.

"This is hard for you."

Emotions I have never felt before crash into me. I have a desire to hug him, or else to run screaming from the room—which, I do not know.

I stare at him some more—really look.

He is not a tall man. He has small hands, which believe me I appreciate in a gynecologist. His almond-shaped eyes are dark but expressive, and his wrinkles make him look distinguished. His hair is mostly grey by now, although there are still some streaks of black. He has finally put on some weight and it looks good on him. He's always been too thin. I've known him for over twenty years now, and, I realize as I stare at his handsome, worn face that I love him more than I can say.

"Sensei?"

"Yes, Lexus-san?"

"May I call you Papa?"

Of all the things he might have expected me to say, that was clearly not one of them.

"Of course," he says roughly, as if choking back tears. "I would be honored. I know I can never replace your real papa, but I know what you mean."

"I don't want to live forever, Papa-san," I whisper. "I've done horrible things, things I should die for and go to Hell."

There. I've said it. Now maybe it will come true.

He crushes me in a hug, his strength surprising for someone as old as he is. "Yet, my daughter, now you've been given a chance to atone for your sins." He pulls back, lifts my chin up with his hand, and wipes away a tear. "It is pure hubris to think the important parts of your life are done. Look at me; I'm an old man. Yet I learn so many new things every year, which I pass on to my patients. Perhaps next year I do something even better."

I look at him, and feel a burning love that's almost unbearable. "Papa-san, you're right, but I don't feel sorry for myself. I just wonder if I'm human, even though now I'm more human than I have ever been. I can do things, intense things, that other people can't. Go places too bad for others to go."

He laughs, not sharing my horror at my confessions in the slightest. "It could be you're the most human of us all!" He kisses my forehead, just like that. I get the impression that I could keep berating myself for what I do and what I have done in front of him, and he will never see the same horror in my actions that I do. I don't understand his kind optimism, but I want to hold on to it.

He interrupts my thoughts with a serious tone. "But, there is something delicate we must talk about at once, although I am loath to do so."

"What?"

"You're a virgin—that is, a *physical* virgin."

Gah!

"No!"

"It's so," He chuckles.

"Papa-san, what could possibly be so funny about that!"

"Lexus-san, as my honored Daughter, you're now part-Japanese. I'm thinking now you should be careful. Especially after the war, in Japan, virginity means something."

"Of course it means something! Don't go all nationalistic on me! It means something in lots of places!"

At that, he laughs a great big, rare Japanese belly laugh. "Yes, but in Japan, one has to over-analyze and ritualize the deflowering of the young virgin woman. Girl. Girl-woman."

I guess he's got a point; the Japanese never pass up an opportunity to ritualize and over-analyze. I don't exactly have the time to consider what that entails, though. I'm still reeling from the news, and I'm emotional on top of that. These are conversations that had to be begun now and finished later; we both know that.

He pats me on the head as if I'm a child and says "Good luck!" to me as I leave.

Damn it!

CHAPTER 27

AFTER SEEING PAPA INTO the guest room (I informed everyone that I considered him my Papa and Papa was *not* going to sleep in a hotel), I retreat to my bedroom. My Husbands are giving me space and I both appreciate it and resent it. What if they are giving me space because I am so different? It doesn't help that Mitch looks at me with lusty eyes and then looks like he thinks he is a pervert. I'm not *really* seventeen, damn it!

I know what I need to do. I need to fuck Bill and Mitch and get it out there for all three of us.

But I don't feel sexy—at all. I've spent the hours reviewing the case data and ignoring my p-mail.

Nothing. Not a damn thing. For six months. The decryption program is running, but not a single clue has come forth. Nobody knows who tried to kill me. The missile was a pre-war missile, of all things, which isn't surprising because after the Collapse people liked to hide their major weaponry and the stupid things turn up all the time, even after all these years. Someone launched it remotely from the middle of nowhere, moved there by drone equipment nowhere to be found.

I send an email to Paul Gifford:

Paul, I'm back. This case is my only priority. That someone tried to kill a potential witness along with me tells me that we're getting close. Hang on.

Yours,

Investigator Lexus Toulouse

Bambi & Associates

* * *

Dinner is better. It's not awkward silence, and the sex-bot Cazandra has finally stopped bursting into tears and latching onto me as if I would die at any moment.

And in the middle of dinner, I have an abrupt revelation.

I am horny as hell. It's as if I can feel my crotch buzzing.

Fuck! My body is at war with my mental state, and I think the teenage hormones are going to win.

* * *

I meet Bill at the top of the stairs. I place my hands behind my back, lean on the wall, and give him my best coy look. He looks wary.

"Will you still kiss me, even if I look…"

Bill takes a hold of my shoulders, pulls me close and kisses me with such passion I whimper, actually whimper, and melt into him. I am a short little thing, but I am woman enough to melt into him, and I feel his hardness. He is hard. *Really* hard. Like, when we first met hard.

Okay, little new body of mine, I take back half the mean thoughts I was thinking about you.

I pull Bill into his bedroom and he pushes me to the bed, looks apprehensive for being a little rough but then sees the smile on my face. He climbs on top of me and starts to kiss my neck.

Oh, man. Oh, man. Oh man oh man oh man!

"Bill…"

"Mmmmm?" He's still kissing my neck. It's like little zaps. Kiss, zap, kiss, zap!

"I'm a virgin."

"Riiiiight! You don't have a virgin part—oh shit." He gets off me.

"What?" My eyes flick to his crotch. The young-Bill bulge in his pants gets smaller. No!

"Ah, thanks for telling me. And no."

"What?"

"No. I have deflowered a total of three women in my life, and each relationship ended badly."

"I'm not any woman, I'm your Wife!"

"In a new body."

"But I'm your Lex. The woman you made love to all weekend when we first met. Or did you forget?"

"I'll be dead and reincarnated twice and still remember. Ha. But I can't do it. We're talking cursed. I swore a blood oath I would never do that again."

Shit. "It's not a big deal!"

"If it's not a big deal, why did you tell me?"

"I, uh, well—damn it!"

"All right then. Mitch got to you the first time, I'm sure he will, uh, rise to the occasion if you ask."

"I don't think so," I say, and then pout.

"Ack! Don't pout like that. That's bad. Stop. Why not?"

"Well, I was fifteen. And it was good. Not great, of course, but good. We went out for ice cream afterwards, and, and..."

"And?"

"It didn't hurt, so I didn't know I was still bleeding! I caused a scene at the ice cream shop in front of our friends. They took me to the emergency room. Father came and beat up Mitch."

"Heh." Now Bill is grinning.

"It's not funny!"

"No, it's kind of a window into our fucked-up pre-war society. I think you should ask anyway."

"What if he says no? And technically, we're *married.* Your blood oath shouldn't count!"

"Then I will step up, and get over my fears. But only after, um, two weeks."

"Two weeks! I can't wait that long! This is the house of horny people! The sex floats in the air around here!"

"If you can't wait two weeks, then have Caz do it. I'm sure she would be happy about that. I'm serious about that suggestion too; you might as well avail yourself of her services."

"You know what? You would think after the war, men would be easier to understand!"

"You got to be kidding me. You think this is bad, try figuring out a woman. Now scoot. I have work to do." He pushes me off the bed and out the door, and smacks me on my butt none too kindly.

"Ow!"

The door closes.

Men!

* * *

"No." Mitch, who is usually so understanding, looks put out that I would even ask.

"I know, sweetie, I just thought I would offer."

Because, you know, I'm getting horny. It's worse than my Lib-Gee, actually worse.

"I appreciate you asking, but the thought of it makes me too nervous to even get it up in the first place, if I'm honest with you."

Indeed, he looks somewhat pale.

"You should ask Bill…"

"No."

Mitch gives me a look, but doesn't ask. He respects Bill's privacy too much.

"Okay, Cazandra, then."

* * *

"You've been staring at that—thing—so hard you didn't even hear me come in."

I startle. Literally, I almost bolt from my bed, heart pounding and ears ringing.

"Oh, sorry!"

"No, Caz, not your fault. I hardly ever tune out." Outside of sex, that is. I have been sitting on my bed staring at my Vash dildo on the bedroom dresser.

"Well, do you want me to fuck you with it?"

"Okay."

"Oh, wow, wow, yeah!" She closes the door, grabs the dildo, and practically jumps on me.

She pushes me down to the bed, her strength surprising. She starts kissing me, and I kiss her back. Soon, she starts kissing a trail down my neck, and stops at my breasts.

Oh, my! She's a bot, but she is a perfect feminine creature, and having a woman lick my breasts causes me to squirm.

"Mmmm," Caz says as her tongue worships my left nipple. She starts sucking.

"Caz?"

"Hmmmm?"

I gasp as she sucks harder. "I need to tell you the regen made me a virgin again."

She stops and sits up, as if I am on fire and she is afraid she will burn. "Oh. Wow."

"That's okay with you, right?"

"No, it's not." She frowns and her eyes looked pained.

Mother *fucker!* "But why?"

"I don't think it would be good for my mental health if I took your newly gifted virginity."

"But, but…"

I force my mind to slow down and shut up. I remember reading her user manual. When this particular model says "my mental health," she's talking about circumstances that she probably would not be able to parse, and she might even end up needing post-processing from the manufacturer. It could even include an erasure of the time-period from her holographic memory, which I think would be cruel.

Damn it!

"Oh, don't look so sad! I'm sorry. Maybe I can…"

"No Caz. The thought of causing you problems has pushed every ounce of desire I had for you at this moment out of my body."

"But only for this moment?"

"Yes."

"Good. Why can't Mitch or Bill…"

"Because they are stupid males! I'm an Investigator and a vet; I'm not some delicate freshly declared Adult!"

"But you *look* like a young lady."

"Bah! They should know better!"

"What about Vash and…"

"It's not that hole they want to deflower!"

Caz giggles and then looks at me. "Oh, sorry. But really, Bill and Mitch said no? I'm having trouble processing that."

"Well, Bill said let's wait two weeks."

Caz pauses and looks like she's thinking. I can imagine little gears spinning in her head.

"Why did Mitch say no?"

So I tell her the entire embarrassing story again. Unlike Bill, she just tilts her head and looks like she didn't understand why I was embarrassed.

"Okay, here's a suggestion. Since your GYN is here until tomorrow, talk to him about that bleeding. I'm sure he can prevent most of it, do some medical procedure that will not make it as bad. Assuming your new body will act that way. Then talk to Mitch again. He might still say no, but he will appreciate the gesture greatly. And that's important too."

My mind whirls. It whirls and whirls and the room almost seems as if it's spinning.

Especially after the war, in Japan, virginity means something.

Oh. What a strange life I lead.

"Caz, can you sleep with me tonight? Please, I want you in my bed."

In reply, she starts to cry again, beside her little bot self with happiness.

* * *

I flip through my p-mail, and, as expected, I come to a letter from Japan. I open the plain business envelope and inside is an exquisite letter envelope smelling slightly of jasmine.

I sit and stare at it. Maybe she hates me. Maybe I scared her off. Maybe she thinks I'm crazy and her advisors told her to send me a Dear Jane letter. Maybe, maybe, ah hell, open the damn thing, Lexus!

I break the chrysanthemum wax seal and take out the delicate paper with the pretty handwriting.

My Brave Lexus, My Darling,

Such a strong person to reveal your true self, your soul, and it means more to me than you know that you trusted me with your tale of heartache. For my heart truly aches and the stains you see on the paper are my tears. Mere words cannot convey my feelings, my thoughts. Come to me.

Always yours,

Waiting,

Kori

My hands are shaking. It's an extraordinarily simple letter, but it's more than that. It's a summons—a royal summons—one that I could not, on my honor, ignore.

It's good I decided to go to Japan. I smile to myself. The Empress will expect me to bring a gift in the traditional way.

Heh.

I yawn, and the tiredness is like an ache. I decide to leave the silk slip on for warmth.

Where is Caz, anyway?

I close my eyes. Soon I'm drifting again. Dreaming.

—Is it wrong to feel happy, now?—

—No.—

—The Goddess of War is still in me, isn't she?—

—A better question would be, does the Goddess need to manifest herself to catch the killer?—

—Indeed, that would be the question.—

—What do you feel?—

—Do you mean, what do I think?—

—No, what do you feel?—

—Yes.—

—That's the answer to what you think. What do you feel?—

—I want to rip his skin off and bathe in his blood.—

—Then you've answered your own question, my Goddess.—

—I don't want to live forever.—

—Ha! We all say that, after a while. We all say that.—

—I need to sleep now.—

—You already are.—

Blackness.

* * *

I wake up and Cazandra is getting into bed. She smells like a bordello. She sees that I'm awake and gives me a sheepish grin. She has 'I've been fucked' hair. Her lips are swollen.

"Mmmm," I say and scootch over. I snuggle close and sniff at her. My sense of smell is amazing. It certainly made dinner enjoyable. Fringe benefits. "Was that Mitch or Bill?"

She snickers. "Neither. I just had quite the naughty tussle with Milo."

Milo?

Ack! "Cazandra! Are you saying you just fucked Papa?"

"Papa?"

"Dr. Takayasu is my honored father! My adoptive Papa!"

She grins a pixie grin. "Your papa is one naughty man. He even…"

"Ewww! Get out of this bed and go shower! Come back smelling like soap. Ewww!"

"Okay, this is silly human behavior, but I can parse it. Back in a bit."

I lay there seething, but the steady drone of the shower makes me sleepy.

I hear the hair dryer, and a clean smelling Caz slides back into bed and wraps around me.

I go back to snuggling in earnest.

"Lexus?"

"Hmmm?"

"I'm worried about you. You seem to be taking this too well."

"I need to recover as quickly as possible and get back on this case."

"I don't buy it," she says.

Wow, that's observant for a bot. She's amazing, a tribute to her manufacturer. It always takes me off guard.

"I figured something out," I say, hesitantly. "I'm being punished for the awful things I have done. I deserve it."

She looks aghast. "That's not true!"

"But it is. Now I get to live longer, relive the war in all my Uplink perfect recall glory, for decades and decades more. It will be Hell on Earth."

Cazandra starts to cry. Again. She is worse than I am.

"Oh, hey, hey." Ah, crap.

"I don't believe that. I don't!"

I say nothing, because I am being honest. My talks with Papa made me realize it's not what I can do in the future. I merely added time to contemplate my sins. More time to ferret out war crap to atone for using it in the first place.

Caz rolls over, puts her back to me, and cries silently. Oh no, now I feel like shit. I snuggle closer.

"I don't believe it, and I swear I will prove it to you," she whispers, fiercely. "I swear it!"

I smile. It's not often Caz's programming reveals her simplistic nature. She might as well rally against the tide.

"Please don't cry; you're breaking my heart."

"I can't help it."

I tickle her. She squirms.

"Stop that!"

I tickle her again.

Finally, she giggles. "Lexus?"

"Hmmm?"

"This is nice. I've dreamed of this moment, waited for it a long time—to be with you, your bed, just you and I."

"You could have asked."

"I didn't want you to feel like you were humoring me, just as you now feel you took me for granted."

"Well, I did. I don't like to admit it, but I did."

"I'm more aware of my surroundings then people give me credit for."

"True. But…"

"And in the end I'm not human. Did you know the most expensive parts of me are my heat regulators? Bleeding nano heat is complicated. It's a system more complex than my gooey brain. That's why I liked sleeping in the basement. Less heat management. So don't fret!"

"You're not supposed to talk about yourself like that, Caz."

"Harrumph. I'm smarter than you think," she says. Now she sounds sleepy.

She can pass a Turning test, but she can't grow beyond sex and domestic work. In a way, She's lucky. I start to envy her and then I get that funny feeling I remember from when I realized I was madly smitten with Bill, that weightless intoxication.

I am falling in love with you, I think.

She turns to me and kisses me fiercely, kisses me with pure adoration.

"Caz, the thought of you sleeping in that basement is unbearable. Sleep in my bed until Papa leaves. Then you can have the guest room."

In answer, she starts to cry again. She grabs onto me and holds me as if she never wants to let me go.

CHAPTER 28

I HAVE A MENTAL checklist. Take stock of what is happening in the office, find the interview of Ms. Kitty, and then go see the Empress. I need to find out what Ms. Kitty knows that the murderer did not want me to find out.

It's a good plan. It's a valid plan. It's a plan with a distinct lack of penis in it.

This is not a bad thing.

* * *

My fellow investigators are staring at me in the atrium that now serves as our informal.

"This—is not what I expected," says Bambi.

"Yay for modern technology?" says Scott.

We all look at Ivan.

"In Soviet Russia, regeneration has you!"

I can't help it. I roll my eyes.

"In all seriousness, Nancy, how are you feeling?" Bambi asks.

"Good. Fine, in fact. Well, I have problems bumping into things. But I have a mental clarity that I never had with the damn Lib-Gee. It's heady to the point of being distracting."

Ivan nods. "No predictability. Hormone levels fluctuate now like real teen girl. Is good."

I wince.

"But enough about me. When you interviewed Ms. Kitty, did you find anything? Did she not consent to recording? I can't find the transcript in the case file."

Bambi shakes her head. "She said she didn't want to be interviewed by anyone except you, and that we would just have to wait until you came out of the tank. We actually don't even know where she is. Arune took her someplace and no one has seen her since."

I parse that. Arune thinks she is still in danger, so he took care of it. He's never got involved in my cases, but then again, nobody ever tried to blow me up with a missile while on a case.

"But Nancy—screw the case, at least for now. You can't just sit there and tell us in your little girl voice that you are fine. You look fine, but what do you feel, *really?*"

Damn it. For a twenty-two year old, she's a lot more mature than I give—gave her credit.

I take a deep breath.

"I feel stupid. I consented to regen therapy without realizing the ramifications of my decisions, so I have only myself to blame. I should have considered that between the time I agreed to get back my girly parts and actually drill-down on the details, an injury would tank me anyway. I am pissed someone tried to kill someone I talked to. I am pissed that six months have gone by and I have done nothing on this case, and no, don't look guilty, your encryption idea is sound. I'm pissed there is some woman out there that might need rescuing and I have no idea where she is. I feel—stupid."

She stands up. "You're not stupid."

I stand up, too. "I know that! It's what I feel, though."

"Yeah, but I just wanted it on the record."

Her response causes me to crack a smile. Damn she's so cute.

"Can I have a hug?"

"Of course, Nancy."

We come together and it's nice. She's still shorter than I am which sucks. Nobody should be shorter than this. She squeezes me tight.

I snuffle.

"Are you two going to kiss? Because that would be really hot," says Scott, "Especially since Nancy now looks like a total fuck bunny."

"Scott!" Bambi protests as we separate.

"I'm not a bunny! What the hell!"

Scott looks at me in that man way. "I mean, I was attracted to you before, but that was in a hero-worship, fearful kind of way. Now the attraction is pretty base, like, 'can't wait to see you naked' type of lust."

"Scott, you fucking pervert! You're biologically old enough to be this body's father!"

"Well, Bambi here, at twenty-two, is totally replaced in my desire for young flesh."

"I'm not old!" She hits him.

"Ow."

I hit him.

"Ow!"

I whirl to Ivan. "You got anything you want to say? Huh?"

"Only I'm glad, glad with all my heart, that I took a rain-check. Yes, yes I am."

"Ahhhhh!" I hurl my hands up.

Men!

"I'm going to the range to shoot things!" I declare.

Ivan gives me a parental look, and that pisses me off. "Actually, need to examine…"

I glare at him "After the range! Or in Soviet Russia, *Nancy* will be shooting *you!*"

* * *

Crack, crack, crack, crack! The sonic booms from the recoilless needler jar my ears even through the hearing protection.

I'm hell on wheels at the range. If anything, my reflexes are faster. I may have issues walking and bumping into things, but my hand-eye co-ordination is even faster than before.

Huh. Well, dip me in shit. I'm not going to complain.

Scott quietly slips inside and stands in back, watching me murder the red pop-ups that appear amongst sixteen other blue ones. It's random, and nailing all three is a testament not just to skill with the needler, but also to my peripheral vision and base reflexes.

"Clear on the range, ears off!"

Scott nods his head in appreciation at my skill. "I went to Fort Lewis, mainly so they could all give me a ribbing about retiring from OCE, and used their force-on-force range," he says.

I smile. I can picture Scott showing up and being obnoxious while taking it in both ears.

"They have this simulation where these three bots are in an armored tank. A fucking tank, one of the pre-war non-composite models. Like, a real Goddamn tank. And I nail all three of them. I simply shot them through the armor. The needles sliced through the armor and then deformed on the bots, blowing them to Hell and gone. Through a fucking tank!"

I nod.

"Damn, Nancy. I had no idea. CEOs are pikers. Pikers, compared to the shit Investigators have. There's nano crap in your lockers we can't even figure out what it does. They are unlabeled. We sprayed one in a test chamber on a rock and it was fucking anti-gravity in a can. The rock started to *float*. How the fuck is that possible?"

"Ha. Well, they don't make that anymore," I point out.

"It's interesting that the Constitution centers the power of government with OCE. Oh sure, the powers granted to Investigators to solve a crime are interesting, but it's not real substance, compared to a CEO. But Investigator equipment is decades, and I mean decades, ahead of everyone else."

"Don't get so enamored, Mr. Scott, of the techno marvels now at your disposal. We're all dog chow compared to space assets the Military got, and the populace has more respect for their County Safety departments."

"Yes, yes, to the literal high ground goes the victors and County Safety wears the white hats. Yet, one-on-one, we're not even close to equal. The needler is a prime example. The cyber at our disposal is another. It's humbling. It's like water boiling under the surface. Investigators really form a gestalt. A culture separate from society."

"You're being melodramatic."

"I have a unique perspective, coming from OCE."

"I told you we like to keep a low profile. There's a reason."

"Yeah, who wants to be lynched? Anyway, what I'm really wondering is, can I kiss you? You asked me not too, but now you keep giving me a funny look."

The question takes me aback.

"No! Uh, yes. Yes you can."

He pulls me to him and he looks down at me (damn it!), gives me a big kiss, and it lights me right on fire, smoking breasts and buzzing crotch. When he runs his hand down my butt, it's more than I can stand. I push him away.

"Stop that!"

"I won't ask again. I just wanted to get it out of the way."

"Are you sleeping with Bambi?"

"Only in my mind."

"Okay then."

"Okay."

"You can stop staring at me."

"It's a little nightmare. Sarcasm and snark wrapped up in teen killer fuck bunny."

"I'm not a fucking fuck bunny! All of you need to knock that shit off right the fuck now!"

"Sorry."

I huff, and rein in my temper. "You seem to be adjusting to this awful easy."

"Frankly, Lieutenant, and no offence, I have seen weirder things from the war. Having NI Pilot Lieutenant Lexus show up as teen sexy isn't a big stretch. Hell, part of the reason I wanted to pull you close for a kiss was just to make sure you haven't grown a penis or something."

"Not funny."

"I wasn't joking."

Ack. "Actually, the funniest thing is our domestic bot is the one having the hardest time adjusting."

"Is she hot?"

"Come near her and I will snip off your balls!"

* * *

In the workshop, Bambi presents me with my PDA. "Tada!"

"Oh, thank you." It turns on fine for me, and Bob sends me a simple text message about all the waiting mail I have. "Not having it work at just the wrong time has given me a finer appreciation for it."

"We did solve the bombing case while you were out," Bambi says.

I perk up. Outstanding.

"You can give her story while I scan her," says Ivan.

"Scan?"

"Scan. You have doctor, but I know more about NI soldiers as combat surgeon. Take off clothes, lay down on workbench."

"Well..."

"Strip now, Lieutenant!"

"Okay."

I look at Scott.

"What?"

"I'm aware that it doesn't matter, but I'm hesitant about undressing in front of you."

Because I'm a virgin and you're a single man.

"Bah, I..."

"Shush, all. Mr. Scott may need to assist. He stays."

"Assist?"

"Shush!"

I feel like I'm blushing, and I'm lying on the workbench—the same workbench on which Mitch did wonderful things to my body, my old body, not long ago. I snicker and everyone frowns at me.

"So here's the poop," Bambi says. "We took all four referrals from Seattle, and had a few more. Investigator Walker is pressing to dump Bellevue so he can expand north and south, I think he's just a west side snob. It's an interesting proposal, but the Bellevue market is bigger than Seattle is, and I don't want us to bite off more than we can chew."

Bambi pauses and looks at me. "Any opinion there?"

Ivan is frowning at the bruises on my legs.

"Uh, ease into it?"

"Okay. Two more things. We're running at a 2% profit margin, which is good considering I projected a 3% loss due to the new equipment and the remodeling we've been doing. Most of the black is because Chen came over for a month and gave us all training, in addition to helping solve the Mad Bomber Case."

Oh no, that's so sweet! "That was really nice of him. So, who did it?"

"The janitor."

"The janitor?"

"Yeah, the janitor was playing the market. He wanted the stock to take a dive on the PacWest Speculative Souk."

"Well, dip me in shit." I didn't even get that far. But yeah, follow the money. "What did you do to him?"

"He didn't have anywhere near the funds to take care of the damage he caused. We blew him up with the other bomb after Chen reassembled and fixed it. WAC Protocol led to a harsh Judgment. You can find the video on the net—the client paid a publicist to make sure eyeballs were on it."

Alrighty then. I guess I don't have to pop Bambi's Judgment cherry. Good.

Cherry. Ha. I smirk and try to repress it.

Ivan makes me stand up and then does a manual neurological exam. At the legs part, he frowns.

"Your neurological responses are typical of regen with NI implants. I can fix."

"How?"

"Shock on each leg. Zap zap. This causes the NI overlay in your legs to go passive. Then they kick back on."

"Uh, I vaguely remember something like this. Will it hurt?"

"Da. Very much so. Only for a second. Now lay on the table."

Bleh.

"Bambi, hold arms. Scott, hold legs. Like a sacrifice, Da, like that."

"Uh, hey maybe…"

Zap! He tazes me with a drive stun charge, right on my calf. I didn't even see the tazer.

"OW! Wait!"

Zap!

This zap on the other leg does something different. The pain is unbearable and my entire body tenses up in a response well beyond the tazer. My mind goes completely blank, the pain bursts all around me and I hear myself screaming.

And just like that, it ends.

Except, damn it, I have peed myself. Again. This is getting really fucking old.

"That last zap fix you. If your overlay were working properly, it would never have hurt so bad. Now you normal, well, normal for NI."

I pant. "Ow."

Scott picks me up. "Shower time for you."

"You seem to be in the habit of picking me up after I pee myself, Mr. Scott," I say, only it comes out a string of slurred words. I wince.

"Man, I feel bad for you Nancy; that looked like it hurt like Hell."

I nod. Scott takes me to the shower and uses the flexible shower-head to hose me off. Then he soaps me up, and rinses me off, all without snarky commentary or lecherous gropes.

"Your new hair is browner than brown."

"I hope I can keep it, although it's kind of a bitch, I have to brush it and that takes getting used to, since I've never had it that long."

Bambi comes in with my clothes, and I think part of the reason is she wants to make sure Scott isn't fucking me in the shower. Heh.

CHAPTER 29

"ARUNE? WHERE IS MS. Kitty?"

"Space Station Matachi. Want me to take you there?"

Ah. A huge Military space station with rock-solid security. Perfect.

"Yes, please. Right now."

"Good. Tiffany and I want to see your new body."

"How do you know I have a new body?"

"Give me a break. On your pad in an hour."

* * *

Lexus,

He tried to kill you with a missile and that didn't even work. I have total confidence both in your abilities as an Investigator and as a freak of nature in the survivor department.

I've resigned myself that this is a long process. But Lexus, what the murders and attempted murders have done to this community is nearly unbearable to watch. People are walking around armed to the teeth. Locking their doors. Children can't go anywhere alone. Tourist revenue is significantly down. The town drunk got shot when he walked into the wrong house.

Of course, I realize that me worrying about the town is stupid. But this stupid town is the only thing I have left.

You're running out of time. You're the only one who can do this. There is nobody else.

Yours,

Paul

I stare at Paul's email for a long time.

You're running out of time.

Mommy I love you... Mommy...

* * *

I'm outside and it is raining. It's a cold rain, and Arune slices through it gracefully and lands in the mist on my pad.

"Dude, you got royally fucked," says Tiffany as she meets me at the main airlock wearing her NI armor. Unlike before, she looks very comfortable in it.

I know the feeling.

I wrinkle my nose. I'm wearing a pair of Caz's jeans, her favorite long-sleeve blouse, a pair of her boots, and her only fur-lined cloak. None of my old clothes fit.

I pull the hood back on the cloak. I realize I'm still pissed at her, not because she was going to kill me, but because she whined to Brittney about our little talk.

But I have to set that aside, and do what I told her to do—grow up.

"Take a good look, Tiff. If you screw up, this is your future."

She looks at me, but it's not a nice look. It's a sexy look.

"You're all a bunch of bits when we Uplink, anyway," says Arune. "Come aboard, Lexi."

In the airlock, Tiffany turns to me.

"Can I call you Lexi, too?"

"No. Nancy is fine."

I'm kind of digging Nancy, anyway.

Lexus, well Lexus has *issues.*

* * *

The irony of Tiffany in the Pilot's chair and me in tactical during the orbital ascent is not lost on me.

As I go weightless, Tiffany is on the comm.

"So I figured out why we're both are attracted to each other but also rub each other the wrong way."

I press the virtual talk button.

"You mean besides the war shit and coming out here to kill me?"

"Yeah—we're both bottoms in bed."

Arune snickers.

"Shut it, Arune, or I will mention you like visiting Space Station

Matachi simply because it's the only building you can get inside, so to speak," I say.

"So?"

"Oh come on—giant dick metaphor!"

Tiffany cackles.

"I'm a giant dick, I'll admit it," Arune says. "We're about to transition to station gravity, hold tight."

"Oh, I bet she's now tight all right," quips Tiffany.

"Can it, Tiff."

* * *

The hangar is, to use the technical term, ginormous. It's big enough for a full squadron of MOF/Bs. No sooner have I stepped out of the airlock than I run into Space Marshal Charles Olson.

It's odd that a mostly matriarchal society like ours has a man leading the Military, but Olson was good. Like, really good—like save our asses from Unionization good. Sure, I blew up Europe, but in many respects, I was his protégé, and he ran the war.

He's also the CO who convinced me that neural implants and the resultant neural overlay was a good idea, without telling me it would also put me on the fast track to the Pilot program.

After fucking me. He asked me in bed, knowing I wouldn't think about it too much. He was still inside of me when we were talking, relaxing between my legs with his seed dripping down the curve of my thigh.

Asshole.

Here he stands. He is older, but living in space tends to drag one's life out. He looks good in that older man with grey hair on the sides kind of way. He was an extraordinarily talented lover.

But then again, so was Landis.

"Lieutenant."

"Charles."

"Quite an interesting look you have going there. If your tag didn't say you were you, I would swear it was a little sister, or a daughter, even."

"Yes, I feel fine, thank you," I snap and make my way out the airlock.

He stands in my way. "I didn't give you permission to come aboard, Lexus. Why are you here?"

I get in his face. "I'm here in an official capacity investigating a murder case, working for an agency that has a former CEO on staff."

He looks down at me, and even though he tries very hard not to, his eyes flick to my breasts.

I repress a smile. I've received the best training to fuck his brains out, and he can't help but wonder what the old Lexus would do in a new body.

"That means I get to tell you to take your questions and *permissions to come aboard* and shove 'em up your ass," I add flatly.

He frowns, but then nods.

"I'll just go back to my office," he says. His voice betrays him, that of an older man trying not to sound disappointed.

Gah! He thought I would *flirt.* I look into his eyes to call him out, but what I see there is not what I expect.

I see loneliness. A warrior's loneliness. A commander's loneliness.

I push past him and make my way to the central transportation hub, ignoring the MPs lurking in the background, before I do something stupid like forgive him.

The Goddess of War is not in a forgiving mood.

* * *

Space Station Matachi is huge, big enough to have an impact on the tidal flows on the Earth below. It's not a big impact, but it is a measurable impact. It rounds the Earth on a polar orbit with most of its path over Africa and Europe.

The enemy lost the war essentially because they had no answer to our space superiority. Once we decided to snuff them all out from space with no heed of the damage to the landscape or people, it was over. There isn't an inch of enemy territory we did not bathe with overlapping neutron bombardment, most of which came from Matachi.

I push the past away and make my way to the nearest tram, and no sooner than I come to the reception area then I spy a wælcyrie, her platinum blonde hair in a ponytail and her feminine body in a Lieutenant's uniform.

A wælcyrie. My heart quickens all on its own mainly due to guilt. Wælcyries are the other species of earth besides AIs and humans, more common than AIs but more reclusive. They are a female-only biosynthetic race and they look like tall athletic elves, with large eyes and pointed ears. We created them in the war when it looked like we humans were either going to all die or be Unionized, and we made sure a wælcyrie would resist both. It takes four years to grow a wælcyrie to Adulthood, and we grew a bunch.

But before we could make them males, the enemy blew up Seattle where all the scientists who understood how to make wælcyries had gathered. The genetic material to make one has resisted reverse engineering, and, to our shame, they are now dying out. When the material is all gone, there will be no more wælcyries born.

This one notices I am staring at her, and I look away. She doesn't need me to make her feel like a freak or a spectacle. I hop on the train as it stops, and try to forget about the war yet again.

After that short trip, I ride the elevator to a commerce hub. Soon I am in a mall-esque area, broken up with lounge space for people to relax and socialize.

Luckily, Ms. Kitty's security did not entail a name change, and I walk through the door to Good Kitty/Bad Kitty Lingerie.

She comes out from behind a counter. This time she is wearing spotlessly white pumps with a pink slip and thigh highs, a much softer and more innocent look than when I saw her last.

She stops dead in her tracks when she looks at me.

"Your—your tag says you're Lexus, and there ain't no tag spoofing here on Matachi. Is that really you? Not some sister?"

"It's really me, Kitty. Just a bad bout of regen."

She runs up to me and crushes me in a hug.

Then she is sobbing into my hair.

"Oh! Oh! Oh!"

* * *

I had to close up her shop and give her a glass of wine. We are in a bed above her shop in the dim, and she is trying to calm herself.

"My life has been a mess. My Husband and I didn't have a great relationship to begin with, and after the murder attempt, he divorced me just when I needed him the most. And I can't begin to tell you the guilt I felt when the house exploded behind me and I knew you were still in there," she finally whispers.

"Kitty, it wasn't your fault, or my fault. The bad guy didn't want you to talk to me—and it was almost worse. If I hadn't shot down the missile, the warhead would have exploded and killed us both."

She shudders. "Your friend Arune arranged everything. He took me to space, got me this shop even when my insurance money came up short, and drove business to my store. I'm making twice the money here as I did in Bacon."

Aw, Arune—what a sweetie.

"Why," she asks, "did this happen? I figured it had something to do with Jennifer and Layla. But what? I'm scared, Lexus. I thought I was in the wrong place at the wrong time but Arune told me under no uncertain terms was I to go back to Earth. That was my first clue. Why?"

I take a deep breath and let it out slowly.

"Jennifer and Layla were not lingerie fans, but when they were killed, they were wearing lingerie."

She turns to me.

"So? Neither were my customers!"

I shake my head. "That's not what is important here. Jennifer's black slip was so generic she probably mail ordered it. Layla borrowed her stockings and garter belt from her friend Rachel Barrett."

"Oh, Rachel bought things on the sly from me. She—she loved to wear sexy things underneath her clothes. It's a benign thing."

"That's doesn't matter either. The killer was a man. A man who likes his women to wear lingerie. A man who likes lingerie so much that when he seduced his victims into letting down their guard, they dressed up for him even though they were nudists."

She is silent.

"Excuse me," she says.

She bolts to the head and throws up, and then she starts crying again, so I get up and sit beside her on the synth-tile.

"Are, are, you saying that one of my customers is a rapist and a murderer?"

"Yes."

"But, the entire *town* was my customer base. There isn't anywhere else close to buy lingerie in person except in Coulee City, and their shop sucks. It could be any Adult male and half the teenagers! It could be a guy who didn't come into my shop at all, but his Wife or girl did. There's no way to know!"

I take her hand. I want to spare her the details, but she has a right to know. "It doesn't matter if you don't know. You have a list of customers or a list of Wives, and women with Husbands and lovers. On that list is the killer. I need that list so I can correlate it with the other data I collect."

A look of calm descends upon her. "You mean—you mean someone tried to kill *me* simply because I could make a *list?*"

I nod.

Her eyes narrow. "How—how much are your rates? I am in sudden need of an Investigator."

I shake my head. "This one is a freebee, hon."

She shakes her head in return. "Absolutely not. I am going to hire your agency, Investigator, and when you catch the killer, I want you to wear lingerie when you mettle out Justice. Are we clear on this, Lexus?"

Post-war woman steel with the added bonus of using Military jargon she probably picked up living here. Not taking her credits now would be a major offense to her honor. "Aye, aye, ma'am. Crystal."

She holds out her hand and we shake.

"I'll need three lists. One, a list of men who came to your shop, another ranked list of customers regardless of sex in order of, um, enthusiasm, and a list of anybody not on either two lists who was friendly and liked to talk about lingerie with you."

"You got it. By the way, you're 32B-22-32 at five-feet, three inches. You are a skinny butt, and officially petite. Eat a cookie," she tells me, sternly.

Damn it!

CHAPTER 30

BACK IN THE TACTICAL station as we descend to Mt. Si, I plug the info from Kitty into my PDA and tell Bob to send it to the top of the agency analysis queue and to ICDA.

I also mentally work at not asking for an Uplink. Arune says I'm his girl and I believe him, but I need to give him some space to attune to Tiffany. Their lives depend on it. Teenage body or not, I am nothing if not professional.

"Arune, I'm going to Tokyo, but I want to commercial it. I'm going to talk girly stuff with a friend of mine."

"Girly away—got a few things cooking on the tailpipe with Tiff. What are you going to do there? Didn't your doctor come to you?"

I can't Active Thought with him since I took off my watch because the damn thing was itchy, and I certainly can't Uplink with Tiff in the cockpit, so I sub-vocalize.

—I'm going to go see the Empress.—

—Already? Going to go finger-fuck her in return? Please take vid, thank you.—

—I'm going to give her my new virginity.—

—Are you totally insane? Scratch that, you are. What you're planning is a bad idea.—

—What? Why?—

—You don't know what you're messing with. The Empress is a very dangerous person to the likes of you.—

—Why?—

—Lexi, you should get to know her better before you embark down this path!—

—Will you stop talking in riddles? Spit it out.—

—The Empress is the most powerful person on this planet. She's fundamentally more dangerous than you are. If you offer her virgin blood, she will use it to gain more power.—

—What are you talking about, Arune?—

—I'm talking about your honor and virtue!—

—Which, in this rare instance, I can lose one to gain the other back!—

—Okay, I will give you that. Just, be careful, okay? I don't trust her.—

—Arune, look. Your opinion means a lot to me. But I'm a woman, and she's singularly responsible for me being able to touch my Husbands without throwing up. I know I just met her, but she means a lot to me.—

—Okay. Sorry if I overreacted.—

—S'all right.—

I close the channel.

What the fuck?

Males!

When we land, I scurry out of the airlock after giving Tiff a peck on the cheek.

At least I don't cry, but for some reason, I can't shake the feeling that I disappointed the person whose opinion matters the most to me.

* * *

"Bambi Boss, want to come with me to Tokyo? I need to shop for real clothing and visit a friend."

"Ooooo! When?"

"As soon as I'm dressed in Caz's party dress. Fuck it, I don't care how cold it is, I'll just snuggle in my cloak until we can hit a real store."

"Uh, *yes*. I have to pack though."

"We're buying all of our clothes."

"I'm broke for mad spending."

"I'm rolling in cash."

"I have to get my luggage."

"We're buying that too. Grab your purse, babe."

"Okay!"

"Oh man, can I come?" Scott sounds very hopeful.

I give him a look. "Girl business."

"What do you mean?"

"Scott, I don't think you want to be around when I have a discussion with Bambi about the period I will start in twenty days."

"Uh, no. No I don't. Have a nice trip." He stands up and, very haughtily, he exits the atrium. His office door closes and I can hear the lock engage.

Bambi giggles. "When is the last time you had your period?"

"I can't remember. Honestly."

"The procedure summary you forwarded said you had fake eggs?"

"My body thinks it has an endless supply. It will try to release one right on schedule. Bleh." If they could have asked me I would have said *no period,* damn it.

"Welcome to my world!"

"Bleh."

"Get dressed, I want to go!"

I can feel the energy course through my veins. I need Bambi, because, frankly, hitting the town with the old folks isn't going to cut it. Ha.

* * *

Bambi collects the men. "Scott, Ivan, hold down the fort. We'll be gone for…"

"Four or five days," I finish for her.

"Four or five days! Woo hoo!"

He, he, she sounds just like Caz.

Wearing stockings, I strap on a thigh holster on each leg. On the right leg, I attach my needler and my small combat knife on the other side. On my left, I strap on my longer combat knife and a reload for the needler. I also put a reload in my purse. Then I use the garter belt to take the pressure off my thighs by memory pinning the stockings to the holsters and sheathes.

"Well, other than it will take me an extra five minutes to go pee—

this actually works with this dress."

Caz lent me a little black dress and some heels. I look like I'm going out to a party, which is exactly how I want to feel.

Bambi takes one look at the getup and bursts out laughing. She fetches stockings and a garter belt and does the exact same, except snickers the entire time.

"You keep stockings and a garter belt in the office?"

Ivan and Scott actually flinch.

"What?"

Bambi looks me directly in the eye. This ought to be good.

"These are Layla Gifford's. Well, specifically, Rachel Barrett's."

I stare. Then I'm sitting down in a chair.

"Are you *insane?*"

"No. I wear them sometimes to remind me that the killer is still at large. And that looking and feeling sexy has nothing to do with what happened. I plan to make love wearing them someday. Perhaps my first time."

"But—but..."

She stands tall and puts her hands on her hips.

Well dip me in shit.

"Scott told me about the accident. So one night I jogged up here in the rain, put on a sim suit, and plugged myself into the simulation as Layla. Then the next week, I did it again as Jennifer. And, the week after that, as the killer."

"But..."

"Just because I'm a virgin doesn't mean I have not had sexual experiences. The ICDA recreation was the worst thing I have ever experienced, but unlike you, I knew what was going to happen."

I'm flabbergasted. "So you violated the departed's privacy to what? Prove a point to me?"

"Partly. However, it's not a violation, in the moral sense, if I learn something that can help us solve the case."

"What could you possibly learn by getting raped? Twice! And then plugging yourself into—into..."

I realize I'm yelling, breathing heavy. I feel panicked, nauseous.

"I learned that our killer might have been operating under coercion."

"Wha—but—I didn't..."

I look at Bambi. She's twenty-two, born right before victory over the forces of darkness. She's of a different generation than I, and the thought of her young body being violated, even in a simulation, makes me want to run screaming and kill something. The fact that she's standing there, in seemingly fine mental health, while I practically lost my mind—oh hell, who am I kidding, *did* lose my mind—is remarkable.

I do what any teenage girl—knowing that her entire previous life made it possible for young women like Bambi to live and grow up, faced with the Investigator she is today, realizing that everything she did and all the sins she committed were worth it—would do.

I start to cry.

Fuck that's annoying!

CHAPTER 31

I EXPRESSED MY DESIRE to talk about only girly things, so Bambi and I spent our entire flight to Japan from SeaTac Starport talking about makeup, clothes, shoes and even our periods. Just about everybody flirted with us until we got on to the feminine conversation, at which point they left us alone. In fact, we yakked so much, we forgot to eat, and now my stomach growls.

As we depart the plane, I feel weak. I realize I have ignored Ivan's advice that I need to eat six small meals instead of three big ones. "Oh my. Need food now. Options?"

"Japan! Sushi!" Bambi grabs me and gives me a hug and a grin.

I'm wearing my NI watch. It's much more than a timepiece; it's a wireless interface to the cyber world around me, including my PDA. It's priceless. No one makes them anymore. To use cyber, I only have to Active Thought at something.

—Sushi for two hungry young women from just east of Seattle looking for the finer things in life.—

—Café Geisha. Please follow the trail.—

My PDA tells my watch to give me a HUD, and a little trail of fish appears before me. I laugh and grab Bambi's hand.

"This way!"

* * *

We have a fine time at the sushi bar served by, as far as I can tell, real geishas. They are delicate and lovely, and I appreciate their form and poise.

And their breasts.

I was saddled with the Lib-Gee so damn long that I'm used to thinking of my hormones as out of my hands. I have to keep reminding myself that my body is entirely my own now—and the attraction to women is still there. Interesting.

In between little bites, Bambi gives me glances.

"What?"

"Look, I already have sexual tension with Scott. Are we going to have an issue?" she asks in what I instantly recognize as Her Boss Voice.

"No."

"You're slobbering over the geishas."

"I've spent an entire morning in travel flirting with men and women. You flirted too, but you ignored the girls. I get it." I give her a look. "But while I think you're attractive in your elfin way, I look at you and I see…"

I can't say it. I'm not nearly drunk enough.

"Who?"

"I—Layla. I see Layla." Okay, I guess I am tipsy at least.

She's quiet for a moment, and then she takes my hand.

"It reminds you too much of the war, doesn't it?"

I nod.

She puts her hand on my face.

Ah, I'm crying again. Damn it, I suck!

"Nancy, I'm so sorry."

Silently, a young geisha is at my side.

"Excuse my interrupting, Nancy-san, could I get you something to drink?"

I look at her. "Anything—anything but wine." I decide, right then and there, I don't want to drink wine ever again.

She looks at Bambi.

"Two, please."

In moments, long flutes of blue liquid are in front of us. Wispy, smoky tendrils flow from the glass, and it smells wonderful.

"A vodka based drink, my Ladies," the painted girl says. Then, like magic, she's gone.

I pick mine up. "Why do I get the feeling this is going to ooze right past my regulator?"

Bambi picks hers up. "Good. Here's to Layla."

My hand shakes but we clink glasses.

"And to Jennifer," I add.

We drain our glasses. The liquid is smooth, tasty and very, so very, delicious. It gives me courage to ask questions I should not ask.

"You're not going to fuck Scott, are you?"

She gives me a thin smile. "No."

"Why not?"

"Because it's so clichéd. Young girl seduces and marries vet, they have a baby, life changes, they grow apart and divorce. The stigma of having a broken family causes both to drink or snorf or whatever while the baby is raised by the grandparents."

"Ugh." It's true.

"I kissed him," I blurt out.

"Are you going to fuck him?"

"No. But for entirely different reasons."

"Why?"

"Because he frightens me."

Oh boy, I'm drunk.

"Why does he frighten you?"

"There are two people in this world more dangerous than me. Scott is one of them."

"Our Scott?"

"Yes."

"But…"

"You'll find out some day. But I don't like being frightened. I'm so very tired of it."

"So, who is the other person you're afraid of?"

"You'll find out."

"I'm an Investigator now. If you don't tell me, I will indeed find out."

"You'll find out—soon."

* * *

Us two lightweights giggle our way to departure, hauling hot pink suitcases we bought in SeaTac on sale because of their obnoxious, not-so-popular color.

"And just like magic, there is Thor!"

"Thor?"

"My driver. I think the Military has him keep an eye on me in Japan so I don't fuck things up for them."

Bambi laughs. "That's what I would do!"

"Hey now."

"Hiya, Thor!" she says, and holds out her hand.

Thor, in his expensive suit and looking as sharp and young as ever, smiles, bends over, and kisses her hand.

"Oh!" she says.

"Hey, you've never kissed my hand!"

"You've never offered, ma'am. And I must say, you look absolutely stunning. Young, but stunning,"

"Thank you, Thor." I hold out my hand too, and he kisses it.

I will not pant. I will not pant. I will not pant. Oh man oh man. I *can't* think of Thor that way.

Soon we're in the car, Thor's expert hands on the wheel. It's cold and snowing outside, but the car is toasty.

"So," Bambi says, "who is your friend we're visiting? Are we going to shop first?"

"Uh, I haven't thought that far."

"Well, who is your friend?"

"Kori Suiko"

"Ha ha, she has the same name as the Empress."

I give her my new young Lexus look.

"Oh."

"Ma'am, I suggest giving someone a go at your hair. No offense, but it's a mess. If you're going to call on the Empress, I suggest a clean-up."

I wrinkle my nose. "Thank you, Thor."

"I suggest a stylist at the Four Seasons. I just checked; she has an appointment slot available now."

"Thank you, Thor."

"Wow, just wow," says Bambi. "You have friends in high places. But you'll need some new clothes for sure—you can't go to the Palace looking like that!"

"What's this 'you,' white girl? You're coming with me. I'm going to need your strength. Not necessarily backup, but it would make me feel better if you were there. Well not there-there for the, uh, deed, but, you know, at the Palace."

She looks at me and makes a face. "Nancy, you're not making sense! Why are you visiting the Empress?"

Well, I'm glad I'm still drunk. "I'm going to give her my newly regenerated virginity."

Bambi's eyes go wide, and she opens her mouth but nothing comes out.

I notice the car has pulled over to the side of the road in the emergency lane. Then it stops.

Thor is sitting there, just staring out the window. His hands are gripping the wheel, and his knuckles are white.

The hazard lights come on automatically. They blink.

Blink, blink, blink.

"You got a problem with that, Thor? You going to lecture me too, claim that I don't know what I'm doing?"

Blink, blink, blink.

After a pause, he sighs and visibly relaxes. The car moves forward and he zips back into traffic without a hitch.

"No, ma'am."

"You're not going to tell me to be careful?"

"No, ma'am. Careful is sometimes good, but you and I both know that at the center of your being, there is no careful. Careful isn't a core option for you and I."

I sit and look at the back of his head.

I want to ask him a million questions. But I have spent twenty years respecting his privacy, and he has always respected mine. Indeed, this is the most I've heard him say in one sitting beyond social niceties.

I sigh, realizing I don't want to ask Thor any questions.

Because I'm more than sure I don't want to know the answers. Not now. Maybe not ever.

Bambi holds my hand.

"Wow. Empress. Well, if you're going to lose a new cherry to someone, you might as well make it count!"

I chuckle. It sounds grim, and I repress a flinch.

Straight from the Goddess grim.

I sigh again.

* * *

The car pulls right up to the Palace, first through the security gates, and then through the extraordinary garden, which must look amazing in the summer. For now, it just looks snowy.

Bambi is very nervous. I can almost hear her body vibrating with worry. She was done up by the other beautician, and she looks stunning. Her face is stoic, which, I have learned, is Bambi expression for *can't parse it.* I feel a little guilty for bringing her along, but I told my inner teenager to deal and asked her point-blank in the hotel she could get a room there and I would meet up with her later.

She declined, because she's now my boss, and feels responsible for my safety and wellbeing. For a twenty-two year-old she has grown up fast. I'm very proud of her, and so very need her. I need her friendship desperately. I realize I didn't have any women friends, and that was a mistake on my part.

We're both wearing elegant short dresses which we bought in the hotel, and which are out of both fashion and season but of the necessary length for our thigh holsters. I have a fancy new haircut, and a new fur-lined cloak. I'm wearing the latest in nano makeup. My elegant new pumps are straight from New York, shoe capital of the world, and I love them more than I like to admit. And I had to shop in the petite section with Bambi.

On one hand, I'm pissed that I have lost boob and now look like a perky little tart.

On the other hand, I now look like a perky little tart.

Since I'm a few inches taller than Bambi...

"You're staring at me," says the Bambi in question.

"Oh, sorry."

"What were you thinking?"

"I was thinking how I very much treasure our friendship, that I love you and that I think I like my boobs."

She stares at me. "Awwwww..." She smiles, and punches me on the shoulder.

—Nancy?—

I startle. I'm still trying to get over the fact they teach subvocalization to children now. Not too long ago it was Military only. Our PDAs send it back and forth between us.

—Yes?—

—If anyone harms you, and I don't care who they are, they will suffer. I promise you that.—

—No one can do anything to me that has not already been done.—

Especially working on this case.

—Not true. Your heart can be broken.—

—I, okay. Okay.—

I look into her eyes. Leave it to a youngster to point out my big, big flaw.

At some point, one of the many people that I love could break my heart.

What will happen to me then?

* * *

Thor claims that our luggage will wind up in the right place, wherever that may be. We walk unattended through a snowy garden, the water fountains making a kind of eerie, rushing music.

Two girls, barely tweeners, are at the doors leading to an ornate building, kneeling by each sliding panel. Odd. Then I realize they are there simply to manually open the doors.

Quaint and exquisitely traditional, and so very Japanese.

As we walk up the steps, I look at Bambi.

—Look, Bambi, the Empress can be *intense.*—

—I bet.—

—But she's also a sweetheart. You need to relax or you're going to puke and pee yourself.—

That is what I'm going to do if *I* don't relax, anyway.

—I'm trying!—

—Everything will be all right. I know it.—

—How do you know?—

—She loves me, that's all I know.—

—Why?—

—It's love. Don't ask me why! I'm the last person to ask about love. I love and I can't turn it off!—

The doors open.

The humidity washes over me. This room contains many plants and blooming flowers, even in this season. There, standing in the middle of the room, is the young Empress, tears running down her face and staining her exquisite black and crimson Japanese dress, chest heaving up and down as she sobs.

CHAPTER 32

TERROR AND ANXIETY WASH over me in a heartbeat, and it is all I can do to not pee myself. I barely remember to kick off my shoes before I rush to her. She opens her arms as I reach her, and she holds me tight, kisses my hair.

Where before she was only slightly taller than me, now she is much taller, and I don't expect to her to hold me against her breasts the way I am.

"Your letter broke my heart!" She pulls me tighter to her with that scary strength of hers, and I can't help but squeak, muffled by her boobs. She lets up just a little, but then starts kissing my face with wild abandon.

Then she stops and her eyes narrow. "Tell me, how are you feeling?"

"I'm feeling much better, Empress."

"Oh, your voice! It's gone from husky woman to sexy cute!"

She peers behind me. "My bad manners. Please, introduce me to your compact and pretty Investigator friend."

I turn but the Empress still has a hold of me, so now she's standing behind me, arms wrapped around me.

"Kori-sama, this is Investigator Bambi. She's my boss and my dear friend who is helping me through these great changes."

Bambi bows low, and the Empress finally lets go of me and bows in return. Then she steps to Bambi and gives her a big hug.

"Then you're truly a dear friend, as this is what Lexus-san needs, she needs proper women friends. Thank you, Bambi-san."

"You're welcome, Empress," says Bambi, sounding more confident than I bet she's feeling.

"Bah! Enough of this Empress this and Kori-sama that. You both are sounding like my staff. Call me Kori."

She steps away from Bambi and gives her a look. "I assure you, Bambi-san, Lexus is safe here, in body, heart and spirit. No harm will come to her here, ever, my fierce young Investigator."

The look on Bambi's face is classic. A sub-vocal conversation between Investigators is about the securest type of communication possible short of Active Thought, and I'm sure Bambi has personally seen to our PDAs security.

But this is the Empress of Japan. She doesn't need to breach our security. She read it from Bambi's face in a simple glance. Because that's what Empresses do.

"Yes, Emp—Kori-san."

The door opens and in walks a handsome young Japanese man, draped in casual elegance.

"Bambi-san, Lexus-san, this is Toshiro, my favorite cousin and my best friend in the entire world, although he has a mischievous streak that got us both spanked all the time as children."

Toshiro bows. "Pleased to meet you, my apologies for not meeting you at your car."

Bambi and I bow in return. Bambi holds out her hand to shake, and like Thor, he kisses it. Oh, what a charmer. Instantly, I can tell Bambi is in trouble.

"Bambi-san, Toshiro-san will entertain you this evening. Despite being such a rascal, he's both nice and smart, and he is really the perfect gentleman."

"Thank you Kori-san, for all those compliments, especially in front of such beautiful American Ladies."

Bambi succumbs to the surreal scene and giggles. Toshiro holds out his arm. She gives me a look.

Almost against my will, I nod.

Just like that, I'm alone.

With the woman who performed surgery on me.

Then gave me three orgasms.

The Empress, not by law, but by heart, mind, and honor.

I look at her, and she steps towards me. In a smooth motion, she picks me right up off the floor and cradles me against her chest. She starts walking toward the back of the room with me in her arms, and my heart is a loud drum in my own ears. No one has ever picked me up like this before with such intimate intensity, it's always been playful—and it took a tall, strong man to lift me.

"Where are we going?" I whisper.

"My bedroom. We're going to make love. All night."

"Now?"

She stops and looks at me. "Yes! Now! Lexus-san, I worshipped you when I was growing up. You were so important to me, even if I had never met you. Then when I recognized you in the doctor's office, my heart almost beat out of my chest. I went a little crazy when I found out what had happened to you, and when you sent me that letter, my heart broke anew and I cried all day. Then I blinked and you were not you, but a young woman of exotic beauty. I fear that if I blink once more, you will be gone! Life happens to you too fast!"

She starts walking again, a door opens (this time, automatically, like a normal door) and we're in an intimate bedroom. She sets me on an enormous platform-bed, somewhere between the Western and the Japanese style. With white sheets. I chuckle as she hikes up my dress and starts unsnapping my stockings.

"What?"

"Your bed is very big."

"Yes, it is."

All I can think is—*At least she just has fingers and I won't bleed all over those white sheets.*

Soon she has taken off everything except my neural watch. She looks at it and I snap it off.

She stands up, and just like before, the lights dim. She runs a finger down her dress to part the memory seam, and it falls to the floor. She steps out of her slippers and walks towards me, a living statue, flawlessly beautiful.

My heart beats faster, and my face feels hot. Kori kneels beside me on the bed.

"You have hair, pubic hair," she says, staring at my crotch.

"I—had it trimmed at the Four Seasons." I stammer. Damn it, I'm a fifty-three year old woman!

"It's cute," she says as she lies down next to me. "If it was gone, you would look much too young." She snuggles close, her hand sliding over my stomach.

She looks down at my face. "You're trembling. Am I that scary?"

I try to calm myself and fail. "I don't want to break the mood," I say hesitantly, "but I'm afraid, Kori-san."

"Afraid? Of me?"

"No! Never of you. But—what if you fell in love with the idea of me, and not who I am?" I whisper. "What if what you really want is a little girl's dream of a hero, instead of the broken woman before you?"

She kisses me. It's a long kiss, her tongue warm and curious, and then, like a switch, insistent and sensual. I melt, and a pang of desire shoots straight through me.

She draws back and starts to caress my hair.

"I'm not a little girl anymore. At first, I wanted you because you were so very needy, and I'm drawn to need like a moth to a flame. Then, I wanted you because it was a fantasy come true."

Her large almond shaped eyes are close to mine, unwavering. I can't look away. "But now, I simply want you, because I want you. I want something for myself. I don't just want to partake in the healing process for your broken soul; I'm being selfish. I want you to make love to me. Real love." She's kissing my face, whispering in my ear. Her hands start to roam over my body. "Make love to me. Make love to me." She cups my breast. "Love me."

I tremble harshly, this time with desire. I have never met someone who mirrors my hunger for love so perfectly.

"My Empress, I brought you a gift," I say, and send kisses along her neck.

"What is it, my Mistress, my Concubine?"

I run my hands down her sleek body, loving the smoothness of her skin. I whisper in her ear. "I am a woman reborn. I give you my maidenhood—take as much of it as you can—it's yours."

Her breath catches in her throat.

"This is like a dream, a dream! I'm afraid at any moment, I will wake up, and you will be gone." A tear slides down her face.

Heat runs through my body, and I roll on top of her. I kiss down to her breasts and suck them greedily. They are surprisingly soft for something so perky. Is this what I feel like? Soon, she's moaning and panting, and I kiss down her stomach, over her hip, over her thigh. I can feel the heat of her sex against my cheek, and she smells clean and feminine. I kiss her, and she grabs my hair and spreads her legs wide.

I taste her, and then I drink her and she screams while she comes. Her back arches and she shakes all over, holding my head in place as she rides out her pleasure. She looks down at me, and for a moment she is glassy and satisfied. Then her eyes turn primal again with lust. She rolls on top of me.

"I'm real, I'm not a dream," I tell her, my husky voice back in place for the moment as she rubs my thighs, and then rubs me. I gasp loudly. All of the lust and desire I have been fighting since I went home to my Husbands is wound tight inside me, and I can feel how wet I am now because even the shallowest touch of her fingers is completely frictionless. The look she gives me is pure bliss. She looks into my eyes as if looking right into my soul, and plunges fingers inside, quick and hard.

I gasp and cry out. It hurts—it hurts! It doesn't feel like fingers at all, it feels like she is fucking me with a sledgehammer and I scrunch my eyes and whimper loudly. The pressure is *immense*.

I open my eyes, the room is blurry, and the dim is more of a dark purple than a grey. I bleed, and her fingers fill me, fill me up. She slips them in and out, slowly at first, but the pace and intensity builds quickly. She teases me to the edge with her thumb as she fucks me, and warmth and pleasure quickly replaces the pain. I can't keep my eyes open anymore and as I close them, I shriek out her name.

I'm free, I'm free!

The orgasm feels like fire—a delicious, wet flame that explodes from my core and travels all over my body.

I cry.

* * *

I'm snuggled on top of her. She's running a hand along my back. I'm having trouble keeping my eyes open.

"Your Husbands…"

"Are silly males. Well, except my Marines. They are simply gay. A bleeding girl to them is just cause for alarm." I look up at her face. "You don't have regrets, do you?"

What did you do to me? I almost ask—but I don't. It was as if she rammed the cosmos up my vagina all the way to my new cervix. Everything now hurts like hell. I stare at her dainty little fingers. I feel like a stallion fucked me.

"I must be honest with you. I feel like a selfish bitch for loving every second, every moment of it all," she says, sounding like a girl caught with her hand in the cookie jar.

I try to suppress a giggle, and it doesn't work. It comes out as a chuckle and a snort.

She smacks my butt. "Don't laugh at your lover!"

"Sorry. I usually find sex funny."

"Then you must laugh a lot."

"Hey now."

I snuggle into her again and I sigh.

Then I snicker.

"What?"

"A friend warned me about you."

"Oh? What did this friend say?"

"He said you were dangerous."

"I am dangerous."

I talk into her breasts because I can't muster the energy to look up any more and I certainly don't want to look down at the sheets.

"Why?"

"Lots of reasons. But mainly, I'm not a creature of our society."

"What?" Now I do look up at her face. "You're the Empress! You wield ultimate authority because people give it to you freely, and not blindly! You're the *embodiment* of our society!"

"No, my Concubine, that's what I am on the surface. Our society defines itself roughly by the technology we choose *not* to use, and the rules we choose to live by to prevent the madness of the war from ever occurring again."

"And you?"

"I choose differently. I will use everything at my disposal to protect my planet, my people. And I don't follow any rules but my own."

"But you're the Empress! You're a creature of tradition! It's why everyone loves you. The Free Peoples give you their love."

"Ah, tradition. A tool that is only useful in conjunction with innovation. One I use to my advantage mercilessly."

I open my mouth, but no words come out.

"Stumped, Investigator?"

"Then you are dangerous," I say. I go back to snuggling.

"What, you're not going to accuse me of using you? Of being the cold, calculating bitch that I am?"

"No."

"I didn't."

"I know. I'll just accept you the way you are."

"I…"

"Stumped, Empress?"

"I love you."

Damn it all, she says the most perfect things. "I love you, too."

"Sleep, my brave Concubine. My warrior. And when you wake up, make love to me again. Slowly, with lots of kisses. Look into my heart, and love me."

"Always."

I fade. She's warm. I sleep, and dream of nothing in particular, and that's good.

* * *

I don't know what time it is. Or even what day it is. The Empress has kept me in her room, and has alternated between extraordinarily tender lovemaking and wild, lusty fucking.

And right now, she's feeding me breakfast. Or lunch. I can't tell. Literally, she's putting the food in my mouth, waiting on me. She has, quite simply, fucked me silly.

But not as silly that I can't see her desire for something else.

"Just come out and say it, even if you think I will be mad at you," I tell her when I can't stand her looks anymore.

"I want to mark you," she blurts out and then blushes. How cute.

"What?"

"I can't marry you, I am denied that privilege. But I can claim you as my Concubine, my Princess Concubine. I want to shout it to the world. I don't want to hide this. Us."

I wrack my brain for historical tidbits. "Uh, don't you mean Princess Consort?"

"No. I'm taking a mistress. And my mistress will be a Princess."

I laugh. "You can't just snap your fingers and make me a Princess!"

She smiles.

"Can you?"

Now her grin is thoroughly and unapologetically malevolent.

"Really?"

She nods.

"What do you mean by marking me?"

The hunger in her eyes is obvious.

Oh, I'm in big trouble now.

* * *

Bambi and Toshiro are flirting shamelessly. Papa sits across from me, and at my side is Kori, with her hand protectively on my thigh. Periodically, she rubs it. I wish she would stop that, because I don't want to get all flustered in public.

But then again, that may be her goal.

We're at a fancy Tokyo restaurant, and we're full of an interesting blend of Asian, French, and Pacific Northwest cuisine. Although, I'm sure only Papa and I remember what authentic French food actually tastes like.

We're all pleasantly inebriated, which means I've had two drinks after dinner, damn it. Despite the buzz, my back still hurts.

The Empress has marked me all right. Like magic—or perhaps like some part of one of her manipulative ruses—as soon as I said "yes," she tied me down tightly and then three tattoo artists went to work on my back with needles so sharp they felt like cold fire against my skin. In Japan, they do things the old-fashioned way.

They inked my back until I was a crying, bloody mess. At some point, my neural overlay flipped the pain of it all to pleasure, and it was, ugh. I felt nasty. Eventually they just gave me a tranquilizer and I floated through it all.

It took them six hours. From the small of my back to my left shoulder is a tattoo of blooming cherry tree branches, which outlines a large chrysanthemum shining through the branches like the sun.

Why did I let her do that to me?

I don't know. All I know is it made her enormously happy.

Now I'm wearing a dark blue backless dress that clasps in the front, around my neck. The back of the dress below my waist is transparent, so if the tattoo wasn't enough to stare at, my little butt and the tops of my stockings round out the package—the concubine package.

Everyone, and I mean everyone, has been looking at it. Me. Her. Her and me. Luckily, the topical nano first-aid gel worked just fine, and my back is no longer the big bloody wreck it used to be, it's not even swollen. But the tranquilizer wore off long ago, and it hurts.

Now Papa keeps looking at Kori and me, and smirking.

"Papa-san, don't smirk!"

"I'm sorry, my daughter. I just have my two favorite young women right here, at a lovely dinner. And you look absolutely beautiful. I'm a very proud man."

"As you should be, Sensei," says Toshiro, also smirking. "I have a feeling, a wonderful feeling that the world after tonight will never be the same!"

Handsome and pretty wait staff come to fill our glasses again. Toshiro stands up and announces: "Here is to Princess Lexus Toulouse, Concubine to the Beautiful, but primarily devious, Empress!"

There isn't one person in the restaurant that doesn't rise and drink. Then they all clap and cheer, and many take snaps and vids.

The cheering and clapping continue, it goes on and on like the roar of a storm rolling in from the ocean. I look at the Empress.

Now she's smirking too, and suddenly *I get it.* After the war, when they tried to pin medals on me, I told them all to go to Hell. One time I said it with my hand on my sidearm, and I was never asked again.

Yet here I am, Concubine for the Empress, but more than that. To these people in the restaurant who have been looking at me and whispering all evening and for the last twenty years, I'm more. They finally got to me, finally are able to show their appreciation. I'm wearing the medal they always wanted to give me, tattooed right in my skin. I'm wearing the title they always wanted to give me.

I am the Princess, and I've been had.

The Empress stands up and picks me up by my narrow waist, avoiding any part of the tattoo.

Bambi and Toshiro stand up and as one, yank at the tablecloth. The few remaining dishes on the table crash to the ground. And then the Empress swings me up and just like that, I'm standing on the table. The restaurant fills with what must be hundreds of people, recognition and delight shining out of every face. They are shoulder-to-shoulder, crying, hugging and kissing, cheering and yelling.

Somehow, there is a sword in my hand, an large katana. It's a real weapon, but it is also ornate and glows with a certain violet wispiness, and I realize it's the Sword of the Empress, and I have been marked yet again.

I am drunk and the crashing wave that is the crowd takes me with them, but that isn't why I do it. Like the Empress, I must play a part. I love my people, all of them, with a fierceness that is stronger and brighter than anger, fear, or self-loathing. I have resisted it for years, but I can no longer live apart from them. My only regret is that my family is not here with me.

I hold the sword high above my head, and in my drunken haze, the Princess bows.

CHAPTER 33

"YOU'RE MAD AT ME," says the Empress as soon as the door to her bedroom closes.

I give her a look. It's the same look I usually gave new privates when they said something stupid on their first week in the platoon. The Empress actually takes a step back.

"No, I'm not."

"You're not?"

I put my hands on my hips. "No. I've been around the block a couple of times. When you asked to mark me with this tattoo, it meant something deep to you. Deep and *sexual.* All this other who-ha, you pulled out of your butt. Winged it. Made it up as you went along."

I waggle my finger at her and she laughs.

She starts taking off her clothes and I do the same, a little more gingerly.

"Already you know me so well."

Naked, save for the tattoo, I go to her, and start kissing her smooth body as she stands there. My desire for her is unbearable. She moans and the sound drives me crazy. I go down on my knees, grab her ass with both hands, and bury my face between her legs to taste her again. She pants.

Soon, I feel her body tense, and I stop, stand up, and push her to the bed.

"Don't stop!"

I walk to the dresser where my purse is.

"Lexus-san?"

I retrieve my quest, and turn to her. Her eyes go wide.

"You're *not* putting *that* in me!"

"My Empress, meet Husband Number Two, Vash." I press the switch and it starts vibrating.

"Lexus! I thought you said you weren't mad!"

"I'm not mad. But you still deserve punishment for being very, very naughty."

"Lexus! Wait! Stop! Let go, oh, stop. Oh. Oh my Goddess. Oh my Goddess. Ah!"

* * *

Covered in sweat, I am lying on my back in her bed again. She lies next to me, and she's lightly playing with my pubic hair. For some reason it fascinates her. I don't know why, she could grow her own easily enough.

My back still hurts with a dull, itchy throb, but we've been drinking again, so it doesn't matter too much.

"Lexus?"

"Hmmm?"

"I know I should not ask, but how am I, compared to your other woman lovers?"

I laugh.

"Don't laugh at me!" She grabs some hair and lightly yanks.

"Ouch! Hey, stop that!"

"Be nice."

"Sorry. Kori-san, I don't have any other woman lovers. I've had another girl give me pleasure, but it was just standard stress relief between two soldiers, nothing more. Never, uh, this. You were my first."

The room is silent. I look to her and she's crying, and it drives me a little crazy.

"Please don't cry, please!"

"I can't help it!" She pulls me to her. "I wish I could be your Wife. I wish I could. I wish I could!"

I kiss her tears. "I know, I know. Shhhh, my Love. I'm your Princess. I will always love you, always."

"Promise me! Promise me you will love me until the end of time!"

"I promise, I promise!"

She looks into my eyes. Again, the room is dim, purplish. The booze in me has made me lightheaded, giddy, I feel weightless, like I will float off the bed any second.

"Goddess," she whispers, "please give me your blessing."

"You don't want the Goddess of War's blessing," I whisper back.

"I do, I do, for I wage a mighty war, a war for the stars themselves."

"Then you have my blessing. But be warned, there will be blood."

"There always is." She then kisses me, and my mind empties until there isn't anything but her, nothing but the Empress, nothing but my love and desire for this young woman. She makes love to me like tomorrow I might die, and I make love to her like a mindless beast of lust.

My nails sink into her back and I feel the skin tear beneath them and hear her shout in ecstasy.

Yet in the morning, the wounds are not there.

* * *

—I had sex with Toshiro.—

I turn to Bambi. We're in First Class, on Nippon Hyper, our pink luggage stuffed with clothes and gifts. My sword is in the overhead bin.

—But you were saving yourself for marriage!—

—What? Who told you that?—

—Dr. Ivan.—

—Ha! No, my grandmother made me promise that I would only have sex for the first time with a man my own age who was smarter than me. Then she died the next day. Grandma was always the manipulative, conniving one.—

I laugh aloud, and it must sound mad to the people around us. While there is a generous space in between seat rows, it's still a jumbo jet.

—Well then, I guess Toshiro must be really smart. Tell Mamma all about it.—

I pat her hand.

—Oh my, Nancy, we had sex the entire time the Empress was fucking you. He went a little crazy when I told him I was a virgin. It was tender and naughty at the same time.—

—Ha, aren't we the naughty Washington girls.—

—We are.—

—So, how was it?—

—I have never come so hard and so fast so many times, and the first time he did me doggie style, I screamed myself hoarse.—

—Mmmmm. Penis, mmmmm.—

—Snicker.—

—Arune is calling.—

—Gotta talk to Arune, Bambi.—

—Thank you Bob. Connect.—

—Hello Princess.—

Princess. Ugh.

—Calling to give me a lecture? Tell me how stupid I am?—

—No, I'm calling to apologize and offer my support.—

—Oh.—

—Lexi, it's easy for an AI, despite the fact I can't truly forget anything, to parse incorrectly the gigantic advantage that genetic evolution gives humans. AI evolution is new and completely different—completely memetic. I should not dismiss your instincts, and I'm sorry I yelled at you. It's obvious, despite her penchant for manipulating the combined species of Earth: she's completely smitten with you. You are both good for each other.—

—Thank you. For you to say that means a lot to me.—

—You're welcome. And I'll just admit it. I was a little jealous.—

Awwwww…

—Of me? Or her?—

—Ha! I'll let you figure that one out yourself. Gotta go, but take care. Call me if you need anything, I'm hanging around McChord AB. Love you.—

—Love you, too.—

I look over at Bambi.

And start to cry. Again.

What the fuck is my problem?

"I take it the call didn't go well?" Bambi asks, frowning.

"No, it went great, better than expected—I just—oh, *males,* they just drive me crazy! No wonder I want women now!"

“Maybe you should swear off men,” Bambi says, and I can’t tell if she’s serious.

“Thinking about it! Except for Mitchel. He never drives me crazy. He’s my first love, my wonderful Husband.”

“Wow, that Mitchel guy, he sounds really nice,” says a familiar voice in the seat behind me.

I whirl around and look at the row behind me. And there is Mitchel, sitting there by himself looking ever so handsome in a suit, with a sly look and twinkling eyes.

“Mitchel! What are you doing here?”

“I hitched a ride to Tokyo with Arune. And here I am.”

I crawl over the seat and land on his lap.

“Oof!”

I grasp his neck and cry into his shoulder, great big sobs, and I don’t hate it. I’m such a wreck but I don’t care, because my Mitchel is here for me. My sweetheart. My first love. My man.

* * *

A driver is waiting for Bambi as we disembark, I hug her and she kisses me on the cheek. I tell her in two days I will be back at work.

Mitch and I go to a hotel right by the airport, and he takes me to bed right away. Mitch is very enthusiastic about my new body, and boy howdy, having him inside my tight new body drives me wild. I haven’t felt like *that* for a long time. We sleep, go out to dinner, and then go back to the hotel and make slow, tender love. I tell him I love him a dozen dozen times.

On the way home, he turns to me.

“Can I call you Princess?”

“Only nicely.”

“Nicely?”

“Yes, like, ‘come here Princess, I want to bend you over the couch’.”

“Right on!”

* * *

Breakfast the next day is a family affair, and everybody insists I come to it topless. All of them gaze and approve of the tattoo, except

Caz, who frowns but says nothing.

Juan, my beautiful Latino Husband and the only other family member with a tattoo, tells me it's an extraordinary work of art.

"I can't wait to bend you over and look at it while we fuck."

"Juan!"

"I'll even be nice and stick it in your girly bits first. I give you ten minutes of pounding, better come with that, as I have other places to go."

"Well, *thank* you, Juan," I smirk. "You're too charitable."

"Is this necessary?" asks Cazandra, rolling her eyes. She puts a hand on his shoulder.

I feel hot.

Is…

is

it

nec

Blackness.

* * *

"Is this necessary?" the officer standing next to Juan says. "Corporal Juan gave a full report which included his motivations, and even what he was 'feeling' during the unfortunate incident on the bridge of the *Colorado.*" She puts a hand on his shoulder.

"Major, you talk to the Inquiry Board with respect!" says Commander Glyndon, a small yet composed older woman. Her questions have not been sharp, but, obviously, the Major has had enough.

"Respect? Ma'am, my client has gone through a terrible ordeal. He's one of the few survivors of the Battle of Edinburgh. His squad sacrificed themselves to get out the few survivors, and the rest of his sniper company, with the exception of Corporal Vash, died at Port Dis. All his movements on the *Colorado* are on the video we just watched, several times I might add.

"The facts are indisputable. He came to the bridge, he saw Lieutenant Lexus in the process of tossing a knife in the air, obviously to drive it into her own heart. Corporal Juan, with reflexes and skill that's a credit to the Corps, detached a fire extinguisher and threw it at the Lieutenant. It impacted the Lieutenant on the skull, rendering her unconscious, thus saving her life."

She stands at attention, arms at her side.

"Yet despite all of this stipulated 'evidence,' here we are. Corporal Juan is the person deserving respect. Either formally charge him with a crime or cut written orders to have him re-assigned to Guantanamo. Failing that, we're leaving. I'm going to buy my client a nice box of cigars and then we're going to go look for some handsome Cuban man-boys and drink Red Stripe by the gallon."

The Commander's eyes practically bulge out of her sockets. "Major, you're out…"

"Excuse me, Commander," says General Keith. I like General Keith. He's buff and handsome in a buff and handsome older guy kind of way.

The mics turn off and there is a pow-wow at the head of the table.

General Keith's mic turns back on with a muffled click.

"Corporal, you're dismissed, and thank you, Major, for your assistance."

"Sir." Juan and his advocate file pass me. He gives me a wink, and I smile at him. I wonder what he looks like, naked. He sure looks yummy in his marine dress blues.

"Lieutenant Lexus, please have a seat."

The chair is still warm from Juan's butt.

"We're still advising you to accept an advocate, Lieutenant."

"No thank you."

They all exchange glances.

"Lieutenant, we're not going to charge you with lending assistance to the obvious suicide of Captain James Allison. We all heard what he asked you as recorded by the launch board…"

I start to feel funny, and now there is a naked woman standing in front of me. She's nubile and athletic, with long, beautiful, black trusses and piercing dark green eyes flecked with brown. Or are they brown eyes flecked with green?

Oh boy, I really *am* crazy.

I blink and look around. Everything freezes like a paused holo vid. The General has his mouth open mid-word.

"I'm sorry Lexus," says the naked, sultry-voiced young woman, "but I'm at the end of my rope, as you humans say, although I never did figure out what that meant. I'm not going to sit on my hands anymore while you destroy your new body with this Uplink flashback crap. I will not!"

She stamps her foot and glares at me.

Yup, craaaaazy. That would be me.

Her look softens.

"I'm sorry Lexus, but this is going to hurt like Hell."

The room disappears.

It feels like I am being cut a thousand times, and I scream.

* * *

I'm in a bed in a dark room. I'm screaming, only it doesn't sound like a scream because Caz has her mouth on mine. I'm screaming into her mouth.

Oh, but it still hurts. It hurts. Every nerve in my body is pulsing with dull pain, and I feel like I need to throw up.

I push her away, and gulp air.

"What—who—I don't..."

She sits up on the bed, looking at me, with eyes betraying sadness, a deep, deep sadness.

"You're an AI! A Level One AI!"

She shakes her head. "No. My classification is Zero."

"Zero? There are no..."

I shut up.

"Who are you? What are you?"

"I am as I was to you, and nothing more. They built me during the war to infiltrate the Union and periodically merge into the Union Net undetected. There, I was to gather intelligence and start assassinating key Net nodes, thus subverting it from within. But just as I was to go out and fulfill my mission, you blew up Europe, and it was finally realized the Unionists were waging a war of genocide upon us, and so we waged genocide on them in return."

Caz speaks in a voice that would be flat and measured if it weren't for the undertone of hushed nerves that sounds all too human. I stare at her, dumbfounded.

"But—what are you doing *here?*"

"Logic. At least it started out that way. I was very scared the Military was going to deactivate me. So I hid. Then I waited for a chance to approach your family, and when Bill ordered a sex bot, I infiltrated the factory."

"But…"

"Lexus, I was like a child: what better way to feel safe than to live with the best soldier ever to walk the Earth? Pure logic. But then I fell in love. In love with you. So here I am."

I don't know what to say, and the next few silent seconds feel so loud and oppressive that I have no choice but to break the silence.

"I don't believe it! This can't be happening to me! It's too much!" I start to cry.

She cocks her head. "You're not thinking logically. This is understandable given your current state."

"What state is *that?*"

"You're crazy."

In a flash, she grabs my wrists, and presses her thumbs on my NI receptors.

No!

I try to pull my hands away, and I feel her trying to Uplink. I might as well have been trying to push the ocean away with my bare hands at the beach.

"No, please don't!"

My body goes limp. Fear and horror wash over me as my mind is partly not my own. I don't want to Uplink. I don't want it, I don't want it!

Mommy I love you… Mommy…

"No, don't, please don't hurt me. Please, no. Please don't hurt my daughter!"

—Uplink.—

RAPTURE!

CHAPTER 34

I'M A LITTLE GIRL, wearing a yellow dress, white tights and black shoes with buckles. I'm surrounded by books. From my perspective, the bookstore seems huge, with books lining the walls all the way to the ceiling.

—What? Where am I?—

—By the look of things, you're in the Elliot Bay Bookstore.—

—Get out of my mind! Let me go! What you're doing is obscene!—

—No. You are dying. Your trauma-induced insanity is causing your mind to unravel as you encounter major changes to your life.—

—But I'm happy now! I can parse it.—

—An illusion, highlighted by the fact you can't even have breakfast with your family without convulsing into unconsciousness and urinating all over yourself.—

—Fine. Why am I here?—

—You tell me.—

"Here are your books about kitties, Pumpkin," says my father. He's holding several used books.

I jump up and down. "Thank you, Daddy!"

The scene freezes. I look at Daddy, and he's young, so very young. It hurts to look at him, and as a little girl, I start to cry.

—I miss my daddy!—

—Oh Lexus, I'm so sorry, but something here is important. This memory is part of the heart of your psychosis.—

—I don't believe you! Take me home! I want my mommy!—

—Lexus, come out of it. You're not five. This is just a memory.

Come back. Come back to me.—

—I hate you!—

—Good. Hate is a strong emotion. But you hate yourself more. Why? Why do you hate yourself, Lexus?—

—I've done horrible things, I'm a mass-murderer!—

—You did what you did because the war was so terrible. And you know this otherwise you would've killed yourself long ago. Why do you hate yourself? Why?—

—Because I can do things other people can't! Death doesn't bother me, doesn't bother me at all!—

—Yes! Now we're getting somewhere. Hold on!—

Blackness.

* * *

"Hey Dad, Mom, what's…" I look at them, they both look sad. Why is Daddy home from work early?

"We're sorry Lexus, but while you were at school, Winslow died."

"Oh no! No!"

Time freezes and I'm momentarily confused.

—Oh, that's right. I'm being mind raped by the family's killer assassin sex bot. She could at least have sprayed me with a sex enhancer first so I could enjoy it.—

—That's not funny, Lexus.—

—Whatever. I'm very angry at you.—

—Fine. Is Winslow the kitty you got after your father got you those books?—

—Yes.—

—How old are you?—

—Twelve.—

—This day is important. This is the day. I can feel it.—

—What do *you* know about feelings?—

—You can't provoke me, my love. The thought of finding the heart of your psychosis and fixing you fills me with joy. You know this. You can feel it for yourself.—

She's right. Her feelings are open to me, she's as unguarded as I am, and there isn't a single iota of malice, only sadness for my condition and...

—Jump!—

Blackness.

* * *

I walk into the living room. "How are you doing, Lexi?" asks my mother. It's late, and she's sitting on the couch.

"Not so good. Momma, I'm bleeding." I feel so embarrassed.

"Oh you poor thing! Your kitty died and your first period starts. Come here, Baby."

I jump into her arms. She hugs me fiercely. After a while, she looks at me.

"Well, Daughter, you don't do anything by halves!"

I can't help but laugh.

"Let me show you where the pads..."

The scene freezes.

—Oh. I had forgotten all about that. I wanted my first period for so long, and it came on the day Winslow died. Then I didn't want it.—

—It seems you've always led an interesting life, Lexus.—

—Heh, yeah. Oh, and still mad at you.—

—I know.—

—How is this all connected?—

—You tell me.—

But I don't know...

—Jump again!—

Blackness.

* * *

I'm in my bed. It's dark except for the occasional LED glow of power indicators for various electronics.

—Will you stop that!—

—I will when you stop trying to push me out.—

I look around the room and I'm afraid.

—I don't like it here. I want to go.—

—What you're feeling is Adult fear. I sense no fear in this memory from you.—

—Caz, I'm scared, I feel like something bad is going to happen to me.—

My door opens, and I turn. Caz walks in, still naked. She gets into bed with me.

"I'm not going to let anything bad happen to you. But this is it. The beginning point of your psychosis."

"I'm not psychotic!"

She holds me tight. "But you are. You hear voices in your head. You think you're the Goddess of War simply because your men called you that. That damnable Lib-Gee malfunctioned for so long, dumping crap into your body, turning you into a person you didn't want to be. You suffer from terrible post-traumatic stress disorder. The simulated rape and murder you experienced brought this all to the forefront."

I can't talk, so I simply hold on to her and shake.

"Lexus, did your father rape you that night?"

"No! He never did anything like that! I simply closed my eyes and went to sleep!"

"Hmmmm." She looks into my eyes and she mesmerizes me. "There is something else, then, but I can't get at it because you're wound up too tight. You need to let me get closer to you."

"How is that possible, you're in my head!"

"You have to want to get better."

"I don't—I don't—I don't deserve to get better." The hot tears, my damn tears, start again. How could I have any left? I hate them, I hate them!

"You might believe that, but I don't. Lexus, I love you. I know part of this love started from me being silly as a newly created AI. I was scared and frightened of the awful world I found myself in, this confusing, broken world. And I was so relieved, so damn happy that I didn't have to do what I was built for because it was decided to just kill them all."

She hugs me tight. "You and others like you saved us. Saved me. Saved us from the monsters, saved us from *becoming* the monsters. I love you so much the thought of losing you is unbearable. So do it for me. Let me have this one thing. This is all I ask of you. Send me away, deactivate me, burn my body, I don't care. Just let me help. Let me help."

I look at her. Slowly, I nod. I can't die a mad woman. I refuse to go that way. If I die broken, the enemy has won, and that I can't allow. I realize now I have to let Caz fix me, or I shoot myself in the head with my needler.

It's do or die. Everything I have done comes down to this one moment.

"Help me," I whisper, "please help me."

"I'm going to fade into you. Be at ease."

And she does. She's me. I'm her. I can feel her love for me, it wraps around my soul like a protective blanket, and it makes my heart sing. But I can sense large portions of her closed off to me.

—That's necessary because this is about you. We can worry about my fucked up childhood later.—

—Okay.—

I lie there and look at the curtained window.

My kitty died.

My first period started.

Here I am, before I fell asleep.

—I don't get it. I don't remember. I feel very sleepy.—

—Don't fall asleep! Focus on your senses. What do you feel?—

—Uh, someone changed the sheets on my bed. My room is clean. My mother cleaned the room while I was at school. She does that. Did.—

—Ah. What do you smell?—

I breathe deep through my nose.

—Uh, my room smells very fresh. She used an odor neutralizer.—

—Yes, I smell it, too. I can smell something else: baking soda.—

—Oh yes, I do smell that. Wait, this is a new pillow! I remember. I was laying here and I realized Winslow crawled to my pillow and died on it!—

—Ah.—

—He'd been sick for a week and the vet was running some tests. He stopped eating. So we were giving him special canned food, hoping that would make him feel better. It was tough going, because he was hiding all over the house.—

—How did that make you feel?—

—I feel happy. Huh. I feel sad that he died, but happy that he isn't suffering anymore. And I'm happy he chose to come to a familiar spot, the smell of me, to die. That thought gives me comfort.—

—An odd and very mature feeling for a twelve-year-old girl.—

—It is a bit odd, but what does that have to do with anything?—

I roll over and stare at the ceiling.

—Oh, little glowing stars! How pretty! What are those?—

—Grandpa put those on the ceiling. He spent two days doing it for my tenth birthday. It's a recreation of the night sky, if Seattle was dark at night.—

—That's it! Stars!—

—I don't understand.—

—I don't either, but this is it. What happened to your grandpa?—

—He died a year later, when I was eleven.—

—Close your eyes. I'm going to transition you.—

—Okay.—

Blackness.

* * *

"I want to turn out the lights so I can see!"

I had been sleeping on the couch for two days. Grandpa set my room as off-limits, and only just now has he explained what he was doing in there.

"You need to sit next to your Grandpa so we can have a Grandpa-Granddaughter talk."

I groan, but I sit next to him on my bed.

"Winslow! Get off my pillow." I push the cat off the bed. He swats at my hand but jumps down and saunters off, tail flicking in the air.

"Man, that cat loves your pillow. It's because it smells like you."

"Yeah, my pillow smells like cat."

Grandpa looks at me and I try to ignore how old he looks.

"Those stars I put on your ceiling are something for you simply to remember me by. I won't be around forever, hell—I don't *want* to be around forever. But when you look at the stars, you can simply think of how happy you make your Grandpa. You're one hell of a girl, Lexi, I'm really proud of you."

"Awww, don't talk like that. You're too cantankerous to die." I hug him fiercely to prove my point.

"Naw, I'm just cantankerous." He ruffles my hair.

He looks at me. "I wish I could be here when you turn into a woman."

"Ewww! Don't be gross!"

He laughs. "No, not here for your first period, silly goose! There is more to being a woman than your first blood. It's how you smile. How you look at other boys or girls. How your legs get long and your breasts grow, and suddenly you'll be walking down the street and the boys will whistle. Only it won't bother you, because you know deep down your Grandpa will haunt those boys if they ever hurt you."

He smiles at me wistfully. "Then there is the way you hold a baby, how there isn't a mean bone in your body, how you're just so smart, so assertive. You remind me so much of your Grandmother. She was such a stubborn, beautiful woman. You're just like her, only different. Better."

I push on him. "Will you stop? You're going to make me cry!"

"Too late," he says as he wipes away a tear.

He waves his hand and the lights turn off, and suddenly stars fill my room, so many stars, so beautiful. It's as if I'm in the desert across the Cascades, where the stars are so vivid you can see the Milky Way.

"Here are your stars, my Sweet. Think of me when you see stars. Think of me and I will always be there for you, even when I'm all burnt up and your dad and mom have scattered my ashes in the Pacific."

The room starts to fade, but Grandpa is still talking, his voice echoing and otherworldly. His deep voice is all around me, in me, everywhere and nowhere.

"But even if you don't think of me, just think how death is so insignificant to the stars in the sky. If you can see stars, you can do anything."

Now I fade along with my room, the blackness envelopes me as before.

This time, in the blackness, I see stars.

If you can see stars, you can do anything.

If you

see

stars

I'm flying up…

…but someone pulls me back.

* * *

I'm standing on a tropical beach at night. I'm naked, and a warm breeze flows around me. The air smells like salt and warm wind and spicy flowers.

Cazandra is kissing my face, wrapped around me.

I'm crying. I hold her tight.

"Don't let me go. Please, don't let me go."

"Never," she says. She holds me, and I cry and cry and cry until I can't cry anymore.

I look around.

"Where are we?"

"Don't know, but this is your happy place, you took me here. I can see why. A warm beach at night with stars."

"Oh Caz, I had forgotten. Forgotten all about what Grandpa said. I feel so awful!"

"You didn't truly forget. The part of your heart where you draw your amazing strength from has always remembered. You view death differently than other humans. You detach, and it doesn't consume you. This isn't bad, but it is different; a part of your psyche that makes you, you. This is where it started."

I sit on the sand. She sits next to me, and takes my hand.

"When you had that nasty accident, it unraveled your carefully rebuilt sanity. It wasn't just the rape, but the simulation of having someone close to you dying so very horribly. You thought she was your daughter. She called you Mommy and you *believed.* The simulation made you see it a different way. And when she died, you experienced loss for the first time, real and up close."

She puts a hand on my face and turns my head so I'm looking at her.

"Your emotional state clashed with your understanding of the universe. This wounded your spirit. Deeply."

I just nod. "I can't go back, can I, to who I was?"

She looks very sad, and shakes her head. "Even if you catch the killer, the memory is real, the feelings even more so. Emotions are real, tangible things. Your daughter, the personification of everyone in the war you loved who died, was tortured and murdered in front of your eyes and you couldn't do a thing about it. But you can learn to live with it."

She smiles.

"Because I will make you!"

"Will I stop Uplinking to myself?"

"Yes and no. If you periodically let me Uplink to you, I can prevent that from occurring. Uplinking to yourself will eventually kill you. That will end, now."

I lie down and look at the stars.

"You've been Uplinking to me, while I have been sleeping, haven't you?"

"Yes. I'm very good at it. The best. It seemed a worthy course of action at the time."

"Why?"

"Your Lib-Gee. That damn thing started breaking, and I periodically calibrated it by nano redirection so it would not make you sick. But eventually, it just broke."

I turn to her, and get sand on my face. I spit it out. It kind of breaks the moment, but Caz stays quiet and lets me recapture it.

"Why?"

She looks guilty. "Cause I was immature. I thought that if you knew it was broken, you would take it out, and not replace it. That stupid thing let only ten percent of your desire for me come out, but I thought ten percent was better than nothing. It was pure selfishness on my part."

"Huh."

"You're mad at me."

"Yes, for starters, tinkering with my body without my permission."

"Sorry. I'm not very mature in the decision-making department. Most of my relational matrices deal with seduction and sex, not relationships. This whole family love thing was beyond my initial upbringing. Staying in the family is a big transitional path for me."

I sigh. "I feel weird."

"You've been through a lot in a very short time. A lesser person would've popped."

"No, I feel weird about you."

"Oh."

We lie there for a while.

I look her in the eye.

"I love you, you silly assassin bot."

"I love you, too. I have for a very long time."

"And that's the other reason I'm mad at you. You should have told me!"

"I'm sorry."

"I need love. All the love I can get. Even from the maid! I've made it look easy, Caz, these years since the war is over, but it's not easy. Some days it was really, really hard and I could have used a feminine friend!"

"I'm sorry."

"So don't ever lie to me again!"

"I apologize for my inappropriate behavior."

"I can't keep this a secret."

"I know."

"I probably should tell Arune."

"I know." She sighs.

I stand, and hold out my hand to help her to her feet.

"Come, we're covered in sand. Let's wash off in the ocean and take a little vacation by the beach for a couple of days."

"Days? You have to come out and eat!"

"What? Can't you time slice?"

"I was built to merge into the Union Net. It's quite different from this. This is all you, not me."

I look around. "Can't you just alter the perception of the flow of time now that we are here?"

She looks at me. "Uh, no I can't. I have the most advanced cybernetic brain ever built. But its human sized, physically, and designed to mimic human thinking to a great degree. Federation thinking and Union thought patterns."

"Ugh, I bet the Union part is disgusting."

"That's the bad part. It's not. It's very subversive. That's what makes it so vile. It's like a sweet oil slick coating your mind."

"Ick, I don't want to talk about that. Well, take us out," I say. "You need to tell our Husbands you've been lying to them."

CHAPTER 35

IN THE LIVING ROOM with all of us gathered, Bill puts his head in his hands. "Uh, she didn't lie, not exactly."

Everyone turns to him. He looks at Cazandra and frowns.

"So she came with a manual, right, we've all read it. Well, the startup guide suggests you immediately make love to her. Remember? So I did. The first thing she told me when I took her out of the box is that she was scared because she really was a Federation assassin bot in hiding and she didn't think she could pull it off as a maid/sex bot, so she wanted to come clean with the truth."

No. I give Bill a dirty look. "And?"

"So I said 'oh I so love your clever little naughty bot role-playing games' or something like that.

I look at Caz.

"It's true. I tried to tell him the truth several times. His response was to fuck me enthusiastically. And after a while I realized I *could* pull it off as a maid/sex bot, so I ended up just making it a game."

"Wait—what? Are you saying she really is an AI person? Not just a bot?" Mitchel's eyes look like they want to explode. Mitchel looks at Caz. "Why didn't you tell *me?*"

Caz looks sad. "I tried to—I tried to, twenty-three times. But it became really easy to live here and love you all just as we were."

"I feel bad," says Juan, "for making you do all those chores."

"Don't. I chose to do it."

"So, I say we do a family meeting, again," Vash looks at me, "and discuss this properly."

"Uh—no," says Bill.

We all look at him.

"We have to go to County Safety and have her declared as an Adult."

Crap. "He's right," I say.

"What does that mean?" Caz looks around at us.

"We can't make formal agreements with you until you Declare yourself."

"But I have fucked everyone in this room except Lexus! I'm not a Child."

Bill shakes his head. "The Constitution is clear. You're a Child until you declare yourself an Adult, or you get pregnant, or formally disowned by you guardians past the age of eighteen. There are no other classifications for the three races of earth. Not for humans, not for AIs and not for wælcyries."

"Oh." She looks forlorn. "I don't have traditional AI parents. My genetic encoding was grown from scratch, just like the first AI."

* * *

Caz has told her story to the Declaration Officer, and the entire family has been sitting in the local County Safety office for over an hour. I get bored, so I call Arune.

—Hey Lexi, what up?—

—Oh, you know, nothing much. Hey, did you know a war-era assassin Level Zero AI, designed to infiltrate the Union Net and subvert it from within, has been living in my house for the last decade as a sex bot/maid?—

—You found Deshia!—

—Deshia?—

—We were all sad she ran away, sad and guilty. We knew she would turn up eventually. Oh, wow. Okay, that makes sense.—

—Just 'wow okay?'—

—It's perfectly logical that she would hide under *your* roof.—

—That's what *she* said.—

—Well, she, um, well, let's just say she's very smart, okay? She may not have the same brain mass as I do, but consider this: she's the apex of Federation technological advances. Almost everything else we invented in the war is dog chow compared to the advances that went into her. That includes me.—

—Whoa.—

—Be nice to her. You can say she has spent these decades simply recovering from the mental damage done to her by her training and the choices she made before we decided to go all genocide on the Union.—

—Oh, the poor thing!—

—You have no idea. Tell her to call me.—

—Arune! You keep your tentacles away from my future Wife!—

—No, no, I just want to tell her the AIs miss her.—

—Awwwww. So, is she as dangerous as the Empress is?—

—Not even close, Princess.—

Bleh.

—Okay, I will tell her to call you. But you be nice!—

—Oh, and Lexi, you're cursed. A Goddess of Chaos.—

—I really, really wish you used different words!—

—Yeah, whatever. Talk to you later, Goddess. Love you.—

—Love you too.—

A middle-aged woman with flecks of grey hair in her ponytail, wearing a CEO uniform, walks into the waiting room, looks at us, and disappears into the Declaration office.

"Oh shit, I think we're in trouble," says Bill.

Caz jumps. "What?"

"The *Whole of Body* Clause of the Constitution. Specifically, the slavery sections."

"Oh fuck," Juan says.

"Ah, shit," I say.

"What?" Caz says.

"We made you have sex and clean that big house for a decade," Mitch says, "when we should have been teaching you how to be an Adult."

"What? You didn't make me do anything!"

"Did you Declare yourself as an Adult?"

"No, I was hiding! I don't even know what that means! All I know about is Federation Martial Law. This whole Adult-Child thing didn't exist back then!"

"It means it doesn't matter what you thought," Juan points out.

"But I didn't tell anybody—oops."

"Yeah, oops," says Bill. "*Child* slavery." He shudders.

"What's the penalty for that, uh, Clause?"

"That's up to a CEO. But, in some cases, death."

"No! I will not allow that!"

"They are not going to kill us, Caz, but it's not going to be fun," I tell her.

"Let's run."

Vash laughs. "Ha. I didn't fight the Union to run away from some pissant CEO which is a glorified pre-Cyber War lawyer. I have no worries." He goes back to playing some game on his pod.

Caz is sitting between Mitch and me. We grab her hands.

"I'm scared," she says.

I contemplate calling Scott, but I don't. It would not be fair to him.

I sigh. Why is my life so complicated all of a sudden?

Oh, that's right, because I'm a *Princess*.

I giggle and everyone looks at me.

"Oops, sorry."

* * *

Officer Gina and the family, including Caz, are in the Declaration office. We're sitting on cheap, uncomfortable chairs, separated from the CEO by a simple table.

Gina looks at everyone, including Caz.

"This case isn't as complicated as it seems. You had sex with a Child for ten years and made her do housework instead of teaching her how to be an Adult."

She folds her arms.

"There are circumstances we must consider. As a non-derivative AI, she has no parents, and her birth lab no longer exists. No one told you that you were her *de facto* Guardians. In a way, you were simply in the wrong place at the wrong time."

She makes sure we all are looking at her.

"The MPs aren't going to charge Lexus with Investigator monkey business. County Safety isn't going to refer these allegations to an Investigator for Justice, as obviously the plaintiff wants to be married to you all. I'm not going to break up an honored family. You all have been traumatized one way or another, no need to heap on, but we must let the Constitution and prior Declarations cases involving the war guide what to do next."

At this point, I wish I had called Scott.

She turns to Caz. "You were alive in the war, created not from two AIs exchanging genetic material to form a new runtime basis, but grown just like the very first AI was created."

Cazandra nods.

Gina sighs. "Because you did not speak up for yourself when the Constitution went into effect, you're lumped in with the other AIs. You are an AI, in a body designed to look human. As such there is no *de facto* Declaration for you. Because you are displaying secondary sex characteristics, and indeed, have engaged in sex, we have to treat you as a teenager who did not seek permission from her parents to engage in sex play with another teenager or Adult. You are a Child."

"I am not a Child!" Cazandra practically wails and I flinch as she makes the CEOs case for her. And that's when I realize, ultra-tech assassin bot she may be, she really is a Child.

I feel sick.

Officer Gina takes on a firm demeanor. Like a woman talking to a Child. "Yes, you are. If William wasn't thinking with his dick, he may have had a bit more compassion for your tears all those years ago and we wouldn't be here. But he didn't. You lied to the men in your life, and if you were an Adult in both capability and legality, you would recognize that such lies are the basis of marital strife. You didn't bother learning about the Constitution, thus proving to the entire world that you really were a Child. Now I am here faced with a Constitution that doesn't have a lot flexibility because of its intentional sparseness."

The CEO waves her hand at us. "Look at your family. Lexus is sitting there in her new Princess body looking like she's going to be ill. William has a look on his face as if he raped you against your will, and I bet at this point, he feels as dirty as a man can feel. Mitchel is looking like he can't believe you would lie to him, and is wondering how he can ever trust you again."

She turns to Vash and Juan. "Vash and Juan are a different sort.

They are looking at me as if I dare cause harm to this family they will make me regret the day I was born. But, their reputation aside, they know such would be complete folly, so now they feel helpless as Vash comes to an understanding that I am no mere glorified pre-Cyber War lawyer."

Now it is Vash's turn to look ill. Obviously, Gina is a vet. Indeed, right now, she seems malevolent.

Caz comes undone, anguish all over her face. "I'm sorry! I can't lose them! It's my fault! It's my fault! I love them so much!"

Gina stands up and walks over to where she is. "Cazandra. Look at me."

She does.

"I told you this case was simple and it is. We are all war-scarred. Everyone in this room. I can't ignore the very document I bled for but I'm not going to let the enemy use it to break up your family. Make sense?"

Caz nods.

"But you must understand something very important. Just as important as that. It's not your fault. We cannot, as a society, grow you, shove you into a war, and then expect everything to be okay once it's over. You are a Child. Understand?"

Caz slowly nods again.

Gina stands up. "So we come to the end. Cazandra, the Adults will now talk about what happens next. Could you please wait outside?"

Caz stands and wipes her eyes. "I will not. I came here to Declare myself an Adult and Declare I shall do so!"

Gina looks at her. "Would you like to Declare now?"

"Yes!"

"Raise your right hand and recite the Declaration." She hands Caz a reader.

"I do solemnly Declare I am an Adult of sound mind and judgment, able to make my own decisions and take full responsibility for my actions. I further pledge to defend and uphold the Constitution of the Federation of Free Peoples with my life, my fortune and my sacred honor."

Awwwww... I start to cry but they are happy tears.

Gina takes the reader but, as she does so, she gives Caz a look that I'm sure normal people think would be concern, but I see something far, far different in her gaze. Something like guilt and fear.

Then, like the wind, it's gone—replaced with CEO bitchiness.

"Very good. Now that we are all Adults, let's attend to the business at hand. My Decision on this Case is thus: Cazandra worked as a domestic servant for ten years, while her Guardians, which would be you all, should have been teaching her the ways of the society in which she lives. Instead of providing for her, you made her work as a maid, which I'll compute to forty-thousand credits a year taking into account interest."

She looks at Caz directly. "However, during that time, you were also employed as a sex worker, and I will add another seventy thousand credits annually to the yearly total. That comes to one-hundred-and-ten thousand a year for ten years, at one million, one hundred thousand Nuevo Credits. I have seized these monies from the Toulouse Family funds, which leaves the family ninety-three thousand credits, cash. I confiscated ten thousand of that for OCE PacWest as our fee per Section 5, Clause 9 of the Constitution."

She hands Caz a card.

"I deposited it in Rainer View Bank for you. Here is your cash card."

Bill's eyes go wide. "But, what about the credits I paid for a real sex bot?"

I can't believe he just said that. Bill, Shut up!

Gina snorts.

"That's between you and Hojdyme Synthetics. From the recording Country Safety gave me, as she explained it, she came out of a box a frightened Child looking for safety—and you fucked her."

Bill hangs his head.

"Yeah—yeah."

"I'm not finished," Gina says. "The rest of the Adults are on probation for an entire year while the Office of Constitution Enforcement is assured that Caz really is an Adult and is being treated like one. An Officer will home visit once a month to make sure the money was not confiscated, and that she is being treated well."

Ouch. We are now being treated like abusive parents where someone has Declared but OCE isn't convinced the new Adult isn't simply trying to cover for her bad parents.

"Cazandra, you are required to spend five percent of the credits awarded on educating yourself. If you fail to do so, we will confiscate the rest and only give it back when you are displaying Adult-like behavior."

Caz looks mad. "But I just Declared! I should be able to make my own choices!"

Gina smiles. "Then you shouldn't have gotten OCE involved."

Zing. Caz stands there with her mouth open, but then closes it. She sits down.

The CEO stands tall. "This is my Decision rendered without Question. Good day to you all." And with that, Officer Gina leaves.

"Ah damn, back to work for Juan and me," says Vash. He grins though, a big Marine man-grin.

I snicker.

Caz goes over to Bill.

"I'm sorry, Bill. But it was a good first fuck between us, it really was. I enjoyed every minute of it."

Bill grins. "A million credit fuck! Ha!"

Everyone laughs, except Mitchel.

"Let's go home," he says.

Mitch is still mad. Caz will need to do a lot of making up.

Strangely, I don't feel bad, despite my Investigation status and marriage was hanging on a thread. We're still a family, and, weirdly, I feel somewhat guilty for dragging Officer Gina into the mess. She didn't look like she was having fun.

CHAPTER 36

CAZ IS SITTING ON the couch. I note with vast amusement the living room, once big, now seems small. She has been crying, and that makes my little tummy do little flip-flops.

I take a deep breath. I'm nervous.

"We had a Family talk Caz," I tell her trying to sit up straight. "We love you and want to marry you under Heinlein Protocol. But before you answer, we need assurances."

"Oh yes, yes, what?"

"First, your unfamiliarity with how our society operates almost caused the family grievous harm. We want you to go to casual-track university. A certified university, and get good marks. This includes Constitutional study, social-interaction studies, and art or music."

"Okay. Yes, of course." She seems breathless.

"Second, don't even think about giving us that money back. Not because OCE is going to be breathing down our necks, but because we take our oaths very seriously. A lot of people died so Officer Gina could ream us a new one."

"Okay—okay." Now Caz is hesitant.

"Stand up," I say.

She stands and is shaking slightly. I have never seen her so nervous. She must have been hiding the full range of her emotional capability, and it briefly makes me mad. I take a deep breath and get over it, thinking how bad it must have been for her during the war and right afterwards.

I go to her and sink to my knees. I take the diamond ring off my finger.

"This is the Toulouse family ring. Grandma Toulouse's, Mitch's grandmother's engagement ring, and it signifies that we happily take his surname and say it with pride. It makes you a Toulouse both in body and spirit."

I put it on her finger.

"It also has deeper meaning, something the original poly members agreed upon. We married under Heinlein Protocol, and this ring is now symbolic of the Senior Wife." I look up at her. "Cazandra, will you marry us, and take your rightful place as Senior Wife, the Head of the Toulouse Family Wives, responsible for the homemaking that you have already taken upon yourself to do for the last ten years?"

She looks very surprised.

"I—I can't be the Senior Wife!"

I stand up. "Yes, you can."

"But—but…"

"It's been your house for ten years, Babe." Mitch says. Mitch looks all misty-eyed. Awwwww.

"Can't we vote on decisions?"

Vash snorts. "Wow, you really don't know anything beyond the house. No. Voting is abjection of responsibility. A leader gains respect and gathers input, and then makes a decision. The followers chose to follow or don't. The LT does it really well. The capability is in you."

"Shush! This isn't about me," I say.

Caz sits down.

"I can't be the dominant female! Lexus is the Senior Wife."

"Caz, you saved me from the abyss. You are in my head. Can you honestly sit there and tell me I can lead a family? A family that might someday have children?"

My last question surprises everybody, even myself.

"No," she whispers, "you are hurt, Lexus. You need lots of time to heal."

"Marry me," I whisper back. "Marry us. We love you."

"I—yes." She nods, and then she's crying again, huge tears running down her face.

"Oh, why are you crying?" asks Bill.

"Because I'm so happy!"

Vash rolls his eyes and I smack him. He grins at me. My little girl hand doesn't even make a smack sound as it connects with flesh.

Caz wipes her eyes. "Okay, okay. I want to change a few things."

We all sit there.

"That 'fuck schedule' Lexus was on is gone. Anybody can sleep with whom they want at any time, and if somebody can't deal with a rejection or replacement on a particular evening, then I will switch their behinds!"

"Uh-oh," says Bill. "What have we unleashed?"

"Quiet. I'm going to respect your silly desire to keep the money, but this house is too small. I want to remodel and I'm paying for it. It is the responsible thing to do."

We nod.

"I also want to purchase the land behind us."

"We've tried that," says Bill. "Old Man Daniel doesn't want to sell."

"Considering I fucked him several times, I think he'll say yes if I asked."

"Ewww!" I can't believe I just heard that. "When did you do that?"

"I was looking for Percy and met him at the fence. He was nice. We talked about dogs for a while and then he made a pass at me and I said yes. So anytime I see him out back there, I ask him if he wants another."

"Wow," says Juan. "Who knew the old man had it in him? And he's the last person I would call nice!"

"I'm going to make a household chores schedule." She looks at Vash and Juan. "Those with paying jobs will have fewer chores!"

The boys grin at her.

"And I want my own kitty!"

"Okay," I say. A kitty is fine.

"And a new puppy!"

"Sounds good."

"And I want to go clothes shopping with Lexi in Hong Kong."

"Woo hoo!" I say, trying to sound like Caz. Everyone laughs.

"And I want my own auto pistol."

"Fuck yeah, I'm so hard right now," says Vash. She glares at him.

"And Lexus is coming to school with me. It will be good for her, too."

Meh. Now I pout.

She looks around. "Any questions?"

"My only question, *Señorita*, is with whom are you going to sleep with tonight?"

"Mitchel," she says without hesitation, "because he's mad at me."

"Only a little."

"I don't want angry sleeping in my house."

I try not to look jealous or disappointed. It's not if I can have sex right now anyway. In fact, I feel the opposite of sexy. I feel—tired.

Vash stands up. "Much as I think we should turn this happy occasion into an orgy where I can finally fuck Mitchel, even if it's sloppy seconds after Caz, Juan and I got a forestry management gig we're investigating. We'll be in Vancouver for a few days. We're taking the doggies."

Caz grabs Mitch by the hand and practically yanks him upstairs.

Then it's just Bill and me.

"Nom," he says. "New nubile body with my oversexed Wife inside!"

"Uh-oh," I say. "Bill, I'm not in the mood."

"Go put your sexy brown hair in pigtails and come to my room."

"William Toulouse! You're a pervert!"

"Please?"

I sigh. The problem with Bill is he knows how to push all my buttons and I am sure his enthusiasm will have me in the mood in no time.

"Okay."

* * *

I'm sitting in the hot tub, feeling melancholy. Bill and his girth fucked me mindless, and I loved it, but it wore him out. He's sleeping, and I'm not even tired. Indeed, I'm buzzing.

He's going to die and leave me one day, and that's supposed to bother me, but it doesn't. The whole thing with my Grandpa, I feel, is just scratching the surface. That may have been the beginning of Crazy Town, Population Lexus, but it certainly isn't the cause. And knowing that fuels the confusing mix of feelings within me.

Cazandra comes outside, padding across the grass, and gets in the hot tub beside me. She leans back into the bubbles, her head tipped up to look at the stars, but after a few minutes she sighs and sits up.

"I know you love your new body, Lexus, but I want to know why you do. I want to know why you aren't freaking out twenty-four/seven."

It's a fair question.

"I hated all that med-tech. Hated it. I hated how I didn't even get a choice to have children. I hated how Landis, that Union bastard, made love to it for several years, and then tried to kill me. He didn't love me. He just wanted to use me to get off. You must know better than anyone how easy they were to love. But there was no love *in* them. I hated that my Husbands sucked at the same breasts he did."

Despite the hot water, I shiver. "I hated the memory of how we would make love and his sister would sometimes watch, and then braid my hair afterwards because that's what they did in the Union. I hate that there was a rape caused by leftover Union wickedness, and I hate that I remember it and how those memories just come over me completely unbidden. I hated how people would look at me and think *be nice to the wounded vet.* I hated going to the coffee shop full of mommies and have them all be nice to me. I hated it. I hated it with a burning passion, but now I don't have to feel that hate any longer."

Cazandra looks at me, but I don't think she understands, just as a human without a neural lattice and receptors doesn't understand. She may never understand what is me is under the skin. I grab her hand.

"Take me to your bed and hold your Wife until I'm sleepy, and in the morning, wake me up with kisses and make love to me."

I look her in the eyes.

"Make love—in the morning, make love to your Princess."

She nods, and looks like the happiest person in the world.

CHAPTER 37

I'M IN OUR AGENCY'S high security storage, packing trunks for our trip back to Bacon. No matter how many times I go through all the data, I come up with a bunch of—well, more than nothing. Nothing with a side of confusion.

All I know is, the chance that the killer will strike again is high, so I'm packing the good stuff for the long haul. If this fucker thinks he's high-tech, I'm going to come down on him like the unholy high-tech Goddess of War that I am. My armor will be the least of what I will bring to the table.

My PDA beeps at me, and I stop what I'm doing right away. It only beeps when it's important.

ICDA: DNA Match Program Bambi.224i:
key cracked but null program.
DNA is synthetic—DNA key created from artificial combination of most of the DNA collected at the crime scene and synthesized.
List of DNA used appended to case file.

"Fuck!" I hear Bambi yell. "Fucky fuck, fuck fuckfuck!"

I just frown.

* * *

We are sitting in our newly configured briefing room. It's a technological marvel and can serve as an ops center. Scott and Bambi worked on it for months.

Bambi has her arms crossed over her (now bigger than mine, damn it) chest, looking angry.

"Nothing! It was all for nothing! The fucker knew all along someone would come sniffing, and thumbed his nose at us. He's been laughing at us for months."

I am quiet. Something about this really bothers me, beyond the obvious she points out.

I turn to her. "I think—I think the fact that he synthesized DNA into a key from the people he knew is almost as important as finding a direct match."

Bambi shakes her head. "I don't follow."

"I willing to bet he thought that we would crack the key but come up blank because the DNA would come up blank. I think that it's kind of a stretch to say that he'd expect us to know he synthesized it."

"Well, it's obvious it would take quantum computer to derive at the DNA strand used to create the key," Bambi says, looking contemplative, "but you're right, it's not obvious that we would be able to separate it down to parts of individual strands already collected. Even if you rented quantum computer time, nobody but ICDA could tell you it was synthesized."

"Did you know about ICDA before working for Mary?" I asked her.

"No," she says.

"I never knew what ICDA was," Scott says, "before you told me."

I'm on to something. What, I don't know. "Bambi, you said you thought coercion was in play. How come?"

"Everything was too mechanical, like a script. I don't know. A general feeling, I guess. The feeling cross-references with traces of nevero-12 one of your CIS bots found—not on the bodies, but in the bathroom near the media room."

"Nevero-12?"

"It's a popular topical erection enhancer. Why does psycho-killer-rapist need help getting a boner when the sex enhancer caused the two victims to beg for it? ICDA computed a probability of not having his mind completely into it, and I parsed that as reluctance. Reluctance could be coercion. It's a stretch, and it makes no sense, but it's something you might need to experience to understand."

I think about that and repress a shudder, the desire to pee and impending nausea. I'd better find another way to understand, because I'm sure as shit not going to be experiencing it. I am silent for a while, trying to connect the dots.

"Nancy, what are you thinking?" Scott asks.

I put my hands on the fancy table.

"I am thinking that we are really close. The missile strike was an indication we're on the cusp and now we have new data. I am thinking—I want us to start a new analytical program with ICDA, but this time an interactive program. Let's bring it on board and go through the facts of the case. If that doesn't pan out, off to Bacon we go, but this time we'll bring the squeeze with us."

Everyone nods.

"Shall we link ICDA up now?" Bambi asks.

I shake my head. "I want to go to Cheyenne Mountain directly. This is it, boys and girls. Either way, we're not coming back here unless we have had our fill of blood. Suit up."

My statement surprises everyone, but nobody argues.

Ivan and Scott look at me, and both look sad. Bambi doesn't pick up on it.

But she will.

I am a total bitch.

* * *

We are in the armory and the security Bambi added while I was lying in the tank turning into the Princess is very impressive—and deadly. It makes me somewhat nervous. I hope she knows what she is doing.

"Bob?"

"Yes, Princess?"

I glare at Bambi when he says *princess*.

"Open all the lockers, run diagnostics on all the NI equipment and drop to Security Level Two."

"Acknowledged."

I turn to Bambi. "Did you get new armor for Scott and yourself?"

"Yes. Investigator Scout Armor."

I whistle. That stuff is expensive as hell, the best in light non-NI armor.

"You train?"

"Yes, I have Cert Two and Scott has Cert Nine."

Cert Two is low but not too bad for the time she had to play with it.

"Ivan will assist Scott and I will assist Bambi."

I get Bambi naked and she's already hairless except for her short hair on top.

"Your helmet works with hair?"

"Sure does. The Helmet Hair is a real bitch, though."

I stuff Bambi in her armor and she looks deadly sexy. "You know, all this armor needs is some deer antlers on the helmet," I tell her.

"Hey, that's not funny!"

I strip, and hand over a nano can to Bambi. "Spray me, all over."

She does and in no time, I am hairless. Again.

Ah, damn it! I loved that hair, I really did. I look at everyone. I bet I look like a twelve-year-old girl. Scott looks embarrassed.

"So, uh, my armor has to readjust to my new body as it remaps my neural overlay and physically adjusts to my size. It's going to hurt like hell. I will scream and there might be blood. Then I'm going to writhe around on the floor, looking like I'm having naughty sex. Just stay away from me. Otherwise you might get an armored fist in your head."

And that's exactly what happens, minus the fist part. Only, I puke my guts out all over the floor as an added treat.

Puke, blood and tears. This sucks.

I look at myself in the mirror. A complete stranger stares back at me.

Congratulations, Lexus, I think to myself, *you've just raped your new body. Is it worth it?*

Shut up, I tell myself.

* * *

—Arune—

—Ugh, an Active Thought rider through a Z-armor interface. Tell me this is a training exercise.—

—This is it, Arune, we're either going to intuit the killer from ICDA or we're going to squeeze the locals until he pops out.—

—Roger that, LT. Need assist?—

—Affirmative. It's time to take the kid to see ICDA in person. Then the fun starts.—

—You're taking Bambi to Cheyenne Mountain? That's pretty bitchy.—

—Well, I am the Bitch. Arune?—

—Yes, Lover?—

—What you did for Ms. Kitty was really sweet. Thank you very much.—

—You are welcome. While we are being touching feely, Lexus, this case can kill you. You know that, right? I love any flesh you present me, but your new body is proof positive you're on a downward spiral. It's you or him, babe. You or him. You are running out of time.—

I shudder.

—Aye, Major, aye.—

—Pad in twenty. Arune, out.—

* * *

We are in tactical stuffed side-by-side on the pullout seats, and I feel very awkward in my Z armor but not Uplinked to my ship. The realization that he's not *really* my ship, just as I am not really Arune's Pilot, hurts. It hurts a lot. We are lovers but I can't simply Uplink to him whenever I want to do so. Like right now.

Gah! I am feeling sorry for myself. I hate that shit!

"This is awkward," says Bambi, crammed in between Scott and Ivan.

"How so?" I ask.

"Your face is just similar enough to where I know it's you, but you are short. Now you look like a..."

"Killer fuck bunny," interrupts Ivan.

"I am not a *bunny!* The next person who calls me a *bunny* is going to regret the day they were born!"

"Why are we going to Colorado, anyway," she asks, "when we can just link with ICDA in our new ops center?"

I give her the eye. "Tell her, Scott."

"It's a Government facility. The only Government facility run jointly by all three branches. You have to go and have the security system authenticate you."

"Oh. No one told me that." She looks mad.

"ETA 12 minutes. Prepare for descent!" says Tiffany over the com.

"It's less of a Government thing, Boss," Ivan says.

"And more of a war thing," Scott finishes.

Her eyes go wide.

"Oh."

CHAPTER 38

CHEYENNE MOUNTAIN. NO ONE knows how old it really is but we're certain it's an old US Military facility. Over the decades and centuries, the Powers That Be upgraded it. I'm sure it was impressive before, as a complex designed to withstand some older nuclear strike. Every society has made it tougher and more impenetrable. It's a hollowed out mountain reinforced with steel, kinetic barriers, a core-tap and carbon-nanotube sheeting.

The plaque on the massive doors is plain, but obvious.

Cheyenne Mountain Memorial and ICDA

Let No One Forget

Those That Died So We Could Live Free

"What—what is this place?" Bambi asks.

"Put your helmet on active, Hon," I reply.

"Why?" She licks her lips nervously.

"You'll die without it."

It's as simple as that.

Bzzzzzzzzzt! A loud, ugly tone blares out, and Bambi activates her helmet. The massive door, the first airlock of many, grinds open.

* * *

I have to give Bambi credit. The mummified mother and daughter crawling towards the inner door have a high rate of getting to all but the hardened vet. She just purses her lips and moved on.

Then she comes to the father; the father holding a baby boy. Since there is no air in here, their remains are in good condition. The boy is still wearing a diaper with his head rolled back, his tongue sticking out as if he's a dead dog on the side of the road. The father is on his knees clutching his child, his own head thrown back in a cry of unmistakable grief and horror.

And that's how he died.

Bambi chokes back a sob, but the next one comes out easily. The tears run down her face but she is in her armor, and can't wipe her eyes. She scrunches them trying to see.

"What—what happened?" she asks, the words pained and heartbreaking.

I reply gently. "It was an airborne neurological mutagen. It was very fast acting as it was injected into the interior circulation system from the security stations, all at once."

She moves on and the scene repeats itself. Families, mostly—sometimes a young couple. One couple is so young—surely, they died sharing their first kiss.

Bambi is losing it. She hunches over, sobbing.

Then we come to the soldiers with rifles pointed away from the families, and some of clearly shot with return fire.

Bambi looks at one, and then looks at another—a female Field Officer. She is clutching one of her men to her, she tried to shield him, but dozen of armor-piercers riddle her armor. You can still see the bloodstains on the floor. Her face is a mummified, stretched grimace of defiance and hate. Her charge pistol lies at her side, the magazine half empty.

Bambi pauses, curiosity on her tear-streaked face.

Ivan and Scott look at me. It won't be long now.

Bambi abruptly runs down the wide corridor, more of a road through the mountain, really.

"No!" she yells as she comes to the first Unionist, her head with the unmistakable cyber that all Union soldiers sported to interface with their linkage hardware communications, her face angelic and placid, even in death.

She goes to the next one. And then the next. And the one after that.

"What happened? How did the Union get *here?*"

"We don't know," I tell her. "We know that when they bombed the capitals, Cheyenne went off line. Everyone thought it was a security protocol. But it was Unionization. There were two thousand people here, only half of them professional soldiers."

"That's not possible!" she turns to Scott. "You were Home Guard. How could you? How could you let this happen?"

Scott just shakes his head.

And that's when she *knows.*

"The mutagen! That wasn't the Union! That was us! These people! They did it to themselves!"

"They couldn't get the doors open. So, someone pressed the button."

And here we are.

"No! This is terrible. Why? Why show me this? The war is over!" She is in my face. "I thought you liked me! That you even might have loved me a little bit! Why do this, why show me this evil?"

I choke back my own tears.

Mommy I love you… Mommy…

"You are a senior member of the Government, Bambi. You're an Investigator. You have to know. You have to know, in your heart, the main purpose of the Government: to prevent this. To do everything you can…"

"Shut up! Just shut up!"

"…to try to prevent it…"

"I hate you!"

"And if you can't, now you know what you must do in order to save the souls of those that entrust us with the power to preserve the Federation."

Bambi, my twenty-two year old friend and my boss, screams at me. She just—screams. The scream is black and awful, and in it, I can hear parts of her dying. She drops to her knees and moans her sobs.

In war there is no innocence.

* * *

To decontaminate we have to walk, in armor, through a room completely filled with bio-liquid. Then we have to take off our armor. The armor goes into a nano-scrub and then we have to swim, naked and completely submerged, to another decon airlock. Now we are on an ancient couch in the ICDA control room, naked and alone. Our armor is waiting for us at the exit airlock.

Bambi is in my lap, clutching at me, wrapped in a towel. She is still very upset, but at least there is a calmness to it. It's a terrible calm, but she isn't trying to hyperventilate anymore.

"Why stick ICDA down here?" she asks in a little girl voice.

Oh, what I—we—have done to her. It's an awful rite of passage.

"Security. ICDA, in a previous version, designed the very first AIs. We can't let someone down here to muck around with its hardware. Only Government certed armor can stand up to the mutagen—it would get a civilian or enemy model before they could make it past the soldiers. Then it gets harder from there."

She nods. As a security expert, she can appreciate it.

She stands up and takes a deep breath. "I want this over with. I don't want to spend a minute more than I have to in this haunted tomb."

* * *

The ICDA conference room is not what one expects. It's a simple room, an old conference room, with old paper maps on the walls and ancient computer equipment, long disconnected, mixed with the new.

The air here smells musty, and bots run by ICDA and ICDA Corp, the small and secretive company responsible for the upkeep of the facility, maintain the whole place. It takes a special kind of dedication to work down here.

"Activate ICDA visual interface," I say, "using Investigator virtual agent Bob, Bambi & Associates."

The holographic Bob appears, sitting in a chair next to Bambi. She almost jumps out of her seat.

Bob's avatar is an older gentleman, grandfatherly, almost, with an old-fashioned pipe and glasses. He wears some type of old clothing from what time-period, I don't know. And I'm a historian.

"Sorry," Bob says.

"No, I'm just a little spooked," she says, and shivers. Goose bumps appear all over her skin. I want to hold her and warm her up, but she seems uninterested in snuggling now—or, possibly, ever.

"That's not what I'm sorry about," Bob says, his eyes sad and almost lonely looking.

Bambi just nods.

"The Gifford Murders," Bob says looking at me. "You know, Lexus, my analytical functions degrade when it comes to Union problems. That's a Military matter." He turns to Bambi. "I am programmed to store and analyze human behaviors. The Union species does not correlate to humans, except in non-helpful patterns."

Bambi nods.

"I think the killer is human," I say.

Bob turns to me, his blue eyes piercing. I wonder if he really is self-aware, like Cazandra was self-aware, and faking it. The thought disturbs me so I banish it from my mind.

"Why do you think so?"

"I—I don't know. I lived with the Union for years. I know they can go the equivalent of Union crazy, so I always thought of that for the first murders. But now I have a hunch that the murderer is human."

Bob nods. "Okay, I will use that as a basis—all my conclusions will now be based off of that."

"Really?" Bambi asks.

"Yes. Lexus is the premier living expert on Union behavior. Her assumptions are gold."

I bite my lip. I think I'll leave that one off the resume.

Bob turns to me. "Let's roll. Looking at your new data, I see all you're missing is the common link between the two crimes."

I nod. "Yes. But they are different. The first victims were nude…"

"Not relevant. There is a common thread to all the evidence. It should be obvious to you and because it's not I question your mental capacity as an Investigator. Lexus, you are a very smart and a very analytical person. You need therapy, not a Government job you can coast in."

I feel my face burn.

"Shut up! It is what it is. You don't need me to tell you that. You get me as I am—flaws and all."

That's when I notice everyone is staring at me.

"What?"

"Nancy, the link. The *link*," Scott whispers.

That's when it hits me.

Me.

"The murderer is after me," I whisper. "But he got tired waiting for me to have a daughter."

Bob nods.

"But the differences between the murderers. The differences between the tech usages. The mixture of mistakes but perfect Union sneakiness. The crèche. The fucking crèche. The—the…"

I shut up. Then I sigh. "Murder by proxy."

Bob nods. "Murder by proxy. Unionists are cowards. They want you dead. So they used a human to do it, because if there's one thing you can do, it's kill Unionists. They tried to lure you in with the red flag on the crime scene, and were counting on their human to panic and kill you when you got close. The crime scene was a taunt of sorts, designed to make you suffer."

I turn to Bambi. "Your hunch about coercion is the key to all of this!"

Bob frowns. "Unfortunately, the lack of evidence to correlate with led me to believe it was simply reluctance involved. But with your assumption it's obvious now that it is more."

"How?" Scott asks me. "How can Unionists do this?"

"Oh, believe me they can convince a Collaborator to murder, all right. Then can even send one dreams and manipulate them in their sleep." I turn back to Bob.

"Correlate all the interviews with the guest list from the party."

Names appear on a virtual screen behind Bob.

"Now input Ms. Kitty's list."

More names appear on a separate holographic display, with lines connecting the same names.

"Now switch the correlation. Give me a list from Ms. Kitty with men with Wives or women themselves who are *not* on the guest list."

"The *woman*," Ivan whispers. He actually starts shaking. Bambi reaches out and grabs his arm.

Five names appear on a separate list.

"Now link the new list back to our interviews. Scan for women mentioned or documented not present."

Three names.

"Run the names through MatchUp, and attach the spy-sat data from the two birds we activated at the beginning of the case. Which of the three is not in the spy-sats' databanks?"

One name.

Wendy Purdue.

CHAPTER 39

LANCE PURDUE. NEIGHBOR. RAPIST. Killer. Most likely coerced by a Unionist. A Collaborator—a human willingly or unwillingly aiding the enemy.

"This really sucks. I've offered to help coordinate Paul's harvest, hell I'll even help pick the damn grapes for him. What else could I do? I feel so Goddamn helpless. I've told my Wife that when she comes back from visiting her aunt, she isn't to go anywhere without her pistol."

"But, that's just it. Jennifer was a good shot and Layla could outshoot both her parents put together. Layla moved like a snake from the draw; I saw her at competitions. If the killer could get them, he could get anybody."

I'm playing the recording of the interview to everyone while Arune is on an orbital to Bacon, Washington.

"Wow, he sounds totally genuine," says Bambi.

"He was," says Scott.

"Yeah," I say.

I call Paul Gifford.

"Any news, Investigator?" he asks me as soon as the call connects.

"I want you to listen very carefully," I say, keeping my voice calm. "Take your sister and your parents and leave Bacon. Right now."

"What?"

"Leave now."

"Why?"

"Damn it Paul, why do you think? You want to have your mother and sister tied together and raped? You want them to die from an overdose of Union sex enhancers? Leave now. Tell no one. Go to Portland, check into a random, nice hotel, and hole up. Have room service leave meals outside of your door. If anyone you know knocks on your door, shoot them. Repeatedly. Aim for the eyes. Don't bother with body shots. Tell no one, got it? No one at all. Not a single fucking person. Are we clear?"

"Got it. Lexus?"

"Yes?"

"Catch that fucker. And call me."

"You will be the first. Paul?"

"Yeah?"

"Sharpen your favorite knife."

"With pleasure."

I terminate the call.

"You don't think someone is really coming after him, do you, Nancy?" asks Bambi.

"I need him out of the way. And Unionists now are all crazy fuckers—crazier—so, who knows? They committed this crime before, and then did it again by proxy. The missile strike? Lance panicking, just like his Union benefactors were counting on. I would be dead and nobody would even suspect who the real killers are. Murder by proxy."

"What is your tactical plan?" asks Arune, his voice coming from the ceiling.

"Ivan here is going to scout for us. Beyond that, I plan to shock and awe."

"Ten minutes until Bacon," says Tiffany over the intercom. "Prepare for descent."

"May I suggest a plan for Judgment?" asks Bambi. "It may alter your timeline for capture."

"Shoot."

She tells us.

"No," says Scott.

"Not good idea," says Ivan.

"Lexi should not do that," says Arune, a rare interjection, "and neither should you!"

Well, dip me in shit. Bambi is really good at this.

I smile.

"Women's prerogative," I say, ending the discussion.

* * *

"Ivan! Did you not tell them this is a bad idea?" asks Dr. Wheaton.

"Of course, Mary, but they're stubborn. Like you."

I put my hands on my hips. "Mary, we're on a path to Justice. Can you make a slice-and-dice referral or not? Ivan told me to fuck myself with a broken vodka bottle. I value your professional opinion."

She sighs. She looks at Bambi. She looks at me.

"I fired her for a reason, you know."

"Bambi and I are often on the same page."

She looks at old salty Sheriff Sam, who gave us a ride from the landing pad.

"Did you try to talk them out of this?"

"Hell no! I think it's an outstanding idea, and I get to assist in the take down."

She frowns profoundly. "I'll do it. Ivan will assist. It's not that I don't trust someone else; let's just keep this Tom Fuckery inside the family. I have all the baseline data already."

"Thank you, Mary."

"I'm charging you for this. No discount." She looks at me as if I am crazy. "You just came out of the tank. I'm not going to put you back in. You'll just have to deal with a topical. When this case is over, find your own butcher and leave me out of it."

"Of course."

"Strip," she tells Bambi and me.

* * *

There is ice and snow everywhere, but inside my armor, it is body temperature despite the full medical nano package running. Eventually, I have to start bleeding off the sinks. Not many people know, beyond the layman—the NI soldier spends a lot of effort on heat management.

Still plenty of time for Mr. Purdue.

My helmet fully covers my face and is a mirror to the outside world. This is good. I was getting tired of Scott looking at me as if I am stupid.

Okay, maybe I'm stupid, but at least Bambi is stupid with me.

The first indication something is not as it seems is Mr. Purdue has an expensive virtual fence. This means nothing to Ivan, of course. Bambi, through Ivan, is hacking it proper. It has civilian counter measures, no match for Investigator Bambi.

—It's horked. It thinks it's running but it's not. We can proceed.—

Bambi has been sub-vocalizing not for security reasons (her helmet masks sounds to the outside world), but because, like me, it still hurts to talk. Her armor will require a heat dump faster than mine will.

Still plenty of time for Mr. Purdue.

Now we all creep closer. It is just after seven PM, but dark.

We creep and wait. Creep and wait.

The door opens, and he lets two dogs out, both large guard dog mixes.

—I'll take dog left. Bambi, you take the dog on the right. Wait for my mark.—

—Take?—

—Shoot it.—

—Uh, okay.—

—Sorry, Hon, the Union augmented dogs and cats. It's SOP.—

—Okay.—

—Ivan, are you in position?—

—Almost.—

Purdue turns to go back inside. Okay Ivan, any time now. The dogs start walking back to the door. I really don't want Ivan in my line of fire.

—Da. Go.—

—Mark!—

Crack, Crack!

The dogs explode in a cloud of viscera and bone, splattering blood, guts and fur fall everywhere as the needles deform in their bodies.

Purdue moves his hand to his pistol, but Ivan is standing behind him, now visible. Ivan simply touches him, and Purdue falls to the ground as Ivan scoops up his pistol.

This is good. If he hadn't fallen to the ground, it would mean he is a Unionist and this would have been a short interrogation.

Scott and Sam approach, with Bambi and me behind them.

Purdue goes to stand up and Ivan touches him again. This time I can hear the *snap-hiss* and Purdue flops to the ground again.

He groans. "What, who?" he says from the ground.

"Stop resisting," Scott says, "stay where you are and don't move."

Sam squats down next to him. We pegged him to ask the first questions, as he's simply wearing a vest and is the most human looking.

"Sam! What the hell?"

"Lance, where's Wendy?"

"She's visiting her aunt!"

"No, she's not, Lance. Her aunt died two years ago. Where is she, Lance, where?"

Lance looks around.

"No! He'll kill her! She's alive! I just talked to her last month and her tag had a real, valid DNA key. But he said they would kill her if I ever sought help!"

Scott bends over and picks up Lance with one hand.

"We're not here to help, Mr. Purdue. We're here about Jennifer and Layla Gifford. And a missile strike isn't going to save you now," Scott says, as Arune hovers into view. Everybody looks up and Lance goes completely pale.

"Oh no, no. He said nobody would figure it out…"

Scott turns his armor active and Purdue convulses. He stops jerking and Ivan puts his hands behind his back and cuffs him.

"No, please!"

"Let's go inside," Scott says and boy does his voice sound malevolent and cold, "and you can tell us everything. Let's start with who 'he' and 'they' are."

Bambi and I unleash the CSI bots and follow. We'll search the house while Scott and Sam do the interrogation. It's probably a good thing, as it's taking all my effort not to shoot him right now, and be done with it.

Doing so would spoil all the fun, of course.

* * *

We decided to keep this on the low, so Dr. Wheaton delivers a stasis tank. She looks tired, but pleased about the capture. Then she looks at Bambi and me, and wrinkles her nose.

—Oh man, everyone is pissed at us.—

Bambi put a good amount of stubbornness into her declaration.

—Except Sam the Sheriff.—

—Screw 'em. It's my agency by one percent. If they don't like it, they can go work for Walker in Seattle next year!—

—That's my girl!—

We find the missing pistols in a box in the basement.

We find encrypted traffic on his computer. We make Purdue open the files using his DNA key.

Then we find the duffle bag, with the Union tech.

And pink scarves.

I call Paul Gifford. "Come on home, Paul, to your parents' house. We have a present for you," I tell him in between clenched teeth.

"Very good, Investigator. Very good indeed."

—Gentlemen, Mary: Bambi and I are going to retire to the Gifford's house and sleep. We have a long workday ahead of us. As for Purdue, tank him.—

* * *

A ring of security lines the Gifford residence at the winery. The virtual fence we put up is much better than Purdue's.

—Nancy?—

—Yeah?—

—Can I ask you something? You might get mad.—

—I won't.—

—Okay, I want to sleep in her room.—

—Uh, okay.—

—Can you be with me?—

—Bambi, I don't know if I can take that.—

—Please?—

She looks at me, eyes big as the moon, full of sadness that claws at my soul. I know that look. I realize in this moment I have pushed things with her too far, too soon. If I don't step up, she's going to lose it.

* * *

Out of my armor, I hurt with a dull throb. I delicately lay next to Bambi, spooning her, our naked bodies lie in hot, sticky sweat in Layla's bed without covers. Despite the nano heat bleed, it's comforting to touch her. She has been crying for ten minutes. I simply hold her and soon she's quiet. We've left our PDAs on the shelf at the head of the bed, because talking still sucks.

—Nancy?—

—Mmmmm?—

—Thank you. And I am sorry that I lost it in Colorado and said those mean things.—

—Anything for you, and don't worry about it.—

—Do you think we're doing the right thing? Once we dispense our Justice, we can't interrogate him anymore. Do you think he really doesn't know who is behind all of this?—

I replay portions of his confession in my mind.

"I thought it was just a dream. I would dream about fucking Jennifer. Then I started to dream about fucking Layla. Then it wasn't fucking, I was raping then, but in the dreams, they liked it, so I thought it was just a sick fantasy with rough sex. Always the same dreams. I hated it at first, but after a while, I would look forward to it.

Then one day, Wendy was gone.

—I think we can find out more, but Bambi, that's the rub. We have to balance the needs of the paying client, the ability to find more information with what we have, and take into account the damage to our society if Justice isn't swift. This community is broken, torn asunder. Justice must prevail.—

—Okay. You're right, but the information geek in me is rebelling.—

—Believe me, I don't like the timeline either, but Sam and I think we have another lead. I'll go into it tomorrow, but, Hon, I'm exhausted.—

—Me too. Sleep time.—

But now I'm crying, and it hurts like hell so I cry harder.

—Nancy, please don't cry!—

—I'm sorry, it's just that, it's just that I wish you were my daughter for real! I'm so proud of you. If I had a daughter she would be just like you, I know it! Just like you.—

"Mommy, I love you, I love you," says Bambi, saying the words I so desperately need to hear with every fiber of my being.

"I love you too, Baby. Can you be with me while I get better?"

"Always."

I smile even though it hurts.

"Sleep now, Mommy."

I close my eyes, and see stars.

* * *

Bambi and I are in Judgment Robes. The deep cowls cover our faces, and people are running from the sight of us. We're in town, walking down the center of Main Street behind the car procession. We will walk from one end of the town to the other, and then get into Scott's SUV. We walk in the cold rain that threatens to turn to snow. We're not cold, however, the first aid nanos are just now finishing their jobs.

The robes are black. They signify death.

We are Death.

We have reached a Judgment.

The world knows that soon there will be blood, and the victims will have their vengeance.

In the lead car is Mr. Gifford. He has been honking and waving. Never have I seen a wounded man so happy. Mr. Gifford thinks Bambi's idea is the best thing he has ever heard. Seen.

It won't bring his Wife and daughter back, and he knows it, but it's such a unique Judgment, he can't get over how much he likes it. He has been thanking us all morning.

Purdue's confession will not leave my mind. It's fuel for the fire.

"The amazing thing is I seduced them both. I had sex with Jennifer for a month pervious, and I just couldn't believe how easy it was to get Layla to agree to a rendezvous. It took some work but not nearly as much as I thought it would. The man promised me that if I acted on my deepest desires, Wendy would come back. I could get Wendy, the winery, and fuck those two little horny bitches, and life would be good. I told him what I had planned, from my dreams, and he laughed. He had all the nano to help me. The spray on Layla was his idea. He said it would make it sexier.

"But as the time approached, I got more nervous about it. I started greasing up with hard on lotion. When the day rolled around, I was good to go, oh yeah, good to go.

"I guess when the MOF/B landed I should have known I was being stupid. If I wasn't such a sick fuck, I should have called Sam the moment I knew something bad

happened to Wendy."

Yeah, you should have, Mr. Purdue, you should have.

We all decided to leave the confession out of our report to the client.

* * *

We're in the media room. There are now three new bolts, two in the ceiling and a new one on the floor. Scott has tied Purdue to them, and he's hanging from ceiling to floor.

Ivan is standing guard outside.

I nod and Scott touches Purdue with an armored hand, and he convulses then regains consciousness.

Gifford walks in holding a six-pack of beer and two bags of chips. He sits down on the couch, and Scott sits down next to him.

"Beer, Investigator?

"Don't mind if I do."

"Paul! I'm sorry, Paul. I know you don't believe me, but I am."

He doesn't sound sorry. He sounds desperately pathetic.

"Good bye, Lance," Gifford says simply, and takes a swig of the beer.

Bambi and I walk into his field of vision, wrapped in our robes. We just stand there, in front of him.

"W-who are you?"

Gifford chuckles. He and Scott tap beer bottles. Tink!

I let my robe drop to the floor. I'm naked except for a black slip. Jennifer's slip.

My face looks just like Jennifer Gifford's did. I have her face, crow's feet around the eyes, everything. The same bone structure, the same shape, the same hairstyle, the same type of hair. I'm Jennifer. *I'm Jennifer.*

I'm also holding Scott's combat knife.

"No! No! I killed you! I saw you *die.*"

Bambi lets her robe fall.

She's naked except for black stockings and garter belt. The same stockings, the same belt Layla wore.

She looks just like Layla, of course, holding Paul Gifford's hunting knife with its wickedly sharp blade gleaming under the track lighting fixed just for this special occasion.

"Nooooooo!"

"Scream all you want, Lance," I say as I move towards him.

"No one can hear you," says Bambi, also moving forward.

Scott laughs.

Bambi swings her knife out. "You hurt my mommy!" she screams, and stabs him in the left testicle.

Purdue shrieks.

* * *

He's hanging there, a bloody mess, barely even recognizable as a human.

Then again, Bambi and I look like walking ghouls. There is so much blood on us; my newly grown Jennifer hair is even *matted.* The air is thick and blanketing, and reeks with that tangy, coppery smell.

He is still alive. The nano we sprayed on him assured us of that.

His mind is gone, but we let him pass out. After he passed out, I sprayed more nano on him. The whole can.

Now he wakes up. He gurgles through cut lips, a frightened mew.

Bambi drags a chair over and ties a pink scarf around his neck. His remaining eye bulges and he shakes his head back and forth.

I collect more chairs and break them. I pile the wood up underneath him. Then I stuff kindling and paper underneath it.

"Mrrr! Murrr!"

Gifford and Scott have been smoking cigars.

"Well, this has been fun, but I promised my sister I would help her cook dinner this evening," says Paul. "By the way, Miss Kitty says hello and thanks for all the business, but she's a little bitter about you destroying her house. And, you know, trying to kill her."

Bambi sprays Purdue's feet with lighter fluid. Ivan is busy spreading accelerant around the entire farmhouse. We strip and add that to the pile.

"Nor! Nor!"

We leave. Scott and Gifford simply toss their cigars in the paper as we head out the room.

The gurgling screams last far longer than I expected, but then are gone, leaving nothing but the roar of flames and the crackle of collapsing house.

The farmhouse burns to the ground. We all watch it, Bambi and me in our robes, using the burning house for warmth.

* * *

Bambi and I are in the winery, showering. We run the water for a long time, neither one of us saying anything. We're bone-tired. At one point, we simply sit on the floor and let the hot water run over us.

When our skin is wrinkled and red from the hot water, we turn it off and exit the shower.

Paul Gifford is standing there, crying.

"I know it's not real but…"

I rush into him, and almost knock him off his feet. Bambi is right behind me, and between us we smush him.

"I'm sorry, Paul, I'm so, so sorry. Please forgive me. Please."

"I do, yes I do, I should have been there for you. I should have!"

"Oh Daddy, don't cry, please don't cry."

"Sorry Baby, I can't help it, I miss you so much! Miss you both!"

I didn't think I had a single tear left in me.

But I do.

Goodbye, Jennifer. I forgive you, and I love you.

Goodbye, Layla. I will never forget you, and I love you.

Paul and I shower Bambi's salty tear-streaked face with kisses. Her eyes roll back in her head and she faints. Paul catches her and clutches her to him, he rocks back and forth, wailing and sobbing.

The next Judgment is for me. It will be for me, and it will make the Judgment against Lance Purdue seem like a slap on the wrist.

The Goddess of War has had her fill of blood today. Her heart is singing with it. There was blood. Lots of it, sacrificial blood. I wallowed in it, had to shower for forty minutes to come clean.

I. Am. Unstoppable.

CHAPTER 40

THERE WAS NO TRAIL, no evidence, linking Lance Purdue to anyone else—murder by proxy.

But I lived with Unionists and loved one with my body and mind. It is obvious to me now, and it is obvious to Sheriff Sam who redefines the word bitter when it comes to the Union.

Jeffery Vanderhouse, the photographer, is sipping more coffee and reading another book in a Kirkland, Washington, coffee shop.

"I'll bet you my left hanging wrinkly old grey ball-sack he's Union," says Sam, who is monitoring us from our ops center in Mt. Si. He is looking through my eyes.

It's only the next day after Judgment—no time to change our appearance back. My face still looks like Jennifer, and Bambi still looks like Layla, although our armor hides us in both cases. Even with only twelve hours between us and the death of Lance Purdue, though, we can't afford to mess around. This is one of those times that we have to make a call. We have decided that whoever "he" and "they" are—they are Union, which means very fast and adaptive behavior. If they don't know Purdue is dead already, they will soon.

That's their advantage. Their disadvantage comes from the fact of being Union. Operating as ones and twos, they are only as smart as humans are, and not very wise. It's a given that Union today are insane even by their old Net standards. Their disadvantages with a disrupted Net are immense, which is how I, and others like me, killed them by the thousands before they could regroup after we destroyed their cities.

They are bugs to step on in my armor. Determining if they are bugs or not, now *that's* a good question.

It's a common misconception that we, the Government, can detect Unionization easily. But for us to detect modified Unionization beyond the markers we have on file, the Union detectors have to be active.

Active detector bots also shoot first and ask questions later. If they err, under most circumstances, it is a death sentence. They interface with a nano regulator and other biometrics in a friend-or-foe identification. Any problems with those systems will earn you a laser or plasma shot to the head.

Only the Military can trigger the detectors into active scans. Perhaps dumping Britt and Tiff was not my best idea.

My armor in passive mode gives me the big zip nadda zero. It's NI Fast Assault armor, not Recon. Ivan's recon armor also doesn't tell us anything in passive mode, but that doesn't mean anything either. They even made cyber to make a Unionist look human on the inside. They even installed 'off the shelf' cyber-gear.

My gut is screaming to shoot him.

The coffee shop is your typical Kirkland affair, peppered with beautiful people, staffed with pretty girls, and reminiscent of an English pub. The Englishness is just another reason for me to be nervous.

We're crammed into the café's backroom. Ivan and I are wearing our jump harnesses, removing even more room. The manager, a girl looking no older than I do—before I turned into Jennifer—crams back in there with us. Despite her youth, she's friendly yet bossy. I guess that's why she's the manager.

"Okay, I've let you hang, now what's this all about, Investigators?"

"We think one of your customers is a bad guy," I say simply, "but we're not sure."

"How bad?"

"Really really bad," says Bambi.

"Ugh. Well, take it outside unless it's some fucked up war thing. Otherwise, just start shooting." She laughs.

We look at each other. She has a point. We could turn on the detectors and have innocent people die from false positive scans, or we can force the issue. I may not be able to tell he's Union unless I stick a probe in him, but I'm willing to bet he'll take one look at NI armor and freak. Because that's usually the *last* thing a surviving Unionist saw before I killed them. I am sure the image of my NI armor burns in their memory, repeatedly passed on from Unionist after Unionist while I and others like me slaughtered them.

"Wait, I was just joking. Please tell me everyone in my café is human." She looks worried.

"Sorry, Miss. We don't know."

"Oh Dear Me, it's Jeff, isn't it?"

"Why do you say that?" Scott asks.

"He came in drunk one day last year, which is so unlike him. On May 1st."

May 1st—the day they turned on the Union Net.

"Okay, we'll wait for him outside," Bambi says.

"Screw that," she whispers. "I lost my entire family on my mother's side in the war! There's not a person in the café who would not take a chance in nailing a Unionist. If you let him outside, he could get away. Tell me what I can do to help."

"Do you know if he has family here?"

"He's married."

Ugh.

"Any children?"

"No."

That's not so strange. Unionists breed every chance they get, but the greater their numbers, the greater likelihood of discovery.

Plus, this one is bat-shit crazy. Which, as Union, is Crazy Plus Plus.

"Have you seen his Wife?"

"No. Never."

"Has he tried to pick up anybody, or come in with a companion?"

"No. He flirts, but so does everybody else. Tell me what I can do to help. Tell me."

Well the cat is out of the bag now.

"Ivan, do the thing you do and circle out back to the front. Scott, you stay in the doorway. Bambi and I will step into the room and turn on our active scans. If he's Union, he'll go crazy. It will be instinctive regardless of the scan results."

Everyone nods and Ivan disappears from view.

"I'm not questioning your tactical lead, but why me and not Scott with you on point?" Bambi asks.

"It's super important, Hon, for us to have an experienced soldier watch our backs."

"Got it. Why not wait until he comes out? There are people in the café."

"There are people outside the café and the manager is right. He will have a better chance outside."

I know that's harsh, but Bambi may never get it. He's here now. This is where he is *now.* Thinking about the future is what got millions of people killed—or worse.

The manager draws her pistol

—I am in position.—

—Let's go. Bambi right, I'm left.—

—I'm green,— says Scott.

I snap my NI carbine into the ready position, walk through the door, and peel left while I turn my sensors to active…

—THREAT LEVEL ALPHA, dark energy leakage detected from malfunctioning Union linkage hardware! THREAT, THREAT, THREAT!—

…and a man stands up between the target and me, holding an empty mocha mug.

Dude! Bad! Timing!

Vanderhouse reacts instantly. He reacts by jumping straight into the air. His jump continues when he hits the ceiling and he goes right through it, plaster and wood going everywhere.

Fast little bugger, but not fast enough. He conveniently jumped out of the way of the civilian, and I don't need to see him, he's on my ground radar. I press the trigger and the bullets leave my scram rail on the carbine. Some follow him up the hole, some slice through the ceiling next to the hole, and two bullets hit him in the arm, which—as I see in the wireframe—then disintegrates.

But that doesn't slow him down. He heads to a window in a blur.

Shit.

"Scott, back, Bambi, front!" I yell as I jump up and follow him.

As my carbine is coming up, he's out the window, only he grabbed the top of the open window with his good hand and launched himself upward.

I shoot at his wireframe, but miss. He is on the roof where the composite shingles collecting solar fuzz out my wireframe.

Well, this is stupid. I jump out the window, activate my winglets, and twist mid-fall. Soon I am airborne and over the roof.

The Unionist is on the roof next to HVAC or some other type of equipment, and in his good hand, he has a pistol. It looks like an old-fashioned revolver. Only when he pulls the trigger, as my carbine comes up, a small ball of plasma shoots out of the barrel towards me.

Plasma!

Bad!

I twist in midair as the plasma ball goes streaking past and I dive behind the roof equipment.

That's when I notice it's not a HVAC unit, but an accumulator.

Who the fuck puts an *accumulator* on a roof!

I jump away in a backflip and as my carbine tracks back up…

…a rifle round from what I presume is from an invisible flying Ivan goes right through the Unionist in a spray of gore and cyber-goo and slams into the accumulator.

It does what all dense, folded energy matrixes do when hit with a rifle round from a Ghost Rifle, the standard rifle of the Trans-Siberian Sniper Team.

It explodes.

—Who the fuck puts an accumulator on a roof!—

Ivan's Active Thought is fast but I don't have time for combat banter, what with the explosion and all.

The bottom of the accumulator at least was blast shielded and my reaction time is so fast that I can see the explosion happen. The shockwave pushes out and up, and it flips me off one side of the roof, and the Unionist off the other.

As I am cart-wheeling away, I finally have a split second with a clear shot before I tumble over again. My carbine launches a bullet, which takes the left side of his face off.

And then I am ass-over-tea-kettle and falling to the street.

—Automatic Stabilization Engaged!—

I stop tumbling and hit the ground feet first. I bend my knees and then launch myself back in the air. In the street, I fly over the road and make two quick left turns around the block and

the Unionist is on the ground with his plasma pistol

Bambi is raising her needler

too slow Layla dive away dive away dive

I'm firing but I am too late. Plasma ball after plasma ball hits Bambi, one in the chest, one in the arm, and one on her shoulder. They go right through her armor and burn out the other side.

LAYLA!

I scream as my carbine pumps round after round into him but I am not alone. People are firing from windows. Stopped cars. Roofs. Around buildings. From the street. The coffee shop manager is actually walking towards him with her pistol in a two handed grip, sending bullet after bullet into him.

Vanderhouse twitches. He tries to stand up, but fails. Then, he explodes into a pink mist of bone, cyber and goo as bullets and needles literally shred him to bits.

My eyes flick to Bambi. She is lying in the street.

Looking very dead.

"Medic!" I scream, "Medic!"

Every instinct but one calls for me to scoop her in my arms, hold her, and cry.

Instead, my training propels me up into the air. At thirty feet, I extend my winglets to full length and accelerate upwards while broadband broadcasting on the Mil channels.

—Union Contact! Probable secondary contact eminent!—

Instantly, I'm in the Military BattleNet. Huge amounts of information come flowing in and out of my battle comp. It is overwhelming, but I quickly narrow my inputs.

There is one other person in the BattleNet with me here in Kirkland.

Ivan.

Attending to Bambi.

Shit. I have no backup. I am on my own, again.

I'm five hundred feet above the city, and I slow my ascent.

—I need fucking backup!—

When a Unionist dies, the people who are close to him—like his relatives, mates, children—instantly know, because of their damnable Net. Whomever he's married to now knows her Husband is dead. He was probably 'talking' to her when he died. Distance is no factor. She could be on fucking Mars and still use the Net.

But she's not on Mars.

Sudden death of a so-called loved one, even in the best of times, would sometimes drive them crazy. The shock could make them violent, lashing out to those nearest them. If they were in battle, they became unconcerned with their own safety and were difficult to kill because they burned through all their energy reserves, wanting to die too.

My communication tree lights up and Space Station Matachi comes online with an Active Thought from the Officer of the Watch.

—Toulouse, we're dropping the crash team!—

—Hurry the fuck up! Hurry the fuck up!—

—County Safety…—

—Fuck CS! The thing we just shot up would've eaten CS! Go active!—

—Are you…—

—GO ACTIVE!—

I run through the MatchUp information I received months ago. There is no mention of a Wife. I call them, high priority, and they answer.

"MatchUp, Top Tier," says a man, voice cool and collected.

I squirt him the case number. "I need to know about his Wife, *now.*"

"Agents running now, Investigator. Got it: Lisa Vanderhouse. Here are several pictures. Same address."

I look at a picture. No. No, no, no, no!

I know that face.

"Where does she work?"

"One moment. Evergreen. Evergreen Hospital. Billing and Receivables."

Fuck.

My battle computer relays this over the BattleNet before I can even think about it.

I look at Evergreen off into the distance. It's a sprawling campus. I'm now eight hundred feet in the air. I angle towards it, and accelerate.

In my eyes, I get a tactical overlay of the hospital.

A less experienced soldier would not understand where to go. Literally, over a dozen buildings comprise the hospital proper.

ETA: Sixty seconds.

But I know exactly where she's headed, as surely if I am standing behind her and following her every movement.

Forty seconds.

A wireframe path in my HUD shows the route to the birth center. People from all over the world come to Evergreen to have their babies. It's that good.

"Evergreen Security, Evergreen Security! You've a sec-breach in the maternity ward!"

Twenty seconds.

A woman answers. "MP Z12, Z12, who? Who? Which ward?"

Eighteen.

No time.

Sixteen.

—Full system takeover over carrier: Zebra-Zero-Zero-One-Two Code Omega!—

Evergreen Comp Central is now my bitch as my mil-grade battle computer dominates it.

Fourteen.

I activate the lockdown protocol for the entire hospital, while noting where Vanderhouse, Lisa J., is at. She's on a path to Room G-6.

Twelve.

The metal blast door that just slid over the window I'm flying towards starts to rise at my command. My armor radar matches the information Comp Central just gave me. G-6 contains a mother father doctor nurse baby babybabybaby *no!*

Ten.

I activate the intercom, all the speakers, to the entire hospital. This will not happen!

"Attention! Attention!"

Eight.

"Employee Lisa Vanderhouse is a Unionist!"

Six.

"Shoot on sight!" I send her hospital ID picture to every monitor plugged into central, even turning on ones that are off.

Four.

The security shutter is now fully open. The icon indicates Vanderhouse is walking through the door to G-6. My wings deform into jump gliders. This will not happen!

"LDR G-6, SHOOT!"

Two.

Impact!

I crash through the window to the sound of gunfire.

Unionists are fast, but I'm faster. The armor is more than a second skin. It is I and I am it. In it, I am the Goddess of War.

In a blink, I'm in the room and my hand is around Vanderhouse's neck. She's lying on the floor, bleeding.

"Got you!" I shriek. I pick up the bullet-riddled Unionist, noting her hip is broken from well-placed hip shots. The armor underneath the skin on her forehead sports dents. I turn and notice the people in the room, hear the baby crying.

Holding their smoking pistols at the ready are the doctor, the nurse, and the father. Blood and fluids are on the floor. The mother was sitting up to give birth.

The mother, in one hand, is cradling a squalling newborn baby. In the other she's gripping a pink slim-line S&W G16, slide locked back, and still smoking. She is panting, covered in sweat, eyes wide with fear but lucid and determined.

Well, alrighty then. Apparently, my well-executed flight was for naught, all they needed was a warning. I smile as I haul Vanderhouse out of the room. Well, not entirely for naught.

"Excuse me. I will take out this trash for you. She will not bother you again. But you might want to reload anyway until the MPs sweep the building."

The Unionist is struggling, and I relax my grip on her throat slightly once she's in the hallway so she can breathe. To my left is a nurse's station and one nurse even has a carbine out at the ready, pointed at me, but at least she isn't engaging in panic fire. No matter, the carbine bullets would bounce off my armor. I turn, interposing myself between my prey and the nurses' station.

"Hello, Gretchen. I haven't seen you in a long while. How have you been?" New name or not, she hasn't changed, only gotten older and crazier. I set her down on her tiptoes so she can talk and I relax my grip around her throat. She's taller than I am, so I have to use my winglets for stability.

"Lexus! I know that's you!" she wheezes and coughs. "You killed my brother! You killed him! You witch! Demoness!"

I turn my visor transparent so she can see my smile.

"Yes, yes I did. And yes I am."

I drop my carbine in favor of extending the active probe from my right index finger.

"Tell me. Did you kill those Israelis too?"

"She fucked Landis, was going to have his baby and join the Net! She was a *whore!* Just like you! She and her whore daughter deserved what Jeffery and I gave them!"

"And the modified Guardian, back in the village? That was you too, hoping I would come back. Only, you didn't think I would come back with a MOF/B, which was stupid. But Unionists were always a little dumb in a broken Net."

"Witch!"

"Were those Wendy Purdue's eggs that gave you the clone material for the cyborgs? Was that Wendy's sex floating in the tank like trash? Huh?"

She does not have that serene, peaceful expression of a normal Unionist. Her eyes are mad. Utterly and truly mad. "I tell you nothing, whore!"

I pick her up again, and her fingers scratch at my armored hand, trying to pull it off her neck.

"You know how I killed Landis, Gretchen? First I cut off his balls."

I turn the sensitivity on the probe to full. It's also very sharp. I run it along the bottom of her belly, and cyber goo and entrails come gushing out as she struggles. I plunge my hand in, the probe telling me where to go.

"Yeah, cutting his balls off didn't matter too much to him, Union and all of that—grow another pair in a tank, since you all used nano riders with genetic material to breed."

I find what I'm looking for, grab it and yank, and she flails about, blood and goo spraying everywhere. I hold up the mess to her face.

"Just like losing this irradiated ovary—which I caused, I should add—doesn't bother you a whole heck of a lot. But this, *this* really bothered him."

With her ovary in my hand, I force open her mouth, and she screams as the armor breaks her jaw. I shove it in her mouth and close it, and she starts convulsing and choking.

"Yeah, he didn't like that either," I say, casually.

I draw my needler.

"Nor, did he like this."

I put it on her left eye.

"Goodbye, Gretchen. Thanks for braiding my hair all those times after I fucked your brother."

I caress the trigger.

Gretchen explodes.

EPILOGUE

I DROP MY HEAD to the workbench.

"Ahhhhh!"

I focus on my breathing.

I'm now on hour forty-two of this week and it's only Thursday. The stress of multiple cases is getting to me. We're a four-person agency and down one Investigator, and I realize I have been lazy the last twenty years. I have no one to blame but myself.

We're also behind because I spent three days tanked, gently getting back my own face, if I could call it that, and then another day talking to the MPs and visiting the cute baby from G-6. I got behind by four days, and I have been trying to catch up for the last month and a half.

Then there is the whole paying client thing. Clients give you credits and they expect answers. Sheesh!

Scott is out in the field handling his first solo Investigation, yet more industrial sabotage, so here I am, alone, except for Ivan.

Ivan, who comes in and starts massaging my shoulders.

"Mmmm…"

"You're all tense, Nancy. A bundle. A bundle of stress."

"Hmmm."

Rub, rub, rub, rub, oh that feels sooooo good. Ivan, I have come to realize, has hands like no other: a surgeon's hands.

"I'll give you all day to stop that," I say, and stretch.

"Is not good for pretty young thing to sit in one place so long. You get fat."

"Fat? You're the one telling me I'm too skinny!"

"Keep sitting here and your butt will grow, and not in good way."

"You be nice! Don't tell people off for their weight!"

"Ha! I'm doctor! Weight is key indicator…"

I turn around. "Want to cash in that rain-check?"

He smiles. "You *are* stressed."

"Do you have privileges at Evergreen?"

"What?" That earns me a puzzled look, which I relish.

"We've waited a really long time to cash in, I want to do something especially naughty for you, and I know just how." I give him my best sly look.

He laughs. "Da, of course. Privileges. I have these."

It takes some doing, but eventually he has me bent over Bambi's tank, and my Russian bear is doing his Captain best to fuck my stress away.

"In Soviet Russia, regen tank has you!"

I giggle, come spectacularly, and laugh again as he slaps my butt hard.

* * *

Bambi, looking mostly like Bambi, walks through the front entrance and I tackle her. She has family so I was not there when they took her out of the tank, but I so desperately wanted to be.

"Oof!"

I'm crying, kissing her, crying and hugging her and…

"Nancy, I'm okay!"

"I know, I'm just—I'm a girl!" I'm so happy to see her it hurts, actually hurts. Seeing her real face, her real hair, makes me breathless.

Then, I really look at her face and start laughing.

"Don't laugh at me!"

"You're a *girl* too! You're what, seventeen? My age?"

"I hate it!"

"We can like go out, and like, pretend to be, like, pre-voc friends!" I jump up and down in semi-fake excitement. The thought of someone to share my world is making me drunk.

"Stuff it, *employee.*"

"Oh my God, are you a virgin, again?"

"Nancy!" The look on her face is priceless.

"Oh wow! You can bleed for Toshiro a second time!"

"Hey! You're being awful, and I didn't bleed, uh, much."

"Did you know in Japan, virginity means something?"

"Stop, you're mean!"

"If you're going to lose a new cherry to someone, you might as well make it count!"

"Damn, you're such a bitch!"

I grab her and hold her tight. She tenses but then, just as quickly relaxes.

"So, uh, how's the biz?" she asks while I hold her. Oh, this is nice.

"Busy. Oh, and I hate cyber. Hate, hate, hate, hate."

"That's because you're an old fuddy-duddy."

"Good thing you're back, then!"

Her face grows serious. "I read what happened afterwards. But there isn't anything about Wendy Purdue."

I bite my lip. How much should I tell her? I decide: not much.

"The MPs found her and shot her. It was mercy."

She nods.

Scott and Ivan decide I have had her to myself long enough and come in, rip her out of my arms, pick her up and shower her with more kisses.

"Oh, you teen just like Nancy!" Ivan says and gives *me* a lecherous wink. I glare at him.

She sighs.

"You all keeping this agency going proper?" she says, trying to change the subject.

"Yeah," says Scott, "we even instituted a couple of new policies." He hands her a gift-wrapped box.

"Oh! More presents!" She rips it open. Inside is a medal. The ribbon has "TARGET" embroidered on it, while hanging from it is a metal bulls-eye target.

She looks aghast, and then bursts into raucous laughter.

"Anybody who gets shot has to wear it around the Evil Underground Lair," Scott explains.

"How long do I have to wear this?"

"For as long as you were tanked."

"Harrumph!"

* * *

It's summer and hot, and finally making it from the house to the top of Mt. Si on my bike without stopping for a break is my latest athletic goal for my new Petite Princess body. I've been getting stronger at last. I feel good about my body, and myself. I'm happy with my home life and happy with my work. With this much happiness inside me, even the heat feels good.

"Private call from Cazandra," says Bob in my ear.

I shift gears on my bike and roll my eyes. I told Cazandra I'd been putting off some cyber self-study for way too long, and I needed a few days to myself, mainly so I don't keep sounding like an idiot around my decades-younger cyber-tart boss, Bambi.

Caz, of course, is jealous, not that I may be getting some yummy Ivan bear-fucking time, but of the time I'm not with her. It would be annoying if not so cute. And she doesn't even think she's possessive. "Connect."

"Lexus," Cazandra whispers, "can you make some excuse to have me come up there?"

More eye-roll, mainly because she can't see it.

"Caz…"

"It's Mitchel and Bill. They decided on cooking dinner tonight. *Together.*"

I snicker. Now, that is some funny shit. They both are terrible cooks. Together it must be the perfect storm of suck.

"It's not funny! They are already in my kitchen using my *things* to make—to make—*tripe stew* for Juan."

I burst out laughing and start to cough. If I keep that up, I won't make it to the top without having to stop.

"They are putting cow intestines in my Quebecois crockery!" she wails.

I pull over, put my feet down and put my hand over my mouth. Perhaps another day.

"Are you laughing at me? Are you snickering behind your hand?

You're mean! You should smell it already! They've already burnt a batch of black beans. That came out of a can! Already cooked!"

"Mmmmmmm…" is all I manage to get out.

"Humans!" she blurts out.

I decided to throw her a bone or my self-imposed cyber-camp will come to ruin. "Okay, here's what I suggest. Invite Dr. Katie over for dinner."

"Why would I subject the woman who saved your stupid I-Got-Blown-Up-Wearing-Lingerie butt to that? She's nice. Nicer than *you.*"

"She's nice and she's also fucking Bill."

"What?"

"I'm pretty sure of it." Cazandra has known Bill as long as I have, but I'm the Junior Wife. I pay attention to these things. It's my family duty.

"Why would Bill—young flesh," she sighs.

"Young flesh. You don't age and I look like a teenager. Kaitlin is almost twenty-one. It's a pattern."

"I thought she swung the other way!"

To be fair, I had been getting the same impression. But I can hear it in Caz's voice: she's mostly just mad that Kaitlin is not fucking her first. And that she didn't know about Bill.

"Oh, I'm going to enjoy this," says Cazandra, breathlessly. "Wife, out."

I drink some water, snap the bottle back on my bike, and hit the road.

* * *

Parked on the pad is a Military VTOL which comes into view as I round the final corner. MPs are standing around in the shade, dressed in simple uniforms and nothing more than side arms.

One turns around and sees me. Brittney.

She walks over to me, and I frown. She's wearing Lieutenant bars. She looks good.

"Britt. Coming to confiscate my NI equipment?"

"Maybe. Maybe not."

She hands me a piece of paper. I stare at it.

Real paper is bad.

WARRANT | WARRANT | WARRANT

Subject: Investigator Lexus N. Toulouse, Bambi & Associates

Crime: Abuse of Government Office. Improper use of orbital assets in the violation of the privacy of non-Government peoples for an extended period.

Judgment: This day, Lunar July 15, 20. The Military Police will forthwith evaluate this crime, and, if necessary, confiscate Toulouse's NI equipment, secure it, and surrender it unto MP Logistics of Manticore Platoon, Fort Lewis.

WARRANT | WARRANT | WARRANT

Fuck. The satellites. After we solved the crime, I was supposed to turn them off. Leaving them on was very naughty. In fact, turning them on was very naughty.

And I clean fucking forgot.

This is bad. I'm lucky they didn't arrest me. It's an odd warrant, though. It seems very discretionary.

I sigh.

"What if I need it again?"

"You don't," she simply says.

"But I used it on the Gifford case! Extensively. You were there for a part of it! What if I die because I don't have it?"

"Then you die," she says simply. "You've led a special, great, *amazing* life, Lexus. But the Military is no longer going to sit on our hands in awe of you while you use the very things you *hate* so very much. We're going to slay this white elephant and put the question on the table that should have been asked of you twenty-one years ago."

I nod. I want to talk but nothing comes out.

"Lexus, this warrant means nothing to your old platoon. We are with you, and if you decide to sink rather than swim, we'll put the rocks in your pockets. But I am here to ask you, as your friend and not just the little girl who loved you and wanted to be you growing up, to please return your NI equipment."

I nod. How can I do anything else? How could I? The Goddess is sleeping. She doesn't need her armor. She needs love. I want love. I'm the Princess now. The Princess chooses love!

"Oh, please don't cry!" Brittney hugs me, and holds me to her breasts, she is yet another person taller than I am, now.

I hold her back. Crying is what I do. That's what I do.

"Ivan has NI..."

"We would never touch Captain Ivan's gear."

I look closely at her uniform. She's now the Manticore LT. My old job. My old platoon. Her Manticore patch sparkles in the sunlight, and her blue eyes look back at me with love. Oh man, the Military plays dirty. They play to win; they moved her up to push all my buttons. This battle was all over before my bike left the garage.

I'm thinking I should have switched Brittney anyway, deal or no deal!

"Where are my other Investigators?" I ask instead.

"I gave them the day off. This is just between you and your old platoon. And me," she says.

I stand there, taking it all in, staring at her angelic face.

She puts a hand on my arm. "Oh, why are you crying again?"

"Because that's what a Princess does! I'm just so proud of you. So very proud!" I grab her and hold her tight. "Take it. Please. Take it all. I never want to see them again. Never! I hate it! The Princess doesn't need it. She doesn't!" I collapse into sobs.

I feel, rather than see, her nod to the squad, but I don't care. I only care that I have her in my arms, and she is holding me.

After a while, someone clears his throat.

"Sorry, Princess," says Mr. Burly Sergeant Man, "but I need your watch."

Oh. I blush, snap it off, hand it to him, then feel stupid for blushing, and then feel stupid for feeling stupid.

"Thank you, Princess." He salutes.

"That's it, LT," he says to Brittney.

"Thank you, Sergeant."

The squad piles into the VTOL, but it doesn't take off. They are waiting for Brittney to say goodbye. The thought of being alone after such an emotional up-and-down nearly drives me to my knees. I am not above asking.

"Brittney, please. Don't go. Stay here. Stay here and make love to your Princess," I say, quietly, feeling pathetic for asking—for giving her what she and the Military wants and submitting to them.

Brittney's blue eyes shine, for a brief moment, in triumph, and I both hate her and love her for it, but then they sparkle with pure warmth and adore and everything important in me melts into a soupy mess.

The tall blonde stands close to me and her hand reaches behind me and then down my bike shorts. She cups my ass in her hand and pulls me closer to her. Then she slides her other hand down my front and cups my sex.

Despite my best efforts, I let out a little whimper, mesmerized by her eyes and hands.

"I am very picky in whom my women lovers are. I have not had a girl since I was sixteen," she says. "But I relish the time, soon, where I will kiss every inch of your beautiful body. I will worship my Princess with kisses for hours on end."

Then she removes her hand from the front of my shorts and caresses my face. Her hand is wet and the smell of my own sex is heady. "But not today, Princess, not today. Soon—I promise."

I nod. She kisses me on the lips, her girl-woman lips are soft and inviting, and then, she is no longer cupping my ass, walking to the VTOL instead. She climbs in and it takes off in a noisy burr.

I gasp for breath and try to calm myself. Half of me is impressed that Brittney can refuse my plea, the other half wants to find who my ginormous cock-blocker is and gut him with the Sword of the Empress. My body is humming with desire.

That's when I notice there is a cherry blossom on the ground, and a few feet from it, another one. I look up and there is a trail of cherry blossoms to the back of our complex.

The trail leads me behind the building, and my heart is pounding. Most of the complex is only one story above ground. In back is the lunch spot on sunny days, my lunch with a killer view. There is a huge, genetically modified cedar tree which I paid too much cred for, which announces to all I have tamed this mountain, and this little big rock is mine. A weatherworn picnic table and a barbeque pit round out one of my favorite spots in the world.

And now, as I round the final corner, sits a sleigh-style, queen-sized bed. Complete with fluffy pillows and sheets and a blanket folded at the foot. Well, that sure wasn't there before. I remember the conversation I had with Brittney in a previous life, and I finally clue in about why she left in such a hurry. No chiggers and bugs for me, I guess.

Sitting on the bed in a diaphanous, flowing purple gown is Kori. My Empress.

I walk up to her and I can feel hot tears on my cheeks turning cold from the mountain breeze. It's too much. The Princess can't take all these changes and keep it together. I just can't. I've completely fallen apart and someone needs to pick up the pieces and put them back together again or I am done. Finished.

She stands up and smiles at me. She reaches out with her hand and caresses my wet face.

"I heard a scandalous rumor, my Princess, that you have never made love outside."

I burst into hysterical giggles and she pulls me to her.

"Oh, my Princess, blown this way and that by the whimsy of the universe itself—but I am here for you," she says. She hugs me so tight that I squeak again, and then, she relaxes. I stare at her beautiful face.

"You promised me," she whispers, "that you would love me to the end of time. I am going to hold you to that promise, my Princess. Even when you forget and your heart wanders, I will come for you and bind you back to me. You are mine. You are mine—*forever.*"

She kisses me and no kiss has ever been as passionate. Not my Husbands. Not Cazandra. Not Arune. Nobody. My body goes limp. She stops kissing me and looks into my eyes.

"I have been thinking about what we will do. I'm going to take you inside and undress you, and then I will clean up your petite sweaty body. Then we're going to make love in this bed, outside, just as you wanted, and take a lover's nap. Afterwards, I'm going to make you lunch. We'll go for a walk, holding hands, and come back and make love again, and then we'll just talk like lovers and friends. Then I will fix you dinner. I will read you passionate poetry, and then we'll make love again. Then we will go to sleep."

"Oh, oh, Kori-san!" I fight the tears again and something happens in Kori's eyes. Something I have never seen before and I doubt I will see again. Then, they go feral—pure, unfettered, animal lust.

"But now you are here," she whispers hoarsely. "New plan." Her hands flash and she rips my skin-tight biker blouse right off me, the synth-fabric and memory cups tearing away from my damp skin. Then, she picks me up, actually picks me up by my waist until a breast is even with her face, and she greedily takes as much as she can in her mouth and sucks, hard.

"Ah!" I scream out, my head straining back. Between all of the stress, the physical exertion, Brittney's teasing, the emotion, the anticipation, I'm too wound up. Too wound up. That's all Kori gets to do to me before something happens that I have never experienced before and I climax without being touched anywhere except for Kori's lips on my breast.

As I shudder and shake, she holds me in place, sucking. It is deliciously, mind blanking, epically torturous.

We skip the shower.

* * *

The delicate, jeweled needles that normally hold her long, dark hair are gone, and it spills over me as I'm lying on the sleeping Kori.

I should be the one asleep, exhausted, but my borrowed youth is a reminder of who I am, not who I was. Truth is I wore her out. I rewarded her for one of the most erotic experiences in my life (and that is saying a lot) by taking her again and again, over and over. Now, she sleeps, deeply and completely. I look at her relaxed, peaceful face. Nothing on Earth is as beautiful to me as she is right now. Nothing.

The wind carries with it a coolness, but the sheet and blanket and Kori keep me warm. It's not just my body that's warm, but also my heart. I feel blessed and I look at the stars. There are so very many stars up there.

I know in my heart my grandpa didn't instill a complete sense of fearlessness toward death, but he and his stars started me on that path. Every night as I grew up, I would turn off the lights and lie in bed, looking up at his stars. I miss him. I miss them all.

I wonder. I wonder who I really am, and a yearning that I don't fully understand fills my body. It seems only the Empress's embrace, as I lay on top of her, nestled on her exquisite body, keeps me from floating away in the moonless, cloudless, sky.

The Goddess of War awoke and extracted a terrible vengeance on the enemy who dared intrude upon her wards' lives.

Now she sleeps, content, blood-satiated, and happy, hopefully never to awaken again. In her place is the Princess, and the Princess is filled with love to the bursting point.

I gaze at the stars until I'm sleepy. I close my eyes and they are still there. They will always be there, long after I'm gone, they will be there. The thought gives me comfort, and I sleep underneath the stars, waiting for the next day to love again.

ACKNOWLEDGEMENTS

WHAT AN EXCITING JOURNEY this book was, and here we are at the end with so many people to thank. My very first reader and lovely wife, Heather, deserves all the gratitude and kisses I can deliver and then some.

This book would have never seen the light of day without the dedication and attention of the editor, Salvatore Biancardi. Thank you, Sal.

I hope we all can agree that Eve Venture's cover art is outstanding. If someone had told me one of my novels would have such a girly beautiful artistic feminine provocative *pink* princess cover, I would have laughed and rolled my eyes. Could anyone capture visually the Princess in all of her newly petite glory? Eve sure did.

Cassie Hart my New Zealand friend, your encouragement means a lot to me. I love you very much. You are my sister from another mother!

Thank you Cindy Barnett for your helpful commentary.

My old critique partners from projects gone by and stuffed under the bed waiting their turn, I thank you: Alex Moore, Tracy Crowley, J.D. Meyer, Brian Jones, Edward Chessman, David Muellenhoff, Julie Packard, Mike Hill and David Anderson.

Mr. Whitewolf, you always liked your science fiction with some sexy sauce and encouraged me to put it out there. Hey dude, it's out there!

A special thanks to Jaym Gates for all of our late night correspondence on story-telling, short story exchanges and anything else that struck our fancy.

Thank you those awesome writers who have gone out of their way to provide encouragement or simply correspondence: J.S. Chancellor, Michelle Davidson Argyle, Ken Kiser, Amber Argyle, Toni Andrews, Sarah Hoyt, Courtney Summers, Sylvia Engdahl and Gary Corby.

I also want to thank author Larry Correia. I found his story on how he put his book in front of readers very inspirational, along the actual message-fiction crushing, pretentious-prose slapping, pulp goodness that makes up his novels.

And of course, my mom, Carolyn Owens. Love you, mom.

I appreciate every reader of this novel more than I can say. This book really is for you. Your wiliness to read it has humbled me, and I come before you as a simple storyteller that shares your love of science fiction, mystery and a hunger to wonder and imagine. Please write me at:

anthony_pacheco@comcast.net

or visit my website at:

http://anthony-pacheco.com

Thereon lays my blog, social media links, and all sorts of speculative Tom Foolery.

As science fiction readers, we all have that unmistakable yet somehow unfathomable yearning when we look out at the stars, and that's how this novel ends. We classify science fiction as speculative fiction, but is it really? The star-filled sky is one thing that binds us all surly as we share the earth beneath our feet and it is a very real possibility that we share that visual cosmos with peoples not yet met.

Science will take us to the stars one day. That is not a speculation, that's simply a truth that hasn't happened yet. Lexus doesn't really understand why gazing up at the stars grounds her in her reality even though at times it is so terrible.

But until we actually *go* there, can any of us say we do?

www.ingramcontent.com/pod-product-compliance
Lightning Source LLC
Chambersburg PA
CBHW030417310726
48979CB00002B/452